THE SOUND OF
THE HOURS

THE SOUND
OF THE HOURS

KAREN CAMPBELL

BLOOMSBURY CIRCUS
LONDON · OXFORD · NEW YORK · NEW DELHI · SYDNEY

BLOOMSBURY CIRCUS
Bloomsbury Publishing Plc
50 Bedford Square, London, WC1B 3DP, UK

BLOOMSBURY, BLOOMSBURY CIRCUS and the Bloomsbury Circus logo are
trademarks of Bloomsbury Publishing Plc

First published in Great Britain 2019

The writer acknowledges support from Creative Scotland
towards the writing of this title

ISBN: HB: 978-1-4088-5737-3; TPB: 978-1-5266-0599-3; EBOOK: 978-1-4088-0599-3

2 4 6 8 10 9 7 5 3 1

Typeset by Integra Software Services Pvt. Ltd.
Printed and bound in Great Britain by CPI Group (UK) Ltd, Croydon CR0 4YY

To find out more about our authors and books visit www.bloomsbury.com and
sign up for our newsletters

To my sister, Val.

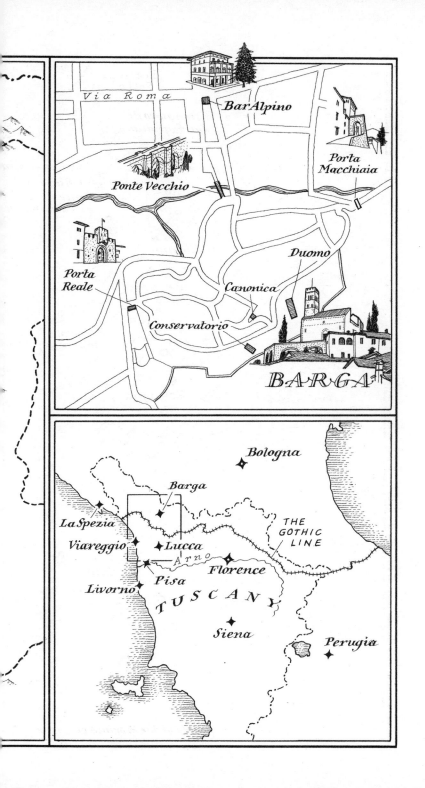

And again the hour sounds, sending down
to me twice now a cry almost fretful,
then back to that slow, tranquil voice.

In my own garden's shade, it persuades me.
It's time. It's late. Yes. Let's return there
to where I am loved, where I love.

From '*L'Ora di Barga*'
by GIOVANNI PASCOLI

Paisley, Endings

Outside, the moon is bright. Obscenely bright. It silvers the rug, patches the eiderdown in wonderful threads. Nonna doesn't want the curtains shut.

'*Il cielo*,' she says.

'Yes. The sky.'

'*Voglio vedere il cielo.*'

'It's still there.'

'*Sì.*'

She's been talking more Italian recently.

Torri's father comes in, stands loosely in the shadow. A beam of moonlight catches his toes. His slippers are torn where the dog's been playing with them; she can see a neon pink sock. *Dad,* she thinks. *What are you like?* He's a professor, but you wouldn't know it. He waits, one hand worrying the base of his neck, lifting, lifting, tiny puffs of grey, until it looks like his ears are gently blowing steam.

They share the same unmanageable hair. While he clips what's left of his into the wood, Torri's is overgrown: she carries a thicket on her head. Only those blessed with hearty hair can know how good it feels on a summer day, fresh out the hairdresser's, and that light lick of air catching, unfamiliar, on the nape of your neck, when you see your tamed head in a window and swear your step is lighter, because two feet of tangles are spread over the salon floor.

On the bed, Nonna shifts some more. Paper-thin eyelids – you can see the dart of her eyeballs underneath. The pink of her scalp, the violet of her blood: her workings are on show. Torri notices how her fingernails splay, how they are like yellow-ridged spades, and it makes her think of moles, digging blindly for air.

'You want some tea, love?'

'Not for me. Non—'

'She can't.'

'Nonna, would you like some tea?'

'Mm.'

'That'll be one tea, please, waiter.'

Her dad shakes his head. 'Water would be fine. All she can taste is the sponge.'

'Nonna would like tea, wouldn't you? I don't know.' Leaning in to kiss her forehead. 'Was he always this disobedient?'

'Hhm.'

Her dad disappears downstairs again. He's happier when there's something to do. Torri plaits her fingers though her grandmother's, careful not to break the skin. This room hasn't changed in years. As a child, she'd sleep here every Friday, when her parents went dancing. Her brother, sometimes her cousins too, in the back room with Papà Joe; her and Nonna here, each chewing mint creams, a hot-water bottle between them, spongy curlers in their hair. Awful music on the radio – accordions or fiddles – and that same patchwork blanket, draped across the bed in faded pleats. Her *tutti-frutti* bedspread, Nonna called it. No pattern to it at all. There is a piece of blue rabbit, there is wedding lace, embroidered hexagons and a weird, humpy creature whose black back rises like a whale. The pink silk lampshades are the same too, the framed pencil sketch on her dressing table, the tapestry rug and the three black-and-white photos on the wall, unchanging in their hierarchy. Although more family has come and gone, it is these three Nonna stares at every night, embraces every morning as dawn comes through curtains that are never closed.

Top picture is Nonna's First Communion: all spindly legs and stiff white dress, her mum and dad tight-lipped proud behind her. They are neat and dark like their daughter; they stand before a stone wall, by the glimpse of an oak door. Nonna has a gap between her front teeth, is grinning wildly at the photographer and clutching her bridal posy so hard you can *see* the flowers wilting. Torri imagines it as a hot day, imagines the sun as fierce as the moon is now, but of course, you can't be sure. The photo is tinged with age, as if tea-washed or left too long in the Tuscan sun. Time has made the people faded, and the heat of memory's passed too. She's never asked Nonna how hot it was that day. She looks at the wee soul on the bed and realises all the things she's never asked her gran, the unrecorded, half-remembered things she might have said, inconsequential words and adages, advice that Torri wants to scrabble up and save, all the old-lady witterings made when Torri and her brother were trying to watch the telly or huffing over homework or adults or life. Later too, when she should have known better, when her nonna deserved at least five minutes of attentive grace.

'How about a hair brush while we're waiting?'

She doesn't use a brush, just her fingers. Tip-touching the scalp, the ghost of bounce present in sparse curls.

It feels like patting air. Nonna sighs, a good, long sigh, not the rattles of earlier. The middle photo is of another bride: Nonna on her wedding day. Papà Joe looms two foot taller, his profile demanding respect, black eyes melting over his *carina*. His little dear one. For all Papà Joe is grand and stately, it is her grandmother who dominates, whose energy spills from the picture frame so she is almost 3D. Her flattened, waved hair gone frizzy in the sunshine; there's a halo of escaping strays; her tea-dress-clad body angled as if she could climb out the frame at any minute. Even her hands are undemure, one finger pointing at something beyond the camera, a blurred, mobile bouquet in the other fist and her mouth open, laughing golden notes into the world. Tucked in the foreground, just on the right of the frame, a child's bare leg kicks out in a blurry run, some disobedient pageboy who will not stand still for photos.

Cameras never lie. Compare the picture to that pencil sketch – such a poor likeness of teenage Nonna. Torri wonders why she keeps it. The face is too long, too sharp; the eyes almond like a cat's.

Dad returns with the tea. He puts it on the bedside table, moving detritus with his elbow.

'Like a bloody nature table, this.'

Torri's great-uncle insists on bringing thyme and cut lemons instead of flowers. He calls it 'sniff 'n' drift', says it's good for Nonna. Last night, he sat with a bag of roasted chestnuts, rubbing the blistered husks to release woodsmoke and burnt caramel. Curls of half-shells remain on the table. She'll bin them once they've had their tea – maybe that's what's unsettling her grandmother.

'Your mum says, do you want a sandwich?'

'No, it's fine. You two get off to bed.'

'Will you—?'

She nods. He doesn't wait to see the torture of drinking, which is fair enough. This is his mum. Nonna's tongue is blackened, swollen. Torri scrapes her mouth with moistened cotton wool. Then she slides her hand under Nonna's neck.

'We don't need the sponge, do we?' Slowly, slowly – you can hear bones creak – she tilts her grandmother slightly, so that when she pours little drops of tea into her mouth it won't run straight back out and into Nonna's ears. They have learned by trial and error. Stroking her throat helps her swallow, but again, the drops must be managed: enough to make a flowing puddle in her mouth, not so much it will drown her.

'That nice? Bet you'd rather have coffee, eh?'

'Mm.'

'But that would make you jittery. Canny have you getting the coffee-shakes, can we?'

Nonna forgets to swallow. Torri catches it with her sleeve as pale tea trickles, but she's not quick enough. Damp spreads on the pillow, only a wee bit but they'll need to change it. She is not having her nonna lying on stains.

The third photo on the wall is of Nonna, Papà Joe and their family. Dad's about eight: same gap-toothed grin as his mamma, arms folded and squinting at his parents. Papà Joe's jacket looks like scratchy tweed. The skyline of Paisley is behind them: a distant outline of the abbey roof, a sandstone wall to their left with a plate-glass window and a door. The door frame has a starburst of coloured glass above and the words *Caffè del Rio*; it is an art deco extravaganza.

In this photo, Nonna looks no different from her wedding day. Less smart of course, she has a flowered overall that crosses her breasts; the housewifely garment makes her look younger than when she was a bride, and her hair's a bit crazy, but she looks so much fun, still a kid herself, with a husband and kids and café to run. Younger than Torri is now. Tucked in either arm is a bundled-up twin. The darker shawl is probably blue, thus Uncle Davide – which makes the one on the right Torri's aunt. Something else she'll never get to ask. *How did you do it, Nonna? All that?*

She hears a car draw up on the street beneath the window. The engine is thick and throaty. A taxi, maybe? The car keeps running. A door slams. Engine stops. Another slam, quick footsteps, then their doorbell rings. Nonna's novelty alarm clock is a windmill from Amsterdam, and the sail is set at eleven. Who comes visiting at eleven at night? Dad's been here all day, and Aunt Lena's on the breakfast shift.

'It's OK. Go back to sleep.'

Her nonna mumbles. Knot-knuckles twisting, leather tongue repeating.

'*Castagne. Voglio le stelle.*'

'I know, Nonna. The stars are still there.'

Autumn 1943

Chapter One

'Vita! Vita!'

Picture the scene. The dance beginning. Quick flicks and flashes, the pale undersides of wrists held high, her sister waving in a swirl of dresses, hair obscuring all but tips of noses and lips counting intricate time-laced steps to call out ancient gods. The bend and sweep, the twirl and sweep. Again and again, women stamping their feet. The unmarried girls pretending to brush, the children clapping, hooking arms through compliant elbows, making space to catch and spin, sweeping, stamping, the jagged edges blurring lines and squares into angular poses, like the posters of the Mother sweeping forth; home behind, all held in the bosom of the land.

Vita spun past Signor Tutto, fingers shiny-plump as he worked his accordion. She didn't understand those posters; why some man had drawn them in hard blocked lines: women, children, wheatsheaves, Il Duce's chin above them, squarer than it was in the photographs. People should be round and generous – she linked arms with her little sister, flung her extra hard – yes, round like the angels in church. Faster, faster, some older women playing the role of absent boys – *Is your Giuseppe not here?* panted Signora Pieri; *My Giuseppe?* – she tried to be bashful, but the moment had passed, and so had Vita, lungs on fire as she swept her elbows high; then the lunge and the push – *It's all about sex*, Renata had said – but it was only sweeping, mimicking how they brushed the forest floor, all of them here, the whole of Catagnana (which wasn't many) – she linked arms briefly with Maria Pieri – the girls from Sommocolonia, some of the Ponte lot too – the ones who could be bothered dragging their lazy backsides up the hill – *Pay attention! Sorry* – that was Signora Nardini's foot, but Vita's zoccoli were falling apart; galumphing clogs with the tops disintegrating, her heels hanging over the soles.

She breathed deep, ribcage a mix of pleasure and pain. Twilight coming. But no sign of Joe. Her skirt billowed – Mamma had insisted she wear an old flowered silk of hers – pretty, but stinking of camphor, and nothing of Mamma's would ever fit her. Ever. *Dress nicely, Vittoria. For once, yes?* There was a plea in her mother's voice, almost an excitement, which had made Vita excited too.

Above the camphor-pangs, she could smell earth, rising like baking bread. Tonight, everyone would take their brooms and brush soft moss and leaves from the forest floor so that, when the chestnuts fell, they'd be gathered cleanly. The men would stand with candles as the women took the first harvest for *Sagra della Mondina*. The Chestnut Festival, a glorious mix of gathering and roasting and milling and more dancing and music – she tugged a strand of hair from her mouth as Signor Tutto, in one fluid swoop, switched from accordion to – yes! tuba; he'd brought his tuba up from Ponte too. His name wasn't Tutto, of course, he was named for his shop, which sold everything. But it suited him;

the roundness of it, the little *oh* of fun attached. Vita stamped and clapped; she couldn't think what his real name was, but it didn't matter because he was Papà's friend and *tutto* meant all and everything, and it was always his music that made their *feste* sing. Her friend Giulia was laughing to herself, laughing and spinning until her skirts flared so high you could see the curve of her backside, and then her mother lunged, slapping the fabric back into place. But even she was laughing. They desperately needed this high day; a day when the music took you, when some unknown hand seized yours and twirled you upside down.

Except the hands this year were mostly women's. Vita could see her mother, standing on the outskirts of the dance, worrying the iron band on her finger like she always did. The awful greyness; all those women with their thick waists. Il Duce's brides. Every time she saw her mother's ring, Vita saw fire. Fire and the slow, grave procession: all the little tots who had held their mothers' hands and stumbled to match pace. *Giornata delle Fede.* Thousands upon thousands of women, from every fold and curve of Italy, offering their wedding bands as sacrifice, to be melted down for war. Along with their ecstatic tears, they were offering themselves too – even as a child Vita had known this. They were saying to Il Duce: *Take me.* And got iron bands in return.

A shiver ran under her skin. The leaves were starting to fade. In one week's time, Vita would be eighteen. She twisted her head, trying to see if Joe had arrived. Woodsmoke crackled in bright air, old men already building bonfires. Soon the first of the chestnuts would be spitting in a giant padella – *But not until we've made them castrati!* shrieked an old lady Vita didn't know. The Madonna swayed past, her blue cloak draped in greenery, on her annual escape from her hillside chapel. A tiny San Cristoforo followed. You could see the arms of the child carrying it shake with effort. Papà had made a smaller bier for the Madonna this year; it too was borne aloft by boys who could not yet shave.

'I'm so dizzy I can see stars!' Cesca looped her arm through Vita's again and they threw each other wide; it was her sister's first time in the dance, finally allowed to sweep and spin with the rest of them. 'Show her no mercy!' Vita shouted. The Pieri sisters took an arm each and lifted the feet from under Cesca. Vita pitched backwards, into old Sergio, who'd his hat clamped over his ears.

'Watch my toes, girl!'

'Scusi, Signor Bertini.'

'I need to go,' he said. 'The noise is too much.'

Vita slumped against the wall. Felt a sudden emptiness now she'd stopped. She'd no air left in her lungs. Why was she trussed in this flowery thing if he wasn't coming? Behind her, a fountain sparkled. Trees flickered to the music. Several of the Sommo girls were sitting out the dance, knees and lips prim. Who were they trying to impress? Only a couple of spotty teenagers, a few walking wounded and poor Pietro from Albiano, home on leave. He sat alone, wiping at the side of his face. Or rather, it was a husk of Pietro, a boy whose fingers had jittered the whole time Vita was trying to say hello. He hadn't answered, just grabbed her shoulder – not in a bad way; a quick dart like he was trying to catch a fish, or press on her a message that he couldn't say.

She flattened down her hair. She'd been sure Joe would come; that she would be one of the few girls dancing with a male under forty. The music quickened, out of time now with the clapping. Leaves drifted, hearts of russet and gold. The dress clung to her legs. It felt sticky.

Despite all this demented, forceful gaiety, there was an emptiness at the centre of the festa. Just as she and Cesca had switched from clapping to dancing, one day she would switch again, and be with the grey women who no longer danced, but stood on the perimeter, stamping veiny, stout legs. She looked up at a big mauve sky. Even the trees were unsettled. Everyone was rustling like the leaves, you could *sense* it. The fretfulness below the skin of them. The air had changed. Italy was holding her breath.

Vita wiped her nose on her arm. She heard one of the Sommo girls giggle. They thought they were something special up here, with their literal looking down on everyone, and their several piazzas and two churches and their castle and their ancient towers. *Sommocolonia. Named by the Romans, don't you know?* Yes, yes. We know. So what? The Sommos were Romans? Everyone knew that proper Tuscans were far more ancient than that.

Listen to the words, carina. Etrus-can. Tus-can-ee. See? Papà knew his history. Her papà knew so many things.

The last parp of the tuba came, a spattering of applause, before a hesitant violin took over. Little Giuliano was treating everyone to a solo, and he was only a baby, and his mother was convinced he was a prodigy, so you had to let him. Signor Tutto mopped his brow, took a swig of wine. The tune resembled an eightsome reel. Vita sang it into herself, eliding the notes Giuliano cranked from his instrument... it was the 'Dashing White Sergeant'. She saw Papà emerge from the patched-up fascio, clapping his hands. Glass of wine, quick game of briscola. He used to say: *I'm not one of those boneheads, carina.* But if you weren't a Party member, you didn't work. And those hills had eyes, even beadier now than before. Who knew which neighbour would decree your mumblings anti-fascist, would pour you a glass of castor oil to purge your mouth, or simply note your name and pass it on?

And what if it was your mother?

'Hee-euch!'

Papà offered Mamma his arm, face lit. He'd taught that tune to Signor Tutto, who in turn taught it to everyone he gave lessons to. Mamma slapped his hand away. 'Not now. Giuliano,' she said loudly. 'Play something more traditional.'

Vita watched Papà touch the bridge of his nose. Held her own face up to the evening warmth. She hated when they fought in public. The light turned golden-pink where the sun caught it, dripping honey across the Valle del Serchio. Vast sky and countless mountains, bottoming to a wide, flat plain so full of trees it was hard to see the river. Nothing but deep blue peaks and Garfagnana green. In this confusion of nature, you'd take your bearings from Monte Forato, that great mountain over there. The sleeping man. The hole in the centre was his eye, caused by, either a sad shepherd lying down to die of love, San Pellegrino fighting with the Devil or natural erosion. Whatever, it was a circle of sky where the sky should not be: a fixed and certain point in a panorama of endless peaks. Twice a year, a double sunset would come to the valley, when the winter sun dropped from the horizon and all went dark. Then the sun reappeared in Forato's eye, and, for a moment, it was day again. Or magic.

Vita used to think it was magic. Halfway down the hillside, she could just make out the rooftops of Catagnana, and the big chestnut behind her house. Narrowing her eyes further, until all she could see was shimmering green. In the middle distance rose a pinnacle of biscuit-coloured villas and dark cypress. Barga. Elegant Barga, a citadel of restaurants and concert halls only half an hour away. The square-towered Duomo loomed over red roofs tumbling in commas and swirls all the way past the city walls, walls which held the bones of San Cristoforo, the nuns of the Conservatorio – and a picture house too. Where the cafés had good coffee and people who were not your cousins, and shops selling dainty lacework, which you could imagine wearing later, as you were putting on your apron and scraping mule shit off your clogs.

She stared down, at all the big things made tiny. Her old, familiar valley. How much had changed in three months. How much, yet nothing at all. Three months ago, Joe returned. Three months ago, Vita had watched this same valley – these people dancing and sweating beside her – tear Il Duce's posters from the walls. Signor Tutto playing his fiddle in time with pealing bells and blue-light fireworks; folk shaking each other in their desire to have it sink in, this whole valley exploding with noise and bonfires and shrieks of laughter; with smashing glass and smashing jaws, with the weeping of the faithful. In this long, deep bowl of space, she had heard Barga howl at the moon.

Il Duce was no more.

In one blistering starburst, the world remade. He'd been arrested by the King. War was over!

Vita blinked, filtering sunlight.

Way down the track, old Sergio was taking his donkey away. She watched him untie the rope from her muzzle. Once the rope was off, he took something from his pocket and fed it to the beast. Then he laid his lips on the mottled grey forehead. Vita circled them both with finger and thumb, so it looked as though she pinched them in mid-air. So close. So far.

Because none of it was true.

German soldiers had set Mussolini free. *So brave*, glittered her mother. *They say he walked down the mountain in his bare feet.*

Now the world was deeper in chaos than before, and Vita couldn't even trust the mountains. The horizon might slip and send them all hurtling off the earth. Italy was ripped in two. Rome lay riven in a fault-line: the King and the Allies to the south, Il Duce and the Germans in the north. Her breast rose and fell. Without moving one step, she'd woken in some 'republic'. Barga was the exact same place it had always been, yet somehow they were on a different side. And the war? This forever war? Papà promised it would end, once they all saw sense. It must.

A butterfly swept a helix above her, dancing through gaps of green. Where even was the war? It might be everywhere, but it wasn't here. Often, when Vita was in bed, she would hear the murmur of Radio Londra, which meant Papà was awake too. And there were nights when the bombing at La Spezia would make the windows shudder. But it had always been a distant storm. La Spezia was a hundred kilometres off, and it was ships and the sea, it was distant. Beyond the circle of Barga's mountains, there were raids on the coast. Boh – where was that? It was ships, it was sea. It was distant. Beyond the circle of Barga's mountains, ghostly lights might burst, and the roar – there was a definite roar beyond the mountains, so the roar and the lights and the sharp rattle of teeth, yes, but it was seldom and distant; it was ships and the sea, and it had been four years still and they were wrapped in forests.

The butterfly flitted higher, flashing an underside of gold. Vita circled her finger round Monte Forato. To die of love. What a daft, wasteful thing. Surely it was better to live for it?

'You coming?' Cesca tapped her arm. 'We're off to Casa Biondi.'

Over at the top of the steps, Signor Tutto was waving his hanky at Vita. 'Why?' she asked.

'Gelato.'

She felt a sensation of heat in her face. That's where Joe was. Signor Tutto disappeared, skipping down the rampa with an agility that belied his bulk.

'Don't say "gelato" out loud, or Mamma will kill you.'

Il Duce had banned ice cream, because it was too American, or made you lazy and stupid or something. Which made it all the more delicious.

'She's going down to Barga anyway.'

'Good. Why?'

'One, she says Papà is embarrassing her, and two, something about a bill from the libreria? She wants to have it out with them before they close. Did you get more books without telling her?'

'For Godsake. Two books. I need them for my exams. Papà said I could.'

Cesca shrugged. 'And yet Mamma says you can't. I wonder who will win. Right, you coming? I've had enough pretendy broom-dancing.'

Vita wanted to go, and she didn't. 'Who asked us? How d'you know they're making ice cream?'

'Spies,' Cesca whispered. 'Everywhere, there are spies.'

'Francesca, that's not funny.'

'Vittoria. It was.'

She followed her sister down the ramp. Sommocolonia was built in tight circles round the highest part, circles that grew more generous as you left the church and towers, and descended the cobbled stairs to where the village walls rose. High stone walls that held the very streets in place. It was cool there, cool against your cheek as you skirted thorns, and the drape of ferns and thyme spilling, looking at the flow of mountain upon mountain, and purple chives and yellow marigolds.

'Was it Joe?'

'Ooh, Joe.' Cesca nudged her. 'Oh, Joe – ooh, mio bello Joe.'

'Shut up.'

'But you lo—ove him. Renata says you two—'

''Course I do. He's a Guidi.'

'You love Joe because he's lovely. You know,' Cesca kicked a pebble, 'I checked with Sister Cristina. He's more the Biondis' than ours. Because of Zia Antonia-rest-in-peace.'

It was a family tradition to refer to their dead aunt thus. What a terrible thing, to be remembered only for dying in childbirth.

'So?'

'So, Joe's dad was Zia Antonia's brother.'

'So?'

'But they were only Papà's cousins. That means Joe's our second cousin, and second cousins are fine to marry. Not even a Hail Mary required. Sister Cristina said if Giuseppe wasn't already spoken for, she'd probably marry him herself.'

A mosquito buzzed at Vita's neck. She slapped it. Too many assumptions since Joe had returned to Barga. Plenty of sharp tongues and elbows.

—*Oh, he's come back for you, Vita.*

—*Renata had a baby by your age.*

—*You won't need to bother with this teaching nonsense now.*

—*No, teaching's for spinsters. And nuns!* (Pause for laughter.)

Vittoria Guidi: a fruit waiting to be plucked.

'Why have you gone so red?'

'Because I'm hot.'

She wiped her face. Cesca was only fourteen. What did she know? Everybody loved Giuseppe, their dark and funny Scottish cousin who'd returned quietly in the confusion of this uneasy summer, just like it was any other. And yes, Vita's fingers had curled with pleasure, and she'd primped her hair, and lined up to embrace him along with everyone else. It was good – no, it was wonderful – to see him again.

How are you? she'd whispered in his ear.

All the better for seeing you.

But they'd barely had a proper conversation since, beyond his daft jokes and winks. Mostly, Joe was with the older men, joking, labouring, playing cards; he'd often spend evenings alone. Yet, whenever the family did eat together, she could sense him watch her; sense the rest of them watching him watch her too, and this stupid, scarlet shame would rise in her skin.

The poor orphan is very hungry. Mamma missed nothing. *Pass him the polenta, Vita.* Yes, everyone loved Giuseppe.

Joe's parents were dead, and his Barga family was all he had left. So they'd absorbed him as quietly as he had arrived. And he was Joe, not foreign at all. Indeed, he was almost a hero – no one had seen family from Scotland since the war began. *But how did he get here? Does he know if Adela's family. . . Ssh! Keep it quiet. Everybody keep it quiet.*

Maybe that was it. Maybe Papà or Zio Orlando had told him to stay away. Squadristi sometimes visited hilltop festivals, if they were bored or thirsty. Her jaw relaxed.

'I wish he was staying at our house,' said Cesca.

'Nae luck.'

Vita tried to capture the nasal way Joe spoke. Every summer when he used to visit, they'd swap words and stories: Vita, Giuseppe and assorted Biondis. If Cesca was toddling round, annoying them, they'd switch from swear words to something less profane. Joe would tell them about Paisley Abbey and the cotton mills. How the mill girls wore zoccoli too, only they called them clogs. *But they don't have ankles as pretty as yours.* And he'd raise up Vita's foot, and she'd giggle and blush.

'He's staying with them because he's a master *creatore di gelato.* The Biondis are learning all his secrets.'

The Biondis lived down here, in one of the first houses in Sommocolonia. Where La Limonaia – the Guidi house – had its rolling garden, Casa Biondi had terraced rock, patches of heather by the door and a shared piece of land further up the mountain.

Vita rapped the shutter. 'Renata!'

'In the kitchen.'

Bars of light slid across the flagstones. Facing them was the massive fireplace, with its charcoal burners in a recessed metal grate. In these fornelli, Renata cooked the most delicious food. A pot stood ready, full of water. Renata was only a handful of years older than Vita, yet so capable and sure: sprinkling flour, rolling pasta on a marble slab. The big wooden madia behind her was open, its pile of flour for that week's bread almost hidden by the large sack of farina dolce. Zio Orlando's prized radio sat beside it, sending out waves of *'Caro Papà'.* He and Papà were the only two men on the hillside to own such treasures.

'Ciao.' Vita kissed her. Renata was a good friend, but, beside her cousin's wife, Vita always felt a little useless. Books did not impress a woman who ran her own home, and was mother to a five-year-old girl. 'You not coming to the festa?'

'Soon as I've finished making this.'

'We heard there might be some gelato-making?' said Cesca. 'Where's Zio Orlando?'

Orlando made gelato to sell in the hamlets round about. But it was mostly weak-tasting snow, with the odd bit of straw in. The best that could be said was that it saved you the walk to Barga. Joe, however, really was an expert. Funny how ice cream was their invention, yet here was this daft Scotsman, telling them how to do it better.

'In the cave,' said Renata. 'In the huff.'

'Why?'

'Oh, you'll see. It's a surprise.' Renata lifted her rolling pin, to drape the pasta.

'Excellent,' said Cesca. 'I like surprises.'

'Any word from Gianni?' Her cousin was fighting for Il Duce, somewhere in Rome.

Renata shook her head.

'Well,' said Vita, 'no news is good news, eh?'

Renata paused, a spray of tagliatelle in her hand.

'You know what I mean. I mean like—'

'I know what you mean.' Renata dropped the pasta in the pot. 'On you go. They're desperate for an audience.'

They entered the long, windowless room that burrowed into the hill. Walls of pure, cold rock. Vita heard laughter. Joe. She was glad of the cool, and the momentary dark. An ornate wooden bedstead stood beside some sacks. Candles in wine bottles on top of a pile of wooden crates. In the shadows were Renata's daughter, Rosa, and Zio Orlando, arms folded. An electric wire had been strung to the ceiling, one single bulb shining on the stars of the show.

'Buona sera, ladies!' Signor Tutto kissed his fingers. He had his other arm round Joe, who didn't even look up. 'Come and enjoy our little demonstration. This beauty is the latest thing.'

'This beauty' was a wooden bucket, with rope lugs and a metal churn in the middle. Signor Tutto tapped the side. 'From a friend, who owed me a little favour.'

'That thing is unhygienic,' said Zio Orlando. 'You must use mountain snow. And beat it by hand.'

'No. This is how we do it back home. Ciao, Cesca.' Joe bowed to them, pushing his black hair from his eyes. 'Ciao, Dolce Vita. Nice dress.'

'I thought you were coming to the dance?' In the cave, Vita's voice sounded shrill.

'Ah, but ice cream called... Now, see down the side here?' Without asking, Joe grabbed her hand, slipped it in the gap between churn and pail. 'First, we fill the sides with ice. Crushed ice.' With his other hand, he thumped a hammer down hard on the tea towel, causing Cesca to shriek and all of them to jump. Vita removed her hand from the pail. 'You're an idiot.' Her skin was thrumming.

'Why, thank you.' Carefully, he unfolded the towel and poured the broken ice crystals into the gap. 'And then, a spoonful of salt.'

'Salt? That's disgusting,' said Orlando.

'Don't worry, zio, it's not for tasting; it keeps the freezing point down. Keeps it nice and slick. Next, we add our fior di latte... what?'

Rosa was laughing. 'You said "lahg-ee"! You sound like Sergio's donkey.'

'When it's sick,' added Cesca.

'Right, we add our run-ee creem then – that better?'

This set them off again.

Italian with a Glasgow twang: bargaweegie, Joe called it. In Barga, it was commonplace – it was how her own father spoke. Lots of barghigiani had made the journey from Italy to Scotland. Folk like Papà's grandfather, leaving dirt-poor Tuscany for the opportunity of foreign shores. Only took one brave soul to jump, tell those back home: *Sì*, it was cold, but it wasn't so bad. Or *wisny. They say 'wisny' here. You should come. The people are nice. They seem to like us, like our gesso figurines, our gelato.* So others came and joined their kin, made their pennies, sent them home with their sons to buy land and wives, grow families, and those families returned their sons and daughters to Scotland, weaving to and fro in a backstitch of generations. Blending gelato and selling chips.

But there were no easy blends in Italy any more.

'Fine. This is all for me and Dolce Vita, then.'

'Stop calling me that.'

'Alright, Dolce.' He winked at Cesca. 'She turned out strict, didn't she?'

'Well, she is going to be a teacher.'

'Ach, girls don't need to work. Not the pretty ones.'

His hair needed to be cut; it kept falling over his face. Suddenly, his good-natured silliness became as clanging as his accent. Her cousin Gianni was missing, there were boys out there in pain, and here was Joe, having a great laugh. Surely his country was at war too? With them, in fact. The racing in Vita's blood became unpleasant.

'I mean it, Giuseppe.'

'Oh-ho,' said Zio Orlando. 'That girl is going to be such a match for you, boy.'

Joe stared at her. She stared back.

'Anyway...' Signor Tutto's voice echoed in the cave. 'Now for the magic ingredient.' He held a couple of small bottles aloft. 'Sugar syrup. We've been experimenting.'

'What's wrong with plain?' said Orlando. 'Plain, chocolate and strawberry.'

'But why?' said Cesca. 'What about every flavour in the world?'

'I agree. So let's have tutti-frutti – with a rosemary twist.' Joe trickled some ruby-coloured liquid inside the pail. 'Drum roll, ladies.' The girls banged their fists on the table. Joe pressed the lid onto the bucket, firming it round to make a tight seal. He spun it vigorously, the veins on his forearms blue. He had such pale skin compared to the rest of them. Same Guidi nose though. He took off the lid, churned it more with a wooden stick.

'What do you think?'

Zio Orlando peered in. 'Looks alright.'

'Who wants to try?' said Joe.

'Me! Me!' In the clamour, Rosa bumped Cesca into a basket of aubergines; purple fruits tumbling on the floor.

'Careful!'

'Ach, don't bother putting them back in. Stick them in your pinny, Ces. Half are for Auntie El anyway – my earnings for clearing Signor Bertini's field. Now,' Joe beckoned Vita, 'age before beauty.'

The gelato had turned rose pink, with a sweet berry-scent. Her irritation melted as Joe's head moved closer to hers. But she would never get to taste the deliciousness that was surely there, because Renata ran in, just then, just at the point Joe was lifting the spoon to Vita's mouth, and it would have been good and cool to taste it in the darkness of the cave. She was sure it would have been good.

'Never mind that!' Renata was shouting. 'The King's just declared war. On the Germans!'

The cave filled with silence. Vita felt Joe's hand reach for hers. It was Cesca who spoke first.

'Does that mean he's at war with Il Duce? Is the King at war with us?'

Chapter Two

'Baby.'

Frank's mom, buttoning up his coat though the sky was a high, bright California blue. A group of white girls sat on their suitcases, watching. The redhead in the middle gave a little wave. Frank turned away, mortified.

Momma wore her Sunday coat, and her yellow-sprigged dress. 'I am so proud. Now, you eat well and keep clean, OK?'

'I am. I'm wearing my best shirt.'

'I know you are, honey. And you look just fine.' She brushed his shoulders with the back of her hand. 'And don't get into any fights – and don't go looking out the window when you pass through Mississippi.'

'Why?'

'The white folks there just don't like us, is all.'

'Momma, they don't know us.'

'I mean, *us*. They don't like Negroes.'

'Oh, Momma. Come on.'

'I'm just saying, Francis.'

'Francis, do as your mother says.' In the brief closing of his father's eye, Frank saw solidarity, amusement. A desire for peace. Was his pop about to hug him?

'Be good now, son.' Firm handshake. Gruff. 'ASTP, huh? Specialised training? And you definitely get commissioned after?'

'I guess.'

'Well. Be good,' he repeated.

'Bye, Pop.'

'You listen to your father, Francis. Be good. Always. Be good, and say your prayers – and wash, you hear me? Keep your teeth clean.'

'Yes, Momma.' Bending to kiss her, then seizing her whole in his arms, so tight that her mauve heels left the station platform.

'Oh, my baby boy.'

'Noreen. That's enough. Let the boy go.'

Only it was him holding on to her. Frank wanted to stay right there, inside the feathery collar of his mother's coat, with her perfume sweet and strong. Gloved hands that were smooth over his, reaching up and kneading his cheek.

'Baby. Home is where you are loved the best. And missed the most. Remember that, you hear? Now you kiss your little brother.'

Willis Junior was tucked, blurry, behind Pop; there was a slick of moisture over Frank – he couldn't see them all, 'cause of the heat and... hell, he must be sweating hard for it to be this sticky. Little Willis found him first, his toecap making contact with Frank's shin.

'You don't kiss me, Francis Chapel. Don't you dare!'

'Hey! I wasn't going to *kiss* you, peanut brain. And get cooties? I don't think so.' He scooched down a little, so he was eye-level with the kid. 'Hand?'

Willis offered it, grudgingly. His skin was hot.

'Will you look after Momma when Pop's at work? You know how to fix her iced tea, don't you?'

'Yup. And I can mow the yard good as you.'

'Well then.'

'Well then.'

'Shit!'

'Francis!'

Grabbing his little brother, hard round the middle. 'Love you, buddy.' Could feel the thin frame shaking. 'Hey! What's this?'

'You coming back, Francis?'

''Course I am.'

'Billy Clerkin's big brother didn't come back.'

'He was up in one of those dumb airplanes. I'm gonna be right on the ground, probably stuck in an office someplace. They're sending me to college, remember? I'm gonna be an engineer.'

'What if the airplanes come at you, though? Like they did on them boats?'

'Well, you know how fast I am. I'll just run. They'll never catch me.'

'You promise?'

'Yup.'

'But what about all the fire trails and 'splosions? I *seen* it at the movie theatre. All the big lights banging. That's when it gets you.'

'You know what? That's just them painting up the sky – it's like a secret war code, so's the soldiers can talk to each other.'

'Yeah, sure.' Willis blew the air out his nose like a little bull.

'Yes, *sure*. Willis, you are looking at the man who scored A1 on the top army intelligence tests. And they *told* me that stuff already. So.'

'So.' Willis shook his head, slowly, but there was the beginning of a smile. 'So. Michael Carrera says you are full of—'

'Willis!' said his mother. 'That's enough. Francis needs to get on his train.'

Good a way as any to leave them: Momma proud and teary, Pop quietly above it all, and Willis thinking he was full of shit. Frank jumped aboard, sat on the bottom berth in a compartment of the pullman. The car was tagged at the end of the regular passenger train, set aside for military.

Four weeks ago, Frank had been a college freshman. Straight-A black kid at white-towered Berkeley, on a campus teeming with girls, slick college girls who made his clever mouth dry at the edges. Studying math and science and wishing it was art, and wanting something big to happen. Been wanting that for years. He was sick of being invisible.

The poster on the bulletin board said if you signed up before you turned eighteen, you'd get a sixth-month deferment. From a war you'd no cause to fight.

Lesson one: they lie.

Since the Japs bombed Pearl Harbour, this war had been churning on, a constant presence like the ocean: over there, a thought, occasionally, when the scent on the breeze turned. A theoretical possibility you might have dipped into. Perhaps. Young men going to do their country proud. You heard a lot about the marching off, not so much about what happened after.

Only now, the theory was fact. They'd used up so many US soldiers, they were moving to draft black folks. *Soldiering's for white men*, said a white boy in his class. *You'll only be shifting and shovelling anyway.*

'Is that right?' he'd asked his buddy Charlie. 'Don't we get to fight?' He'd added the 'get to' at the last minute, figuring it sounded better. Frank could run fast, and he could box. Track and field were permissible activites – you could even shoot hoops, and practise catch, but some invisible line excluded black students from joining teams. Which was fine. Team games alarmed him, mostly due to the fact there'd be others to let down beside himself. He wasn't any kind of leader. Killing might the ultimate loner activity. But it contained, on its flip side, the possibility of being killed. Being killed was not the change of which Frank dreamed.

'Nuh,' said Charlie. 'My cousin's over in Europe right now. All they do is keep stuff oiled. War be over soon anyway – damn Eyeties even started fighting with themselves.'

Charlie was so sure about the world. Practise as he might, Frank could not capture the easiness with which his buddy rolled through life, and women. Charlie reckoned if they drafted you, you'd be gone within the month. *This way, we enlist, we show willing – and get six months longer here.* Six months was half a year: half a year when Frank could perfect his swagger, maybe kiss a girl and join the OTC and practise being a man. A uniform might help. If you had a uniform, that was a shorthand. Meant you didn't have to speak. And a uniform was a uniform was a uniform. It might break through that other invisibility, the one nobody really spoke about in Berkeley because they were college kids and so, so smart. A uniform would make you an American. Hell, a uniform might give you a vote.

Frank removed his jacket, folded it neat inside the tiny locker. Space was so cramped you didn't need to stretch. He'd told his folks not to wait. The little window faced the opposite side of the tracks, so he'd no idea if they were still there. Two berths in this slim chamber, but he'd heard some guys slept top to tail. The thought repulsed him, someone's dirty feet in his face. Charlie had got his six-month stay of execution after all. Whoever bunked with Frank would be a stranger.

Most of the other guys swilling on the platform had been in uniform. He guessed he'd get his at Fort Benning, which was no big deal but it would have been nice to start out looking like he belonged. Should he take the top berth or the bottom? Some guy's butt above you, or your face two inches from the roof? Bottom felt more roomy. As he dithered, he could hear the clip, clip of boots down the corridor. Then a slowing, then a pause. He part-stood, sharp flash-thought; it would mean relinquishing owner-ship of the bottom berth, so, no. And down again. Deep breath as the door opened. This was it, this was it, he could be anyone at all in this new place. Man, he could be Charlie.

A stocky boy stepped inside: roll-up cigarette, duffel bag almost half the size of him slung over one shoulder. He wore a yellow shirt, sleeves rolled high and tight so the packed balls of muscle burst like pea-pods below. 'How you doing?' The boy drew on his cigarette. 'I'm Luiz.'

'Good to meet you. I'm Frank.'

'I'll take the top, yeah?' He chucked his bag up.

'Sure. I...' Frank's fingers, spreading on the coverlet. 'I'm fine here.'

The train jolted forward and they were off. He wanted to run to the corridor, wave to his momma as they sped away – what if they were waiting still? – but this Luiz guy was eyeing him through smoke, so.

So he didn't. And he would always be sorry for that.

They rumbled on for an hour or so; he guessed Luiz was sleeping. He sure wasn't talking. Frank flicked through a paperback, but he couldn't concentrate. He'd packed a blank notebook too, to record this for posterity. *Here's me, on my berth.* Shouldn't they be doing something? Was there a roll call, a bunch of instructions to be given? Regulations to read? Was he officially 'in' the army now, or could he jump off at the next station if he chose?

Did he have choices? He thought of the lieutenant in the recruiting office. Pleasant man, full of Southern courtesy.

'You know,' the man had spoken languorously, 'you boys are something of a dilemma. One we did not seek.'

'Sir.'

'Plenty shouting from your Negro papers, your Negro politicians. Plenty stamping feet. But some folks think coloured troops ain't...' He'd smiled, tapping his pen on his teeth. 'Well, that you don't have the temperament for war. What you say to that, Chapelle?'

'It's Chapel, lieutenant.'

'You done much fighting, boy?'

'No, sir.'

'But you smart? You a college boy, yes?'

'Yes, sir.'

'So how you feel, being bellyached at day and night. Folks yelling instead of asking?'

'I guess that's the army, sir.'

'You want to serve your country, Chapelle?'

'Yes, sir.'

'If I tell you you'll be cleaning latrines for the next two years, that you be cleaning up white boys' shit for you service, you OK with that?'

'Yes, sir.'

'If I tell you you spooks ain't no better than a bunch of women and all we got for you is nursemaiding in the hospital, you be all right with that?'

'Yes, sir.'

'If I said you niggers can't fight because you split at the first sign of trouble and your motherfucking brains is in your dicks, you be all right with that, Chapelle?'

'No, sir!'

'No, sir, why, sir? You wan' fight me, boy?'

Frank's hands were trembling. 'No, sir. I want you to shut up.'

A knock at the door, and then an orderly had entered with Frank's test scores, except Frank thought it was probably to arrest him, and he'd steeled himself, waiting for the hustle out, and then the lieutenant had coughed and gone: 'Heh, heh. Show me some bite, boy.' Tapping his pen on his teeth again. Blue ink on his finger. In a minute it would spread to the side of his mouth. 'You get yourself shot, you blood will run just the same ruby red as mine. You got me?'

'Sir. Yes, sir.'

The lieutenant's eyes had swept down to the blotter on his desk. 'Uh-huh, Chapelle. Dismiss.'

Lesson two: let it go.

Another hour of bumping and rolling, and Frank began to doze. Then the legs of Luiz appeared in front of him. He'd changed into uniform green. Tunic made him seem taller. You could still see the tightness of his arms underneath.

'Wanna get some eats?'

'Can we?'

'It's the army. They ain't gonna starve you, man. Come on.'

Not understanding how Luiz knew these things and he didn't, Frank followed. Had there been an induction message he missed? All his letter said was he'd to report to this train. They walked along the corridor of the sleeping car; he could hear a few voices, the twang of a guitar behind a door. Through the next car, a passenger car, where people turned and watched them go. Then it was the dining car.

'Help you, boys?' said the waitress.

'Yes, ma'am. We're headed to Fort Benning, and I wanted to check what provision had been made for us to dine here?'

This? This urbane soldier was duffel-bag Luiz?

'Sure. Well, there's a few of your boys over there.' She pointed at a full-up table, where young, pink-faced soldiers were tearing into a basket of bread rolls. 'Let me see. You can get one appetiser and one entree, or one entree and one dessert. Water and two cups of coffee too. Why don't you get yourselves seated and I'll bring the menu over?'

'Thank you, ma'am.'

She looked at Frank. 'Mm-hm.'

The tables next to the soldiers were all occupied, so they chose one further down. Across the aisle was an elderly couple, and behind Frank a family was sharing out salad greens. He touched his forehead to the old lady opposite as he sat. 'Ma'am.'

Luiz took the menu card from the waitress, barely glanced at it. 'Soup and steak, please.'

Frank spent longer studying the card, so long in fact that the waitress was summoned by the old couple, and had moved over to them.

'Where d'you reckon we are now?' he asked Luiz.

'No idea.'

All I know is, once we hit south, my momma said—'

He was interrupted by the waitress. 'Excuse me, boys. I'm afraid I'm gonna have to ask you to leave.'

'Excuse me?' Luiz placed his water glass, carefully, on the table.

The waitress was in her fifties, a faded beauty with puffy hands. She lowered her voice. 'I'm real sorry, but I can't serve you. Not here.'

'Not here? Why?'

'Well,' she chewed on her lip, 'I can serve you, son.' She turned to Frank. 'But not you.'

'I'm a soldier too! I just don't have my uniform yet.'

'It's not that...' Her glance slid sideways, to the elderly couple who were straight-backed, slurping soup.

A sudden wash of shame. He could feel the sweat prickle on him, sharp little stabs on every portion of his skin, and inside his head, where they became sharp little hammers, beating on his eyeballs. He stood up to go, but Luiz tapped his wrist. 'Hold up, buddy.' He raised his voice. 'You want to tell me why you won't serve a soldier of the US Army, ma'am?'

Frank shook his head. He was staged like a marionette, for all the world to see. Like a wet eel writhing on a hook. 'Please, man. Don't.'

Further up the car, the other soldiers were taking notice; he could see the nudging, whispers. One big, meaty grin. They were legion; around twenty white faces in the car, all staring up at *him*. The boy who did not wish to be invisible.

'It's fine, ma'am,' he said. 'Can I have soup and steak in the pullman car?'

'You go on. I'll bring it right along.'

He felt his way back down through the dining car, past the old couple who were just rigid bars, past a family not-eating, through the passenger car where he heard crystal laughter, caught a glimpse of red hair, down the corridor of the sleeping car, groping round the door, sliding it shut. Keeping his spine hugged there, tight up against the peeling wood. The flesh on his knuckles taut. Shiny black knuckles.

Frank was not naïve. He might be cushioned in laid-back California, where, so long as you didn't cross the line, there was a veneer of egalitarianism. School was mixed and – technically – you could dance with white girls. The US Army was segregated; he'd accepted that. But to be forbidden to eat in public? That the fact of his teeth on show, that his jaw working, would offend the sensibilities of good folks around him? How unclean did they want him to feel? Not just him, but his momma? Folks like his momma? Would they look at that sweet, Godly woman who polished and scrubbed all day and see only dirt?

There was a knocking on his door. Frank stood himself straight, slid it open. Not the waitress but a soldier, a white man with silver bars on his tunic, same as the soldier in recruitment.

'Chapel?'

'Sir.'

'Come on through. Chowtime.'

'But the lady—'

'Chapel.' He was staring at his clipboard. 'You might think you're some fancy-assed college boy who deserves room service, but not on my train. Now shift your butt through to that dining car. And get your goddam uniform on.'

'I don't have one, sir.'

'How come you don't have one?'

'Not been issued, sir. I was rushed straight through.'

Aptitude scores that were 'off the scale', mechanical and classification tests so good, they were sending him straight to ASTP. 'Not been to Fort MacArthur either. It's on my record, sir. Francis Chapel.'

'Oh.' First time the lieutenant properly looked at him. 'OK. *You're* the one. Big Brain. Kind of expected you'd be...'

'Sir?'

''Scuse me, lieutenant.' It was the waitress. 'That's us ready.'

'Move it.' The officer pushed him forward. 'Quick-time.' He never did tell Frank what kind of a smart-ass he should have been.

The return journey was worse, the lieutenant ushering him on like he was a prisoner. There was no victory in this parade. Swivel-heads following their progress, a tinder-trail of commentary behind. Frank was so thirsty though, he could think of nothing better than to pour a draught of cool water down his throat. When they reached the dining car, he looked for Luiz, saw that he'd squeezed in beside the other soldiers. Why wouldn't you? Who would want to eat alone? In the midst of all their various shaved-pinks and golds, Luiz looked simply tan. Table for one then. Fine. Leastways, it was a table. The old couple, thankfully, had gone. Though if he were to meet them, face on, he didn't know what he'd say.

Man, he would say nothing. Frank went to take a seat at an empty table. The waitress scuttled up. 'Uh...'

'Chapel,' called the lieutenant. 'You sit here.'

It was a table at the end of the row. And they'd rigged up a curtain on a pole, so it could be drawn round Francis Morgan Chapel as he ate.

It remained that way for the duration of the journey: Frank behind his curtain, the rest of the guys taking in the view. Outside of mealtimes, Frank was allowed to walk through the train. One time they stopped in Alabama, and the lieutenant took them off for lunch. Said Frank could come too.

'You sure, sir?'

'Sure. Last time we stopped here, Bull Connor sent a bunch of his boys by to say hi to you Negro recruits.'

'What happened?'

'Oh, there was no trouble.'

'Well, OK then, sir. I'll come. Thank you.' Frank grabbed his coat, eager for the chance to walk on unmoving carpets, get the air on his face. And it might be a chance to know the other recruits better. On untainted ground, where there were no compartments. Luiz was a decent guy, had tried to get Frank to come play cards in another of the berths – he meant well, Frank reckoned. But he didn't want to be Luiz's pet.

'Who's Bull Connor anyway?' Frank asked.

'Chief of Police,' said the lieutenant.

Frank didn't get off the train. By all accounts they had a great feed. Frank rang the changes with a hamburger on a bun, then yellow ice cream for dessert. He was starting to like his curtain, was adept at noticing the changes in the blue and green pattern when light struck through the weave, or when a person moved past. One time, he heard a woman – she sounded old, so he pictured her as the old biddy who'd had him curtained in the first place – say to one of the soldiers: 'You brave boys – you make me so proud. God bless you.'

But this black boy made her ashamed. (If it *was* her – but, for the purposes of his digression, it was.) 'Brave' was a word Frank heard a lot; you did in times of war. It had a ready glow to it, was an honourable, solid word, hung big and certain as a medal on your chest. Folk cast it like a cloak to cover many things – often the things you didn't want to contemplate, not even to stand close to. Was it brave to do what you were told? Because that's all these 'boys' were doing. Was it brave if you weren't scared, if you thought you were on some glorious adventure; if you knew it was not an adventure, but a terrible unknown place, if you showed that terror on your face, if you sat here and cried; if you joked too loud and cared for nothing but what flavour ice cream there was today, if you listened and did not join in, if you made yourself be first, be funniest, if you hid behind a curtain, if you pulled your curtain wide?

You had to be scared before you could be brave. Otherwise, it meant jack-shit. Frank ate his soup. Listened to the soldiers some more.

Eventually, the train arrived in dusty Georgia. 'Men,' said the lieutenant, saluting the red earth and the vast blue, wakening sky. 'Welcome to Fort Benning. Since 1918, this here has been the home of the US Infantry. Be proud, soldiers. Be very proud.'

Sun-up, and the place was alive. Men marching, men shouting. Men running, men at ease. A huge factory of men. The complex covered thousands of acres. It was a city of soldiers, groupings of white buildings and well-tended gardens; here a chapel, dust, trucks, dust; there, assault courses, barracks, dust, tents, towers, showers, dust, brick-coloured dust that puffed in clouds from your boots, got in your hair, your teeth.

Frank was hived off from the rest of them, unsure at first if it was for special training or segregation. It was the latter. Luiz too, surprisingly, but it seemed there were gradations of colour, and, if you were dark Hispanic, you were not white. There were American Japanese (also problematic) and American Indians, who were welcomed into the cowboy fold, no longer the enemy at all, except for this one guy with whom the sergeant did not know what to do.

'You there. You one of them windtalkers, Comanche?'

'Excuse me?'

'Excuse me, sergeant!'

'Sergeant.'

'Name?'

'Barfoot, sir. Sergeant. Jack Barfoot.'

'What kinda name's that? Barfoot? You an injun, son, or a nigger?'

'My grandfather is a Choctaw—'

'What the fuck you doing here, boy?'

'My father was a Negro, sergeant. I was told—'

'Jesus. You one mixed-up fuck, aren't you? You mama one of them Eskimos?'

'Sergeant?'

The sergeant was using his little finger to pick at his back teeth. Some remnant of breakfast still there, or the remains of the last recruit he'd chewed the head off. The stubby pink digit worked away.

'All you coloured boys – get your bedding and line up here.'

There were six of them, plus Luiz, who mutely shuffled to the left. Barfoot stood in the middle of the parade ground. 'Yo! You too, Mr Comanche-Mulatto-Son-of-Eskimo-Nell.' The sergeant quit picking. 'Hoo-ee. Some wonderful bunch of heroes I got me to work with. Corporal, go get me a turkey feather for the injun's hat. You ready, boys? You ready to serve your country? You ready to serve the land of THE MOTHERFUCKING FREE?'

Frank started at the use of that cuss word. He'd never heard it yelled by a white man. It was not a word you shouted. The sergeant dragged Barfoot into line. 'The home of the beautiful BRAVE? Yee-ha! Come on, boys. Come in, to your new home.'

From a barrack window, a voice hollered: 'Hey, Jody! Run while you can!'

Lesson three: they mean you.

Chapter Three

No buonsenso, anywhere.

The streets of Barga's Giardino swarmed, folk milling and gathering, lorries rushing, a whistle blowing. Decrees being pasted on walls; Vita saw a woman argue with an Italian soldier, pulling at his brush as he stuck up a poster. Bold black *RSI*, an angular eagle spread across the flag, its wings stretching from green to red.

'What do the posters say?' said Cesca. 'What are we meant to do?'

'I don't know,' said Mamma. 'There's too many people here. Let's go to the Comune. They'll tell us more there. There's bound to be an announcement soon.'

Folk had been saying that for days. They had waited in vain for instructions, quiet and troubled in their homes; Papà's hand curved over the radio like it was a cage to catch the words, or hold them at bay. Waiting for common sense to prevail. This morning, Mamma had snapped. She was not a patient woman.

They pushed past bewildered soldiers, watching as a gang of youths smashed the window of a droghiere. Only Vita gave chase, yelling as the boys ran off with armfuls of fruit and tins.

'Just leave them!' Papà shouted, and she stopped, abruptly, shocked at her own reaction. Was this how it would be? Your country at war with itself.

Her mother slapped her arm. 'Don't ever do that again.'

Straight over Ponte Vecchio she marched them, up the steep alley that heralded the start of the narrow passages of the old town, past Caffè Capretz with its stone loggia, dodging the salvoes and whistle-stop snatches – *Rome... on fire – Deserting... us or them?*

The wooden doors of the Comune were shut fast. A crowd stood outside. Before anyone could stop her, Mamma shoved her way through, seizing the great brass knocker.

'Open up, you fools. You're meant to be our leaders.'

People were staring. But the woman who wrote frequent letters to Il Duce would always aim straight for the top.

'Elena, come away. They're not going to let you in.'

'This is hopeless. We have the girls... Mario, what are we to do? Is the fighting coming here?'

Fury, then fear. Mercury-fast, the way only her mother could be. Papà let her scold and cry a little, then led her from the Comune, steering her by the elbow, navigating the churning streets.

At Bar Alpino, they passed another line of soldiers, climbing into a truck. These were different. They had unfamiliar greeny-grey tunics and puffy trousers, tucked into long black boots.

Papà spoke softly. 'Let's go home. We need to find Giuseppe.'

Vita had never seen German soldiers so close before. They were loading up picks and spades, clearing out Barga's ferramenta.

'Yes.' Mamma dabbed her eyes. Recalibrating. 'Good. About time they showed their faces here.'

'Mamma, how can you say that? If we're supposed to be at war with them?'

'No. *We* are not at war with Germany.'

Papà addressed the ironmonger, who was watching his store being emptied. 'Be able to retire after this, eh, Enzo?'

'Sì, sì. A great day's business. Except I don't think I'm being paid.'

'Ah.'

'There's more of them coming. They say six Wehrmacht divisions have arrived in the north. Same troops Mussolini was begging Hitler for, before. Funny how they're only arriving—'

'But they are here now, Enzo, and that is wonderful. We must give thanks to Il Duce for his foresight, no?' Mamma's tears had dried to nothing; she was brighter in fact, puffed up, almost, as if her misery had soaked her through and filled her with renewed conviction.

'Well, some aren't too happy.' The ironmonger jerked his head. 'Watch the rats deserting.'

A young woman edged past the truck, pulling at her headscarf. She carried a hessian sack.

'Is that Devora?'

'Think so. Helping herself before she leaves. The Monsignor is far too generous...'

The way those pale soldiers were clattering the tools onto the truck. Methodical. Relentless. There was something majestic in their stoic arms, their neat swings and dips – one whistled at her, and Vita looked sharply to the sky.

'Mario, why don't you take the girls home?' said Mamma. 'There's an errand I need to do.' Scrutinising Vita, the way she might measure her for a dress.

Papà was still scrutinising the soldiers. 'No. We'll wait. I don't want you wandering alone in this...' He waved his hand. How to describe the oscillation of bodies and faces? In every strut, there was a cower. In every smile, you could see the skull behind.

'Fine. I won't be long.' Then Mamma disappeared into the crowds. Methodical. Relentless. As she watched her mother go, Vita caught sight of Devora again, hunched in a doorway. She seemed shrunken, deep in conversation with a person Vita couldn't see. It was a man, she could make out his arm, slung round Devora's shoulders, and her, nodding. Very unseemly for the housekeeper of the Canonica to be—

The man was first to step from the doorway. It was Joe.

'Cara, did you hear me?' said Papà. 'Let's get some limonata.'

They sat on the terrace of L'Alpino: men and the radio chattering inside the bar, outside, engines running, people running, everywhere was sound and motion.

'You not thirsty, Vita?' her father asked.

'No.'

'Look at the face on her.' Cesca slipped into bargaweegie. 'Who stole your scone?'

'Don't speak English,' said Papà. 'Not here.'

The Germans moved off, folk scattering as the truck clattered down Via Roma. A few tedeschi soldiers remained outside the ironmonger's. Smoking, surveying the street. Vita chewed her thumbnail. It was up to Joe who he spoke to. One of the soldiers caught her gaze and smiled. Hurriedly, Vita picked up her drink. She looked through her lashes at her father, trying to see beyond his thinning hair and sad eyes. There was a photograph at home she loved, of him as a child, outside their café in Scotland. Centre stage was his nonna, who must have followed her husband to Paisley.

But he was no longer in the picture. Instead, their sons stood either side, with their sons: Joe's dad and Vita's papà. Short trousers and gappy teeth, Papà grinning and holding a bottle of limonata aloft, while Roberto held baby Antonia.

Joe looked like his father. Vita's memories of Zio Roberto were vague. He and his wife rarely left the café, and Joe would be sent here for long summers on his own. Vita was thrilled to walk with this handsome Scottish Guidi, eat granita at Piazza Angelio, Joe the centre of a laughing crowd, with every girl secretly a little in love with him. But it was always Vita whose arm he took. He was such a flash of light to be around. Gallus, her papà called him. Look at him now, sauntering, brazen, past the soldiers.

'Buongiorno, Guidis!' Joe reached over the low trellis to kiss Vita's hand. If they were to get married, he would kiss her lips. He would kiss her everywhere – that's what Renata said men did. Everywhere. She'd imagined it plenty. Joe dropped her hand. Took a swig of her limonata, his throat pulsing; she could trace the long draught going down. It was like looking at a lovely piece of art. Her tongue worked at a shred of lemon.

'Giuseppe,' said Papà. 'I told you not to come into town. It's not safe.'

'Ach! Bugger the Bosch.' Joe winked at Vita. There was a darkening under his eyes the way an apple spoils.

'Did you hear me, son?'

'Dolce – walk with me?'

She shook her head. Pulled her hand away – she should have done it earlier, to show she was jealous.

'Oh, go on. It'll do you good.'

'I'll go with you—'

45

'No, Cesca,' said Papà. 'Joe. Get your arse back up the hill before I kick it, you hear?'

Vita took another drink. 'I'm sure Joe's got lots of girls to go walking with.'

'Fine. I'll away then.' He said it loudly and deliberately in English. Saluted them, then began to march slowly down the road towards Ponte di Catagnana. Proper marching, from a man who wasn't fighting.

'Bloody idiot.' Papà rubbed his calf. 'That boy's a liability.'

'No, he's not,' said Cesca. 'He's funny.'

'He's full of himself is what he is. Is your leg sore again, Papà?'

'I'm fine.'

You weren't supposed to notice his leg. He'd hurt it in Abyssinia. When he was tired, his wide stride wavered, and he limped. Vita thought that was why he was up most nights, listening to Radio Londra or the sad music he called laments.

Cesca crunched the ice at the bottom of her glass. 'I need to pee.'

'Don't drink so quickly, then.'

'I'm not. And why were you so mean to Joe?'

'Shut up, Cesca.'

'No, you shut up. You're not my mamma.'

'Both of you. Just stop. Here.' Papà handed Cesca some money. 'Pay for the drinks when you're inside. Please.' He took out his tobacco and pipe. 'You two are as bad as your mother. What have I done to deserve three argumentative women?'

At the end of the road, just as it dipped, Joe turned and waved at them.

'You mean passionate, Papà.' Spontaneously, Vita stood. Blew Joe a kiss. He looked so small in the distance. She felt a rush of tenderness, sharp as if she'd pressed a bruise. But Joe kept walking, she'd not been quick enough; he hadn't seen her.

'He's something else, that boy. You could do worse.'

'Why did he come here, Papà?' She sat down.

'He's never talked to you about it?'

'He never talks to me about anything. Not even his mamma and papà.'

Her father stretched out his bad leg. 'Was it a bomb?' she ventured. 'Renata said it was a bomb?'

A puff of grey ash. The fragrant smoke made a thread in the air. 'No. Roberto drowned. A shipwreck.'

'In the war?'

'Kind of.' Papà paused. 'The shock was too much for poor Giovanna. They took forever to... well, finding out what happened took an age. It was terrible. She never kept well, even here. Then, when Roberto took her with him to Scotland, the damp air... Och, it's very sad.'

'But why did Joe come here?'

Her father patted her hand. 'You should speak to him about that, Vita.'

'I've tried.'

'Well, try harder. You're no a wee lassie any more.'

'I thought we'd only to speak Italian.'

'Sometimes I forget what I'm speaking.'

You can be more than one thing, cara. He'd always told her that. Whenever there was a pageant, or San Cristoforo's parade, Papà would wear a piece of tartan over his tabard. Mamma laughed at him, yet it was she who stitched the plaid. Vita thought he was proud of being both. But maybe he'd been defending his differences.

'Do you miss it? Scotland?'

'Why d'you ask?'

47

'Just... it must be strange. Growing up somewhere, then living somewhere else.'

'It is. But here's home too.'

She tried to imagine life without her family, her home. The weight of imagining it frightened her. *Do you want me to marry Joe, Papà? That's* what she really wanted to ask. *Am I to marry him, or be a teacher?* But she knew he'd answer like he always did. *Good question, Vita. What do you think?*

'What will this mean for Joe? If more Germans come?'

Until now, he'd been safe enough, because Scottish or not, he was barghigiano. And nobody bothered with Barga. Young, able-bodied men were at a premium, so he'd even been welcomed on their neighbours' land – provided he worked while the shadows were lengthening.

Papà didn't answer. He relit his pipe, humming to himself. It sounded desperate, not happy. '*Su fratelli e su compagni*' – the old Socialist anthem. They used to sing it to annoy Mamma, then when she stopped being annoyed and started getting furious, they would only sing it when alone.

He'd been a teacher of English, once. Before Cesca was born, in the days when their house was filled with people talking. Vita could remember lots of feet and trousers. Mamma sparkling. Coloured liquids and clinking glass. Nicer clothes. It was the days when you could choose if you went to Party meetings or not, and Papà chose not to, and they chose not to let him keep his job.

'Papà,' she said quietly. He needed to stop humming. 'Is the King really going to fight against Il Duce?'

He shrugged.

'Whose side will we be on?'

'Good question. What do you think?'

'I don't know.' She finished her drink. The limonata was weak and bitter. 'It was the King who ran away.'

Papà lowered his voice. 'Wouldn't you if you could? It's meant to be so simple. All of us following the leader. But look at their squadristi, their book burnings. The fascisti are blunt and dull. And they dull us too.'

'What about Mamma?' Nobody could call her mother dull.

'Faith and obedience, that's what your mamma knows.' He stared at his pipe. 'Your mamma believes in many things. People like to do what they're told. They think it makes them good.'

Yet they were all obedient to Mamma. She was the hub around which their house ran, the arbiter to whom each decision was passed for approval. The voice you dreaded, the presence you felt.

'I've disappointed her. She thought she was marrying an adventure.' He gave a mirthless laugh. 'I'm the one time she was disobedient – and look where it got her. Never marry a disappointment, cara. Ah, speak of the devil.'

Mamma was standing over them. 'Limonata? Oh, to have time and money for limonata, Mario, when we've lemons aplenty at the house.'

'Light of my life.' Papà knocked his pipe on the table edge. 'Any news?'

'Yes, actually. Excellent news. Vittoria, I've found you a job.'

'But I don't have time. Not this term; I'll have too much studying.'

'You're not going back to the Conservatorio.'

An odd, flat feeling in Vita's stomach.

'Elena. What job is this?'

'It's a good one. With the Monsignor. He's in urgent need of a housekeeper. Where is Francesca?'

'Housekeeper? In Barga? Every day, trek down here?'

'Sì. If you like it so much. I said – oh, there you are, Cesca. Right, let's go. I've work to do. Overalls to sew and a letter to write to Il Duce. Francesca, you may write one too. He likes it when children—'

'To come every day to Barga, but not to the Conservatorio?' Vita's limbs felt unconnected to her body. 'But I need to finish school. How else can I be a teacher?'

'There's a war on.'

'I know there's a bloody war on!'

'Don't speak to your mother like that.'

'It's a good job, Vita. And with all this turmoil... and Papà not working...' Mamma's voice came from far away. Everything was receding. Vita gone flat, transparent, as if some great weight had rolled over and over her. 'We need the money. The Monsignor is very respected. You'll be safe there. You can stay at the Canonica if need be. Cesca too...' Mamma kept clipping and unclipping her handbag. 'Now. Enough on the subject. We are in public. Come.'

Not be a teacher? Skivvy for a priest? Not just any priest: the Monsignor, an austere presence who would float sporadically through the Conservatorio, to whom you must not speak unless spoken to. To whom the nuns virtually bowed. Ensconced in the Duomo, he was detached from the crushed-up living of real folk. The Monsignor wore long black gowns and strange hats. He was not fat or merry like a village priest, did not drink, play cards. Vita wasn't sure what he did, only that he presided over greater matters. A bit like God.

'Safe from what?'

Papà got to his feet. 'Your mamma means safe from the madness. The madness that's going to unfold if her beloved Duce doesn't do the right thing.'

'He *is* doing the right thing. More Germans are arriving, I've heard. They'll push back the enemy. And rescue the King.'

'Would you listen?' Papà put his head close, like they were about to kiss. 'The King is gone. He's not been kidnapped. He's under Allied protection. The King and the generals have left us to our fate.'

'Rubbish. We've thousands of troops to defend us. Oh—' Her hand flew to her mouth. 'Mario, you'll need to speak to Orlando. The situation wth Giuseppe. It can't continue. Him being here, or...' She looked at Vita.

'Make your mind up, woman. Last month you and Orlando were scheming—'

'Well, not now. He can't stay here.'

'And where would you suggest he go?'

'I don't know. Il Duce will—'

'Elena, Il Duce is nowhere in the equation. He's a puppet. Don't you understand, our troops are deserting?' In his agitation, Papà struck the café table. Glasses falling, showering the chair leg, the wall. People staring. A German soldier watched them, drawing on his cigarette. Vita prayed he didn't speak Italian. She should stop them, go to Cesca; she could see her sister pressed against the terrace wall. She should lead her away from this embarassment. But her eyes were smarting. The sunlight blurred, tilting the sky to the ground.

Be a housekeeper?

'Traitors,' Mamma was saying. 'Not our boys. Il Duce will not allow us to be slaughtered by americani.'

'Gesù, it's not the Americans you should be worrying about. Nazis are fighting our soldiers in Rome right now.'

'Lies! That's your Radio Propaganda for you. I have told you and told you, I forbid it in the house!'

'And I forbid Vittoria to leave school!'

Jaunty music blared from the café radio, some woman crooning '*Faccetta Nera*', before a shout went up to *show respect*.

'*You* forbid?'

'She's going to be a teacher. Like her father.'

It felt as if all of Barga was looking down on them. Vita knelt to clean up the mess. Wanting to melt into the dust, and dissolve up into the light. Away, from them. From this.

'Where? What teacher? I don't see a teacher. I see one lazy, foolish man. And one lazy, disrespectful girl – who is finally going to do some work.'

The glass, sparkly on her hands. They mean you.

Summer 1944

Chapter Four

Italy. Land of Michelangelo and Galileo. The troops had been convinced, on their voyage across the Atlantic, that they were headed for Africa – and they did stop in Algeria, but only to load more cargo and men, then on, baking below deck as your throat dried, more puking over the side of the ship, more ocean, and playing cards and endless ocean before they landed. In Naples.

Nothing had prepared Frank for the filth and poverty of that wrecked city. A harbour filled with sunken ships, skyline busted like rows of shattered teeth. Rat-folks living by the docks; girls as young as Willis, selling themselves for a cigarette or soap. Old men and women, begging by the roadside as the US Army passed in a roar of trucks and the clip-clipping of horse wagons, pulling guns and boxes of ammo, and crate upon crate of corned beef. Some of the soldiers threw what they had – gum or hard biscuits – but plenty kept their eyes front and their minds on keeping out the smell.

Frank had become part of the 370th Infantry Regiment, which was part of the 370th Regimental Combat Team, which was part of the 92nd Division, which was part of the

US Fifth Army, which was part of the Allied effort to run the Krauts out of town. Even before they'd disembarked from the ship, the 370th were making waves. They were a rarity, this plume of black men in white men's garb, given white men's guns and status. No commission though. No engineer school. Frank had remained a private.

Months of training, then the ASTP got disbanded. Smart, sharp, dumb, slow; didn't matter. If you was black, *you was a Buffalo, damn.* Frank's brain was no longer required, merely his body. No point asking why. The war machine needed fodder – though that had to be segregated too. Frank was learning one perfect truth, over and over. Do not question. Obey. Like sinking into quicksand: if you struggled, it got worse. You were in the army now. When you surrendered, there was a kind of calm. He was sure it was deliberate, the deadening, the marching, the drilling, the dumbing: a way of grinding down all the disparate souls before rebuilding them into a single unit. At least the Buffaloes had been deemed men enough to fight.

Plenty of other black faces had waited at Naples docks, but these were service troops: guys who fuelled the trucks and unloaded crates. They had hollered and whooped, then fallen silent as the Buffaloes marched past. It made Frank chill, right there in the foetid heat of the Naples docks. All that after-cheering quietness. Had the Buffs been put on a pedestal – or a scaffold, waiting for the drop?

'We such fine soldiers they can't wait to get us in the field,' a soldier next to him had said. 'Show them dead boys what they been doing wrong.'

Theirs was a strange caravan. Bunched in open-top trucks, clouds of steam rising like an aura as the sweat pooled. Each day shimmered forward as they crossed an Italy of ruined smoke and heartbreaking beauty. But no combat in sight. Not yet. At times, it felt like a cross between a vacation and a movie playing past his eyes. Since they'd landed here, Frank had sailed past Vesuvius and swum in the Tyrrhenian Sea. He had driven past the wreckage of Anzio Annie – the huge German gun that had hammered beachhead landings all the way from Rome – and seen a flock of C-47s massing to invade the South of France.

The closer they moved towards the front, the more surreal the world became. They would bivouac in little communities untouched by war, where locals joined the chowline for leftovers; next day stay in ruined villas, abandoned by their bombed-out owners. Some of the country boys would catch rabbits, or chickens left behind, cook them up in grease so they could all have a feast. Made a change from K-rations. Frank found it weird, this mix of men. Bundled together purely by reason of the colour of their skin, not intellect or ability. So far, big slow Claude the pig-herd was way smarter than Frank when it came to keeping them fed.

There were Allied command posts studded in a chain across the country, places where battalions could muster, be relieved, redirected. Other soldiers they encountered, battle scarred and cynical, would break into sudden smiles as they realised the men of the 370th were green as grass. The all-white veterans delighted in sharing stories and advice – none of it meant to shock or impress that Frank could see. Without these soldiers, who were generous with their maps and overlays of positions, their timely reminders to stay silent and always watch the hills, the fragmented vision Frank had of his purpose in this war would have remained chaotic.

Though it made no difference to the outcome, Frank would like some idea of whatever the fuck it was he was meant to be doing.

The US Army was experimenting. The entire fighting force of the 92nd was to be Negro. That was the official term, anyway. And while plenty of folks were rooting for them back home, just as many were waiting for them to fail. When the command had come to head overseas, word was even General Almond questioned their readiness to fight – and it was his goddam show. Still, the army's lack of faith gave the Buffs something to bond over.

'You hear the latest?'

Night-shifting two abreast, through reeds in open countryside. Quite literally in the dark.

'Know what Almond say now? "No white man wants to be accused of leaving the battle line. But the Negro don't care."'

'Hail to our great white chief.'

'Where the fuck are the battle lines anyways? I'm sicka this...'

'We'll find 'em soon enough,' whispered the guy along-side Frank. 'My brother's out in France. He say they going through boys like bam-bam-bam. Just mow 'em down like corn in a field. Be same here—'

'Almond's a dick, man. We just gotta suck it up.'

'I gonna get me some sucking soon. You seen some of those Italian mamas?'

'Suck on your tongue, soldier,' said a lieutenant up front. 'If I hear General Almond's name being taken in vain one more time, I will put you on a charge. After I fried me up your balls for breakfast. You got me?'

Lieutenant Garfield. You did not eyeball that man; he was one long, lean streak of tight-coiled fury. He'd more reason to hate Almond than most. Garfield had been a captain when they started out. But, hell, the natural order had been upset plenty. Black men with guns? Then it followed that their overseers must be white. Some black officers got reclassified, others transferred, so no white officer ever had to answer to a black one. Garfield's demotion cleared the way for their new white captain to lead. From behind or in the middle, wherever was safest at the time. A pasty bank manager named Dedeaux, who would never walk with his men, Frank had barely seen his captain, far less spoken to him.

'Now, when I give the signal, you get on your bellies and crawl to the river's edge.'

Dog-hunched on the dirt, the Buffaloes were south of the River Arno. 1st Armoured was pushing up from newly liberated Rome; its men weary, its tanks no good for the mountainous terrain to come. The Buffaloes had been tasked with relieving them. Cross the river, then head north to break through the German line. Simple.

The first batch must be crossing already; Frank could hear the gentle plash of water. He waited, knees sore. Second row moved forward. Then the third. His row waited, the firm, poised squat of athletic men become a droop. It was still warm, even in the dark, Frank could smell the sweat of his comrades; could feel his own, dripping down his neck, into the cracks of his elbows, his groin. Thighs tense. In *action*. What they shout at the start of a movie. As if you'd not been moving before, just hanging in air, waiting for life to be snapped on, for a jolt to make you real.

'COVER! Fucking *down*, you showera shit.'
Bright
white
flaring.

The slow-mo splash of a drip hitting water; except this was dirt, black dirt, and shards of rock and tree flying up; the stony ground before Frank's boots tearing open, an upside-down fountain of crap; and all the black and white light was shot with red as he rolled himself hard, wide, tumbling downhill away from the crater. Two almighty bangs, more dirt spattering his mouth, filling up nostrils and ears and lungs. He was eating dirt, leastways his teeth were crunching it, jittering down on themselves like they were alive.

Of course his teeth were alive. Was he?

Flat on his back, the moon bleaching his eyes. Only dark stars and sunspots. Could feel the rim of a foxhole under him. In the distance, he could hear bells, and an unearthly voice from way across the riverbank. A woman.

'You ready to stop yet, boys?'

Bells and yells and more bangs, but it could all have been underwater, yawning and booming like it had nothing to do with him.

'Fuck me.' Least that's what he tried to say, but the ringing in his ears sent the words down some echoey well. He waited for something to bounce back. Turned to the guy next to him. The moon lit up half a jaw, the wild spinning eyes of a spooked animal, the most God-awful, goddam gurgling, scratching, sputtering on his face, gore of some other man all across Frank's face and he wanted to run from this horror, but he couldn't find his legs, fuck: his legs... no, hands... were his hands his or this half-faced guy's? His, his... patting down, he had legs: *Bend your legs. Get up, fuck, no, roll!* Which way was up? They were on a riverbank, in an avalanche of shelling: stay down till the shooting stops, but this guy, this poor fuck, was trying to scream.

Frank held on to his arm. 'Hey, buddy. Hey. Hold still. It's OK. It's fine. We'll get you out of here.'

The kid was jerking like he'd been given a shot of electricity. Choking, he was choking on what was left of his face. 'Medic!' yelled Frank, disregarding the command to *Stay quiet. Don't even let your helmet clink against your rifle.* Hell, Jerry had seen them clear enough. 'Medic! Can we get some help over here? Hey! In the foxhole!'

Or maybe the words never came out of him, maybe they were just spinning like the sky above, but this poor kid was spinning faster, writhing to escape himself, and Frank tried to remember what he was supposed to do. It was a suh. There was a thing called a 'suh', *you gotta get the suh on*, and he remembered what the medics had told them. There was a green pouch on his belt, a green pouch with a red tin. Sulpha powder.

'Hold up, buddy.' Frank curled sidey-ways, tore the white paper open with his teeth. You'd to sprinkle it on an open wound, to prevent infection. But this was an open face. Did it stop pain as well as germs? He flung it over the guy's jaw. Nothing was going to stop him bucking. Jesus.

'Medic! Medic!' he bawled, louder and louder. Fuck this. The kid needed morphine.

'Stay with me, buddy. I'm gonna lift you up, OK?'

Frank knelt up in the foxhole. Either he was stone deaf now, or the shelling and the gunfire had stopped.

'Stay with me, kid. What's your—'

Stupid. Stupid. Frank heaved the boy's arms up, tried to straighten him, facing, so he could drape him in a fireman's carry, while they were both still on their knees. Half dragging, half carrying, he began to move forward.

'Medic!'

Moon was dipping behind dark-folded sky. In the half-light, it was hard to see where the rest of the troops had ended up. But the line, those Krauts – they weren't supposed to be here. A recce had been done of the river, this point deemed safe. All the way to Lugnano was supposed to be fucking clear; the reconnaissance patrol had sent up a flare. Green for fucking go.

Man, he had to stop this swearing; it was coming like vomit. From other pits and gullies, shadows of men were emerging. Frank could see a couple of stretcher bearers silhouetted.

'Somebody, help!'

They were on the other side of the river. All the ones who were moving. On the goddam other side. The boy slumped heavier on him, a damp and desperate weight. Frank had two choices. Stay here and hope someone risked coming back for them, or try to wade across. He took a breath. Could make out another man, still in the water, but nearly at the northern bank. Looked waist-deep, no more. Forward, then. Forward was always better than back.

'Sorry, man. We're going for a swim.'

Shuffling towards the river. Hard to make out where land finished and the water began. Footstep. Heartbeat. Double heartbeat, the boy's echoing through his, and a spreading density of heat with it, liquid heat with a metal-lic smell. Poor bastard. Frank's boots slipped beneath him, plunging through mud, and the river found them. He felt the boy's groan, tried to stop them both from sliding out of control. After the first suck of mud, the riverbed became stony, and he was able to get his balance, pick his way forward. The current nudged but didn't push too hard. Knees, thighs, waist immersed. Chill water, soaking up his olive drab, dragging the boy's legs away from him.

'Hey! We need some help here!'

Another soldier, the one who'd just reached the rising bank, looked round. Rest of the guys had disappeared from view. If there were still Jerries lurking, Frank was a floating target. The other soldier slid back into the river. Splashed up beside Frank, took one of the kid's arms over his shoulder.

'OK? Let him slip. I got his other side.' Together, they waded to the northern bank. Frank scrambled out first, pulled the kid's arms as the other soldier shoved him from below. They got him close to where the stretcher bearers were working on a pile of heaped, soft forms; you couldn't be sure where one body ended and the next began. The stink of cordite was everywhere, and underneath it, burnt earth and blood.

'Can you help this soldier? He's in a real bad way.'

A medic grunted. 'Put him down there, beside the others.'

They laid him on the dirt. The kid had stopped mewling now; he'd gone beyond the pain. But he was still clinging on, Frank reckoned.

'You got morphine? Can you give him some morphine, please? Or can I?'

'Come on,' said the other soldier who'd been helping him. It was that injun, Comanche. You could tell by the feather in his helmet. 'They know what they're doing.'

'Hey, man. Thanks. For coming back, I mean.'

Comanche shrugged. 'How come you didn't leave him? You'd've got over fine on your own.' He was leading Frank away, into a thicket of trees. 'Up here. Sergeant's up ahead. Cigarette?'

'I don't...' Frank took one anyway. He might as well; they issued them with their rations. Non-edible essentials: smokes, gum and toilet paper. Frank had been trading his cigarettes for extra crackers. Tonight would be a night of firsts. First combat. First rescue. First Lucky Strike. Still, he hesitated. 'Are we not meant to... I mean, the tip. Jerry'll see the glow.'

'Jesus, Chapel. I think the motherfuckers found us already. Light?'

Frank tried to hold the cigarette steady as Comanche leaned in, but his hands were so alive they were definitely someone else's. The unlit cigarette fell to earth.

'Sorry. I'm just... It's cold.'

'Keep moving then. You'll be dry by sun-up.'

They found the rest of their squad resting under a broad-leaved tree. A dozen men in each squad. Four squads to a platoon, four platoons to a company. There was a mathematical neatness to the divisions, men being quartered and quartered until they were part of the dry dust too.

'What kept you lazy fuckers, huh?' Their sergeant, a six-foot mass named Bear, was enjoying a fat cigar. He puffed at it like a movie star. Frank had never had sex and he'd never had a cigarette, but he knew that's what you did, afterwards. Bear had that same satisfied languor about him.

'You been swimming lengthways 'stead of 'cross?'

The sergeant's real name was McClung, James T. McClung. To them all, he was simply 'Bear'. He'd earned his name not for bravery, but on account of the fact that mornings were not his best time. *Bear with a shitting sore head, that's me. I give you fair warning, boys.* They knew not to speak to him before he'd had two cups of joe and his first Cuban.

Bear blew a lazy smoke ring at the moon. 'You got five minutes to shit, piss, shake down, patch up. Then we move on. We got mountains to climb, my sunny band of brothers. A literal fucking mountain.' He made another ring. 'You know, I'm thinking 'bout switching to Toscanos. When in Rome an' all. They ferment the tobacco. You boys find any left behind, you let me know, OK?'

'Yes sarge.'

'Yes sarge.'

'Sarge,' said Luiz. 'What happened there? How comes we got hit? I thought we was clear to get across.'

'What happened? War happened, little man. The dregs of war. Don't worry – we got the fuckers now. All of them. You have my word. From here on in, there will be no more nasty Bosch popping up to give my poo' children nightmares. Mama Bear promises. Cross heart and hope to die.'

'It's just—'

'Is just shit-all to do with you, *amigo*. You go where I tell you and you do what you are trained to do. And you is not trained to think, Garcia. That is my job.'

'Yes, sergeant.'

'Now shift your sorry asses and let's get this show on the road.'

The squad began to lift up their packs and rifles.

'Yo. Chapel.'

'Sarge?'

'Well done back there. With Ellington.'

'Ellington?'

'The half-head you dragged out the river. Now go get your feet dried and replenish your sulpha powder.'

'Yes, Sarge.'

Frank's boots hissed as he walked, like the current was sucking down on them still. He watched Luiz slap Claude's ass, watched the confusion as Claude turned to see *who done that*, Luiz knocking off Claude's doughboy, the helmet spinning like a turtle in the dirt. Thank God they'd to keep moving. He didn't think he could bear to stop. It was why they relished the drilling, the marching, relished the mindlessness of it, and the mild, collegiate hysteria, because if you powered on and on and you went to sleep punch-drunk and you woke up to order, then you didn't have to think about what was real. About the mess on your shirt drying hard.

Chapter Five

'We saw your Giuseppe earlier.'

The nuns eschewed all forms of ornamentation, yet Sister Agatha was allowed to hoard a collection of owls – glass ones, wooden ones, this chunky ceramic effort all the way from Assisi.

'That's nice.' Vita moistened her lips. Jabbed the duster into the corners of the highest shelf, skiting the tip with a too-heavy hand, so it set all the trinkets jangling.

'Yes. Lurking by Via Mura. Looked like he'd been sleeping in the woods. Is he ill?' Sister Agatha did a little cough of concern. 'Should we give him some clothes from the charity box?'

Vita steadied her breath. 'Did you speak to him?'

'No. I thought he was a tramp.'

Vita continued her assault on the bookcase. Next, she would rub beeswax into the wood, buff it to a shine. Move books she yearned to read. Dust lightly. Return. Turn her attention to the refectory table. Dust. Rub. Repeat.

'You missed a bit. Devora always used to start at the top.'

'Did she?'

A dash of light-dark-light at the top of the stairs. More sisters sailed past like holy penguins. Hands inside their sleeves, heads at a modest incline. Dark ring of footsteps, smell of polish rising, so thick she could taste the yellow paste in the back of her throat.

'Oh, there's Sister Cristina. I'll ask her. It really is a shame your mamma can't help—'

'My mamma helps many people.'

'Yes. I suppose. But Giuseppe *is* a Guidi, no?'

Vita beat her duster into the furthest reaches of the ceiling, dislodging a spume of cobweb. 'Careful, Sister. Might get dirty.'

'You know, you were a much better student than you are a housekeeper, Vittoria.'

Off she went, focused on her next errand of mercy. Vita twisted her wrist to capture all the threads. Flicked the duster again; watched a tawny owl take flight, begin its long, slow dive to oblivion. It looked so free as it was falling, so she watched it fall, continued to watch it, all the way from shelf to floorboard, where it bounced gracefully, once, and split in three.

At least he was alive. Something unknotted inside her. It always did, when Joe returned. Joe, who was not hers at all. She no longer knew what to feel. Relief – and something close to fury. She hadn't seen him in over a month. He appeared rarely at the Biondis', would vanish for weeks and weeks at a time and didn't feel the need to tell anyone. *Has your Giuseppe enlisted?* folk would ask. What could she reply? It was a brutta figura; what Joe would have called 'a redneck'.

As the months went by, she noticed she was caring less.

When he'd first come to Barga, it had felt like the horizon unfolding. Joe, bringing a momentary, mad lurch of optimism, and options. *So, Vittoria, would you like to be a teacher or a bride? Please your mother or your father?* Maybe you don't know what you want until it's taken away. Now she had neither, she was confused about what she missed the most. And she was tired. Really tired.

She lifted her bucket of cloths and brushes, dragging the broom behind. This wasn't even the Canonica. Vita was supposed to be the Monsignor's housekeeper, but he hawked her out to the nuns. *My needs are frugal,* he would say. Then he'd add extra requirements to her list of duties, then offer her up to the nuns. At least there were no pupils. She kicked the broken owl under the bookcase. School had been suspended, and if it were to restart, she would refuse to come here. She would not look the Monsignor in the eye, for he terrified her, but she would draw herself tall and say no all the same. Imagine emptying waste bins as her classmates recited poems.

Polishing done, Vita went outside, the cool dark of wood and marble blasted by brilliant sun. She took off her headscarf, stood on the steps, letting light soak her skin. There was a faint, sweetish odour inside the Conservatorio, which all the polish in the world could not erase. It smelled of cloistered lives.

From here, she could see the ochre walls of the Canonica, and the Duomo that rose beyond. The square bell tower sat like a giant chimney on the roof. Overshadowing eveything was Barga's walls. Huge walls, a magnificent canvas of grey stone shining dark to light, lovely greenish light that grew from moss and the reflected glow of trees. The walls wrapped the town, soared round the cobbled approach to the Duomo, dominating and demanding that you look up, and be in awe.

Vita glanced at her wool stockings, her shapeless smock. Half a year of being a skivvy. Papà had promised her it was temporary. This was Vita's war work. Most girls she knew were in the same position. She could have been milking cows or mopping blood. The Pieri girls were off training to be nurses. Giulia was working in a munitions factory on the coast. Vita flexed raw knuckles. At least she was bringing some money home – and a tiny bit of status. Not the respect due a teacher, but being the Monsignor's housekeeper did get you served first in shops. And conferred on you a kind of holy insight. Often, folk would ask: *What does the Monsignor think?* Even Renata sought her opinion.

Life carried on. There had been no great invasion. Only this long-held breath. Every day, more people cascaded into church. Standing room only in the Duomo. The Monsignor brought in extra altar boys; Communion was a perpetual crush. Don Sabatini at Tiglio had run out of wafers, and the sisters were skittish as they rinsed goblets and laundered linen cloths. Either the wily old Church knew just when to trickle into the fissures – more than possible, given it had survived so long – or it was the opposite, and it was the people who were seeping back to the bedrock of their faith. Desperate to be told what they should do. Vita understood this. She, too, would stand in the rear of the chapel, close her eyes and let the smell of cabbage be replaced by incense. The hum of bodies, the chants of her childhood, of beyond that, all pressed together in unseen layers. You went in exhausted and lonely, you came out safe. Like gelato, God made you feel better. Maybe Mussolini would ban Him next.

Raised voices. At the foot of the steps, two women were arguing.

'Il Duce will repel them.'

'Are you stupid? The americani are coming to help. The King is winning!'

Was he? News to Vita. People had been yabbering back and forth like this since the Allies took Rome a few weeks ago. Invaded it? Liberated? That depended if you listened to your mother or your father, and then your head swam, until it was simpler to listen to neither.

'*Me ne frego.*' She recognised the woman speaking: Signora Nardini, a friend of her mother's.

'You watch your mouth.'

The women began to grapple. 'You don't give a damn?' The other woman was pulling at Signora Nardini's dress. 'Fine. Off with the bug!'

A silver lapel pin hit Vita's foot; a bundle of sticks, crossed with an axe. She retrieved it. 'For shame, ladies. Should I fetch Mother Virginia?'

The other woman spat on the ground, walked off. Signora Nardini snatched up her brooch. 'Tell your mother we haven't seen her at the Massaie Rurali for a while, Vittoria. Her presence has been missed.'

'I will, signora. And will I ask the Monsignor to expect you at Confession?'

The signora spread her fingers as if she might lash out, then struck her hand against her own thigh. 'You. You Guidis think you are so special.'

'Buonasera, signore.' A soldier passed, saluting them both. 'Ciao, belle.'

Best to ignore the soldiers. It was hard to keep up with the different uniforms. Once more, all the men were being summoned – though this time it was the Republic calling, not the King. Boys from her childhood; going, going, gone. Some had found their way home from the front, only to be sent back in different uniforms to fight again. Like some giant maw was snuffling through the valley, scooping them up, leaves, twigs, truffles, boys, and it kept coming back and swallowing more. Didn't matter

70

that they marched off in glory. They were still swallowed whole. Vita had seen parts of the forest stripped by loggers until there was nothing left but stumps, and the plaintive calls of homeless birds, which turned to silence after a while. All the girls trapped here would become those birds. Poor Chiara from Sommo had already lost her sweetheart to this re-energised war. And yet Joe evaded it all.

'Hey, bella!' The man was calling after Signora Nardini. Must be drunk.

Vita turned away. The neat soldiers were usually fine. It was the bedraggled ones you'd to avoid; those you saw limping on the tracks above Catagnana. Pale, distant-looking men in part-uniform, flitting like spectres through the mountain passes. Mamma said they were deserters. Each haunted face, you wanted to help them. Last month, an older man had grabbed Vita with his filthy nails. Panicked, she'd given him the bread she was carrying, which only made him weep. After that, she didn't go near any soldiers.

People were avoiding the mountains altogether if they could. Any crops that could be gathered early were being harvested or hidden. The air remained charged; small fires and thuds continued to happen, where bold men became subdued. Farmers, bolting their storehouses, tethering their beasts. It felt, every day, like a storm coming.

Yet still, nothing changed.

A skein of aeroplanes passed overhead. Off to bomb the bits of Italy they sought to free. She held her hand to the glowing sky. But never here. You'd look up as the squadrons shifted – always, thank God, to another place. Say a prayer, put your head down, eyes on where the next bag of flour was coming from. Folk had grown used to the drone of them. 'Strafing', though, that was new. The Allies had started machine-gunning the rail tracks from

Fornaci to Calavorno, taking potshots at Pisa. How was that liberation?

A clang came from the campanile. Then another. She closed her eyes, let the sound roll over her. Their bells had a lovely, buttery tumble to them. Whether you were in the valley or up in the mountains, it was the Duomo that called you home, marking time and blessings and death. The barghigiani were very proud of their bells. Right at the start of the war, the Comune tried to melt them down. They were cutting metal from railings, shutters, even copper milk-buckets, until the women threatened riots. When the three huge Duomo bells were earmarked too, the Monsignor called it an attack on God's music. Folk raged, angry letters were sent and, ultimately, the bells were saved.

Four o'clock. She'd better shift. She was meeting old Sergio at ten-past.

As she stepped out, a stream of cars and trucks rattled by, full of Germans. A dark car scraped the edge of the building, barely slowing, Vita pushing her spine into the wall behind.

'Porco zio! Slow down.'

The soldiers waved, but kept going, bumping up the ramp to the front of the Duomo. There were no tedeschi stationed here, but their visits had become more concentrated. Observers, planners, engineers. Official-looking personnel, who spent whole days on Barga's bell towers.

'What are they doing?' she'd whispered to the Monsignor, that first time, when she was still curious.

'Calculating the triangulation of the hills.' He'd smiled. 'No. I don't know what that means either. But I suspect it is not good.'

'Do we have to let them? It's our Duomo.'

'I'm rather afraid we do, my dear.'

The soldiers were especially interested in Vita's own hills, in Monte Lama and the places beyond Catagnana. 'Are we going to be attacked?' she'd asked.

'No, Vita. We will be fine. I hate to say this, but, to them, Barga is a backwater. We are just a little pawn. War might hit the mountains over the plains of Lucca, but it won't come here.'

Vita had grown quite fond of this austere man. She liked the way the straightness of his profile allied to his clean, sharp actions. When he spoke, he spoke with gravitas. Even so, even with his direct line to God, how could anyone know for sure?

'Watch they don't think you're a spy.'

'Christ, Joe. Don't *do* that.'

Perched on a low parapet, legs dangling. 'What?'

Tongue thick, her brain tumbling with the *what to say*. He was thin, filthy. Each time she saw him, he was skinnier and darker. He rubbed his nose, bones protruding from his wrist like pearls. His thinness was pitiful.

'You shouldn't swear, Dolce Vita. It's very unbecoming. I thought you'd be pleased to see me?'

He sounded a little pathetic, and it spiked her anger again.

'What if those Germans see you?' she said. 'You being a draft dodger and all.'

'Me? I'm a local hero.' He jumped from the wall. 'So. How you been?'

Vita started to walk downhill, but he was walking faster. The heat of his mouth was at her ear. 'Here. Do you want to know a secret? I know what they're doing.'

'Good for you.' *Cara, I've missed you. Cara, how beautiful you are.*

'They're building a great big wall.'

'Is that right?' *Don't make fun of me, Joe. Say something kind.*

'Yup. Way across the mountains. It stretches for miles.'

'Rubbish. If it was that big, we'd see it.' She was trembling. All she wanted to do was cry.

'Oh, but you can, if you know where to look.' He put his arm through hers.

'Leave me alone.'

'Why? What have I done now?'

Vita increased her speed. Everything wound round and up and down here. Barga was a jumble of dusty stairs and thin, shady passageways, of cluttered palazzi and high walls. She headed down a narrow staircase, navigated a pile of rubbish. Still Joe followed.

'Hey! Dolce! Wait!'

She didn't know why she was running.

'Vita!'

Could hear his footsteps echo behind. She ducked under a low arch, but he grabbed her wrist.

'Vittoria, wait!'

'What is it? What? I'm late.'

'Late for what?'

'Joe, I can't stand this any more. Why are you here?'

'I thought this was my home.'

'How can it be, when you're never here?'

He took her hand. 'Because I love it, right? The colour of this place... And maybe I'm trying to fit in – but I never do, do I? Your mamma doesn't think so for starters.'

'That's not fair.'

His grip was clumsy. 'It's true. Jesus, I can't win. See in Scotland, I'm the Tally-boy. '

'Ssh, please.'

Vita's hands were greasy with sweat. She pulled away from him. Turned the corner, and a line of white sheets filled the alley. They were beautiful, how they bounced and swelled like sails.

'Then I come to Barga, and I'm a halfling too. Or maybe a secret agent—'

'Will you stop shouting?'

'See? Definitely an embarassment – according to my own family. Your mamma turned on me quick enough. Fuck, even my girl runs away from me.'

'*Your* girl?' She seized one of the dancing sheets. 'You think I'm your girl?'

'Aren't you?'

As her anger flamed, that curious sensation came again, of observing herself, of noticing how even her voice sounded cold. 'When have you ever asked me, Joe? When have you ever even kissed me, or talked to me like an adult? Do you want to know the truth? I think you're a coward.'

Silence, intensifying. She gazed at her hands: full of damp white linen, creasing fabric some woman had worked to clean.

'What would you have had me do? Enlist in the Royal Italian Army? Only they don't exist now, do they? Stick on my kilt and march with the Highlanders?'

There was a harsh edge to his voice she couldn't bear. 'What proud Jock wouldn't have signed up, eh? All those Union Jacks. All those cheering crowds outside, only they were jeers. My mamma in the kitchen, crying. The glass fanlight over the café door. Bastards smashed it. Did you know my papà got arrested, Vita?'

He moved the washing aside so he could pass. Didn't wait for her reply.

'Joe, please. I'm sorry.'

'Hundreds of men like my papà – me too – arrested on our doorsteps. Strip-searched, jailed. Sent to a concentration camp, only we'd not to call it that. *Internment*, they told my mamma. She was clutching her heart, Vita. Clutching her heart and crying in our own front room. *Stop your hysterics, woman!* I heard them shout that as they put us in the van.'

'Oh, Joe.' Wanting to unsay it. Wanting to comfort him, to run her finger along the side of his face. But she was afraid.

'Took us all the way to the Isle of Man, so they did. Nice beachfront hotel, ringed with barbed wire and dogs. Ten to a two-bed room. Papà kept begging: *Is my wife all right? Please, she doesn't keep well.* Paid good money to see the commandant. They told us she was fine. She was, then.'

Sunlight dazzled. They had reached the wide crossroads at L'Alpino. An ambulance idled there, the driver with the window open, watching the world through cigarette smoke. When the man saw them, he sat up, ground his cigarette against the side of the van. He signalled to Joe, a slicing motion across his throat.

'Look, I have to go.'

She caught his arm. One or both of them were shaking. 'Joe, I'm so sorry. I didn't know.'

The engine revved, and the back door opened. Another man peered out, sporting a red beret. 'Ho! Gelato Boy!'

'Who are they? Is that who you've been hanging out with? Bandits?'

'They're not bandits. What's it to you anyway?' Joe ran across the road, barely looking back. 'I'll see you, Dolce. Maybe.'

He threw himself into the rear of the ambulance before it sped away, lights flashing. Too bright. Too loud. She squeezed her eyes shut for a minute and leaned her hand against the wall of the bar. When she looked up again, she saw Sergio, waiting at the top of the Giardino, with his donkey and cart. Vita walked over.

'Did you see them?' she asked, absently scratching the donkey's muzzle. There was a ringing in her ears.

'Who?'

'Those men with Joe. Ciao, Andromeda.' She could feel a pain behind her eyes, ringing and pounding, as if she'd been standing close to bells. She pushed her face into the donkey's fur.

'Ach, child, I'm too old to be seeing anything much. Now.' He climbed down. 'You promise you'll be careful with her?'

'I promise.'

'She likes it if you sing.'

'Signor Bertini, I will guard her with my life. Is your appointment not at quarter-past?'

Poor Sergio was getting the last of his teeth pulled.

'Sì,' he said mournfully. 'And you'll come back for me at six?'

'I will. My mamma says to say thank you very much for this.' She swung herself onto the cart.

'Watch you don't tug her mouth—'

'Grazie, Signor Bertini. Grazie.' Vita clicked her tongue. The cart creaked off, drowning out Sergio's instructions.

It seemed half the valley had come to Barga-Gallicano station, bringing their rolls of bedding, their squawking chickens, their goats and dogs and children who were weaving through the throngs, clumps of soldiers, families embracing, weeping. As many folk leaving as arriving; so hard-crammed you could barely move, and the noise a physical pulse. At least Vita's head had stopped ringing.

Gone dull and heavy; a not-quite ache that spread to her jaw.

Joe wasn't a liar; at least, she didn't think he was. So, Mamma had been right. The Allies were their enemy. Scottish policemen had locked her family in a jail. Scottish people had smashed up their shop. She felt sick. Sicker still for what she'd yelled at Joe. She flinched as a whistle shrilled. The stationmaster stood at the front of the platform, shouting at a woman. 'I told you. The train's not going to Piazza al Serchio. It's stopping here, then straight back to Lucca.'

'But that's no good to me. One train a day, and you can't even run the proper route?'

'Signora, it's no good for any of us.' The stationmaster pinched the bridge of his nose. 'But it's not me machine-gunning the tracks. Now, are you getting on or not? Be grateful anything's moving at all. There might be no more trains this week.'

He clutched his whistle, moved on. Vita tried to get past two women and an old man sitting on a bench, but their suitcases cluttered the way.

'Permesso?'

They ignored her; focused on the train, on a teenage boy at the edge of the platform. He was swaying slightly, and wearing only a vest and muddy trousers. A brace of German soldiers moved towards him. It was such a casual saunter; they were chatting, lightly holding their rifles as they might a baby. No sense of wariness: a person could easily have ambushed them and seized their weapons. Yet the crowd parted to let them through. These neat foreign soldiers, occupying their station. Folk coughed. Looked away. They lowered their heads, and looked away.

'This is not your land,' said a young boy beside Vita. '*Tedeschi*.' His mother smacked the back of his head.

'Mah.' The old man got unsteadily to his feet. Leaning on a walking stick, he picked his way across the platform. '*Meine Herren.* Can you help? I think I've lost my ticket. Do you have more tickets?'

It seemed as if the hordes had suddenly grown even greater, a high tide of people swelling, putting distance between the boy, the old man and the Germans. Vita was distracted by another voice.

'Papà, I can't.'

A young soldier was hesitating, one boot on the train, the other planted on the platform. He wore the feathered cap and emerald flashes of the new Monterosa. It was Pietro from Albiano. Jittery Pietro, who used to speak with horses, who had a plan to grow sunflowers and make better oil than any olives. 'Please don't make me go.'

The German soldiers were laughing. Wringing their fists, one of them pretending to cry. She watched Pietro's father pull his son's head towards his own, until they were brow to brow. Heard him say: 'You are no coward, son.'

Then Pietro nodded. Broke away, and was swept onto the train with the other boys. What she'd said to Joe; it kept repeating, over and over, like these seethes of people. But it was true. Boys who'd been injured, boys like Pietro – they still had to fight.

Vita didn't want to look at Pietro's father. She was here to meet her mamma's cousins, come all the way from Rome. Except she'd no idea what they looked like. She searched for a woman and two small boys. Mamma had already claimed Vita's room for them. So many folk here she didn't recognise; the station was all steam and bobbing heads, battered suitcases, a girl dropping a potted plant – a plant, you would bring your aspidistra all the way from Rome? Another lot of soldiers moved towards the train. These wore black shirts. Red fasces on their tunic lapels, and death heads on their breasts. Brigate Nere. Shiny and sharp, the soldiers broke the air around them with metallic vigour, their steps ringing like tin cups on the platform. They were the kind of swaggering men at whom her mother beamed, and her father scowled. Any Fascist who had fled was back, bigger, bolder – and this new force of soldiers had arrived with them. The Black Brigade.

'Hello! Vittoria? Hello there!' A small, fat woman waved through a cloud of steam. Two little boys emerged alongside. 'Cousin Vittoria?'

'Carla?'

She seized Vita, kissing her once, twice, thrice. 'Oh, dear Vittoria. You look *so* like your mamma.'

For that, cousin, you can carry your own suitcases.

Carla's powdered face was sheened with sweat. 'Dario, Marino, say hello to Vittoria.'

They were only babies; both boys pink and curly, as if they'd stepped from a Botticelli canvas. The smaller was clearly exhausted. Nudged by his mamma's hand, he stumbled into the path of one of the Brigate, who shoved him back to his mother again, harder. Caught off-balance, the little one trod on the soldier's boot.

'Ho, *stupido*! Watch the polish, you!'

The sugar-mouse cheeks flared red. Dario burst into tears. Small legs bowed, the crying releasing his whole pent-up little frame. A stream of piss hit the platform, splashing upwards, Vita moving backwards, away from the mess, Carla fussing her son. Laughter from the watching soldiers. The older boy, Marino, set at them like a terrier. 'Shut it! Just shut it or—'

'You'll do nothing,' Vita whispered in his ear. The soldier who'd pushed Dario stared at her, his mates catcalling, whistling. He had a stupid, soft face, made hard by the scar across his lip.

'Come on.' Vita steered her cousins to the exit. 'Let's get you home.'

Sergio's donkey was chewing the vine that grew up the front of the station house. She'd managed to pull off a hunk of plaster too. A lush frond hung either side of her muzzle; it made an impressive moustache.

'Horse!' Dario ran to where the donkey was tethered.

'She's called Andromeda. And she's a donkey. Watch she doesn't bite. Right. Up you go.' Vita tried to lift Marino into the cart. He went rigid. Carla was way behind them, lugging cases.

'You need to sit down.'

'You should have kicked that soldier! He *made* Dario pee his—'

'I know. I'm sorry. You were really brave. But it's best not to argue with the soldiers.'

'Why? If they're bad?'

'Because. . . can you just please sit down?'

She put Dario into the cart beside his brother, only touching him under his arms. Mamma was worried about 'Roman diseases' and fleas. Well, now she'd have the perfect excuse to scrub these kiddies Catagnana-clean.

There wasn't room in the cart for everyone. Vita was halfway into the driving seat when she noticed the tremble in her cousin's hand. Carla's coat shifted open – she was wearing her winter coat in summer. Two cardigans underneath and a dirty blouse, and the bones, the bones of her neck like blades. A body held together by face powder and air.

'Here,' Vita said. 'Andromeda's a lamb. I'll walk. You take the reins and I'll hold her bridle.'

Carla made a non-specific half-gesture. 'Oh, no.'

'Please.' She helped Carla up, then clicked her tongue at the donkey. Andromeda sighed her whiskery sigh, plodded on. They crossed the road behind the station.

More tedeschi had parked their truck on the diagonal. Vita tried to guide the donkey round them.

'*Nein! Nur rechts.*'

'Scusi?'

'Go right.'

'But we need to go this way. It's just up—'

The soldier was insistent. '*Strasse geschlossen.*'

'Why? Look, I don't want to go left. I just want to cross, then go straight up. Up, *ja?*'

'Is closed.'

You couldn't see his face beneath his helmet, just the chin, thrusting out.

Carla was anxious. 'Just do what they say. Please.'

'Oh, for Godsake. We'll have to go all the way round. It'll take ages.'

'Vittoria?' said a small, steady voice from above. It was the older one – Marino.

'Yes?'

'I thought we hadn't to argue with the soldiers.'

It was a long, slow climb to Barga. Vita's breathing synchronised with the donkey's, willing her not to stop. If the laden cart pulled them backwards... well, it wouldn't. Not with Vita pulling and pushing her on. The wheels made a rhythm of clunk and roll, like a slow, creaking train. She thought of the train taking all those boys away from Barga, and her cheeks ached. Would it not make you want to fight? The unfairness? The anger? Would someone putting handcuffs on your father not stiffen your resolve? Joe should have told her. She pressed under her eyelids, expecting tears, but none came.

In the cart, her cousins were very quiet. Vita looked up. 'How was your journey?'

Carla's eyes were closed. 'Long.' A tiny shivering shake. 'My goodness.' She sat up, brightly. Stroked Dario's curls.

'I didn't expect it to be so busy here. We thought we were coming to the peace and quiet of the country, didn't we, boys? Are there many… people like us?'

'Refugees? Yes. They've started coming in from every-where – Pisa, Viareggio.'

'But no war?'

'No. Plenty planes flying over, but no war. Though they have started firing at the trains. You were lucky you made it.'

'Yes.'

'Was it hard?'

'Hard?' Carla echoed. Frowning at Vita as if it was some foreign word she'd used. 'We were under siege for half a year.'

'Sorry. No. Of course. I meant, was it hard to get out? To escape.'

'Not really. The Nazis left, the shooting stopped and we managed to get on a train. And that train took us to one station, then we walked for miles, then another train, and so on.'

Two suitcases in the cart. Carla's husband had been killed last year. So that was it, those cases. That was her salvage. Vita saved her breath for the remainder of the climb. The road wound in bends, Carla hopeless at navigating Andromeda round its steep corners. Vita nudged the donkey with her hip, the boys cheering her on. At last, they entered Piazzale del Fosso. Here, at the top of the tortuous hill you'd just scaled, your eyes were drawn away from the view, and onto the towering, upward spring of Barga's walls; their blank, lofty importance hinting at grand palazzi and the Duomo beyond.

'Are we here?' Carla wiped her brow.

'No, sorry. We've the same again to go yet, to get to Catagnana.'

Marino leaned in to whisper to his mother.

'Ssh, darling. It's fine.'

'But I'm *hungry*.'

'Am hungry too!' cried Dario.

'I'm sorry,' said Carla. 'We've been travelling for so long. And there wasn't much time.' Mouth slack, face powder crusting at the corners.

They were five minutes from the Canonica.

'Come on, folks,' said Vita. 'Click her reins again, Carla.'

'Is that a castle?' Marino pointed at the crenellated towers of Porta Reale as they passed below its arch.

'A castle!' echoed Dario.

How quickly these children moved from flat to animated. There was an unstable, brittle paperiness to them all. Being blasted out of your city might do that to you.

'No. It's one of the old gates. See how there's a big wall round the town? In the olden days they'd lock these gates at night, to keep the people safe.'

'Can they still do that?' Marino sounded hopeful.

'No, darling,' said Carla. 'There are no gates here any more, just the big arch. Isn't that right, Vittoria?'

'Afraid so. But there is a lovely big church nearby, where I work. Would you like to see it?'

Both boys sighed. 'Bo-ring.' Marino slumped further into the cart.

'Not the church – the place where the priest lives. There's lots of good things to eat there. Why don't we go and see the Monsignor? There's bread and cheese. And soup. There's always soup.'

'Nice soup?' said Dario.

'Cabbage soup.'

'Cabbage soup… makes you poop. Cabbage soup… makes you poop.'

'That would be lovely,' said Carla.

'Come on, then. We might even find you an egg.'

'Do they still exist?'

Accompanied by several choruses of *cabbage soup...
makes you poop* (this was the chorus and all the verses too),
they headed for the Canonica. Vita led them up Via Mura,
which hugged the wall all the way to the Conservatorio's
back door. It was narrow, you could just about get a donkey
and cart through. But the shelter, and the high tightness of
it, felt safe. This street would demonstrate to her cousins
how solid Barga was. From the Conservatorio, it was a
simple matter of turning left, and *ecco*: the Canonica. But,
before they could reach the entrance to the piazza, more
uniforms appeared. Silvery click of boots. Blackshirts with
red fasces, small frames in padded shoulders.

'You can't go through here.' Two Brigate Nere, bristling
with self-importance. Acne on this one's chin.

'Why not?' said Vita.

'Because I'm telling you. Now move it.'

'But I need to get through. I've got two little ones...'

'Should've kept your legs closed.'

'Don't speak to me like that.'

The other soldier moved his rifle a little higher, so that
it gleamed across his upper body. She heard one of the
children whimper.

'You not understand? I think my colleague said to fuck
off!'

They grinned at their own bravado.

'Vita!' Carla said. 'We don't need—'

Through the gap, Vita could see other blackshirts,
men in different uniforms, men in suits. In one corner
stood a cluster of cassocks. Atop one of the cassocks was
the familiar, wide-brimmed hat the Monsignor wore
outdoors: in rain to keep his hair dry, in shine to give him

shade. She sucked as much air into her lungs as she could, then yelled: 'Monsignor! Ho! Monsignor! They won't let me through!'

The second soldier seized Andromeda's reins as Acne Boy hit Vita hard in the breast. Knuckle on breast and bone.

'Don't!' Marino shouted.

The shock of pain sent her to her knees, set off a chain of other tiny spasms, like stabbing bells, making her eyes smart with tears. She could hear crying, Carla or one of the kids. Vita widened her nostrils, teeth clenched to stop the flow.

'Whatever is the matter?' The faint, dusty smell of the Monsignor's cloak, an arm reaching in as the brim of his hat dipped over her face. 'You,' she heard him say. 'Did you hit this young woman?'

'Monsignor. Is there a problem?' Another face peering; a heavy-set man with swept-back hair.

'Indeed, there is.' The Monsignor helped Vita to her feet. 'One of your men just struck my housekeeper. Is this how we treat womenfolk in our brave new world, generale?'

'Sir. It was security. You said we were to—'

The generale raised a finger. Acne Boy fell silent. 'Monsignor. Signorina.' He clicked his heels the way the tedeschi did. 'My apologies. Please, allow me to escort you and your... little band through our checkpoint. Maybe you could watch the ceremony, as my guests?'

'No, sir,' said the Monsignor. 'That is not necessary. Vittoria – go to the house immediately. Take... Cook and the children with you. You are already late for work. This really is not good enough.'

'Yes, sir.' Unfathomably, she bobbed a curtsey. The Monsignor raised an eyebrow, then turned away.

They made their way across the piazza. A few soldiers turned, but most seemed preoccupied with untangling flags, or lining themselves up in rows. That and fiddling with a large tarpaulin covering some great bulky thing in front of the Canonica. Her heartbeat drove into her ribs.

'Oh, goodness. I thought we'd be safe here. Are you all right, Vita?' Carla asked her.

'Yes, yes. I'm fine.'

Nicodemo came out, wiping his hands on a dirty rag. He was the Monsignor's 'man', forever oiling and tinkering, bustling about on bowed legs. Speaking few words to the Monsignor, even fewer to Vita. She was never so glad to see him. 'Come inside, Vita. Leave the beast – I'll see to it.'

'She needs water.'

'Yes, yes. Now get inside.'

The cool, dark hallway of the Canonica, folding round her. 'You're shaking, child.'

'Nico, what's going on?'

'Would your friends like some water too?'

'Oh, sorry. Nicodemo, this is my cousin Carla and her little boys. They've just got out of Rome.'

'Ah. The Eternal City. How is the Holy Father? Have you seen much of him?'

'What? No. Of course not.'

'Nico, can we give them something to eat?'

'Please, into the kitchen.'

'This is very kind,' said Carla.

Vita remained, watching through the hall window. Flat of her hand pressed on her bosom. That ugly, pock-marked boy, striking her there, where it was private.

'Vittoria,' said Nico. 'Come away.'

The generale was laughing with two taller men. One of them inclined his neck, hand scratching at the nape, then removed his military cap. His hair was faintest blond, more milk-coloured than gold. With a bow, he offered the cap to the generale. The generale accepted it, placed it on his own head, and all three laughed again. Much backslapping accompanied the little pantomime.

'Who is that man?'

'Him? Generale Utimperghe. Head of the Black Brigade.'

'And those other men? With the silver on their collars?'

'Germans. Officers of some sort. Apparently they're going to be stationed here. Now come into the kitchen, Vita.'

'Stay away from them,' said Carla. 'That's the *Schutzstaffel*.'

'Who?'

'SS. You wait. We'll be having curfews next.'

'Signora, that is not true,' said Nico. 'These men are our guests. They're hosting a reception for them in Palazzo Comunale. The Commissario is to take the salute.'

Vita stared as a bunch of tedeschi soldiers pulled the tarpaulin away. It soared green, filling all the sky outside the window, then settled, revealing a shiny row of machine guns, padded with bags of sand.

'Why are they putting guns in front of the Canonica?'

She wanted to be home, with the wide green valley opening below. Not everything shrivelled to fit this slit of window.

'To protect us,' said Nico. 'Apparently. Now, boys – although your cousin is the housekeeper, she is being very remiss in her duties. Would you prefer goat milk or water? Or I think we could offer you soup?'

No songs. The little ones had returned to being very quiet as Nico ushered them through the hall.

Chapter Six

Frank woke to a cloud of flies, and a view of the Leaning Tower of Pisa. Fingers strumming, jerking; his blood like quicksilver. Everything was moving, heat dancing inside thick heat, the distance of the mountains merely inches. He shifted up on his elbows. Blinked. It truly was squint: an arcaded spindle slanting five degrees. How it remained upright had been a mystery for centuries. Stamina? Science? He had an urge to get up close, study the tower's geometry, take notes, measurements. Get so near your neck cricked and your head swam at the unlikely loom-ingness of it.

He arched his spine. Sky above was aching blue. Smell of sweet herbs coming on the breeze. Fixing to be a beau-tiful day, a day lit by the same bright sun under which he'd stood in California. That thought was unfathomable. He shook his water canteen. Empty. Amazing, that this line of this horizon dropped off the edge, became a curve, and the curve girdled the globe and would carry this light back to his momma, who would kiss the sky and send it back to him. Frank lay down again. He wished he could run from this hilltop all the way to Pisa, through the golden land and the strange, thin Tuscan evergreens that stuck up in exclamation. But he'd an appointment with a tray of powdered eggs.

He wasn't hungry. How could you be, when eating was an order, and when what you ate was the same shit, three times a day? Reality had shifted. Life outside the army was the one that no longer rang true, and this world of marching and digging and eating and marching was the only world that did. He wrote home, of course, and his mother wrote back. The exchange was always light and cheerful. His momma was a dream. As their bull-necked officers never tired of yelling: *Army's your mama now.*

He let his eyelids close. Italian sun soaking his bones, his stiffness melting off. And then the rush of yesterday came pouring in: the smell of new-singed skin, the noise in torrents. He needed a sluice gate to slice down and keep his head clear of yesterdays. And tomorrows.

The blood on his clothes. He had to keep not looking at it, not imagining it flaking as he moved, falling into his mess kit, his mouth. He glanced around, at the stubbly grass, the dusty, ruined wall. There was no one else about. Frank reached into the pack he'd been leaning on, extracted his journal. He'd been trying to keep it up to date and hidden at the same time, which was no easy feat. No one had said, but he figured a journal would be against regulations. But there were no military secrets in the little book, just Frank's thoughts on stuff he'd seen, the odd brief drawing or doodle. Quickly, he sketched the view in front of him, wrote *Leaning Tower. Still standing.* Flicked back a few pages: a brief (rude) poem about latrines, a rant about short-arm inspections (*Milk down that member, boy. Lemme see if you got the clap*). Lyrics of a song Bear had sung; an IOU list of people he'd given his cigarettes to – there was always some promise made in return. He didn't care if it was honoured; it was just neat to see it in hard black pencil. Just the fact of the promises suggested a future.

He turned another page: *Crossing the Arno*. That page was blank. Frank had plenty of thoughts, but the notebook didn't seem big enough to contain them. He drew a line through the blankness.

By the height of the sun, he reckoned it was no longer morning. Night had been spent quick-time marching to the next command post, lest Jerry see their position. Even a glinting windshield was a beacon of intent. They'd slept in the shade of another villa. Officers got the inside, men got foxholes and canopies of leaves. Wherever they halted, the mechanical chink of shovel on soil sounded the Buffaloes' arrival. A scrape-out of stubborn earth was enough to build you a burrow. A mummy-bag made you a king.

The engineers had slung Lister bags on tripods, big canvas containers for treated water. A rough latrine had also been dug; guys were shitting, pissing, rinsing faces and teeth. Comanche was mixing coffee, pouring extra powder from a painted tin he'd acquired.

'You want some joe? Is really shit today. Think this is made of sawdust.'

'Nah.' Frank took a cup of water instead. 'You hear anything about Ellington?'

'Who?'

'That kid we pulled from the river. With the face.'

'Why you want to know?'

'Because...' He rubbed his eyes. Swigged more tinny water. 'I just do.'

'Won't do you no good,' said Comanche. 'Or him.'

Since they'd be on the move again today, the field kitchens hadn't been set up. Instead, they were on 10-in-1 packs. You could have it cold, or there were some dinky portable gas stoves to warm the rations through. Cold, hot – powdered egg was vile.

'Your legs OK?' said Comanche.

'Uh-huh.'

'Good. 'Cause we ain't going to Pisa no more. Next stop's up there.' He nodded at the vast ridge on the horizon. 'Monte Pisano.'

Frank's stomach felt hollow. The mountain was steep and exposed. Scrabbling through scree, the Krauts would be up above them, picking them off like bugs.

'And we're moving out at fourteen hundred.'

'But it's still light then.'

'Apparently, the enemy is in retreat.'

'They fucking said that before.'

'Yup. Anyhow,' said Comanche, 'I asked Bear. Kid got moved to a field hospital back down the line.'

'OK. Good.' He was alive. Leastways, when he was moved, he was alive. 'Good,' Frank repeated. He was still shaking the water from his cup, Comanche grimacing at his coffee, when all hell broke loose, a bunch of yelling, and a rumbling shout above all the others: *'Halt! Cover! Get back!'*

Down, or back, he couldn't remember, just a white wall of noise, of rushing noise, and him and Comanche hitting the earth as a shot rang out. A scream came, a stuck-pig scream.

'Mothafucka, holy fuck!'

One of their own. Some fool had run into the command post; got shot in the butt.

They all had the jitterbugs. Strange, this moving free in sunshine. Strange, but kind of wonderful. Like Mardi Gras. As they passed through the little towns east of Pisa,

Frank's shoulders began to ease. Folks came out to cheer them, folks emerging from behind German lines. Women throwing flowers, grapes, themselves, kids jostling for candy, men offering wine.

'*Viva gli americani!*'

Hundreds of them, lining the route in a daylight that embraced the Buffaloes. People kissing their hands, kissing them. The Buffaloes responded by throwing food and chocolate, gone gooey in their hands. The sun beat on, its gaudy light shining on sweating black skin, on an old lady who pointed at their faces, who touched her own face, then crossed herself as the convoy passed. It shone on a gaunt priest grappling momentarily with a young boy over a can of meat.

'*Per favore!*'

Almost instantly, eyes huge, the man collected himself, pressed the food into the boy's hands. Frank grabbed three more cans, leaned down from the truck, which was barely moving at this point through the crowd.

'Here, Father.' He stretched out, dropping the corned beef towards the starving man. '*Sì, sì.* For you. *Per favore.*'

Then another, then another hand reached out, snatching, shoving, voices squawking. It felt like feeding ducks.

'Whoah there, cowboy,' said Bear, pulling him back up into the truck. 'Stay cool. Don't want you drowning in a sea of Eyeties.'

The faces receded, still squawking. The light drove forwards, towards the looming ridge. Monte Pisano was to be their first real test. 'The Arno was just an ickle tickle, children,' said Bear. 'Trust me.'

But the way ahead, the fact they were travelling through towns and villages in light that was golden and clear, made that possibility distant. The Buffaloes were on the advance, the enemy in flight. Against the might of the Fifth Army, how mad would the Sauerkrauts be to stand their ground?

Plenty. The Germans were a machine, so they said. As a science major, Frank should have appreciated that.

Chapter Seven

Warm air, stirring Vita's hair. The jostle of a largely silent crowd: arms-crossed barghigiani, studded with pockets of frantic flag-wavers.

It took a whole weekend for the German 14th Army to occupy Barga, ushered in by the Brigate Nere, who were their hosts or bodyguard, depending how you looked at it. The procession was a piece of theatre. For over an hour, Vita watched as foreign tanks and men streamed up Via Roma. Their strange-shaped helmets made her think of matadors. Column after column they marched, a sea of spindle-legged precision. She wondered if they'd chosen this road deliberately; a broad, modern street in the Giardino. It offered the longest stage possible on which to introduce Barga to her new visitors.

Mamma waved a fascist flag. Cesca too, Mamma scolding her to *wave harder*. Renata was clapping, making Rosa wave and salute. Gianni was a prisoner in Rome; you'd think it was a badge of honour. Mamma had given them wheatsheaves; an extravagant gesture for those with little bread. When Vita refused to throw them under the soldiers' feet, Mamma did it for her, reserving the loudest of her cheers for the Brigate Nere: proud, black-browed men who did not even blink.

Vita searched for Joe in the crowd, in with the boys who laughed and shook their heads – yet shut their mouths as the Brigate neared. But he wasn't there. Mamma made her family stand with the other Fascists. All these gleaming men and women who radiated defiance, who you could *see* inflating as the army passed. Papà had refused to come. 'You're just a sore loser,' said Mamma. 'You'll see. Order will bring stability. Stability will bring peace. Il Duce will—'

Papà swore loudly, slammed from the house to his workshop; Mamma said she'd a mind to set fire to it, and her eyes were wild enough. She was a crackling wire that needed to be directed to where it could do least harm. Carla and the boys stayed at home too. Vita had heard her through the bedroom door, crying.

All that weekend, tedeschi poured in. They commandeered the finest villas on Via Roma, many palazzi in the old town. Plenty of smaller homes too. Each ripple into Barga meant another ripple out. Vita was sent to the Conservatorio, to help the sisters co-ordinate shelter, food, bedding for those who needed it. But how were you meant to salve indignity? This was wrong. Surely this was wrong? Vita hated how her mother excused it all.

Catagnana was too far up the hill for La Limonaia to be requisitioned, Sommocolonia even further. But that didn't stop foragers. So far Mamma – with flags and cake – had kept the German soldiers at bay. But she was sanguine about the possibility of loss.

'They are fine young men. It's only natural they would need supplies.' Patting the back of a soldier, as he stuffed necci into his pouch.

'*Danke. Danke.*'

Thank God Papà had been out. Only after the soldiers left did Carla speak. 'They are not at all fine men, Elena. Believe me.'

'You Romans are all the same. No backbone. These boys are only doing their job. And so smart, so polite – you know they've asked us to a concert on Largo Roma?'

'A concert?'

'Sì. That boy Hans is doing a trumpet solo.'

It was Mamma, too, who pre-empted the soldiers journeying further up the mountain. 'Oh, those Sommos are a mean lot,' she'd said. 'Thin-lipped misers, stuck on rocky soil. They've barely even got chestnut trees. You'll get nothing of value up there.'

Later, when everyone else had gone to bed, Vita reached to trim the lamp wick. Papà was still at the fascio. Mamma leaned forward then, pinching the back of her hand. 'I don't know where Giuseppe's gone now, and I don't *want* to know. But you'd better tell him to move on. And keep moving.' She returned to her knitting, clacking at inhuman speed.

'I don't know where he is either. Why would you think that?'

'That Antonella Nardini was going on about him at Mass. *Is it safe, do you think? For your family to shelter a foreigner, in such dangerous times?*'

Vita's heart tightened. 'And what did you say?'

'I told her Giuseppe was as Italian as she was, and that if she ever took the name of Guidi in vain again, I would cut out her tongue and feed it to her cat.'

'Mamma!'

Flash-flash-flash of glinting needles. Mamma was a shape-shifter; she made you hate and love her with equal passion. The fury of her needles, how did she not stab herself? What would it be like to have your mother as your friend, this person you once lived inside? Vita suspected Mamma barely saw her family as separate entities at all, merely an extension of her own limbs. Or some kind of awkward tail.

'But the old witch is right. Joe needs to disappear – properly this time. Here. Wind this wool.'

Vita took the hank, spreading and turning her fingers. The burnish of lamplight smudged Mamma's frown lines, her eyelashes soft over her work. 'I'm sorry for you, though.'

The room glowed, shadows making the air dense until it felt that, if you pressed against them, the shadows would ripple and press back.

'Do you think there are different kinds of love?' Vita teased out a knot.

'Of course there are. I love you, and your father, I love God—'

'I don't mean that. More, like, a practice?'

Her mother smiled. 'You mean like a crush? Oh, yes. You'll never guess who my crush was.'

'Who?'

'Well, he was at the seminary with Cousin Nello.'

'A priest?'

Mamma winked. 'He wasn't a priest then.'

'Who?'

She shook her head. 'I will tell you one day. Maybe. What? You think I was never young? We all need our secrets.' She looked sharply at her. 'Is Joe your crush?'

'I don't know. Mamma – have I to marry Joe?'

'*Have* you? I thought you wanted to?'

'Do I? Nobody's asked me – och, I don't know.' Vita stared at the home-dyed wool. Some poor soul was getting a beetroot-coloured jumper.

'Well, what do you feel about him?'

'That I don't want to hurt him.'

'So, you care about him?'

'I suppose. But he makes me angry too, and sad and frustrated. I'm not sure he listens to me – well, he doesn't really know me.' She looked up. Felt zinc-bright clarity. 'I still want to be a teacher. That's what I really want.'

'I see. Well, that's one thing about this pitiful war. All normal life is on hold. It gives you space.'

'How did you know, though? With Papà? Did you get a choice?'

'Choice? My choice was a little different. Your nonna did not approve. *How could you live with such a man?*' She mimicked Nonna's mannered accent.

'Wasn't he a student though? Surely that was respectable enough?'

'Oh, yes. But he was also a foreigner.' Mamma shrugged. 'So. I asked myself, not could I live with this man, but, could I live without him? And I decided that I would follow your father into Hades if I had to.' She bit off the end of her wool. 'Now, it's late. Enough talk, yes? What will be will be. Joe must keep himself safe, I must find more flour in the morning, and those children will be up with the rooster.'

'You love it, having boys to feed up.'

'I do actually. Much better than feeding tedeschi.'

The German occupation coated the valley like varnish. The real Barga was underneath and visible, but with a hard new glint on top. Swastikas flew at barghigiani windows; tedeschi police directed traffic on barghigiani roads; tedeschi voices in barghigiani shops and bars. The film settled over the sky too, clipping it shut in a hollow echo. The Monsignor ensured the Conservatorio and

Canonica were unaffected, but he couldn't stop the requisitioning of food and supplies – or his telephone.

'It's most inconvenient, Vita. They've fiddled with the switchboard so only they can use the telephone wires. How are we meant to function?'

She didn't mention that the Pieris' goat had been seized, along with half their chickens.

'Still. A nice diversion, this concert. Very pleasant. And we're to have a public meeting too, in the cinema. I suppose they are doing their best to be approachable.' The Monsignor dabbed his mouth. 'Apart from my telephone.'

She took his coffee tray into the kitchen. The back door was open, Nico dragging in wood.

'Why do we need all that?'

'Woodshed's leaking. And it's going to rain.'

'Rubbish. It's really warm.'

'Exactly.' He heaved his load into the hall, leaving a trail of muck.

'Suppose I'm cleaning this, then?'

She warmed some water, poured it into the sink. Maybe he was right. Outside, the sky was changing colour, a dull grey patch emerging in the west. That leaden feeling had left her; she felt lighter since she'd talked with Mamma. It was like someone had been pressing down hard on her skull, and now they'd stopped.

'Vita.'

She wished the Monsignor made more noise, not perambulate like some benign ghost. 'Is there more coffee? We have visitors.'

'So early?'

Coffee was running low. Carla said to use acorns, but Vita had no clue what she meant. Grind them? Steep them? She assessed the tin, then the gunk inside the macchinetta. Could she reuse the dregs? 'Enough for one more pot. Maybe.'

'That will do. Bring it to the dining room. And some of those little cakes your mother makes?'

'The necci? All gone, Monsignor. Sorry.'

'Ah. Well. Just the coffee then.'

She carried in the tray. A group of men were gathered round the table: Dr Baldacci and other Homburg-hatted men from the Comune, Don Sabatini and old Don Leoni too. Complaints flying. 'Misfits everywhere,' said Don Leoni. 'Speaking gibberish, expecting to be fed and sheltered. What are we to do, Monsignor?'

'What would Our Lord do, Father?'

A long, fraught silence, before the Monsignor answered his own question. 'I would imagine He would say you are to offer them food and shelter. Be blind and deaf to what they are, but awake to what they need.'

'But, Monsignor—' said the old priest.

'Yes, Father, you may have some coffee. Our hospitality is boundless, no? Now, in addition to refugees, I think we must discuss rations, and housing.'

'Monsignor, I'm not just speaking of refugees,' said Don Leoni. 'This latest decree: *Harsh sentences for those who give hospitality to deserters.*'

'Indeed, Father. I too have had such a letter from our friends in Lucca, as I imagine we all have. It's good our illustrious leaders see fit to include us in their daily utterances. And particularly good to have such copious amounts of paper in ready supply, don't you think? Once I have enjoyed the contents, I can use the other side of these epistles on which to write. A most satisfactory arrangement.' The Monsignor's voice gleamed.

Vita decided to take in the torta di riso she'd made for lunch. Crisp, fluted crust: it was a triumph. Even Mamma would have been impressed. The Monsignor frowned. 'Such largesse, Vittoria. When our parishioners survive on crumbs?'

She was ready for him. 'The chard's from our garden, sir, and the eggs are from my mother.' The smell of pecorino was too much for Don Leoni. 'Tre becchi, Vita.' She cut him a slice three beaks wide.

'The Allies are in the Pisan hills now,' said Dr Baldacci. 'Near Cecina, I believe.'

'So close? That's nearly the edge of our own diocese.'

'Why don't the tedeschi keep moving then? If they get over the mountains—'

'I fear they're digging in.' Baldacci stirred his coffee.

'Here? In Barga?'

'You've heard the rumours? This wall they're building? Has it crossed your mind they might be entrenching?'

'But we can't possibly sustain them – we've barely enough to feed our own, what with all these extra bodies. If the Germans start taking food out of our mouths—'

'They already are,' said Vita. 'They've been up in Catagnana.'

'Vittoria!' The Monsignor's cup rattled in its saucer. 'Go back to the kitchen. None of this concerns you.'

But it did. Why did these tired, earnest men think food was their concern? Who eked it out and cooked it? She pressed her ear to the door, trying to hear. Baldacci was saying they'd enough grain stored to last until September. So what were they worrying about? The tedeschi would never stay that long.

'We'll call on all the parish priests,' said the Monsignor. 'They can do an inventory of what we have, whom we might prevail upon. Gentlemen, you must excuse me. I will do the rounds of our parish Masses now.'

'This morning, Monsignor?'

'Indeed. Time is as pressing as our hunger. I think the Gospel of the loaves and fishes is in order. Nico! Nico!'

Nicodemo was squirelling his wood somewhere. Vita waited a second before responding. The men were collecting their stuff. One by one, they filed past. Dr Baldacci raised his hat.

'Ah, Vittoria.' The Monsignor was standing by the window. You could not ignore the black tip of the guns outside the Canonica, their terrible one-eyed gaze. 'I need Nico to go and borrow the sisters' donkey. And can you fetch me my travelling cloak, please?'

His disposition was completely pleasant, as if he had never been sharp. That big smelly thing? She'd forgotten to wash it. 'It's very warm, Monsignor. Are you sure?'

'Well, perhaps not. It is muggy.' He tapped either side of his breast, searching.

'Here.' Vita got him a pen from the sideboard. 'You need paper?'

'Thank you. Loaves, fishes. What else might I speak of, Vita?'

'How about telling them to stop talking?' No paper in the first drawer. 'That's all folk do. Stand round gossiping. How about "don't grind your teeth, grind your grain"? Something like that? Here.' There was a pad of cheap paper in the third drawer down.

'That's rather clever, child. Yes. Talk does not make flour. Share your food, not your thoughts. Very good. Very good indeed.' One hand still on his breast, his elbow crooked. Brain cogs turning, he froze in this manner often, when he was composing a sermon or some lengthy prayer. 'Yes. And a three-day petition to San Cristoforo. For the needs of war. We must pray for our parishioners. Ask others to pray for us.'

'Why?'

'Stop asking so many questions. Go find Nico, child. Go, go.'

Monsignor was gone for ages. Vita wasn't sure how old he was, but his energies were boundless. Bereft of her torta, she prepared him a hearty lunch. Two types of cabbage today – workaday green and cavolo nero. Who knew there was such variety? Nico tended their garden with religious devotion: rows of cabbages, fagioli, basil. Weedy vines. More cabbages. The worst thing about the soup wasn't that it made them fart: it was the stink of it that clung to your hair. And soap was such a precious commodity. She prayed for the day cabbages were too.

It had turned properly overcast, wind whipping up dust in the piazza, catching at the tarpaulin-covered boxes where the Germans kept their bombs. Soft splats of rain began to hit the window, just as the Monsignor came home.

'I've made you lunch.'

'No time, no time. That meeting is now.'

'What meeting?'

'The one in Cinema Roma.' He was rummaging in the tin box of junk Nico kept above the sink. 'The German generals are insisting – and no one can find the key. Ach!' He smacked the lid of the box shut. 'Come, Vita.'

'Why have I to go?'

'No exceptions. The whole of Barga is to be present – the sisters are already down there.' This was unlike him. He was discomposed. Agitated.

'Well, *technically*, Monsignor, I'm not barghigiana, am I? Catagnana's the other side of the river...'

'Vittoria. Take off your apron, brush your hair and get your shoes on. You will be representing this household.

Dignitaries are coming from Lucca. Generale Utimperghe too. It will not look good if we stroll in late.'

'But you've not stopped all morning. And you didn't eat the torta. Will you at least have some soup?'

'Soup? Who has time for soup? Except our honoured guests, of course. They're all dining as we speak. A fine *pranzo* in Ristorante Libano. Thirty-five of them, gorging on pasta, steak and cheese – for which the Comune is to pay.'

'Monsignor, are you feeling all right?'

'No! No, I am not. I have spent all morning preaching about the importance of frugality in personal needs, about the Godly joys of sharing what little we *do* have, and these... these German visitors are consuming a month's supply of food at one meal. It's not right.'

The rain grew wild as they walked through the town. Quick licks of wind took Vita's shawl from her shoulders. She gave up trying to hold it in place, tied it in a headscarf. Nico was battling the storm with his umbrella, but the wind bent it before they'd reached the first steps downhill. She held his arm, afraid he'd be caught in a gust and blown down the steep incline.

'Stop pawing me, girl.'

The Monsignor strode ahead, a long smudge against fat grey sky.

They crossed Ponte Vecchio, its low parapet offering little protection from the wind. The thin bridge arched over land, not water, and the drop below was significant. Rain drove in heavy rods. When it hit, it hurt. Again, Vita held on to Nico, clutching until they reached Piazza San Rocco. From there, the going was flat, newer, squarer buildings offering some shelter from the gale.

The cinema straddled one corner of Via Roma, bridging the modern Giardino and the jumble of old Barga.

A film poster fluttered. The 'Roma' sign was unlit, and a large crowd stood outside, miserably folding themselves against the storm.

Dr Baldacci greeted them. 'Still no key. I think we are to have the meeting outside.'

'You think? Surely you are in charge, Dottore?'

He raised his hands. 'Apparently not.'

'Ach, this is a nonsense. On whose authority?'

Generale Utimperghe appeared. Another who moved quietly. 'Problems, gentlemen? Apart from your inability to locate the key.' He showed a row of small white teeth. You couldn't really call it a smile.

'The cinema hasn't been open in weeks,' said Baldacci.

The gale scalded Vita's neck. Rain stabbing into her face, lashes dripping. She could see a hazy figure waving at her from the queue: it was Cesca, with Carla and the boys. But no Mamma or Papà.

'I jest,' said Utimperghe. 'In any case, it seems our German friends have been detained.'

'You mean they're still eating lunch?' The Monsignor brushed globes of rain from his sleeve. 'Are we really to stand out here, generale? There are women... children.'

'All of hardy Barga stock, no doubt.' Those ugly little teeth again, his pink tongue behind them. Utimperghe strode to the head of the crowd, climbed the steps of the cinema. A small man with impressive epaulettes. Behind him, two blackshirts took up position. Cesca came over.

'What's going on, Vi? Are we not getting in? I'm wet to my *bahookie*. Oh, buongiorno, Monsignor.' She bobbed her head. 'Sorry.'

'For?'

'*Bahookie* – it's not a nice word.'

'People of Barga,' shouted Utimperghe. 'Thank you for coming. I won't detain you – the weather is a little inclement, no?' But he looked gleeful in the whipping rain. 'Alas, in times of war, we must all make some sacrifices.'

Surrounding Vita were women who had husbands, brothers, sons at the front, in prison, in Greece, Russia, lost or broken, while this shiny man talked about sacrifice. He didn't pause for a response. Utimperghe was speaking and they would listen. Hands behind his back, barrel-chested into the storm, neither air nor water stopping his flow.

'We are delighted to welcome our German allies. We have absolutely nothing to fear. They are our friends, and our protectors. Along with your sons and countrymen in the Black Brigade, we are here for your safety. And, for your safety, it will be necessary to abide by certain rules.' He unrolled a sheaf of paper, which soon became transparent.

'All citizens are to carry personal papers at all times. If you do not have papers, you must attend the Comune forthwith. All citizens are to comply with the curfew, which will be instigated from tonight.' Utimperghe turned slightly left to right, to acknowledge all the crowd.

'From twenty-two hundred hours until oh-six hundred hours, no persons are permitted to leave their homes, without prior authorisation. All Jews are to report to the Comune for further instruction.'

'Why Jews?' whispered Cesca.

'There is to be full co-operation with our German friends regarding requisition of any property, goods or personnel as required.' Utimperghe's voice was wrestling with the wind, his face gleaming wet. 'This is one more effort for our country – and for Il Duce, who is with us in our struggles. Now, I know *der Kommandant* wanted to take this opportunity to introduce himself. It's unfortunate that he and his colleagues have urgent war business—'

The Monsignor tutted.

'There will be plenty of other opportunities to meet our guests. We hope you will enjoy the concert tonight, and the other cultural activities we have planned. A gesture of friendship, of the close connections we share with our German brothers.'

'Excuse me, sir,' said an old lady in the crowd. 'May I ask—'

Utimperghe continued. 'Remember – all this is for your own protection. The barbarians are almost at our gates. We must stay strong and trust in Il Duce and Our Lord.' He raised his arm to the Monsignor, who shuffled backwards, reluctant to share the stormy spotlight. 'Monsignor. Bless these, your fellow citizens, for the travails yet to come.'

Vita could see the Monsignor's jaw dance. His face remained impassive. 'My fellow barghigiani are always in my prayers. Indeed, I have been with them in prayer all morning. And, if our meeting is now adjourned, generale, you are very welcome to join us at the Duomo, for a rather delayed Mass.'

The generale bowed. 'Very kind, Monsignor. Alas, the duties of office call me.'

Folk began gently to stir. Was this it? Were they done? Pasta was waiting to be cooked, shivering children to be dried. Utimperghe called the crowd to order. 'I urge you, good people of Barga. Be vigilant to spies within your midst, and to those who fail to comply with our wish to keep you safe. My men will be stationed throughout the town, assisting our allies with every aspect of their work.' He was shouting again, bludgeoning the other voices, the people desperate to mutter to their neighbours. 'And it is incumbent on every good Italian to do likewise. It is Il Duce's greatest wish, his express orders to his people. Now. Dismiss!'

Several faces in the crowd looked puzzled. A few people clapped. Most just stared, as the rain lashed harder.

'You may go,' called the Monsignor. 'Go home and dry your clothes.' He too was shivering. 'Mass will now be in thirty minutes' time.'

Utimperghe marched to a waiting automobile. Baldacci followed, but they drove off before he reached them.

'Well,' said Cesca, wringing out a hank of curls. 'What a load of nonsense.'

'Thank you,' the Monsignor said under his breath. 'A lift would be most welcome. Francesca, do not be so dismissive. Generale Utimperghe is Il Duce's representative. As such, we must obey. Are those your Roman cousins over there? So you will all be coming to Mass? If you wait, Nicodemo and I will escort you. It will be nice for your cousins to worship inside the Duomo.'

Help me! mouthed Cesca, behind his back. Vita tried not to laugh.

'Please eat something first, Monsignor. Let me get you a towel at least.'

'No, it's fine.' He adjusted his wide-brimmed hat. 'Do you know what I would love?'

'What?'

'A peach. A fat gold peach.'

'But no one grows peaches here.'

'Sadly, that is true. But I would love one, nonetheless.'

Where could Vita get hold of a peach? Imagine his face if she bowled up clutching one. The rain seemed to be easing, vapours rising from their soaking clothes. Poor Nico was trembling. Vita untied her shawl. It was a good thick one, the underneath was reasonably dry. She put it over his shoulders.

'Oi!'

'Nico, I'm too hot. Can you take it back to the house? I need to go on an errand.'

'Skiving again? You're supposed to be cleaning out the store with me.' But he didn't remove the shawl.

'I'll be twenty minutes. Half an hour at most. Ciao, Cesca! Carla. Enjoy Mass.'

From Cinema Roma to Ponte di Catagnana was not far. If she cut through the low woods and ran, she could be there in ten minutes. If anyone in the world knew where to get peaches, it would be Signor Tutto and his shop of wonders.

The forest was shiny-fresh after the rain. Perhaps it would be nice to go to a German concert, instead of chasing cobwebs with Nico. What about this curfew though? Were they really not allowed out at night? She wasn't a saboteur, she was a housekeeper.

Ponte was very quiet. They should call Sunday Shutter-day. Though Signor Tutto never went to Mass, his shop was not officially open on the Lord's Day. But everyone knew if you tapped on his door, he'd open up. What could she offer for peaches? Money was useless; bartering was the way to go. A primitive currency of four-eggs-for-a-cooking pot, a bit of goat for some cloth, rubber, candles. Signor Tutto set the rate for most transactions, but he wasn't greedy – he seemed to balance his weights and measures depending on need and your ability to pay.

Vita struck the door knocker. Thought she heard a shuffle inside. But there was no reply. Tried a second time. Rattled the door latch. 'Signor Tutto? It's me, Vita. I need peaches. I know it's daft—'

The door opened. It was his wife; hair tangled, her eyes red. 'Come in. Quick.'

Inky dark inside. Darts of daylight filtered through the shutters. A few blinks before Vita could make out what was wrong. The shop was in disarray. Where there should be a counter and bulging shelves were packing crates, baskets piled high, tins toppled, clothes spilling from opened bags. Herbs that usually hung from the rafters were on the ground, their fragrance trampled.

'What am I to do?' A man, high-pitched and desperate. Not jolly Signor Tutto. 'We cannot take it all.'

'We can't take any of it, you old fool. Look, here's Vita.'

'What? No! I don't want anyone.' The voice came from a crouched shape in the corner.

'Maybe she can help. Vita works for the Monsignor, don't you?'

The kneeling shape unfurled. It was Signor Tutto.

'What is it?' Vita said. 'Are you ill?'

'Oh, Vita.' He took her hand.

'Please. What's wrong?'

'So many Germans,' said Signora Tutto. 'We thought they would pass through. Who would come to Barga?'

'I know. Swanking about like they own the place.'

'We've been told to attend the Comune.'

'Is it to do with the shop? Have they commandeered it?' Aware she was talking into a gap, her words falling over an invisible, sharp edge.

'Vita, we are Jewish,' said Signora Tutto. 'Do you know what the Nazis do to Jews?'

'No.' In the darkness, her voice sounded like a child's. There were rules, yes, about Jews not marrying Italians or teaching in schools. But nobody paid them much heed.

'Bella.' Signor Tutto stood on her other side. She was flanked by sadness. 'It's no longer safe for us here. We have to leave.' Vita could see the outline of his hand, rubbing his brow. 'Before we go, we need a favour. Will you do that for us?'

'Tullio, no.'

'What?'

'Will you ask the Monsignor if he can dig up my mamma and papà?'

'You can't ask the girl that.'

'From the Jewish corner. *Please.* Ask if Nicodemo will rebury them in the main cemetery.'

'I don't understand.'

'In case Ronaldo comes back. You remember Ronaldo, don't you?'

Their son had been one of the first boys from the village to go to war. If you could prove your family fought for Italy in the past, they let Jews serve – and Ronaldo's nonno had been a war hero. Signor Tutto had composed a tune in his papà's honour.

'Please. They will check. It won't matter that Ronaldo's a soldier. But if we're not here, and we've no family buried as Jews, he might be safe.'

The perfumed dark was making Vita feel nauseous. Thick scents like creeping oil.

'You'll try?'

'Yes. I'll try.'

'Good girl. We would ask the Monsignor ourselves, but it's not safe for us to go outside.'

'How? They're hardly going to arrest you off the street.'

'They might.'

'Folk wouldn't let them.'

'Darling girl.' Signor Tutto's hand squeezed hers. 'We cannot risk it. We leave tonight.'

'You can't. They've started this curfew—'

'It's fine. We have a friend to help us. A guide.'

'Oh.' The sadness in the room pressed against her; fuzzy, like peach skin. 'But where will you go?'

'Far up into the mountains. Sant'Anna. No one will come there.'

'Tullio! You are not meant to say. Not to a soul.'

'Ah, but it is only Vita. Anyway, it's her—'

'Not a soul. Remember?'

'Signora Tutto, my mamma often says I have no soul, so don't worry.' Vita kicked one of the baskets. 'I wish you didn't have to go. Who'll mind the shop till you get back?'

'It doesn't matter.' Signora Tutto righted the basket Vita had kicked. 'Just leave it unlocked, Tullio. People can take what they need. We can't carry it with us.'

'But we must take this.' Signor Tutto lifted a candlestick from the shelf beside her head. Vita caught a gleam of brass, of many curved arms like a great beetle, before it disappeared inside a sack. 'And what of my music? My instruments?'

'We'll lock them in the attic. I am not carrying a tuba up the mountain.' Signora Tutto opened the shop door. Daylight cut across her wrist. 'You'd better go, child, while the street is quiet.'

'Will we see you before you leave?'

'I don't think so.' The older woman stretched up to kiss her.

Vita didn't return the kiss. Barely registered it, just a press on numb skin. Signor Tutto also kissed her, his rough bristles scratching her face. Why were they being so calm? She wanted to shake him until he chuckled, said it was one of his silly tricks. Then, as they were bundling her into the street, she found her senses and went to hug them both. But it was too late. The door was shut. And she'd forgotten to ask about peaches.

Chapter Eight

As the Buffaloes moved forward, the air grew sultry. An occasional plane circled overhead. Bear would turn his face sideways, not up like the rest of them. He could calculate the speed, distance, make, by the sound of the engine alone. It was one of his 'things'.

'Best sound you can hear is the purr of a Merlin, boys. Ideally in a nice Mustang; they got that big, smooth ring to them. But that ain't one of ours. It's Charlie.'

Bed-check Charlie, the German observation plane that always came out at dusk. It was far above the mountains, seeking future targets, surveying the dance assemble. What could the Buffs do, except keep dancing? The airplane never came near, but they kept close cover anyway, using trees and low riverbeds, the natural dips and shadows of the land. And then, it began to rain. Great, heavy drops, which soaked you through.

'Butt-end of a storm,' said Claude.

'You a weatherman now?'

'I know 'cause a how it's hard.'

They made camp near the foot of Pisano. Order was to wait until just before dawn, then move up, in a pincer movement. *By the light, of the silvery moon,* sang Bear, pretending to dance with the lieutenant.

'What do we do now, sarge?'

The 370th were part of a far greater dance. They might cover ground fast, get themselves into position first, but, until all the players were in place, the Monte Pisano polka would not begin. Some of the 1st were nearing the eastern slope, but other battalions were still to assemble in the west. Bear said more and more Allied troops were pouring across the Arno. The front line was moving, pushing out, constricting the Bosch. The Buffaloes had them fleeing Pisa and holed up in them thar hills. And the rain had blown itself out.

Barring any ambush, Frank's company had bought themselves a chunk of downtime. 'Course, it was not downtime; it was truncated, stolen time, same way sleep was, or shitting. It was a scooped-out hollow where you were neither marching nor shooting. You were waiting. You were listening to airplanes fly overhead, or to mortar-crunch, or bursts of gunfire not directed at you. You were watching pillars of smoke, and knowing that, somewhere else, a bunch of guys were burning. You were fingering your rifle like you loved it; you were feeding little birds or writing home. Patrols were sent out, raiding parties to search remote farmhouses and draw down enemy fire. Nothing doing. Sentries were set around the camp: four on, four off, Frank was due up next, but then another company, high, still damp from their river crossing, reached camp to relieve them.

'Relieved? But we ain't done anything yet.'

'Calm before the storm,' said Comanche. 'I guess.'

A surprise gift of time, this new scoop. Dedeaux showed up to announce the 370th were no longer the forward line. You could tell it pained him to let them loose.

'This comes from on high. Command believes you need some kind of respite, and this area has been secured. But I trust you men will not disgrace your uniforms.'

'You heard the captain. Back by midnight, children,' said Bear. 'Else you turn into pumpkins. Stay in twos and fours, keep your wits about you and your dicks in your pants. And do *not* get drunk.'

'Sarge, any chance of a new shirt?' asked Frank.

Bear laughed. 'Not unless you wanna take it off some dead guy.'

Frank and Comanche followed the herd. It seemed they'd become a pairing. A nearby nameless village with a church and a piazza was all that was on offer. Thin houses, where the occupants came out at the sound of bootsteps, opened up their windows, laid out tables and wine. Dollars, nylons, chocolate for grappa, wizened nuts and grapes.

'Hey there.'

A little girl peeked from a doorway. 'Com, you got any chocolate? *Cioccolato*? You want some?'

She shrieked as Frank came close, slammed the door.

Another soldier's fist came over Frank's shoulder, thumping on the house's shutters. 'We don't motherfucking bite!'

Comanche pushed him. 'Leave it, Ivan. I got plenty candy. We'll just put it on the window ledge, see?'

'No, you fucking leave it, Redskin. Christ, these people should be on they knees, thanking us.'

'She's just a baby, man.'

'Who the fuck you scared of?' Banging on the window. 'You don't gotta be scared, kid. *Avanti!*'

The front door opened again. A mother and her three daughters. She had them all wrapped inside of her coat. Frank could see a glint of metal in her hand.

'*Signora. Scusi, per favore. Va bene, va bene.* No... problemo. *Noi*, um, *assistiamo?*'

'*Non ci mangiare*,' whispered the middle girl.

'*Mangeri*? No, we ain't hungry,' said Comanche. He'd a bucketful of chocolate in his fist. 'It's for you. Is good. Ivan, put your hood down, man. Let her see you.'

'I think she's saying, don't eat *us*,' said Frank. 'Jesus Christ.'

The oldest daughter dipped behind her momma. Came back with a leaflet, a crude drawing of a gorilla in US drab, taking a bite from a white woman's neck. *Bestien* dripped in red letters. Frank shook his head. 'No true. No, no. *Bene, capite? Americani, sì?*'

The mother moved forward. Without a word, she stuck her fingers in Frank's mouth, opening his jaw. '*Belli. Denti belli.*' Then she rubbed the side of his face. Showed her daughters the flat of her hand. '*Il colore non si stacca.*'

'*È il cioccolato?*'

'That's right. Here.' Comanche finally got the kids to take the candy. '*Cioccolato.*'

'Think she's asking if *I'm* chocolate, man.'

The three Buffaloes began to laugh. If you didn't, you would weep.

'Mm, tasty.' Ivan drew his finger down his own cheek, pretended to lick it. Then the kids started laughing, and, eventually, the momma too. But she was still wary as she closed the door.

They drifted on through the town. Left Ivan haggling over a bottle of moonshine. Frank and Comanche walked from one end of the town to the other. Didn't matter that Dedeaux said this place was clear. You couldn't relax in such narrow, shuttered streets. Despite the initial celebrations, folks weren't coming out to play. Who could blame them? If it was Frank's momma behind these walls, he'd keep her holed up too.

In the piazza, an elderly man played a fiddle. The music wavered, as if it were no longer sure. Faded notes, a head-scarf streaming. Girls linking arms. A dance beginning, a different one. There was an open doorway, an arch really, leading down an alley to what might once have been a barn. A couple of women stood there, beckoning. Older soldiers, who knew the steps of this dance. Young bucks following. Giggling, nudging.

'Behold,' said an old-timer, '"Casa Prima della Montagna".'

'Huh?' said Frank. But he knew.

'Fuck knows, kid. I'm only reading the sign.' A card inside the window; a woman's chipped, painted finger-nails pushing it to the centre of the sill. 'Bordello below the hill? Big titty mountains? It looks clean, anyhow.'

To Frank it looked like a beat-up barn, with candles in bottles and lace across cracked glass. Caught in the flow, he was almost at the door before he finally turned away. Couldn't see Comanche, didn't know if he'd already gone inside.

'Hey, deadwood.'

'You wanna die a virgin, Chap-*elle*?'

He rounded on Luiz, leering at him. Hard-glazed eyes from hard liquor.

'Who says I'm a virgin?'

The dumpy guy next to Luiz winked, cheek spilling over his eye. 'You just did.'

'Calm down, *amigo*. Is no big deal. Not that I'd know.' Luiz hitched up his trousers. 'I mean, all the ladies want a Latin lover. But, serious, Chap. You get shot up tomorrow on the hill? Might be your last chance. These ladies, they providing a public service. You gonna be rude and turn your nose up at that, college boy?'

The dumpy guy held the door. 'C'mon, sweetpea. After you.'

Outside: perfumed herbs. Inside: animal smells. Twilight or mirrored dark? Whichever way would be wrong. Frank told himself this was an initiation no different from your first combat, your first kill. That it was no more or less important than cleaning your rifle. And the dirtiness of it, the unasked-for immediacy that it was here, *now*, waiting for him when he thought he'd be eating crap out a tin and hunkering in the mud; that beyond this door or that, a woman might spread her legs and welcome him in, and he had the money in his pocket to do it, was making his blood pump hard the way it did in dreams. Buzzing in his stomach. Another dance starting. And, through the buzz, Frank felt an abrupt, gut-busting urge to cry, because if this was it, if this was life flooding into him just so it could all flood out tomorrow, then that was truly, truly sad. For all of them; if this was it, it was as dirty a death as those poor fucks got by the River Arno. But the dance kept pulling him, pulling him in and making him be that other person who did not want more, who'd never thought of kindred spirits, of the first-time talk and touching and warmth that might lead to love, and they were forming an orderly queue, only half a dozen of them, only two closed doors by the looks of it but Frank was tall, athletic. Good cheekbones, looked real clean; he was a boy to make his momma proud, and there he was, before he knew it (Liar. He fucking knew it), in a room full of candles, on a bed made of silk.

Except the bed was bales of straw, with a slippery coverlet on top. Sharp tips of straw poked through, stabbing him in the back as a woman leaned over, onto him. Businesslike, unbuttoning his flies. She was pretty. Older than him, with fine lines around her eyes and mouth. Mouth pouting, lips in a flower-bud shape as she rambled foreign words. His dick was bursting. As she leaned over the side of the bed, her breast fell out of her dress. Frank shut his eyes. The image of the thin white tit, hanging like a dog ear, the yellow sprigs of fabric nursing it, was like a cold shower across his back. He could feel a condom being rolled down his dick, even as it was shrinking.

'Hey.' He put his hand over hers. 'Hey, signora. What's your name? *Tuo nome?*'

She shook her head.

'I'm Frank. Francis.' He shimmied upright. 'Like Assisi?'

She looked confused. Took a breath, then she bent her head towards his dick.

'No!'

He caught the woman's hair in his hands. It felt greasy. 'Ma'am. No. No.' Whispered in her ear. 'It's OK. Please.' From his pocket in his pants, which were halfway down his legs, he took a fistful of notes, pressed them on her same way he'd given the priest those cans of beef. Guilt money.

'Come on, signora. Up.' She shrank from his grip on her hair. 'Please. *Scusi*, ma'am. I don't want... Here. Just take the money, yeah?'

Sitting on the edge of the bed, watching him. Frank did up his pants.

'I'm sorry for your trouble.'

What his momma would say, a polite apology when folks were angry or in pain. Could there be a less appropriate phrase to offer in a whorehouse? But whores don't wear yellow-sprigged dresses, nor have a band of untanned skin where a wedding ring should be.

He stood. 'I'm just gonna go.'

Now it was her turn to grab him. '*Momento.*' She held up five fingers. Beyond the door, Frank could hear a babble of kite-high voices; it must have been going on all the time they were in here, but he'd been oblivious. Outside was a queue.

'*Cinque minuti.*'

There was a thump at the door. 'C'mon, mo-fo. Hurry it up in there.'

'Hey!' said Frank. 'We're busy. Half an hour at least – I'm on a roll.'

Catcalls and whistles. Another thump. 'Fuckin' roll on and roll off, boy.'

'*Trenta?*' he said. 'How much for *trenta?*'

The woman smiled at him. '*No trenta. Non ci crederebbero mai.*'

He thought a moment. '*Credere?* Believe? You saying no one will believe that?'

She lay back on her bed. '*Dieci,*' she said quietly.

They stayed like that, Frank hunched, the woman resting her eyes, for maybe a quarter hour, until the banging got too insistent and she swung her legs round. '*Grazie.*' Her eyes were still closed. Frank could have been anyone. He picked up his jacket, edged from the room as Luiz's pudgy mate eased himself in.

''Bout fucking time, deadwood.'

Frank returned to the main street, where the impromptu café was doing a roaring trade. He wasn't thirsty. Wasn't anything, really. Sure wasn't that woman's hero. They weren't supposed to head back to camp alone, so he sat on a wall, beside a cluster of grandmas, who took little notice of him, in the way a wary animal takes little notice, when all its fur is on end and it is quivering with the insistence that *you are not there.* A crowd of kids were kicking a soccer ball on wasteland at the end of the village; a few of the Buffaloes had joined them. He could see Comanche at the goal. Frank ran over, caught the ball, deft, with the side of his boot, weaving through two of the soldiers to kick it hard past Comanche.

'Goal!' he shouted.

'Hey! Piss off and find your own game, Chap.' Luiz again, squaring for another fight.

Nobody cheered. The kids stood and watched him, watched the other Buffaloes for a response. Underneath their exuberance, they were as wary as the old women: clued-up for body language, coiled to flee.

Comanche swung his jacket up off the dirt. 'We're done here anyway.'

They fell into step beside each other, leaving the others to carry on their game.

'Man. You supposed to ask their permission first or something?'

Comanche ignored the question. His prowling amble ate up the ground, but effortlessly, like he was gliding over water. Apparently, they were headed back to camp. Fine by Frank.

'Pointless, ain't it?'

'What?' said Frank. Wanting to justify himself, and wondering why it mattered.

'Time off, when you got nowhere to go and no one to see. You have a good time?'

'Not really. Gave a woman a bunch of money and watched her sleep.'

'Shit. You bored her that much?'

'Guess so. You got a girl, Com?'

'I got me a wife,' Comanche said proudly. 'Jilla.' He slipped a small snapshot out of his billfold. It was creased and grubby, but the face staring back was lovely. Long dark hair in a plait, real pretty eyes.

'Jilla. She's a looker.'

'Yup.'

'Kids?'

'Nope. Not yet.'

After they left the perimeter of the village, they didn't speak. By silent consent, one kept watch up front while the other periodically checked behind. All quiet. Tonight, the moon was faint, and the darkness was a quicksand; a soft, thick swallow that might eat you unawares. The heavy night-scent of... what was it? Rosemary? Olives? Whatever; the smell filled you up. They were almost back at camp. Frank could see the sentry, shifting from foot to foot. The line of his gun, propped against the wall that partitioned the villa's garden from the surrounding countryside. You could tell the guy needed a piss.

'Don't say to anyone, will you?' said Frank.

'What? That you went to a whorehouse, spent all your money and didn't get screwed? That what you don't want me to tell?'

'Nope.'

'You got someone, Chap?'

'Just my momma. Shit, man. Why do they do that? Those women. You could tell she hated being there.'

'Like us, you mean? We don't got so many options either.'

'Yeah, but *that*.'

'Fuck, man. What they teach you at college? This is a war, Chapel. War makes good men do bad things. Least this way, the woman gets paid first.'

'Halt! Who goes—'

'Piss off, Ginger. It's us.'

Fact the sentry's Christian name was Roger was just too much of a gift. 'Here's your gun by the way.' Comanche handed him the rifle.

'I knows it was there. Is jus too damn heavy to keep holding it.'

'Well, you better. 'Cos if Jerry shoot you first, then they come shoot us. Which would make me very mad indeed.'

They went inside the cordon, past the jeeps.

'Asshole. People just waiting for us niggers to fuck up.'

Frank flinched at that word, same as he did when folks said *motherfucker*. Both words were common here, flung as hard as any grenade, in the belief that constant exposure inured you.

'Ever thought of going for promotion, Comanche? You'd make a good corp.'

'Nope.'

They found Bear and the rest of the squad, sitting round a pile of boots and rifles in lieu of a campfire.

'Evening, children. You play nice?'

'We did, sarge.'

'Mama don't need to know. Come. Join us. We been telling bedtime stories.'

'Ain't no story, sarge,' said a skinny kid named George. 'Is history. Was Buffs all way back to the Civil War. The Injun Wars. We was *cavalry*, man.'

'Bull*shit*,' said Ivan. Always with his hood up. No matter how hot it was, he wore a hooded jerkin under his uniform. Said it kept the flies away. Fact he sweated like a hog probably attracted more bugs than the hood kept at bay.

'No, Ivan, the boy's right.' Bear was rolling a thin cigarette, leather tobacco pouch balanced on his chest. He was clean out of cigars. 'Your people named us, Comanche. The injuns.'

'They ain't my people.'

Bear chuntered on, licking the edge of the paper. 'On account of our curly hair. Black men been fighting for this nation longer than the Stars and Stripes themselves.'

'How come, sarge?'

'The Brits had us battling away for them when we was still their slaves.'

'Thought you was a Brit, sarge?'

'Me?' He spat a piece of tobacco out. 'Uh-uh. I ain't no Brit.'

'Who's your people then, sarge? What kinda name is McClung?'

'Ain't never hearda the Black Irish?' He struck a match, shielded it with his hand.

'Irish? Where's that?' said Claude.

'It's in England. And you don't get no black faces in England.'

'Wrong and wrong.' Bear got his cigarette lit. Puffed on it a few times, made them wait till he was ready. 'Ireland is in Ireland. The auld country, my grampy called it. Galway, I think. Where his great-great-grandpappy came from.'

'Ireland, huh?' Comanche lay back in the dirt, one hand behind his head. 'So you're a mongrel too then, sarge?'

'Sure am.' He closed the snaps on his tobacco pouch. 'Yup. We be the healthiest stock, us mongrels.' The sergeant winked at Comanche. 'Bedtime now, children. Gotta two-hour snooze before the big boys arrive.'

Several companies had assembled overnight. Tanks and trucks, jeeps and foot soldiers, moving off in the pink glow of daybreak. Some of the infantrymen hitched a ride on the tanks. The whole Italian front flamed into action that day, so the papers said. Frank's momma told him so in a letter. It was reported they punched a twenty-mile hole through enemy lines. When threatened with encirclement, the Germans had 'hastily evacuated Pisa'. Neat as that. Shooing the bastards away. Momma sent him the whole clipping, as if she were telling him what really happened:

> Negro troops of the 92nd, making their first appear-
> ance in battle, stormed up the slopes of Monte
> Pisano, from whose heights the enemy had lobbed
> shells into U.S. lines during the long stalemate.

Didn't feel much like storming to Frank. Felt like crawl-ing naked through glass up a wall of molten rock. Heavy artillery began almost the moment they moved onto Monte Pisano. Shells they'd heard hammering all along their front line, in the background. Blunted. Now they were alive. Tanks only took you so far, then you were on your own. Ordered lines at first, until the thunder started. Thunder louder than the loudest roaring wave, the loudest freight train, a constant barrage of thunder that spewed up the ground as you tried to stand and climb and keep your balance, think tactics, dodge the bullets, the fine line of tracer fire, the mortars, the burp guns – which meant Jerry was close. Those things could burp five hundred rounds a minute at you and you realised that there were, in fact, no tactics, no fear, no sense that made sense except the up and up, slip-scrambling up into the face of the mountain, into where it would hurt the most.

Tramping and stumbling, boots crushing the herbs till they were bitter. A whizz of lighting by his left temple, sweep of bluish-grey; a nest, an arm and flung-back grenade. He steadied himself. One leg anchored high. Took aim as the Jerry's head poked up from the low ridge above his own head and he pulled the trigger, sweet-sweet-slow. The man's head snapped back, a look of pure amazement as the skull split red, Frank ducking, the grenade going off in the hand in which it was still being held. Turned to blink the smarting smoke, to yell a joke to George, to stop from upchucking, and there was George, on his back and his leg, and his leg was away, apart and spilling, great gouts of his blood, showering his face.

And the on and the up. The shrilling. The drops.

Frank stopped seeing the men on either side of him; the ones that fell away screaming, the ones that fell quiet. They ceased being comrades; they were shields, targets that saved him every time. And with each brittle step, a little piece of him fell too.

Just the up and the up. Reaction not thought, left and right and up and down, movement, what colour? Who is where and what and up. The smell of burning. Cloaking clouds of dirt and smoke. Screamed orders: *UP*. And the roar of the thunder and up and the up. That woman's voice again, mocking them. Offering hot coffee and strudel and the up and the up. An angel voice. Perhaps he was dead? She floated again on crackling air:

'*Your country doesn't want you, boys. Come here. Lay down your arms and come over where it's safe.*'

Frank fired and fired, randomly towards the voice, which echoed round the mountain. Saw a German gun, swivelling. Tore a grenade from the cluster at his waist and lobbed it. Count of one, count of two, scrunching down as the bodies fly and the on and the up and the stumble, slip, crash, up and the whizz and the zip and the thunder, the fucking thunder but the fucking dame had stopped her yakking and the up, lob, fire, duck and the up, scree, slip, up and duck and the up and the splatter and the up.

And then it was over. The order came to cease firing. They had taken Pisano.

Frank's legs had no feeling left, his shoulders on fire. The kickback of his rifle had stopped hurting eventually;

it had become another pistoning limb, but now he was limp, and aching. Ears singing. He closed his eyes for a minute, the way that woman had done in the whorehouse. But he couldn't close out the pictures. Of the blood, and the limbs and that split, shocked face.

'Woo-ee!' hollered Bear, thumping him on the back. 'You enjoy that, boy? Alright! Buffs is on a *roll*. All aboard for Lucca. Lovely Lucca, HERE WE FUCKING COME!'

Chapter Nine

Vita locked the cellar door. If tedeschi came to the Canonica, she'd say she'd lost it. She climbed the back stairs, and a sickening, muffled crunch fell somewhere to earth. Her body gave, that involuntary shrinking small and hard, distancing yourself from rattling stone. Through the back door in time to see plates and bowls on the dresser dance, like you'd chanced on an enchantment.

After a moment, the shaking stopped. Vita spat dust from her mouth, waited for the fluttering in her throat to stop. La Spezia's distant guns, that drumbeat of daily life, were now accompanied by these crumps and high-pitched whines. Firepower, not aimed at Barga, but – if Mrs Pieri's sister who laundered shirts for General Kesselring himself was correct – at the Allies, who had broken through, past Pisa. Allied planes were making sieves of the buildings along the railway embankment. From today, the Comune said it was suspending all trains. Buses, delivery vans too. No food supplies, no post, no outside world. No escape. Tough luck if you didn't want to be in Barga.

The Germans were definitely more jumpy. Groups would mass, drill, then move off; then another squad would go through the same rigmarole; then the first lot would march back and start doing drill again. Their efficiency appeared less oiled. They spent hours in the shadow of the Duomo, singing marching songs, and practising lifting stretchers of grapes into trucks, while kids pointed and laughed. *All that waste*, fretted Nico, as the grapes tumbled out. She wondered if Joe carried on like that, away in some secret place, with his ambulance pals. Since they'd fought, she hadn't seen him; nobody had. At least he'd got away in time. Ironic, that, how they'd parted at a crossroads. But it was for the best: each would be better without the other. The drift would happen slowly, like water cooling. They'd become friendly cousins once more, free to suit themselves. Was there such a feeling as happy-sad? Vita's brain was rusted.

She put the key inside her blouse. Divine providence, for the door knocking began almost immediately. Yesterday, the Germans had taken the last of Mamma's chickens, and most of Papà's tools. They were supposed to pay, or give you coupons to take to Lucca. In your imaginary automobile. When you managed to translate them, the coupons said things like 'Many thanks. Mussolini will pay.'

Damned tedeschi, folk muttered under their breaths, as they smiled and acquiesced. What was the alternative? Ach, the tedeschi weren't so bad, Mamma said. Yes, they strutted and pilfered, but they were harmless. God, that Hans was addicted to Mamma's necci, he kept mooching round La Limonaia. Papà said she shouldn't encourage him and Mamma said he was just a boy, and if people saw boys instead of soldiers, then maybe there would be less hurt in the world, and Papà went quiet.

The Brigate Nere frightened Vita more than the Nazis. There was a vicious zeal about them when they demanded papers, a sense they were sizing you up. Plus, they were Italian boys, so they knew the things to say, the comment that would make you blush, stumble. She tried to ignore them, donning a headscarf, slipping down narrow staircases rather than passing them in the street.

The barghigiani were to carry on 'as normal' – that was an order, if normal meant being locked indoors at night, challenged on your way to work. Or having no electricity for days, or the constant, low drone of aircraft, the unremitting flow of military vehicles and more soldiers and more refugees; vast crowds of strangers, sifting and settling.

'I've got it,' she shouted. But it was not soldiers. Long cones of light lanced the entrance to the Canonica, bronzing the floorboards. A couple stood there, the woman nursing a baby in a shawl. The man, skinny and smartly dressed, carried a stiffer bundle. Vita caught the tight plug of sound which rose in her throat. It was a coffin. He bore a tiny coffin, wrapped in a matching shawl.

'Can I... Come in, please. Come in.'

'Thank you,' said the man. 'May we speak with the Monsignor?'

'Yes. Of course. Wait—'

'Might we have a seat? They've walked us all the way from Pisa.'

'*Pisa?*'

'The rastrellamento.'

'Who is it, Vita?' The Monsignor emerged from his study.

'My name is Dr Contini, Monsignor. This is my wife.'

'Ah.' Gently, the Monsignor rested his hand on the small of the woman's back. 'Please. Come into my office. Vittoria – coffee. No. Some broth, I think.'

Vita heated the watery remains of lunch. By the time she returned, the Monsignor had placed an altar cloth over the tiny coffin. It rested on his *prie-dieu*. The doctor sat by his wife, the living baby in her arms.

'Vita. I want you to go your mamma. Tell her to gather some of the Catholic mothers, and ask them to take whatever food and supplies they can to... Albiano, did you say, dottore?'

'Yes, sir. Directly before the village as you approach.'

'Tell your mother there are some poor unfortunates there who have been herded all the way from Pisa. Countrymen of ours. I want us to extend to them whatever comforts we can. I'll speak to the German generale, to ensure his co-operation. But tell her also to be wary of the guards. No men are to go, nor girls – only older women. *Not* you. You understand?'

'Yes, Monsignor.'

'Run along then. Ah... perhaps you might go to the sisters first, and ask if they could attend to Signora Contini?'

'That isn't necessary, Monsignor. I can look after my wife.'

'I rather think it might be... just for...' The Monsignor's composure was slipping, spiralling an impatient hand at Vita, encompassing the room, the urgency, the shivering woman. The puddle of blood beneath her seat.

Mother Virginia herself would look after Signora Contini. 'You are pale, Vita. I think, if you're going home to fetch your mamma, you should stay there.'

'No, Mother, I need to do the laundry, and—'

'Vittoria.' The old lady put her knuckles to Vita's forehead, rising on tiptoe to reach. 'You are very warm. And you have been working too hard. The sisters and I will tend to our menfolk today, and you'll come back to us refreshed in the morning, sì?'

'But—'

'It's not a request, child. It is an order.'

The thought of this sweet, tiny soul ordering anyone made Vita laugh, but then the laughter bubbled into tears. Mother Virginia shoved her. 'Away. Do not let me see you here again today.'

Out into high-walled streets. Barga's stone-faced buildings, the crawling, bright green mosses, the flashing yellow sun. All wrong. That poor, bleeding woman. Was that what they did, those necci-loving soldiers with the iron crosses at their throats? How ugly must your soul be, to make a woman carry her baby's corpse? Eyes shone in places that should be blank, dark shapes in shortcut alleys. A lone girl strolled towards Piazza Angelio, arm-in-arm with a soldier of the Brigate Nere. Vita recognised her from school; felt an instant punch of jealousy.

She hurried down the steps of the old town, across Ponte Vecchio, through the crossroads. Rastrellamento? That word should not be used for people. How could you 'rake' up human beings?

Before she realised where she was going, Vita found herself in Ponte. She'd been avoiding it, taking the shortcut through the woods instead. Signor Tutto's shop stood forlorn. Someone had torn down the shutters, the door wrenched wide. A few scattered, empty baskets lay in the doorway, and painted in bold yellow scrawl across the front: *JUDEN*. Vita was a coward. She'd never asked the Monsignor about the graveyard. How could you? It was a sin to dig up consecrated ground. Pointlessly, she stacked the baskets, closed the door. An orange box rested against the shopfront. Size of a tiny coffin.

Tutto bene, tutto bene. Her mother muttered it often; it was a mantra to keep them sane. All is well, flicking her hands like she was flicking flies. Part of the brittle-thin gloss coating everything. All was not well. There was a sickness in Barga; infectious, corrosive, and just because you do not see things does not mean they are not there. Vita always thought she'd be brave. Turned out, most folk were not heroes. Head down, you clung to quiet survival, where the bravest thing was a nod between acquaintances as you passed, a twist of your mouth that spoke of disaffection and acceptance. No better than the plod of cows for milking.

Insects drowsed on oregano, growing through a crack in the wall. On the other side of the Corsonna river, the road hairpinned to the right, and home. Turn left, round the next bend, and you would find the cobbled road to Albiano. The place where the rastrellati were being held. A hidden network of paths linked these roads; old mule tracks, which were quicker and steeper – why Catagnana girls had such good legs. Some of the Sommos never left their little fortress, and the Ponte girls would rather stroll to Barga than climb. In Catagnana, you were neither up nor down, which gave you choices. And sculpted calves. The clear hard light shone on the start of the mule path. Vita spread her hair to cover her neck from the sun. Took the track to Albiano.

As she neared the village, she could see two army cars and a flatbed truck. A group of men were gathered under the eaves of the school. Some slumped, a few stood as if to attention. They looked more pitiful than the ones sitting, heads in hands. Tattered, dust-laden clothes, boots that were flapping and broken; not one man had decent clothing. Then she realised, the ones who were standing had their hands roped together. Even from behind a rock, she could feel their shame, their exhaustion. Thirty or so men, guarded by a handful of German boys, who swigged water from canteens and never offered it around. One of the captives, a middle-aged man with filthy dress shoes, was shaking uncontrollably. The others were kindly ignoring him. Or maybe they were too spent to care.

Vita slipped back down the rock face, ran all the way across the ridge to Catagnana, the long, hard muscles of her calves like wings as the path rose and dipped. At one point, a distant German patrol shouted at her to stop, but she kept running. If they came after her, she would strike and kick them. But nobody followed.

Catagnana. Just a string of houses clinging halfway up a hill. La Limonaia stood at the end of the lane: yellow walls, blue door. The summer kitchen was open, a beaded curtain to keep the flies away. Mamma and Carla were in there, chopping onions. Vita threw her arms round her mother.

'Vita! What is it? Has someone hurt you?'

'Mamma.' She hid her face in her mother's dress. 'They've got them trussed like cows.'

'Who?'

'Pisans. And there was a baby, a dead baby. Why would people do that?'

Her mother soothed her, rubbing the nape of her neck. Vita was soaking Mamma's dress with tears and snot, and she couldn't stop.

'Mamma! Cesca made us a den!'

'Hush, Dario.'

'Is Vita sore?'

Rocking, Vita bending to fit her mother's embrace. Seeing the man's shaking shoulders, seeing the babies, the one who was alive and the one who was dead. The damp fabric, hot at her mouth. Cesca's arms came round her and Mamma both. 'Don't cry, Vi. It'll be alright.'

She felt a tiny hand pat her leg. 'Alright,' repeated Dario.

Her mother kissed her. 'My beautiful girls.' Another kiss for Cesca. 'It's good to feel, but sometimes, you must seal yourself up. You understand? This war will bring many bad things to our door, and we have to stay strong. We are Guidis, no?'

'We are.'

'Well then. Now, what of these refugees? What can we do to help them?'

Mamma rolled into action, magnificent and fierce. Within thirty minutes she and Carla had amassed the might of Azione Cattolica. They organised food, clothes, even footwear. Dario offered his knitted socks.

'No, darling. You keep them.'

'You make them too scratchy anyway,' said Marino.

Mamma swiped the air above his head. 'And you are too cheeky by far, young man.'

'Did the tedeschi get Papà's wheelbarrow?' asked Cesca. 'Where is he anyway?'

'Doing some carpentry for Sergio. No, I don't think so – he hid it under the house. Come, Carla, we best go. You girls stay here.'

Cesca waited until they'd left.

'Well, I'm going to take the wheelbarrow up to Sommo. Coming, boys? I'll give you a ride.'

'What for?' Vita's head was aching.

'To fetch all Gianni's boots and jumpers too. It's not as if he's using them.'

Marino was pulling on Cesca's arm. 'Can it be a boat? Can we go in it?'

'Me want a goat!' shouted Dario.

'Boat! Why are you so stupid?'

'Look, you rest, Vi.' Cesca disentangled Marino's fingers from her sleeve. 'You look tired.'

'You can't manage those two and a wheelbarrow.'

'I can, you know.' Her sister smoothed Vita's hair from her face. Her palm was lovely and cool. 'Trust me.'

Vita sat awhile in the kitchen, crushing the garlic her mother had left. It turned to paste. The room was quiet, the light in the doorway golden. The chestnut tree outside wavered, tall and fat with leaves. When she was little, Vita used to climb that tree and feel protected. There was a whole army of trees to the rear, marching up the slope. This chestnut was still part of the forest, but part of La Limonaia too. Mamma grew pea-plants at its feet, and their heights were marked in paint on its trunk every birthday. She went to the threshold, shaded her eyes. She could still get up there, if she wanted.

'Vita?' First, the voice, then a raised hand. Her heart lifted. An unwashed Joe was climbing up the path. Hair matted with his beard, filthy, unfamilar clothes and a leather satchel swung across his shoulder. He looked harder somehow; a dark gleam about his skin.

'You not get clean to come and see me?' There were a million things she could have said.

'I've not come to see you. I'm here for Carla.'

'Why?'

He tapped the side of his nose.

'You shouldn't have come back. The Germans have moved in. They've a whole bunch of Pisans tied up in Albiano.'

Joe leaned against the chestnut tree. 'I'm not a coward, you know.' He held her hands, pulled her under the canopy of leaves. The shadows made butterflies in his hair. 'I missed you.'

He took a skein of material from his satchel. 'Got you a present. Might need a wash.' He was blushing, fumbling. Vita ran her hand along the slippery fabric.

'I thought you could make a dress. Or something.'

She held a handful of silk to the light, let it pour through her fingers. 'It's lovely.'

'It's a parachute.'

Vita could hear snapping twigs.

Voices. Male voices and clinking boots, coming up the hill. The hard rasp of a German accent.

'Shit. Fucksake.'

'Quick.' She shoved them both through the fly-curtain, back into the kitchen. Clutching at the beads to stop them tinkling. Pulling the back door, a soft click that rang louder than a gun-crack.

'Hide.'

'Where?'

'I don't know. The cellar?'

No time. Footsteps, flagstones. Shadows at the glass.

'Inside the madia. Here.' The wooden larder was already open. Just enough room inside for Joe to scramble onto the ledge, inhaling as she shut the doors. No key, but if she dragged the table across... she could see the outline of a fist at the frosted glass... wait, wait till the knocking starts.

Rap-tap-tap.

Drag-drag-drag.

'Sì?'

'Is Hans. Open up.'

The satchel. Joe's satchel with the silk spilling, lying on the floor. She kicked it under the table.

'Hans, my mother isn't here. She'll be back later.'

Silence. Then louder. Harsher. 'You hear me? Open up, bitch.'

An approving chuckle.

Hans was a simple, easy boy. Cold needles on her tongue, Jesus, Jesus, *please*, was there any food to fob him off with? She cast her eyes round the kitchen: onions, mashed garlic. Nothing made. No cakes. Her blood drilling; they would hear it through the door. She patted down her apron. Important to keep her voice steady. 'There's no need for that, Hans. I'm coming.'

She positioned herself so his path into the house was blocked. 'What is it?'

'See,' said Hans to whoever was with him. The way Vita was angled, she couldn't see past the German any more than he could see past her. 'I tell you she is pretty. May we come in, Vita?'

'It's not a good time. There's no food, and I've two young children sleeping.' She was thinking, why did he speak in halting Italian, there, to his companion? And, as she was thinking it, the companion was strolling into view.

'Oh, look who it is.' The soldier smiled. 'The little whore.'

Acne Boy. The *fascista* who'd hit her.

'You mind your mouth.' Vita jutted out her arms, trying to fill the gaps between her and the door frame.

'And you mind your manners. *Puttana*.' The soldier came close, so close she could smell his breath; that same sour heat as before. 'Hans tells me this is where you go for... what was it, amico? *Kaffee und kuchen*? Been boasting to all the boys how good it is, haven't you, *mein freund*?'

Hans nodded, beaming.

'Like I said, Mamma isn't here, Hans.' Vita's jaw was quivering; she pretended to yawn. 'She'll be sorry she missed you. She's away for more flour actually. For the necci. It's only me here. I was just getting my cousins down, so if you don't mind...'

'You got me into a lot of trouble, you know,' said Acne Boy. 'From the generale.'

'Think you got yourself into trouble, not me.'

'I wasn't asking your opinion, girl. Does this mean nothing to you?' He tugged at the silver insignia on his shirt. 'When you insult me, you insult Il Duce.'

'And you insult your uniform. My father was fighting for Il Duce when you were still squeezing your zits.'

Why could she not stop talking?

His boots were on the final step.

'What did you say?' He was pressing himself as he spoke. Against her. Deliberate pulses into her breast, his sharp silver buttons imprinting themselves in the place where he had struck her before.

'Only you here. Shame that. You got me into so much shit. For nothing really.'

There was a string of blackheads where his nostrils flared. Symmetrical either side. Weeping milky-yellow spots at his throat; he must slice them every morning when he shaved. One hand was creeping up her skirt; she gripped herself tighter, pushing her backside out to try and escape.

'Hans, I really think you should go now,' she shouted, but she could no longer see Hans. Her eyes were smarting, swimming, the soldier's hand on her thigh, one finger inching up, his rancid, breathed words deep in her ear.

'So much shit. May as well make it worth my while, eh, puttana?' And if she screamed, Joe would come and if Joe came, they might kill him. A finger reaching into her pants, bile and shock and a sly slick flick – but it was her fingers finding him, grasping his groin with her fingernails, just hard enough. A twist, a throttled gasp. Her teeth against his.

'Touch me and I will kill you.' She sang it soft, like an incantation, words vibrating in a secret between their teeth. Singing and grinning. 'I will find you in the night, wherever you are sleeping, even if I am dead because I am a mountain witch, you pustulent, ugly child, and I will come back and I will kill you. But in the meantime, I will let you go. I will let you go and I will not even tell the Monsignor of this, because if I do, he will have your generale have you shot, if anything at *all* happens to me, he will have you shot, because I am a favourite and there is already a spell with your name on it, I have written out a spell and it is hidden but the Monsignor knows where it is, and you will die. Cursed in battle, you *will* die.'

Releasing him, a spring away, so that he tripped backwards down the step, her dress ripping. 'Do you understand me? Hans!' She raised her voice again; the stupid Nazi was standing, eyes downcast. 'Hans. Your friend doesn't like necci, so probably best if you don't bring him here again. Then Mamma will have more for you, yes? Goodbye, boys.'

She slammed the door shut, locked it. Locked it. Locked it. Braced her spine, waiting for a boot or a machine gun to blast its way through, and yes, the glass was rattling, was rattling and they would come inside. Mamma would find her dead, oh sweet Jesus, it was rattling so hard. But the rattling was her.

Creak of cupboard, dunting the table.

'Vita?' Side of Joe's face, all squashed up in the little slit. She could hear him giggle. 'Jeez, that was close. Whatever you said, well done. Can I get out now?'

His eye, peering. 'Hey! Wake up, woman!'

Unblinking.

'Vita! What is it? What's wrong?'

Whimpering as his shoe booted door, table, pots, everything, the madia half-tipping as he struggled out. She could hear Giuseppe, hear him kissing her hair, and the crisp rustle of his shirt as he held her. But she couldn't uncross her legs, nor her arms to hug him back.

Chapter Ten

Four men, crouched above a bridge. Hazed light shimmering like the sea. It lapped over the men, animating the rocks and trees. The youngest scratched his balls, pretending it was a macho thing, but he was desperate for the toilet and he'd only just been. Nerves.

Less than a mile away, in Via Roma, the sunlight nudged through sumptuous curtains. It polished a group of German generals and high-ranking Brigate; it gleamed on dignitaries from Lucca and white-coated surgeons from the Barga hospital; it cast a slight shadow over the Comune hangers-on, who knew they must answer specific, local queries only if asked – *But my, isn't this pranzo good? And isn't General Kesselring smaller, in real life?*

Tucking into slabs of cheese, steak, rich puddings, in a room draped with fresh flowers, in a house where a family no longer lived. The family's fine china was being clashed carelessly, their good silver-plate would be left stained. Some crystal that came from Austria three generations before, in a dowry wrapped in lace, was smashed as a meaty hand reached for more wine, while the question of putting a Red Cross flag above Barga was discussed.

'It will protect you,' Kesselring said. 'Protect your lovely town. They will not strike the centre. Not while the Red Cross is flying.'

'But what of the German positions?' said a thin-lipped Fascist. 'The guns outside the Duomo? Surely they'll attract their fire?'

The men, for it was all men, chatted a little round this, and sipped their *vino santo*, which was holy wine. The meaty hand, which had brushed the glass shards he created off the table, lifted a slice of almond cake. Popped it into a generous mouth. The meaty hand belonged to a meaty general of the Wehrmacht, who felt a fleeting sense of guilt. He recognised the goblet as Austrian. He was a kindly man. His children liked him. Every day, his soldiers brought him a chicken from Catagnana – a place he had heard of, but never seen. He thought he might visit it before he left, to thank the supplier of his daily breast. (He was a leg man too, but so was his aide, who worked very hard for him, so he did not object to sharing.)

The conference was drawing to a close and, as expected, Generalfeldmarschall Kesselring's views held sway. They would do what he deemed best. Although he was a Luftwaffe man first and foremost, as Commander in Chief of the South, Kesselring had been an effective leader, thought the meaty general. He was glad the Führer did not accept Kesselring's resignation last year, over that crass power struggle with Rommel. Despite their current trials, it was a wise decision. Kesselring listened, he was more humane. These Italians did not know how fortunate they were. The general's meaty hand signalled his aide to bring the staff car round. 'We will take a little detour,' he said, manoeuvering himself in.

The same stringy blackshirt who'd accompanied him earlier came too; it was an affectation Utimperghe insisted

143

on, a Fascist bodyguard for their 'guests'. Kesselring thought it funny, so he permitted the delusion. They called them the 'Wheatsheaf Brigade'. But not to their faces, naturally. That would be rude. And *meine Güte*, that blackshirt's face was rude enough; it was a positive road map of pustules.

As they drove, the meaty general held his face up to the rolling sun. Tuscany was truly beautiful. He thought, after the war, he might buy a villa here. Up there, on that very ridge. Hildegarde would love the rolling views, and there were singing caves, he'd heard, inside the mountain, with stalactites and an underground lake. He could tell the children it was a fairy grotto. The car jolted on the rocky road. Ahead was a bridge, a pretty arch of grey stone, with huge boulders and a fringe of trees above. Maybe the cake was chestnut, he mused, not almond after all, because those trees were all *kastanienbaum*; he recognised the broad five-fingered leaves from when he was a boy and his *vater* took him camping. Ah, this was *nice*. His belly was full, he was a little sleepy and he saw one of the boulders shimmer in the heat.

Except it is not a shimmer, it is a sleeve and he is wondering if he should shout as the sleeve rises up and there is a head, a face, and inside that head, there is a boy who is no longer nervous because ice has fallen, it has frozen him shut and there is just the puttering black car on the road and unwavering, resolute light and the nose of the gun before him, the bullets coming out fast, and he thrills with the actual violence of the thing, up till now it has not been real; his job has been to deliver: bundles, ammunition, souls – he has ferried folk as high as the mountains of Versilia, immense, perpendicular, a place where bolts of blue shadow catch you unaware, where heaven is a handbreadth above and you feel you're falling backwards as you climb in a sky so high you can taste the breath of God, the air thinning, and it is thinning now, for when the boy feels the squeezing of his finger on the trigger, he feels the squeezing of other fingers, their imprint on a young girl's thigh and her anguish and how he used to be her hero and then the ice cracks wide and it is press, release, press, release, and the wonderful foreign weapon sings as it is meant, the ice melting, becoming light, and freeing the thing inside which is him, the heart of him, and he had thought that to bring death might invite the horrors back, was terrified that he would be there again, in the burning water, watching his father die, but no. That was the strange thing. As first the pus-laden blackshirt, then the fat general in the open car toppled backwards, as the blackshirt's head skewed left and blood gouted from the general's breast, as the driver veered and crashed, parapet, embankment, river, *splash*, and the pulsating light flowed on, Joe felt only one emotion.

Satisfaction.

Chapter Eleven

They found Joe washing his hands. Vita and Cesca had been gathering early mushrooms, fat pale stems that bulged in the middle. It was nice, working in silence. Deft, satisfying pops as you shook the fungi free from soil. The mushrooms tasted best when they were darker, but these would do. Any food would do. Vita hadn't slept much, skittering awake at the least noise. Even in their own boschetto, a glade of truffles, and trees pollarded and chopped for generations, she felt stupid and scared. She'd told no one about the soldiers coming.

Joe was kneeling by the stream, shirt off, water beaded on his back. His spine was sinuous. Beautiful. For a moment, neither girl spoke. Vita tried to feel the skip in her belly; she willed it, but it didn't come. He couldn't see them, was staring straight ahead, listening to the dark-brown whisperings of the forest, waves of thin muscle flexing and dimpling his shoulder blades as his hands worried, and washed, and rinsed.

Cesca called out. 'Joe!'

He started, turned. A cigarette smouldered in his lips.

'It *is* you! How d'you not tell us you were back? We've missed you!'

He didn't move.

'Are you alright?'

'Yup.' The smoke made his eyes crinkle. Face like a stranger's. His fingers jittered as he extinguished the cigarette.

'You sure?' said Cesca. 'You look… starey.'

'Joe.' Vita spoke softly. 'What's happened?'

'Garnet,' he said. 'That's it, isn't it? Red and purple. With that blue underneath.'

'Has something happened?'

'Right thick colour. Bright and dull at same time.' He reached for his shirt. 'I remember thinking when Papà died, how the blood in his mouth—' He wiped the shirt across his lips, absent for a second. 'The salt had set it, so it was… I don't know the word in Italian. Like jelly – but shining like a jewel, and I couldn't remember – I could never remember what the name of the colour was, but that's it.' He sat back on his heels. 'Garnet. That's what blood is like.'

Vita hadn't seen him since yesterday, since he'd wrapped her shawl round her shoulders and left La Limonaia. *Don't do anything, Joe,* she'd cried. *Please.*

'Will you answer me? What's wrong?'

'Ssh.' Cesca sat down next to him. 'Here.' She took his shirt, helped him into it. She was so much better than Vita, at being natural and kind. Vita watched them, thumbnails pressing into her fists; useless things, just hanging at her sides.

'Tell me about your papà,' said Cesca. Soothing him with straightforward bustle.

'Brave lad.'

'What?'

Joe moved his arm so she could pull the sleeve on. 'That's what he said I was. On the boat. They put us on a ship, see. A huge ship, with stars on the funnels. Thought we were going home. But it was taking us to Canada. Furthest point from Mamma I could imagine.'

Cesca nodded, tongue out as she buttoned his cuff.

'She didn't speak good English. I kept thinking, who'll sort the milk order if I'm not there? We were sitting on deck; it was dawn, and I remember Ireland sliding into view. Papà was telling the man beside us it was called the Emerald Isle, and there was this...' his breathing quickened '... this massive, creaking roar, and the ship buckled – it felt like the deck was folding up.' He shook his head, and a cascade of water droplets fell from his hair. 'It was a torpedo.'

Vita sat on the other side of him.

'A German torpedo. D'you know how stupid that was? We were talking to a German man.' Abruptly, Joe got up. He began to walk round the glade, hands behind his back.

'The lights went out. Hundreds of us, scrambling for lifeboats. And the water... the water kept pouring over the deck. I saw a man on fire. He just hit the railings and cartwheeled into the sea. Someone yelling at me to jump. But I couldn't let go the rails. Then this priest started praying, gathering folk round, then I could hear my papà, shouting, saying, *I won't leave you*, and I thought, If I don't jump, then you'll die too. So I held his arm, and we jumped.'

He threw his arms up, like he was tossing something away.

'It was so quiet, after. When the boat went down. Just this one voice, over and over, calling: *Cibelli! Cibelli!* You'd feel stuff, soft stuff, and kick it away. But I knew. I knew what they were.'

148

Vita pushed her feet deeper into the loam. Crumbs of soft earth, falling into her zoccoli, working between her toes. The Guidi truffle grove was quite an ugly glade. Stunted limbs, pale fungi blooming from the tree stumps, and the circle of sun above, bleaching everything.

Joe was still talking, but it was to himself. 'Then his head... He hit his head on the way down, I can't remember how, but we were hanging on to an upturned lifeboat, and he'd all this blood coming out of his head. I couldn't get him up on the boat; it was too choppy, and I kept trying, thinking if I could turn it over, but he kept slipping, so I just hooked my arms under his armpits. Clamped us to the side.'

A spider walked over her foot. Joe hugged himself. It was desperate. Vita went to go to him, but Cesca laid a hand on her arm.

'Five hours. They worked it out. Five hours we treaded water, in freezing, undrinkable sea. Five hours till a warship came, and I woke up. Saw Papà had slipped out of my arms.'

Flickering on Joe's face, as the trees broke the light above them. The wind caught a handful of rotted leaves, rippled them in the air. You could taste centuries of forest on your tongue. The weather changing.

Cesca walked over, put her arms round him. 'I love you, Joe.'

'I love you too.'

Vita ached to do the same, but she was too hesitant, and then he started speaking again. 'Know what the bastards actually did? Put me on another ship to Canada.'

'But how did you get here?'

He smiled at Cesca, and the spell was broken. 'They don't call me Stowaway Joe for nothing.'

Around them, trees nodded and shook themselves. When they were small, they used to play hide and seek here. The breeze picked up and the sadness grew finer, the way rain becomes mist. Joe kissed the top of Cesca's head. 'Right, come on, you. We'd better get home. I think it's going to rain.'

It was already too late. Drops began to fall as they left the forest. Vita watched Joe's face the whole time, trying to fathom him. Silent and damp, they reached La Limonaia. She couldn't understand why Papà came running; he came out from behind the house. His palm made contact first, skiting the back of Joe's head, and he was yelling: 'What the fuck have you done, Giuseppe?'

In English, but the slap was pure Italian.

'We've been looking for you everywhere. Get inside.' He shoved Joe.

'Papà!'

'I had to do it.'

'Do what?' said Cesca.

'A fucking general?'

'Aim for the top, *zio*.'

Then Mario started hitting him harder, harder, with Vita and Cesca in the middle. Shoving them apart, Joe just curled in on himself.

'Don't, Papà. Please, stop it.'

'He shot a car full of soldiers. Your precious, stupid Joe and his mates just murdered a Nazi and some spotty wee prick of a blackshirt. I'm sorry, darlings. *Scusatemi. Scusate* for the swearing. Please. *Andate.*' Papa was spinning from English to Italian, was shaking Joe. 'Do you realise what you've done? How could you be so fucking stupid?'

'I'm sorry. But I canny keep watching them strut about. I had to do it.'

Vita took her sister's hand. The air prickling as the sweat on her back evaporated; Joe, with his eyes too bright, panting; their breath making clouds on the cool stone walls of the kitchen. Her breath was the only part of her moving. Joe had killed two men.

'I know.' Papa was quieter. 'I know.'

He did it for me, she wanted to shout.

Joe stared at the fornelli. Sweat trickled from hairline to temple; drips meeting, bisecting.

'You're a walking target now, wherever you go. You canny hide out with Lenin any more.'

'Who's Lenin?' Cesca was crying. 'Sure you didn't shoot anyone, Joe? Tell him. Will everyone speak Italian?'

'Scusi, bambina.' Papà was dragging a knapsack from a cupboard, his boots from the soffitta. 'Take these. I'd to hide them from Elena. She's pinched all my shoes for the rastrellati.'

'Where am I going?'

'Where you said you would. With Carla. But this time, you'll not be coming back.'

'Where? Will somebody please explain?' Cesca was growing more distressed.

Papà ignored her. 'We need to get away before curfew.'

'Papà! Where is Joe going?' said Vita.

'Sant'Anna,' said Joe. 'Mario's right. I can't stay here. The tedeschi will come after me.'

Papà stuffed a jumper inside the knapsack. 'He was taking Carla and the kids to the mountains anyway. Vita – pass me that penknife. She's scared they'll get trapped here, like Rome. Our Joe's managed to get a few folk up there already.'

Vita's fingers hovered by the blade. 'It was you who helped Signor Tutto?'

'Yes.' Joe took the knife from her.

She regarded her cousin again. All this time, it was Vita who didn't know Joe. How many people had he saved? She wanted to ask if he'd been scared. And was he scared when he held that gun? How did it feel, to see a body fall, to snap the soul from it? She wanted to ask if he'd prayed when he did it, and did he feel the same ugly thrill that she did? Her hand rose to wipe her eyes. Vita was glad the blackshirt was dead.

'Right.' Papà scratched his head. 'Your mother's still at Albiano with Carla. Orlando's away to get them. You girls, start getting all their stuff together. I've taken the boys to Sergio's. We'll borrow his donkey. I'll take you as close to Gallicano as I can, Joe, then you're on your own. You'll need the donkey, for the mountain pass. The boys'll never make it on foot.'

Unspeaking, they gathered up food, blankets. Papà led them down to Sergio's farm. A stroll Vita did almost every day, hardly noticing the way light slanted on the cobbles, or how the chestnut tree sang as the wind gusted. Now, everything was sharp, and fleeting.

Orlando and the boys were waiting by the barn. 'At last!' he said. 'You need to go. The tedeschi are up on Lama di Sotto already – I couldn't get anywhere near Albiano. I think they're working from the top down.'

'Well, that's one advantage to living in the middle of nowhere,' said Sergio. He held his donkey's head, stroking her muzzle, while Papà tried to attach her harness to the cart. 'Bella, bella,' the old man whispered. 'I will miss you so.'

'What about Carla?' said Cesca.

'If she's here in the next few minutes, fine. If not...' Orlando shrugged. 'You either get Joe and the boys away now...'

'Right, Giuseppe,' said Papà. 'In you get. You'll need to lie flat, mind. The way we did with Tullio.'

Papà was a genius. He'd built a hidden compartment, a dip under the base of the cart; enough room for two folk to lie in. There were some packed sacks beside the wheels. Joe used them for a leg-up, then wedged himself inside the compartment.

'No. Not on your back, son. Lie on your belly. That way you can breathe through the gaps. We'll need to cover you.'

'What with?'

Sergio began to chuckle. 'Oh, you don't know the worst of it, boy. Sacks of flour aren't going to be enough today. Soon you will be a mushroom!'

'Give him a minute more in the fresh air first,' said Papà. 'I'll get the boys on the front. C'mon, young 'un.' He swung Dario onto the bench.

'Where's Mamma?'

Vita smoothed his curls. 'You're going on an adventure.'

'Don't want a venture. I want to stay in my house.'

'I know.' Cesca's voice broke, and she turned her face away from the children.

'Where's my mamma?' Mario looked mutinous.

'I'm going to walk up the track,' said Cesca. 'See if I can see her.'

'Here.' Vita got on the cart beside the boys. 'C'mon, Marino. Sit. It's just for a little while. You're going to a lovely place in the mountains, where there's plenty to eat. Loads of other boys and girls to play with. Not like here, where it's just boring us.'

'I like it boring.'

'And I like cuddles. Come here.' Marino shied away, but Dario curled into her lap. His hand stole a piece of her dress, pulling it towards his mouth. The wind grew stronger. 'She'll be here soon, I promise. Joe,' she whispered, 'you can't go without Carla.'

'I know.'

The three older men were huddled, muttering. Papà's face went scarlet. 'Absolutely not!'

'They see you're fit enough to drive, you're fit enough to work,' said Sergio.

'We're thinking maybe you should drive, Vita,' said Orlando. 'You're less likely to get stopped than your papà.'

'Are you deaf? I told you, no. Down you get,' Papà said. 'Hurry.'

'Well, Carla then,' said Orlando. 'If she ever gets here.'

'Carla? She couldn't ride a bike, far less steer my donkey.'

'No, I'll do it,' said Vita.

'No,' said Papà and Joe, together.

'I bloody will.' A long strand of hair slapped her mouth, catching where her lips split.

'Vittoria!'

In the cart, both boys bowed their heads and giggled.

'Why? Because I'm a girl? Maybe I'm fed up being a girl. Maybe being a girl brings nothing but folk telling you what you can and can't do. Ever thought of that? If being a girl's the one helpful thing I can do, then let me do it. Please.' From her vantage point, she could see Cesca waving, running down the track towards them, all skinny legs and the wild madness of her hair.

The donkey pawed the ground. Dario kicked his brother. 'No, *you* a girl too... Hey! Mamma! Look, there's Mamma!'

Carla was behind Cesca, breathless. 'There's tedeschi everywhere. Elena's still at Albiano – one of the refugees is sick.'

'You need to leave now, if you're going. There might not be another chance.'

'I know, Mario, I know. But I have to get—'

'We've got your bags, in the cart.' Vita got down, handed the reins to Carla. 'You can manage the donkey, can't you?'

Their dresses flowed behind them like sails. Vita held Carla's gaze; folded the reins round Carla's fingers. Fine drizzle, dampening their hair.

'I can.'

A firm kiss for her cousin, then Carla started embracing everyone, then they were all at it. Dario bubbled over, clamouring for hugs. Marino took his lead from Joe, pretending to be brave. That was worse because you couldn't embrace them, these two stiff males staring into the distance. Vita gave Marino instructions for Andromeda, how the donkey's teeth weren't so good now, and if he could mash up scraps before she ate them? Marino nodded gravely, memorising his duties. No fuss. They were a credit to their nation. Italy was heavy with men being brave and women being stoic, and for what? For what?

And then it was Joe, reaching down from the cart. One glancing, butterfly kiss that pressed through her bones.

'We were meant to be each other's rescue.'

'What?'

She hadn't thought she'd said it aloud. 'Take care of yourself, Giuseppe Guidi.'

'I will, Vittoria Guidi.'

The grey sky stretched low. A band of soft rain moved over the face of Monte Forato.

'Vita?'

'Yes?'

'What's the donkey called?'

'She's called Andromeda. Sergio says you can see constellations in her eyes.'

He touched one finger to his forehead. 'Mad. You're all mad.'

'Right, Joe,' said Papà. 'On your belly.'

They covered him first with sacking. Then, the slide of wood. A dragging sound, the heft of breath. Squeals from the children, disgusted squeals and shrieks, exhortations to *be quiet!* before dense-thudded donkey shit hid Giuseppe Guidi from the world.

Water fell from the copper tap, in slow, persistent drips. To make Mamma happy, Papà had drilled pipes through solid rock. He still kept their old secchia, beside the draining board, to be filled from the communal well. *Unhygienic*, said Mamma, who refused to let her children use it. *Delicious*, said Papà, who insisted the secchia remain.

'Vita, call Cesca down.'

From La Limonaia's kitchen, stairs led to the soffitta, where corn and potatoes were stored on wooden slats, and to Cesca's bedroom beyond. The sole of Vita's foot hurt. There must have been a stone inside her zoccolo. Pain was good; it gave her focus, a sharpness to rub against. An excuse for sore eyes.

'Mamma's made food.'

'I'm not hungry.'

'Get down here now and sit at the table,' Mamma yelled. 'Vita, put the bowls out.'

The shutters were closed. Vita could hear the warning bell ring. Fifteen minutes to curfew, when all the barghigiani must be locked away. Nobody sitting on their steps or taking a stroll. She lit a candle on the candelabrum. Always sporadic, since the tedeschi came, power could be off for weeks. Few houses in Catagnana had electricity, so you got no sympathy if you moaned. Mrs Pieri had loaned them tallow lanterns, but they stank the place out. So the Guidis met power cuts with Luccese candelabra.

'Mario. Pass me the wine.' Mamma was making vinata. When the wine was warm, she tipped in the chestnut flour, stirring it to dark-red sludge.

'Couple of bowls of that and you'd be fit for anything.' He kissed the nape of Mamma's neck. Her mother reached behind. Caught Papà's hand and pulled it close to her mouth.

'Why are we all sitting here, pretending?' said Cesca.

'Because it's important—'

A wail of anguish lifted through the dusk, coming from the end of the lane.

'Sit down!' Mamma ladled crimson gloop into their bowls. 'Now eat.'

'*Öffne die Tür! Schnell!*' Three sharp raps. They had come to the front door. Papà rose. Mamma shook her head.

'I'll go.'

She went into the hallway. Vita looked at her father, willing him to do something.

'*Hans! Guten Abend*,' said Mamma.

Papà's knuckles were white, gripping his spoon, which never moved from the bowl.

'Now? But we're eating.'

High, brittle noises, Vita thought she heard her mother yelp, then the kitchen door flew wide, tedeschi pouring in, yelling and screaming into Papà's face.

'*Raus! Raus!*'

Someone wrenched at Vita's hair, chair spilling as she was hauled to her feet. *Think, Vita*, try to think, to find a quiet space of air inside all the screaming, but it was her screaming, her and her little sister, hysterical.

'Don't you touch my daughter!' Papà shouted. Vita struggled to reach him, hair tearing as a soldier swung his rifle butt, smashing it into her father's face. He crumpled, Cesca kicking out at the soldier who had struck him.

'Leave him alone!'

The Nazi hit her half across the room. It was Hans.

'No.' Her mother ran to Cesca, shielding her with her own body, but no more blows came. Not for Cesca.

An officer in a black tunic started shouting at Papà. 'Where is Giuseppe Guidi?'

His nose was bleeding. Voice thick. 'I don't know what you're talking about.'

Again, the rifle fell on her father.

'Where is he? You are harbouring a murderer. You know the punishment?'

'I don't know a Giuseppe Guidi.'

Hans raised his rifle butt a third time. Her father groaned. '*Nein*,' said the officer. He took the soldier's gun and turned it round, pointing it at Vita. Behind him, Mamma held his ankles, crawling and weeping.

'I am *fascista*! I am *fascista*! Please. Leave our family alone.'

The officer swung his elbow, direct and swift, cracking her mother's temple. She dropped against the table. The candelabrum shuddered, blue flame rippling.

The dark room began to shimmer.

'*Lass ihn! Das Haus durchsuchen.*'

The soldier released his grip on Vita's hair, shoving her towards her mother and sister. Mamma, dazed and blinking, Cesca's eyes puffed into slits. Two more soldiers seized her father under the arms and dragged him out. The rest began to search the house, crashing over furniture, smashing pictures and ornaments. One of them took out his penis and pissed into the pot of vinata. Laughing.

Vita laid her head on Mamma's lap. Cesca threaded her fingers through Vita's. They were like a circle of cats, heads and tails entwined, and she could not break the circle. If she moved, the circle would crack. Circles were magic. Circles and stars, the breath of trees, these were the old magics.

The candles fizzled and smoked. Extinguished. Nobody moved. Vita's knees were burning-numb. But you couldn't break the circle. It might be the only thing holding them in place. Eventually, the dreadful noises ebbed away.

'Have they gone?' Cesca breathed.

'I don't know.' Vita struck the tinderbox, lit a candle. The waxen light shone in Mamma's face, showing blood on her mouth, and a yellow-purple cheekbone. 'I'll go and look. Ces, get a cloth for Mamma's face.'

She went into the hall, expecting darkness. But the front door hung like an open mouth. The rain had cleared; the moon, high above the mountain, pouring white, milky light. Dispassionate light, neither warm nor cold. She could see soldiers dragging a man from Casa Pieri, Signora Pieri running after them. Torchlight flickered down at old Sergio's too, and further up the hill, towards Sommocolonia. The heavy tread of tedeschi patrols, owning barghigiani streets. An engine revved. Two open trucks at the end of the street were packed with men.

Somewhere in there was her father. Nose broken, maybe struggling to breathe. Vita sat on the step, her arms over her head. Harsh shouts, a loud slam. She heard the clunk and vroom of vehicles moving off, a door banging, wailing within.

All of this was her fault.

The crying tailed off. She unfurled her arms. With the sound of the trucks petering to nothing, she could be the only human left on earth. No lights were permitted after curfew, you could look all across the Garfagnana and find no signs of life. Bright white, deserted Catagnana: their tiny church, the silvery shape of the Pieris' barn. Papà's workshop.

Men. Men, raking up her father. That was rastrellamento.

She pictured Sergio shivering with fear. She thought of that doctor with the poor dead baby. The forced march had exhausted him. She saw her papà, with his quiet, shabby mantle of defeat. How could people do that to each other? Did they not see another human looking back?

'Vita!' A strange-shaped figure was hirpling up the track. Barefoot, two heads. It was Renata, carrying Rosa on her hip. 'Did they take Mario?'

'Did they take Orlando?'

'Gone. Every man in Sommo. Gone.'

The bridge of Vita's nose ached.

'I tried to follow them – but one of the soldiers hit me.'

'Come inside. You shouldn't be out. It's still curfew. Here. Give Rosa to me.' She took them into the kitchen. Rosa clung to Vita's neck. 'Mamma. It's only Renata. The soldiers have gone.'

Cesca had put a blanket over Mamma, got her onto the low bench under the window. She'd lit one of the Pieris' tallow lamps too. The smell of burning fat crept through the room.

'Oh, Elena! Your face. They hit you too?'

'Well, I wasn't going to stand by while they assaulted my family, was I?' The unsteady flicker of the lamp reflected in Mamma's eyes.

'They came all at once,' said Renata. 'Just grabbing, and hitting. They even took Don Sabatini.'

'They took the *priest*?'

'Moved in like locusts. Pincer movement, isn't it? I remember Gianni saying...' High-pitched and shrill, Renata couldn't stop talking. 'People were running to the mountains, into attics, woodpiles, trees. Everywhere. But there was nowhere to hide. The tedeschi were all over us.'

'I know.' Mamma pulled a little of the blanket over, so it covered Renata too.

Cesca lifted her arm. 'Here, Rosa. You cuddle up by me.'

Vita mixed a little of the chestnut flour with the last drop of milk they had. 'Right, Rose-posie. Drink that.' There was still half a jug of wine left. She poured two glasses, handed them to Renata and her mother. When Mamma had gone to bed, she would take the pot of vinata and hurl it down the mountainside. The pulses of rage inside her were slowing to something deeper.

'What will they do to them?' said Cesca.

'It's alright.' Renata took a long draught from her glass, wine spilling over the edges. 'The Monsignor will stop them. Don Sabatini sent a boy down to the Canonica.'

'If the Monsignor can't save his own priests...' Mamma turned down the lamp till it was barely a glow. 'Do you mind? My head aches.'

'I think we should wait up for him.'

'But it's curfew. What can he do?'

'Intercede,' said Renata. 'Don Sabatini said the Monsignor would intercede.'

'With God or the Germans?' said Vita.

'Both, I think.'

They sat in the crumpled dark. A hand took Vita's. Time folded in on them, looping and closing, giving distance. Each with their own thoughts. The flames on the fornelli dimmed. Only shadows and unseen faces for company.

'Should we pray, Mamma?'

'In the morning, will we go to the Comune?' said Renata.

Mamma was twisting the blanket through her hands. Tugging and twisting in long, furious movements. It might have been a chicken's neck.

'Mamma?'

'What? Oh... yes. If you like.'

'Will we pray to San Giuseppe?' said Renata. 'For times of distress?'

'No, San Rocco. He helps people who're wrongly accused.'

Vita stroked her sister's hair. 'How do you know these things, Ces?'

'Why not San Cristoforo?' said Renata. 'He's our patron saint.'

'Good idea.' Mamma stood, the blanket dropping to the floor. 'Come with me girls. Renata, you stay with Rosa. Keep her warm.'

'Where are you going?'

'Mario's workshop. We won't be long. You think up a good prayer, and we'll do it when we get back. Vittoria, bring the lamp.'

Renata made a face. Mamma rarely passed up the chance for prayer.

They crossed the yard, light bobbing from the lamp. The lock had already been forced. Dark smells raced; shellac, pipe smoke, dust from the wood Papà coaxed into shape, the oil with which he wiped his tools. Smell and memory pleating. Long boards of oak were stacked inside the door, just-hewn planks dripping sap. There was his vice, his plane. The racks for tools. The ceramic scaldino tucked beneath the workbench, its handle turned inwards so you wouldn't trip.

Vita fingered a chisel on the bench. She wanted to kill those men. The chamfered blade nicked her skin. She pulled her finger back, before the blood spilled and spoiled her father's work. It was a piece of marquetry; inlay for a table, spread in careful carved pieces so fine they fluttered in the draught. She tried to set them straight, and a sliver of veneer broke.

'Vittoria! Pay attention. This is important.'

The cabinet where Papà kept his shotguns was open. Mamma was holding one of them. It looked odd to see her mother with a weapon.

'Did you hear what I said? About the weight? You need to spread your feet—'

Vita ran her hand along the smoothness of the shotgun's barrel. 'Can I try?'

Mamma hefted the gun so the butt rested on Vita's shoulder. 'Look through here. See the little dimple? Match it up with the U-shape. Then line it with the thing you want to shoot. But it sprays all over the place, so you need to wait until they're close. Two barrels, remember.'

'What?'

'Remember to squeeze twice.'

'Mamma, how do you know this?'

'Just concentrate.'

The gun felt intense. The slim length of it a magic wand, a stick to point and make others do your bidding. All across Europe, as the war crested and crashed, this scene would be repeated. Parents showing their children where to hide. Where the gun case was. How to plunge a knife as you might stick a pig.

'Vita!' Cesca screamed.

'Godsake, there's nothing in it.'

Mamma slapped Vita's head. '*Never* point that at someone you love.' She took the gun, relocked the cabinet. 'Not a word to anyone. And you only go in if...' For a

163

second, her mother looked lost; the loose-focused eyes of a child.

The workshop door opened. Cesca screamed again.

'Scusate, scusate. I didn't mean to frighten you.'

It was the Monsignor. Here, in their dark and messy workshop, gliding on his saintly wheels as the three of them played with guns.

'Mario is fine. Don't fret.' He laid his hands on Mamma's shoulders. A proprietary, intimate gesture; it was a skill Vita saw him use often, a shepherd calming his sheep. And every time he did it, she wondered: did it feel lonely, being the Monsignor?

'They're all fine. A few hundred in all, from here and Barga. They're taking them to Castelnuovo, along with the Pisans.'

'Then what?'

'I spoke with the commander. He's given me his personal assurances they will be well cared for. I think men like blacksmiths and bakers might be let go, perhaps some professionals too.'

'Is Papà professional?' asked Cesca.

'Not really,' said Vita. 'Not any more.'

'And after Castelnuovo?' said Mamma.

'I believe the plan is to take them to Bologna. Or possibly Germany.'

'Germany? How will they survive? Oh, God, how have they have tricked us like this? The tedeschi are monsters.'

'They're not monsters, Elena. They are simply following orders. The commander was quite reasonable.'

'Reasonable? They took Don Sabatini!'

'No, he elected to go with them. For comfort. And there is that Pisan doctor too.'

Mamma began to cry. A low, boundless wrench, with no Papà to stem the flow.

'Elena, the worst that will happen is that Mario will do manual labour.'

'Slave labour?' She wouldn't stand still to let you comfort her. Up and down, up and down, she strode, weaving her own pattern on the workshop floor. 'But he's not fit enough. Did you tell them about his war injuries?'

'The men will get a medical. If they're unfit to work, they'll be released.'

'Gino, you didn't see them. The *relish* as they hit him. They want to punish us. Don't you see?'

The Monsignor turned to Vita. 'Is it true? The gossip about Giuseppe? I don't want to know the details. I do not wish to be culpable in any act of wrongdoing. But does your mother have cause to be concerned?'

The sickly lamplight shone on the Monsignor. On Vita, wrapped in the warm smell of linseed and papery wood, on Papà's tool bag tucked behind a stool, on the table edge he'd been smoothing. The yellowish cast of lamplight, flowing like brackish water, right inside of you. To the place where that boy touched you, to the sharp burst of joy when you heard he was dead.

She nodded.

'I see. In that case, perhaps you are right to be concerned.'

'About what?' Mamma was like an unknotted thread, loose wisps of her drifting.

'Further reprisals? It's hard to know. Where is Giuseppe now?'

'On his way to Sant'Anna.'

'Ah.' He let a little pause grow. 'I learned something else today. It might explain why the tedeschi are gathering all in their wake. The Allies have taken Lucca.'

'So close?'

'Indeed. And I gather there was little in the way of struggle. Now, your mother still lives in Lucca, Elena?'

'She does.'

'Possibly that is an option? I could get a message to Don Nello.'

'I'm not abandoning my house, Gino. They are not driving me from my home.'

The Monsignor's swivel-neck stare, alighting on Vita. 'What about your daughters?'

'No, Mamma. We're not leaving you. We are not being boarded out at Nonna's.'

'Only if you come too,' said Cesca.

'How can I? What if Papà comes back? Out of the question. If I leave La Limonaia, we will have nothing to come back to. Tedeschi will seize it, or refugees will move in...'

Churning again, the mamma-tide, sweeping up and down the workshop. Even the Monsignor stepped out of her way. Vita had seen this in his repertoire too, where he dropped a notion, like an acorn, then carried on being mighty and steadfast until the notion rooted, deliberately, where it was meant to.

'You really think it will become worse here, Gino?'

'Mamma—'

'Be quiet, Vita.'

'Yes, Vittoria, please stop interrupting. I believe so. I fear the Germans are entrenching themselves. Sealing off the mountains so that any escape that way may prove impossible. Including the route to Sant'Anna, alas. And with the Allies continuing to push forward—'

'When you say "Allies", you mean americani? Is Lucca not overrun by Moors? I will not have my daughters become *marocchinate*.'

'Please. The soldiers there are rough, but I do not believe they are beasts.'

'Americani, francesi... those blacks are all the same.'

Every woman had heard of the marocchinate. Thousands of wretched women and girls at Monte Cassino, given the Moroccan treatment by their liberators. Many had died. Many others killed themselves afterwards.

'Elena, Lucca is a place of relative order and safety. Compared to what you might risk here.'

The Monsignor frowned, Mamma glowered. They were carving up Vita's future, hers and Cesca's. She tried to think clear thoughts. Her scalp throbbed. She wanted to run after the bastards who'd taken her father. And she wanted to take her family and run very far away.

'I'm not going to Lucca. Not without you.'

'But you're always so keen to leave.' Her mother placed her hand on Vita's neck. 'How will Francesca get to Lucca if you do not take her?'

'Hey, I'm right here. Don't I get a say?'

'Monsignor, I have a job. Nico is old.'

'Nicodemo and I can manage, child. Your safety is of more importance.'

A gift-wrapped blow.

'Well, I vote we all go to Lucca,' said Cesca.

'Good counsel,' said the Monsignor. 'There may only be a brief window of opportunity. The Germans are increasing their reinforcements round Borgo a Mozzano.'

Mamma. No longer walking, but waiting, intently, beside her daughters and the workbench and the glint of Papà's chisel. 'What if you two go on ahead with the Monsignor, and I'll wait a few days, in case Papà is released? Then I'll come to Nonna's too. I promise.'

'What about Renata and Rosa?'

'That's up to them.'

'But you just decide for us.'

'Renata's a grown woman.'

'So am I! You can't keep controlling me like this.'

The Monsignor laid his hands on her shoulders. 'And what would you choose to do, Vita? For the sake of your father and your mother? For the sake of your sister, who is not yet a grown woman—'

'I am.'

'—and relies on you all?'

The tallow lamp guttered, its greasy smell masking the fragrance of the wood. Vita snaked her finger through sawdust, tracing a curve. C for *colpa*. For fault.

'I would...' She looked at her sister. Cesca's hair sprang up lopsided at her temple, the way it had when she was a baby. Kiss-curls, Papà called them. 'I suppose I would take Cesca to my nonna's.'

Mamma nodded at the Monsignor. The decision had been made some time ago, without Vita even realising. They were going to Lucca.

Chapter Twelve

To Frank, war was a series of clean surprises. With the suddenness of snapped bone, orders would be counter-manded, about-turns turn to forward marches. Mealtimes might end, not with jello, but with the man next to you becoming dead, and a momentous battle for which you had prepared for days – waking up sweating with the thought, the flavour of blood; doing push-ups and running hills till you'd moved beyond tiredness to some lightness of being – would melt to anticlimax. Be side-stepped by a *partigiano* in an ill-fitting jacket, opening a gate.

Lucca had been liberated. Not by the US Army, but by local partisans. Sure, it was a domino effect; if the Buffaloes hadn't been battling forth and the Nazis hadn't been shitting bricks, *La Resistenza* would have stayed shadows within Lucca's walls, unpicking and disrupting where they could. But with a Buffalo onslaught on the horizon, the partisans had become emboldened.

Since Monte Pisano, the 370th had been pressing forward, through minefields and machine guns, artillery and snipers. A shower of phosphorous bombs hit them just outside of Vorno, a cymbal clang in the threat-filled symphony which bounced off Frank most every day now. Not symphony. His pops listened to classical music after work, on his phonograph. A symphony was a planned, conducted thing, which rang with coherence and could be sublime. This war was discordant screaming.

In their withdrawal north, the Germans had left fields of mines and barbed wire. Blown every bridge across every river. The Buffaloes navigated it all. Frank had seen his first white officer killed at Ripafratta. Shrapnel to the skull. Nice guy, a boxing heavyweight from West Point. You could be two hundred pounds and death would still scoop you up. Human skin was featherweight – and colourless, to a bullet, or a bomb. Man, the bombs? Constant as the weather. The Germans kept shelling their positions, five hundred rounds a day, moving when they moved. The very tanks protecting the Buffaloes, that were deployed to dance cheek-to-cheek with the infantry for maximum impact, were attracting death. The noise and dust they kicked up could be seen from miles off. Every time the tanks rolled in, Jerry guns rained down. But you grew used to the artillery pounding, and the hiss of incoming shells. Where they kissed was a movable feast, but at least you got some warning. Mortars were untrackable. The ground erupting beneath you. That was your warning.

Calluses had formed on Frank's hands and feet. Possibly inside his ears. Rub and chafe and *fire* and chafe. Sweat and chafe. Don't look and chafe; don't cry and chafe. Yeah. He was mostly callus now. Some days he got to ride in a truck or a tank, others he could barely walk as the olive cambric of his boxers sandpapered his balls. That part of him used to be private and plumply happy. Excited about the future. Now he pissed freely on the march, while his balls wizened in the heat. He wished he'd fucked that dame when he'd had the chance. It was plain that he would die here. Claude explained it. A brothel was for reward and refuge, not love. That dumb-ass sharecropper knew more than straight-A Frank. *When you deep in there, you saying, I'm alive, man! Might not be no next time, see?*

Frank wouldn't have the energy to fuck now. Sleep came with a caveat, in that it could never be deep. One part of your brain remained on constant alert, a reptilian eye that kept you alive. Deep sleep meant dreams – and you sure as shit didn't want any of those. *Sweet dreams, boys.* That's what that woman's voice told you, night after goddam night. The sexy voice of reason which came from the sky. No angel; she was a witch, a propaganda witch. Axis Sally, the troops called her, and the Krauts blared her out across loudspeakers, to mess with the Buffaloes' heads. She played soothing music alongside her ravings, so you learned to appreciate the bits of her you could.

For Frank, Lucca would forever be a Sleeping Beauty city, guarded by water and blown bridges instead of thorns. They arrived to find a Committee of Liberation had driven the Germans from the city, then closed the gates. Various factions were quarrelling over control. Shady men snuck out for meetings with Colonel Sherman. *The Bishop of Lucca requests that the americani enter and take command.* The city had little food or water; the Krauts had destroyed the aqueducts before they left. But they still controlled the roads around Lucca, and all the vantage points above.

That night, a platoon from Company F had crossed the canal, seizing both south and west gates. Two other companies encircled the thirty-foot walls, posting a perimeter defence right around the city. Frank's platoon was focused on the rearguard action, of which there was plenty. Inching, shooting. Creeping, blasting. Frustrated you so bad, not to know where your enemy hid, so when you did see the fuckers, man, you just lost it. An army's greatest weapon was fear. Men wound up tighter and tighter with fear, to be fired like skittish missiles into the great beyond.

At one point, Bear crawled uphill to a Kraut machine-gun placement, lobbed two grenades, before getting pinned behind a wall. They thought he'd been shot. 'Fuck this,' said Frank after ten minutes. He and Luiz sprinted over exposed ground, to fetch the lunatic back. Found him puffing on a Toscano. 'What kept ya, children?'

Once the Buffs had established a command post inside Lucca, the game was up for the Germans. Three dead Buffaloes, forty-nine wounded. Objective gained. Same as in Pisa, it would seem Frank was never to set foot inside the city he'd risked his ass for. Two days resting on the outskirts, then they were to launch a new drive. Up the Serchio Valley, and the infamous Gothic Line.

Except the line wasn't a line, it was a hellish fortress. Built like the Great Wall of China, using the Apennines as a bulwark, but with concrete gun-pits, ditches, mortars, vicious iron wire and steel. The Buffs talked about it, hushed and awestruck – *This big… That wide… My buddy flew over it.* An engineer might appreciate its efficient precision – if only it weren't bristling with Nazis. Thousands upon thousands of Sauerkrauts, raining down fire.

The battalion had reverted to regimental reserve. This meant fixing vehicles, cleaning gear, retrieving equipment cached along the route. It meant clipping toenails and reading letters, washing socks and patching skin. It meant counting your losses and filling the gaps. That was another bone-snap. One man's death was another man's promotion. Frank was now a Private First Class. Lieutenant Garfield had called him over, handed him a little cloth chevron. 'Get that stitched on tight, Chapel. 'Fore they take it off you.'

'Yessir.'

Back in the tent, Comanche and Ivan saluted. Luiz gave Frank the finger. 'Son of a bitch. That's 'cos you got to Bear first.'

'Son of a Bitch *First Class*, private.'

'You coming for some chow, *suh*?'

'Nah. Not hungry.'

'PFC wants a little *private* time, private.'

The rest of them trooped out, Luiz flicking the chevron off Frank's belly and onto the dirt. Frank didn't care. Sure, it was nice some lieutenant thought he was a good soldier, same way teacher giving you a gold star was nice. But when some guy dying down the line bumped a corporal to a sergeant and a PFC to a corp? That was bravery? That was shit. Least his pay grade would jump a few cents. Yeah, because he was in this for the money. Still. It would make his mother proud.

He took out his journal. Last two pages: *Dust* and *Bombs*, over and over, real neat. Through the canvas, he could hear the distant spit of machine guns. The climate of constant sun and artillery fire no longer made him flinch. Frank felt like an old, numb man. He'd christened Villa Orsini, where they were camped, the Slough of Despond. Only Comanche and the lieutenant got it. Shamefully, Frank had expected Comanche to be illiterate, because that's what folks told you. *Them redskins can't even read.* Folks told Italians that Buffaloes were devils, that they'd horns and tails. Those posters of fat-mouthed monkey-men about to pop a woman in their mouths were in every town they'd travelled through.

Frank's momma wasn't stuck-up. She was a kind-hearted Christian, who'd raised her kids to love thy neighbour.

Just not necessarily mix with them is all. Their neighbour-hood straddled shoddy to aspirational – what developers called 'on the up' – and the Chapel home sat firmly on respectable road, with its trim lawn and painted mailbox, its white porch and green front door. Momma made sure they went to church, that Francis and Willis had music lessons as well as basketball practice. Study time was every night after supper, because *education is the key* and if you worked hard and spoke nice, you got results. She fed them wholesome food and wholesome wisdom, all of it well meant.

He lit a cigarette. Supposed to be overseeing the strip-ping down of an engine in some captain's jeep. But the captain had been moved already, to make up numbers elsewhere. Or was he the one who'd got shot in the eye? Frank pursed his lips, trying to make a smoke ring like Bear did. It looked so cool. Did he even want to be a PFC? Frank, who would take copious notes, sit straight in class, keep his teeth clean and please his superiors. For so-fucking-what? To wind up dead in a Tuscan ditch? Being promoted would open him to scrutiny and judge-ment. What was the point in being 'good'? Any niche you might have carved for yourself got subsumed by the fact you were black. And when a two-foot mortar tornadoed the ground, spitting shrapnel 360 degrees into black flesh and white, into college boys and farm boys and hoods, none of it mattered anyway.

Tracing the energy of the tornado with his pencil. Round and round in coils, the blackness getting harder, tighter as he pressed. In the looping centre, he drew a little diamond, shadowing the bottom facets for perspec-tive. Truth gleamed from several sides, and maybe his momma just hadn't seen them all yet. Jews weren't dirty; redskins weren't dumb. Foreign food could be delicious, and there was no natural order of things that made you wait your turn.

He went outside the tent. Air thick with bright light, too much gaudy light, all spilling cheerful and full of dust. Sharp, contrasting panes of shadow, the mountains were like a Cubist painting. The foreground was a shipwreck. Smoking funnels of tree stumps. Distant heaps and disjointed spars that could have been broken masts, but were broken homes. This blasted landscape.

Over by the mess tent, he could see his guys crowded outside, with a bunch of other Buffs. This was a big camp. The tank crews were white, and the army excelled in division. Rank and speed and accent and size and money and colour all mattered. In places like this, when the men entered the mess hall, the dividing began again. *All Negroes over here.* Didn't matter who they'd fought and bled alongside. What mattered was they knew their place.

The segregated tables ate mostly in silence, because to do otherwise would draw attention. To the monkey enclosure. You were supposed to laugh at that. But it looked like today, they weren't even getting to go inside.

'What's up?' said Frank to Comanche.

'Usual. Life on the reservation.'

A white corporal stood at the inside flap. 'I told you. Your tables have been taken.'

'Lord,' said Ivan. 'We got to call ahead now? Food here ain't all that.'

'Come on, Corp,' another remonstrated. 'There's spaces at the end.'

The segregated tables were occupied by white men. White men, some in dusty greenish-grey, others in canvas tunics with *PW* stamped on their backs.

'You'll need to wait. Or go round the back and we can feed you outside.'

'Do what?'

'You can't eat till these men are finished.'

'They ain't men. They's Krauts.'

'Listen, boy. You can eat round the back or you don't eat. It's your call.'

'Hey, corporal,' said Frank, shoving to the front. 'Can't we do a deal? If you push those Krauts along the bench, they could all fit on one table. Then our boys could have—'

'*Our* boys? Who the fuck you talkin' to? You think I'm some kinda albino nigger?'

'OK, OK, cool it, man,' said Frank, palms upright.

'You raise your hand—'

'Fu—'

'Yo, Chapel,' Bear's voice boomed behind him. Frank's sergeant slapped him on the back. 'When you last have a wash, boy?'

'Sarge?'

Bear was steering him from the tent. 'You heard me. Five, six days ago?'

He thought about it. 'I dunno. Maybe ten? But, sarge—'

'Go take a shower, chile. You stink.' Still nudging him, fatherly paw in the small of his spine. 'And then I want you to run an errand for me.'

'Sure, sergeant.'

'I want you to go into Lucca.'

'Uh-huh.' He waited for his instructions. Deliver a message? Fetch a crate of oil cans?

'Thas it. Just go into Lucca for me. You didn't get to see Florence, did you? Or Pisa? Where the pizzas come from.'

Frank laughed. 'No, they don't, sarge. They come—'

'From Napoli. I know that, boy.'

Over by the big stucco villa, there was a commotion of vehicles and men saluting. 'Stand by your beds,' said Bear. 'Colonel Sherman's away.'

'What's he doing here anyhow? Thought he was in some *palazzo* miles off?'

'Been so much bellyaching with the socially-communists and the national committee of fuck-knows-who, colonel's come back to umpire 'em. But they all talk so goddam fast none of our interpreters know what they shouting. Italians, man! Worse than the goddam Irish.' Bear slapped him a second time, but softer. 'OK. Go. Get yourself into a church, look up at the towers. Get yourself human, yeah? But wash first. Thas an order.'

Cold shower on a hot day. Rough towel on a sore body. Sluicing off the dirt. Bliss.

They'd set up field showers behind the lines, using water from the canal. Basic, but efficient. Strip at one end, get clean clothes at the other, while your dirty ones were washed and recycled to someone else. You'd to stand under the water bladder, which was meant to be heated by the sun. Squeeze the nozzle, let it fall. Jesus. Cold. Don't let the water splash your mouth, because Godknew what was in it. Frank didn't look at his body as he washed. It wasn't really his.

He hitched a lift with two other privates into Lucca. They were off duty and they were not, that lizard eye always flicking. You were in uniform. You kept a side arm on you at least. But a pocketful of candy and cigarettes – these things were appreciated more than dollars. Frank left the other two at the gates. Months of snoring and shitting in unison. He wanted to be on his own. Needed to. A huge, open-arched gateway was carved into the massive city walls. Frank walked through, and it was like a whole other shower. Slim trees lined broad avenues, trees and greenery everywhere, even on the tops of the walls, where generous paths looped a circle round the city. In an ideal world, he would begin at one end and traverse Lucca from on high. A perfect morning stroll. He picked his way up the stone staircase, over the leavings of partisan guards, the spent cartridges, the stinking blankets. Empty bottles and pools of piss.

Up here was exposed. Experience told him he should crouch and skitter. A sharpshooter could easily take him out. An airplane might dive. Briefly, though, Frank let his shoulders be upright. He stood on the walls of Lucca and took in the view. How beautiful it was. To his right were plains and mountains. To his left, red-tiled roofs and crenellated towers. At his feet, pale stone ramparts that were echoes of other circles, still present in the undulating green land, circles guarding this city since Roman times. He felt a sharp sense of his own perimeters. The shadowed edge of cheek below his eye. The papery breeze tonguing his collar. Sting of raw flesh where he'd cut himself shaving, and all the empty, unanchored pieces that jarred inside. He saw a rust-coloured blot on the stone parapet in front of him. If he bent real close, he'd be able to smell it. The iron-black tang of blood. He thought of the sniper who had stood here yesterday or the day before, eyes narrowed over this same view. The whizz of air as the bullet came *straight back at ya*, or did the sniper trip and bang his head, or were the wounded piled up here to die?

He could see the city walls from Villa Orsini. Frank searched the hills beyond the canal, trying to glimpse their tented village, imagining he could see a string of clean laundry dancing in the breeze, all nice and homey. Why?

Why did he need to see the camp? The instinct of the lost, searching for the familiar so you could wave up at it, like baby-Frank would wave to Momma at the window. But here was only empty spaces, vast craters in a conscience-less world. Sun baking hot, but there was no warmth in it. Hard-gleaming, unblinking light, laying over the wreck-age they had wrought.

On the other side of the walls, mediaeval Lucca seemed relatively unbombed. The tallest tower he could see had a white-faced clock on pinkish brick. The hands did not move. Frank climbed back down the stone staircase. If he had known, then, that there would be a before and after, he would have taken so much more care to note the details. He would have drawn and recorded in intricate precision the threads that were binding and spinning him on. But he was just a guy on a walk in an unknown place.

The broad roads shrank, becoming warrens, a dead-end maze that would suddenly open into the shocking bril-liance of a light-filled square. Forcing your head up to meet the sky, bathing you in deep, sore blue. Strings of US Army trucks scattering people; an urgency at odds with the bruised sleepiness of the streets. Ancient towers and silenced fountains. Faces, faces, carved and wise. The air was flavoured with waste; a just-woken mouth taste sour from the night before. Then a peppery scent of olive oil would sneak from under a shutter, and you could imagine cooking, and life going on. He passed a baroque church dressed in white stone, frosted like Christmas cake, with a painted angel guarding the roof. Down a lane of tower-ing houses so close the upper windows almost touched, then he'd turn and be in the shade of an arcaded pa-lazzo, through a square wreathed with statues and syca-more trees. Following unknown streets, unknown people, who were tired or joyful or curious. A grandmother shielded her grandchildren as he passed, while another offered him purple flowers. He took one, bowed. Gave her a Hershey bar in return. Passed a group of giggling *signorine* who twirled back to have another brazen look. One of them touched her upper lip, tracing a line with her little finger. Self-consciously, Frank touched his own lip, where he'd sculpted a pencil-thin moustache, the sole remnant of the stubble he'd just discarded. It was on a whim, in the damp shiver of after-shower grooming, when he'd been confronted by his parched, savage face, and decided he did not like it. Soon as he got back, he'd shave the damn thing off.

The girls tittered.

Lesson... fuck knows. A zillion and one. Here, you are made exotic. It is the uniform, stupid. Not you.

Frank lowered his eyelids, and the laughing became murmurs. He gleamed the buttons on his tunic with his sleeve; fabric freighted with the power of the invader. Kissed the flower he was holding, presented it to the teenager who'd mocked his moustache. She blew him a kiss in return. Then it was Frank's turn to do the predatory circling, a neat half-turn before a full-beam smile, switched in their direction. Could feel every bristle of his moustache, being electric. Then he sauntered off. Terrified he might trip.

He found himself in a huge, oval-shaped piazza ringed with pink and ochre buildings, three, four storeys high. Neat green shutters, wrought-iron balconies. None of them grand. For a space this size, there were no lavish fountains, no imposing marble recreations of ancient gods fighting ancient monsters. It felt like being inside an arena. He wandered for a while, his mind slackening. Probably the ringing rush in his ears would never disappear. But it was fine. Knots of Buffaloes perambulated the piazza. Plenty other soldiers too. Swarthy *partigiani*, swaggering under the weight of their cartridge belts like they owned the place. Which they kinda did. A bunch of Japanese Americans, some flag-draped men from the Brazilian Expeditionary Force, drinking grappa in a chequerboard hodgepodge of colour. The Brazilian units were not segregated. Frank avoided the lot of them, gravitating to where a market of sorts had been set up. Locals jostled for pickings. Candles. An empty picture frame. One lone shoe. Small knuckles of unidentifiable meat.

Bear hadn't said how long he was to visit Lucca. Frank was glad he'd come. He felt refreshed, reminded of something that wasn't olive drab. Beyond the market was one of the many small arches that cut through the clustered buildings, to let you exit the piazza. He'd head out through that one, walk round to the gate he'd come in, and that would be him done. Vehicles were coming and going; he could hitch a ride back to camp in time for a stolen siesta. Inside the arch, he saw another two Buffaloes, messing with an Italian girl. She was dressed in green, had her back to him and her hair piled high in a loose skein, but it was the neck... oh, man, it was the neck that hit him like a body blow.

Later, he could only suppose that he had felt this, that it would become a memory, or a story he would tell, but now – now it was a zooming ceaseless thrum; it was a sly line of promise from his groin to his gut; it was a conversation he had been waiting for. And it was the most gorgeous, most glorious, of necks.

The Buffs were only joshing with her, but it was becoming insistent, where the balance was tipping slightly, and you could see she just wanted to get by. It was perfect. Frank and his 'tache would intervene. He'd be firm; she'd be grateful. The soldiers would concede (he was a PFC after all); Frank would smile and it would be—

A tornado. A wall of sound rising, echoing and booming, slipping along the tunnel to ricochet across the oval piazza and surprise the world. The glorious neck twisted. A chin rose. In the roughest, most guttural English he had ever heard, the girl screeched: 'Will yous just *piss off* and leave me alane?'

Chapter Thirteen

They had reached Lucca in a day; Vita, riding on Gianni's old cycle, Cesca on the crossbar, bumping under her chin. Freewheeling down winding roads, panting up the hills, smelling sharp air instead of dusty Barga. It was close to exhilarating – if you ignored the death-and-danger looming. They stayed off main roads, using the paths their forebears would have taken. Papà's old mushroom knife rested a hand-grab away, in the pannier of the bike. The curved blade was vicious; the brush at the other end a friendly tail.

When she thought of Papà, Vita's chest grew vast, filled with cracks and rough edges, with a terrible, plummeting emptiness. So she tried to think only good thoughts. She thought of Joe. Him and Carla and the boys; they'd be there by now, safe in Versilia's marble caves. How brave he was, and sad.

She'd called him a coward. The unpaved track bumped as the cycle gathered speed, veering precariously along the rim of a pothole, Cesca squealing. Air flowed effortlessly through Vita's open mouth, and she wanted to shout into the wind.

Every few miles, they would see evidence of movement. Yellow plumes of smoke. Brown dust. Flat-bed trucks painted greyish-green. Refugees lugging their bundled lives, crawling north and scuttling south, because in truth no one knew where safe was. As they neared Borgo a Mozzano, they moved down from the old trails to cross the river. Rolling tanks passed them on the road, lumbering like prehistoric beasts. Metal-headed soldiers marched in squads, soldiers running reels of cable, shouting.

They slowed as they approached the river. 'I need the toilet, Vi.'

'Wait till we're across.'

'What about those tedeschi?'

'Trust me.'

Wading over would get them shot. Nothing for it but to take the bridge.

'You'd better do your teeth again.'

'Oh, for Godsake.'

'Just do it, Vi. Mamma will have some spy tailing us. You know she will.'

This was not a wholly unchaperoned journey. The Monsignor had accompanied them as far as the paper mill at Rocca, riding on the sisters' donkey. At Ponte a Moriano, they would be met by Mamma's cousin Nello, who was a rector in Lucca. This bit in the middle was courtesy of one cunning disguise: the ugly sister.

'Here.' Cesca handed her a stick of charcoal.

'Gesù.'

'Don't swear, Vi. Mamma's right. You're becoming very coarse.'

Vita flapped her voluminous skirt. 'Look at me.' Clad in sackcloth and ashes, literally. The charcoal was to blacken her teeth. They were a priest's housekeeper and her charge, out for some harmless foraging. No law yet against looking for food. But it was wise to take precautions, Mamma said. *And you are such a beautiful girl.* She'd said it thoughtlessly, looked more surprised than Vita when it trailed out.

'Can I just pee here? I'm bursting.'

Keep away from La Macchia, the Monsignor had instructed. Easier said than done. La Macchia was all the broad flatlands near the Serchio riverbed. 'There are mines beneath the soil,' he'd said as he left them. 'And they do not distinguish whose feet tread there. Keep to the high ground. Whenever the way looks easy, eschew it.' He had twinkled merrily. 'A good lesson for us all, Vittoria, no?'

'Yes, Monsignor.' Pretending to be demure, before she hugged him. The man of God went brittle in her embrace, but she clung on regardless, and was rewarded with a brusque patting of her shoulder.

'I'm sorry I cannot accompany you all the way. But there is much to be done in the parish.'

'Monsignor, you've done enough.' She'd felt the frail ribs of him, seen the deep shadows made darker by the brim of his hat, which she'd knocked askew.

There was a crypt beneath the Duomo where the Monsignor went to pray. It was kept locked. The tedeschi respected the sanctity of this place, for didn't the Church offer them succour? The Monsignor had been diligent in providing solace for German soldiers: Mass for those who wished it, the last rites for that awful blackshirt and the general. He was kindly and courteous to all, when other priests might have been firebrands or sycophants, and this allowed him to move freely, within limits. But a watchful housekeeper, who must account for every grain of rice and yolk of egg, notices things. And, if she is a nosy besom like Vita, she follows the breadcrumb trail. Sees it leading to the crypt, and the hidden souls inside. Nico knew, of course.

Like he knew everything, and said nothing. *They are Jews,* he hissed at her. *They won't be here for long. And if you tell anyone, I will bury you in the camposanto.* Nico never joked.

'Vita, I *have* to pee,' said Cesca. '*Please.* You want me to stink like an old fish?'

'Now who's coarse? Fine. May as well have a last supper.'

Her sister went pale.

'I didn't mean that. Look, what about here?'

They stopped just before the skinny arches of the Ponte del Diavolo, in a dip of land, tucked out of sight of the tedeschi on the bridge.

'Pee behind that tree. No one can see you.'

Vita brought out the water and focaccia Mamma had packed. Then their papers, and a pass for the bike. Cesca reappeared, brushing down her skirt. If they stayed calm, it would be fine. Vita's legs were shaking; it was all that cycling, Gesù, these were the animals who'd beaten her mother. Who'd stolen away her father. Blank, she must stay blank, was actively trying out her blank expression as the sky poured in on top of them.

From nowhere, stuttering dreadful growls, two fighter planes coming in fast, swooping so low she could see bright bullseyes painted on their fuselages. She threw her arms over Cesca's head. The planes banked suddenly, swerved to the right in a beautiful arc, before a rain of gunfire hit the bridge. Spitting dust and stone, screams; Vita, seeing a body fall, his helmet clanking off the buttress of the bridge, then his body hitting water. She could not breathe. There was a salvo of hopeless shooting from the bridge, but the planes had zipped far into the sky again, like triumphant birds of prey.

'Vi, you're choking me. Let me up. '

'Shut up till I tell you.' She held her sister until the body floated past, face up in the river. The boy's eyes were

186

open, his chest leaking scarlet. He came to rest ten metres downstream. Two tedeschi ran along the river's edge, waded in to get him.

'Get off.' Cesca, muffled, squirming until she fought herself free.

'Cesca. Please.' Vita didn't know what the soldiers would do. From here, they could see straight to the opposite bank. See two Italian girls having a picnic while they wrestled with their dead.

'Do not move.' She made them be statues, neither looking at nor away from the funeral scene on the other side. The tedeschi were soaked. They managed to drag the body up the bank. Another ran down with a makeshift stretcher. The body was laid on top. The soldier who'd brought the stretcher bent to listen to the boy's heart. Ear to chest, his head angled so his eyes were directly on Vita. She didn't blink. Neither did he. Then the soldier did an uncanny thing. He straightened himself up and saluted her. It was not at the others, or the body on the stretcher. It was at her. She found herself lowering her head. For the dead boy, though. Not the medic.

He had looked surprised, the boy. Astonished by his lack of readiness. Vita listened to the shift of the gleaming river. She had never seen a death so immediate; not the actual moment of it. Could taste metal in her mouth.

She waited until the trucks clanked off before releasing her sister.

'Can we move now? Oh my God, that was awful. Did you see his face?'

'Cesca, just be quiet.'

Her sister seized the bike. 'Well, excuse me for getting a fright because some man just got killed in front of us. God. What is wrong with you Vita?'

'Can we just go? Please?'

A clear run, no one left to challenge them. They wheeled the bike over the thin humps of the Devil's bridge. The river below was emerald green, shimmering eerie faces back at them. Weeping trees lent their colours to the water. Or maybe it was magic, mingled with blood.

On the other bank, the land rose steeply. Sheer rock faces edged the road, dripping with foliage and clinging trees. They began to cycle again, looking for a path back into the hills. Way up ahead, a couple and a little boy were also walking, the three of them limping under bundles and packs. Quickly, the cycle gained on the family, but they seemed to have stopped.

'What on earth is that?'

Vita braked. The road ahead was blocked – a wall stretched right across it, with a curious, curved lip on top. They both got off the bike.

'Is it to stop trucks?'

'We'll need to climb over – or get back down onto the riverbank. What d'you think? It looks quite steep.'

'Wheesht.' Cesca drew her to the side of the road. 'Look.'

From nowhere, a sentry had appeared, rifle flashing in the sunlight. Then another soldier slipped from inside the rock face itself; you could see the long vines part as he emerged. Tunic off, sleeves rolled – he was carrying a brush. He ignored the couple remonstrating with the sentry. Instead, he started daubing at the stone.

'What's he doing?'

'I think he's painting it.'

Pale grey where the soldier was dabbing, turning stony black as he stippled away. Transforming it.

'That rock's not real. That must be it! That's the German wall they all go on about.'

'It's not very big.' Cesca was looking at the concrete blocks on the road.

'It is, if it's all that rock face too. They're actually building fake cliffs—'

A shot rang out, not from the sentry, nor the brush-wielding soldier. It was a quick-glinting barrel higher up the escarpment; Vita saw it slide in and out, heard the heavy plash of water as a missile hit river and the woman ahead screamed. The sentry laughed.

'Quick, Ces.' A wire fence separated them from the river. 'We need to get over there. I'll hand you the bike. Watch in case it's slippy. Hold on to the fence the whole time, sì? And keep your head down.'

She could hear a German voice calling: '*Nein ingresso! Nein ingresso! Capite?*'

There was another crack, and one of the figures fell.

'Go! Hurry up!'

Cesca scrambled over. Vita tried to swing the bike too, but it was sticking, the handlebars lodged in the fence.

'Just leave it! Come on!'

Vita flipped on her belly, climbing over the bike. One last tug, and she managed to yank it free. Shielded by the trees, they crept, dragging the bike along the sloping riverbank, below the line of the road.

'Can they see us?' Cesca whispered.

'I don't know. Crawl.'

'Isn't this where the mines are?'

'Just shut up and move.'

Vita hauled the bike along on its side, alternating arms. Hands and knees bleeding as tiny thorns and twigs punctured in. They crawled and did not speak and did not look up or back. Time flowing round a single, pin-sharp point. Would it be now? Surrounded by green, waiting for a yell, for the thud-ping of gunfire, Vita wondering if she'd have time to fold herself over Cesca; dull with fear and that one burning thought, over and over, and still they crawled.

When Ces couldn't go any further, they lay, face down. Vita's muscles burned.

'Right, piccola. You had enough of being a snake?'

'I'm scared.' Cesca's mouth was in the grass.

'Trust me. We're well away now.'

'What if they're everywhere?'

'All the more reason to get back into the hills. Now, ready? One. Two. Three.' Together, they stood. Blood-rush, head-rush. The fence had become a thick hedge, more difficult to surmount, but they used the bike as a battering ram. The road was clear. Borgo a Mozzano lay behind them; Vita recognised its two square towers.

They climbed back to higher ground. Sometimes they cycled; at other times they pushed the bike along precipitous mule tracks. They were spiders, navigating their country sideways. At some point, the tanks and uniforms changed colour, going from blue-grey to green. The soldiers' skin got darker too: while the Germans had been mostly pale and neat, these new soldiers were rugged. There were men with gleaming hair and sunglasses; there were black-skinned, dangerous-looking Negroes and men with turbans and daggers, doing the exact same dance of march-and-reel-and-dig-and-shout. Vita watched them all from above.

Where did the front line happen? It was a permeable, viscous thing, it seemed to shift and coil like the tide. They stayed alert for random patrols. Apart from a few contadini, and a young boy walking his calf, they encountered no one on the mountain tracks.

As they neared Lucca, evidence of the dull thuds and lights that were faint in Barga became stark. Homes with gaping holes, burnt curtains still fluttering. Great craters in fields and roads. Whole villages that were skeletal and ghostly, unreachable via amputated bridges. Once or twice, they saw the flash of steel as a temporary bridge was lowered into place. This rebuilding was brutal: crude girders replacing weathered stone. Walls were pocked by bullets; you could see their dark splatter on every solid thing, as if a great plague had come and sickened Tuscany. From Vita's vantage point in the foothills, you could pretend it was a film. Glass-clear light up there, and a deep quietness, with the wash of blue shadow down below. If you stared too long, though, the land began to shift and ripple.

'Where is everyone?' said Cesca. 'The people, not the soldiers.'

'Hiding?'

'D'you think Joe will have got them there by now? It's way further than this, isn't it?'

'It's Joe. Of course he will.'

'Are you sad he's gone?'

In the fierce blue sky above them, a bird wheeled, looping the sun. Closer and closer. An Icarus bird.

'I'm sad they've all gone.'

'Guess he didn't fling himself down on one knee before he went then?'

'I didn't want him to.'

Cesca skewed her head round. 'You mean that, don't you?'

The bird soared freely across the sky and the wide grass plain, a runway of green on which they could not step. Looking at it made Vita feel calm.

'Careful, Ces, or we'll fall.'

They met Cousin Nello as arranged. He took them on, through the farms and orchards on the outskirts of Lucca, towards Nonna's house. Up close, the devastation was worse. Lemon groves and vineyards laid waste, ripened fruit blasted on the vine. Sliced-open houses, where you could still see the supper table, or a child's doll in the rubbled yard. People too, small, frightened people who walked in the margins. Folk stopped shuffling as Don Nello approached; deferential nods to the priest in their midst. Don Nello would smile, and carry on. Did they think he would help them? Mamma's cousin was a pleasant man, but Vita resented his presence. He wittered at them, slowing them down to his walking pace. This was their adventure, hers and Cesca's. And they had done it on their own.

Inside the girth of its walls, Lucca was remarkably unscathed compared to the landscape around it. Nonna's house was also untouched; its blue shutters jarring with the rest of the street's douce green. Nonna was waiting for them in her rosy salotto. Her maid, Serafina, led them in, down the corridor of plaster saints and classical busts. Pride of place was still afforded to the photograph of Il Duce, nailed to the arch below the staircase, requiring an act of homage as you dipped below. Next to him was a picture of Mamma's brother. Cesare was almost as lantern-jawed as Il Duce. A large, spidery crack in the plaster spread behind both frames.

'Nonna!' Cesca ran into her grandmother's belly.

'Oof! My goodness, Francesca. Have you no manners? Stand up straight so I can look at you.'

'Buona sera, Nonna,' said Vita.

'Cosi! Francesca, were you not able to wash at all?'

'Nonna,' said Vita, 'we've just cycled fifty kilometres.'

'I hardly think it's that far – is it, Nello?'

'I'm not sure, zia.' Don Nello beamed good-naturedly. 'Are we to have any food? I'm sure the girls are hungry.'

'That depends. Did you bring me anything, from your vast store of goodies?'

'Ah... I only—'

'Come, we all know that priests get fatter while the rest of us starve. You're practically swimming in oil and butter.'

'Zia, I—'

A rapid, indifferent flick of her hand to quieten him. 'What about you girls? Did your mother send anything to help with your keep? Some fresh eggs perhaps? A few vegetables?'

Cesca was about to cry. Standing by the side of her grandmother, she looked lost and exhausted. Could the woman not even offer her a drink? Vita sat down on a blush-coloured sofa, deliberately plumping the cushion with her dirty hand.

'Sit by me, Ces. Nonna, we have nothing. The Germans have taken it all.'

Nonna sighed. 'Well, if your mother had stayed in the city, you wouldn't be in this predicament, would you? Here.' She passed Vita a cotton handkerchief. 'Will you sit on this, please? We've managed to keep ourselves decent, despite the deprivations we've been forced to endure. Haven't we, Serafina? Personally, I have found the German soldiers to be perfectly fine, if you speak to them nicely. It's the Moors I worry about. Filthy blacks, rampaging about the city. How your mother thinks you'll be safer here, I have no idea. And why is she not with you? I told her she must come immediately. Does she have any idea how fraught my nerves are, worrying about you all, stuck in that little hole?'

'She's waiting for our papà.'

Nonna's mouth pressed in on itself. 'What was your father thinking of, getting himself arrested? What did he *do*, for heaven's sake?'

'He didn't do anything,' Cesca shouted. 'Stop being horrible about my papà, Nonna. Just stop it!'

'Well. I hardly think making a simple enquiry is being horrible. Perhaps you are very tired, Francesca. Serafina, will you please take my granddaughter up to her room?'

'Fine.' Cesca slid off the sofa. 'It smells funny in here anyway.'

Vita also stood. 'Don't be rude, Francesca. Nonna, she needs a drink first. And maybe a little bread if you have any? Serafina always makes such lovely bread.'

Nonna wasn't a bad woman, she just had to be managed. Deep under her ribs and layers of black clothing, there was an actual heart. Soften her with a little wine and there was even a sly sense of humour. Vita loved her grandmother. Widowhood had come early; that's what had made her brittle, Vita was sure. She found Nonna easier to love than her own mother, because it was less intense. Nonna did not need to impose her will and Vita did not need to impress her. It freed them simply to like each other.

'Nonna. Are you wearing a *blanket*?'

'No!' Her grandmother regarded the sleeveless cardigan she wore, head pecking as if seeing it for the first time. 'No, it's called a *weste*, dear. Like a gilet? Do you like it? One of the German officers gave it to me, after they'd come here for caffè.' She glanced down at the shapeless thing again, a little shame-faced. 'Perhaps it was... some kind of covering once. But it is clean. They are very clean, the Germans. Not like those Moors.'

'Signora Teresina, shall I get the girls some food?'

God bless Serafina. They were given polenta, some hard cheese and a pudding of wizened grapes. Thus began their sojourn in Lucca. Don Nello didn't stay for dinner after all.

They had been in Lucca forty-eight hours. Vita was growing more worried. No sign of Mamma. Serafina knew a man from Sommocolonia, who'd arrived the day after them. He said La Limonaia was shut up. Why was Mamma not here? Surely she could have sent a message? There was real fighting now at Borgo a Mozzano. *We were lucky to get through*, Serafina's friend told them.

'Be patient,' Nonna said. 'What is the use of agitating? All life will pass in front of you if you are patient.' Vita begged her to send Don Nello back to Barga. They wouldn't hurt a priest. But Nello was too busy: there was a backlog of funerals, he said. Vita thought he was scared. Oh, where was her mother? If Papà hadn't been released, he'd be in one of their labour squads by now. When she thought about that, the panic was overwhelming. It gnawed inside her. It was always there, she realised. Like walking through a field and seeing a bull, and the bull seeing you. You walking, walking faster, then it was moving faster. And if she didn't fight it, the panic swelled and flashed to an anger too big for her to contain. The anger was worse, it was exhausting, because she had to *do* something with the energy of it. No matter how hard you crammed it down, this need to do something gobbled you up until you were nothing but this need, and you understood completely why Joe had killed those men. And then you had to shake yourself, and be a girl again, be useful by going to the market.

Except there was nothing left to eat. Like two mangy curs, she had just fought another woman for a lump of gristle the butcher assured her was pork, and for which he'd charged her handsomely. It would never feed the four of them. Vita had been expecting to see Zio Cesare too, but he'd remained in Amalfi. Doing important war work, Nonna said. Shame it didn't include looking after his mother. Vita was tired. Hot. Lucca was stinking. She needed a wash – the aqueducts were ruined, and there were no mountain streams here to splash in. Now these two moronic soldiers were stopping her from getting home. They didn't think she understood them, drawling their obscenities.

—*You wanna fuckee-fuckee?*

—*Oh, Momma. Lemme suck on those titties.*

Americani. The Moors her mother and Nonna warned about. One of them dangled a bar of chocolate over her head. The other blocked her path.

—*You want candy? You suck my dick, I give you candy? Or beef. You want some corned beef, baby?*

Vita had brought a couple of Nonna's candlesticks, with a view to bartering them when the cash ran out. Since there had been nothing else to barter for, they were still in her basket. Her fingers itched. They were heavy, proper brass. Not plate. Though the passage leading from the Anfiteatro was dark, she could see both ends of it: the piazza in one hemisphere, the street she wished to reach in the other. She wasn't trapped, she wasn't even scared – because these men were pathetic – but they were preventing her from doing what she wanted, and they were laughing while they did it.

Churning, pacing, until a weird release pounced, and took her unawares. A sound came up; it came from inside her clenched, hungry belly. It churned up from her need for her papà, her fear for her mamma, her cousins, the woman she'd just shouted at by the butcher's stall, for the butcher who had nothing left to sell, for Signor Tutto, for her splitting headache and sweating armpits and her terrible aloneness – and it was aimed at every one of these bastardi who did not own her country yet behaved as if they did.

'Will yous just *piss off* and leave me alane?'

The impact was immediate. Beautiful. No need of candlesticks, Vita's words blasted jaws slack and eyes wide.

'Hey! Sorry, ma'am. Didn't realise you were English.'

'I'm no. And how would it matter if I understand yous or no? You are still saying those things. You don't have sisters? Mothers? What would your mammy say if—'

'Hey, baby. It's cool.'

'Don't bloody call me—'

'Damn, you got a mouth on you, girl.'

Oh, she was flying. Fleeing and flying, and she was as high above them as she'd been on the mountain tracks, could feel crisp wind beneath her wings, now she would swoop down low, spit, spit out words she didn't know she knew, in love with their rawness and the Scottish dregs of her, how she was bad to the bone.

'*Scusi, signorina.*'

Another americano voice. It came from behind, so now she was actually a wee bit trapped. Wings slipping. Vita spinning, candlestick in hand, because three against one just wasn't fair, and he caught her at the wrist, this one. This one caught her like a fish, but if was a nice catch, a cupping, holding motion. Soft. The boy's whole face was soft, not like the other two. Soft eyes under his daft, squinty cap. Soft mouth, which had understood the need to twinkle, instinctively. You could tell. Slick-thin moustache that emphasised the softness, like an underlining of it, except above, if that made sense, and it probably didn't because he was grinning like a loon, and the grin was also soft. Was lovely. Where his skin touched hers there was a shading, their two skins making a colour that was entirely theirs; Vita had seen it on a colour chart on the wall at the Conservatorio. Mother Virginia insisted all the girls take art, because art was holy, it was creation, and there was a chart of all the colours, a square rainbow where one colour shaded into the next so you had a spectrum of indigos and blues and greens and golden-fawns and yellows in one glorious burst of possibilities, and here were they, here, this boy and her, making their own colour which was latte, the good, warm kind you want for your second morning cup, the kind Mamma says is babyish but you don't care.

And there was a pause in the air, a space that nothing and nobody filled. Because the thing hadn't happened yet, nothing had happened, and yet it had, in that small safe space in which she was flying, flying forward to the thing that had not yet happened and was happening and had always been happening, or should have been. Yes, she thought. Yes, that's it.

Chapter Fourteen

Frank took the girl back to camp with him. He didn't know how else to stop her slipping into Lucca's labyrinth. Told the two other Buffs to beat it. Amazingly, they did. Frank wanted to think it was down to his new chevrons, but he bet it was the girl. She was crazy. Amazing, but crazy.

'You speak good English.' First thing he said. They both burst out laughing then; it was the kind of delighted glee you got after battle, when you realised you were still alive, and the liveness is infectious, and brighter; it fizzes sharper than it ever did in the hour before you fought. Before is the quiet time, a praying time for those that wanted it, but Frank had moved beyond asking for intervention. There was nothing divine about grabbing your screaming buddy's arm to help him up, and it coming clean off in your hands.

'What's your name?' he asked. Dumb small-talk you would ask in a dance hall. He wanted to say something bigger, but he needed a tether. A name was a thing you could hold on to, could pour stuff into, like a container. With a name, when he was someplace else and she was here, or a page in his notebook, he could imagine her.

'Vittoria,' she said. 'But they call me Vita.'

'Who's they?'

'That's two questions. What about my turn? You have nae manners.'

'Neigh?'

'It's true what they say? All you Moors are savages?'

He pretended to be hurt, but she wasn't buying it. Frank did not think he had ever encountered a human being so sharp. This girl's face had a complex geometry: lines and curves, but even the curves were flat and bony. Gauntness was hiding there – not the emptiness of the emaciated faces he'd seen in Naples, not yet, but it whispered. Or it might just be how Frank was seeing things. Actual features of people were beginning to rub out, the bits and quirks that made them distinctive, so now when he looked at them, he saw only hunger or fear, not people. This girl, this Vita, did not allow for that blurring. She was so alive she shone. But the hunger was there all the same.

He nodded at the candlestick. 'You buying or selling?'

'Neither,' she said, putting it in her basket. 'Just taking it for a walk.'

More laughter, the honest, can't-stop-it-spilling stuff he realised he'd missed. 'What is this place?' His voice echoed in the stone corridor which led from the square.

'The Anfiteatro. It was an amphitheatre in Roman times. That's why the funny shape.'

'Can I walk you home? I'm Frank.'

'So you are. Wee bit cheeky, anyhow. I hardly know you.' She astonished him, this girl. 'Sorry. See, when I'm nervous, I just gabble… And it's no so easy in English, know?' She had coloured then, and it was beautiful.

He let his pinkie finger brush hers as they walked. 'You're nervous? Why?'

200

Because of this? This tense pulse between them, a kind of glittery, pressing pushing. Frank was hearing it, hearing the crisp movement of her skirts and the rustle of her sleeve, hearing the coarse fabric of the stained green cloth scratch her skin and feeling the soft fingernail gap between his hand and hers. To almost-touch was better than anything in the world.

'I don't know.' She laughed again. 'Should I be? My nonna warned me about *i Mori*.'

'Nonna – that's your memaw, yeah?'

'Your gran, aye.'

'Say again? Eye?'

'Aye? Yes.'

'OK. I got you.' She led him down a twisting alley. He might never find his way back. He wouldn't care. 'How come you speak so funny?'

'*I* speak funny? Mee-maw? What kind of word is that?'

'Hey! Be nice. I rescued you from those guys.'

'*You* rescued me? Don't talk teugh.'

He loved the lilt of her, how she rubbed the edges of her strange accent with that Tuscan rhythm, the rhythm he'd felt when folks here were talking, but had never understood. He got it now, the inflection that had spoken of musicality, the shortened vowels and trilling 'r's. Absolutely it was music, it was a glorious song, her mobile hands cutting and conducting air, the fricatives and taps and clicks of her tongue, high and forward in her mouth. Man, that tongue was fluid and it was making him... he was unable to concentrate on what her words were saying.

'... and my papà is Scottish. *E quindi*, my English is very, very good. Not far now.'

Not far scared him. Once she got to the door, some mad papà would come hustle her inside. What could Frank offer her, quick? This was insane. What did he even want? He could shove her in that doorway now, steal a kiss, a feel, take whatever with him. This was war, for Chrissakes, where you eat, kill, shit and fuck.

'You live with your folks?'

'I did. Not now.'

'Your dad back in Scotland?'

'Nope.' That tongue, on her lips. Dabbing. Her hands fell silent. '*Tedeschi* took him. And I think my mamma's went to find him and now she's on her own, and nobody will help me get back to find out. I'm stuck here with my bloody mee-maw.' Fists on hips, pretending she was tough. Where her knuckles pulled her dress tight, you could see the dip of her belly. Outline of her hips. She could be made of fine crystal. 'Don't suppose yous are heading to Barga?'

'Lady, I have no idea where we're headed. Think they tell dumb grunts like me?'

She moved her basket to her other arm. 'Dumb grunt? Ha. That's good. Me too.'

'Yeah? You didn't sound so dumb to me. Back there with those meatheads.'

She didn't laugh. Tick-tock-tick-tock. Slowing thought and pace. Elongating time. Tomorrow, Frank would be gone. Lucca would be off the map and it would be the next town, then the next. Grains of dust slipping through his hands, nothing more than grains of dust and dots on maps, yet for every single one of them, for the Buffs and the Japs, the Krauts, the Indians, the whole shambling mass of foreign bodies that occupied this land, the next town, the next footstep, might be their final resting place. For keeps. You, becoming those grains of dust, this land you never wanted, which would now be made of you, and your land, your place, would be filled by someone else. That Frank might never see his mom again was terrifying.

'This is me,' she said.

'Huh?'

'Here. I live here.' She gestured across the road to a beat-up yellow house with blue shutters. In thirty seconds, in one minute, she would go behind that peeling blue door and Frank would walk to the city walls and he'd go hitch a ride back to camp. Chowtime, maybe a nap. Probably moving off before dawn. Tomorrow, or yesterday, the house with the blue shutters might just as likely be bombed, as the front line pushed and provoked. Next Tuesday Frank would most likely be dead. And if the girl had been at market when her grandma's house got hit, maybe she'd remember him, briefly, before the next passing GI groped her for a laugh.

The air was pulling him into her, yet there was not a breath to be had in this dust-thick road. He wanted to see her face not be hungry. 'You wanna be an interpreter? Work for us?' he asked.

'What?'

'We pay good money.' Did they? He had no clue. But she was brilliant, of course they would pay her. 'And plenty food. You could bring home food for all your family.'

Although they were forging forward, always fucking 'forward' except when it was sideways or back – the Buffs would retain a presence here in Lucca. Bound to. It was a major strategic city. It might keep her safe a little longer. She should not be carrying an empty basket.

'Why?'

'Why what?'

'Why would you do this for me?'

'Hey. No, it's for me. Prove what a great guy I am. Truth. My sarge was just saying how we need good interpreters. I mean, is there some kind of weird Lucca dialect? I dunno, but we can't make out half what these *parmesani* guys are saying. You'd be great.'

She brightened. 'I would, wouldn't I? And it's *partigiani*. Parmesan is cheese.'

'I know.'

Then she shook her head. 'I don't think my nonna would let me. See, to her – yous are the enemy.'

'Ah.' That. The thing he'd thought was not so important here. Frank rubbed ostentatiously at his own skin. 'Well, ain't nothin' I can do 'bout that, see.'

'No.' She put her two hands round his, stopping him from scratching. 'Don't be daft. My nonna – all my Lucca family. They are *fascisti*. This, you being here, is not a good thing for them, know?'

'OK. I see.' He felt stupid. Stupid and liberated, that light, giggling euphoria again, which drives you to be more stupid, so stupid and light that it doesn't matter. So he took up her right hand, and he kissed it. She tasted the way she looked. Delicious.

'I better go now.'

'Yes.'

'Thank you. For rescuing me.' Heavy emphasis on the *rescuing*.

'That is so ungrateful. We did rescue you. We rescued Lucca.'

'Think you will find the *partigiani* let you in, *americano*.'

'Whatever.'

'Goodbye, Francesco.'

She kind of dipped her head, then crossed the road to her house. Green dress swinging, one final glimpse of neck as she bent to unlatch the door. After she had gone inside, he waited. Watching the windows, imagining her in the hallway, or the kitchen maybe. Vita's glass-light shimmer as she stooped and kissed her nonna's hair, the frailty of the old woman as she checked the basket, then sighed. The sense of lack there would be in the house. But cruelly, he hoped she, Vita, would feel it too, for him. Feel a cold bite of gone-ness.

He continued to stand outside until there was no point. Must be well into the afternoon. Bear should have said when he wanted Frank back; it wasn't fair to give you rules, then cut you free. That just fucked with your head. Still, Frank was in no hurry. He thought he might run to camp. Straight up the steep hillside, feel the long lope in his legs until he was pleasantly numb. For now, though, he would walk. Real slow.

He was two streets away, before she came yelling after him.

'Hey! Francesco! Wait! Wait.' Her face was tear-stained, wild. 'Please, wait.'

Frank's heart bucked. Behind Vita, a younger girl was also running, and behind them both, an older woman. Not the soft, downy gran he'd imagined, but a striking dame who was waving a walking cane and also yelling.

'You've got to help me.'

'Vittoria! No!' Her grandmother's chest was heaving. She leaned jointly on her stick and the younger girl, who shrugged her off. All three of them were shouting, at one another, at him, in fast, angry Italian.

'Please,' said Vita. 'Help me. My mother has been arrested.'

'By us? Where?'

'No. By *tedeschi*. Please. You got to help me get to Barga.'

'No!' Tip of the old lady's stick, slapping on the ground. '*È troppo pericoloso*.'

'Dangerous?' Frank nodded at the old woman. 'Your grandma's right. Fighting's moving every day. Getting worse. The Krauts are digging in, all the way up the valley. It's not safe for civilians.'

'Exactly! Why I need to go. I need to help my mamma. You said I could interpret. You must need them when you travel too, huh? Take me to your camp, please. Let me ask at least.'

'Vita. This is stupid. There must be other people who can help your mom.'

'Who? Tell me who? My cousin is gone. My father is gone. Nobody will know where she is. But my neighbour *saw* her. They went to Castelnuovo. They went after the *rastrellamento*. She saw them take Mamma away.'

'What's "*rastamento*"? And what could you do, anyway? You can't help by running back to Barga.'

The younger girl was examining him. Vita's sister? He smiled at her, to show he was a good guy. The kid scowled. Head-toss like a pony.

'I can try. My friend is there. He is the Monsignor. If I speak to him, he will speak to the tedeschi, I know he will.'

'Does he have a telephone, this Monsignor?'

Maybe there was a wire they could send, some kind of cable. The camp was only up the hill. *Yeah, sure, Frank. Let's call up Bosch-occupied Barga.* But there was communication across the lines every day, he'd seen it. Couriers coming in, shady-looking locals going out. Somebody, surely, could get a message to her friend.

'A telephone? Oh, aye. Very pretty black one. Sits on his desk in the Canonica. Doesn't bloody work, but. Not since the *tedeschi* came.'

'How can you no help? How come you're so great and we're all waving stupit starry-stripe flags?' It was the sister speaking; same strangulated English as Vita. 'If yous canny even help?'

The grandmother cuffed the side of the girl's head. '*Silenzio.*' Yet she too glowered at Frank, as if she might devour him.

'Jesus, man.' What was he meant to do?

Another tirade from the grandmother.

'She says: "Don't take the Lord's name in vain." '

'*Scusi. Scusi, Signora. Mi dispiace?* I'm sorry, yeah?' *Walk away, Francis. Go for the next truck out and walk away. In fact, here's one now.* He hollered it down. That asshole Ivan was driving.

'You boys going back to camp?'

'Sure are.'

Vita and her grandma started fighting again. Both gesticulating at him. Ivan grinned, clacked his big fat tongue. 'Got some dame in trouble aready, Chap?'

So, yeah. In a way, he took Vita back to camp with him, although, in truth, she took herself. His trophy of quicksilver. She looked tiny, on the back on the flatbed, tucked beside a herd of Buffs. They'd offered her the seat inside, beside Ivan, but she wanted to sit by Frank. The other guys were laughing and roughhousing. Amidst them, she seemed to have no substance. It was as if he'd netted air. Pressed and folded air, which bumped and jostled her hip against his, all the way uphill. It was the most beautiful kind of torture.

He took her straight to Bear. Bear was Bear. He smoked. He listened. Fixed her a drink to calm down. Vita told him about her mamma. Bear nodded. Said if they could help, they would. Was it really that simple? Vita beamed at Frank. She seemed to think so. Frank had a vague sense of his heart shifting further out of place. Bear asked if they could chat some more, just to see how good Vita's English was. Oh, man, Frank could drink on her voice for the rest of his life. The sergeant asked a bunch of questions; where she lived, how she'd got here?

What it was like in Barga? Her journey here – was it difficult? She described crawling commando-style, and men melting from a cleft rock, and it was like she had stepped from a beautiful fairytale. She and Bear talked for maybe a quarter hour, Vita loosening up a little. Smiling. Still urgent, but more calm. They talked about the Germans, and had she ever seen Kesselring? No – but she knew a woman who did his laundry. Bear laughed. They talked more about her mother. No surprise to hear the mom was wild as her daughter – she had tried to help Vita's poppa escape. That's why the Germans had taken her. A neighbour saw it, was right here in Lucca, now, in her nonna's house when Vita got home. Bear offered her another soda. About her dad – did she know what he'd done to get arrested? She was a little coy then. There'd been a shooting. A Nazi general. Some of her family might have been involved.

'I thought you were fascists?' It was the one time Frank interrupted.

'No me. Not my papà either.'

'And I guess not your momma now too?' Bear wasn't being mean; he said it with a big, shaggy smile. Then he took her on into the villa. Frank was not permitted entry. He loitered outside. She would have to leave by the same door she went in; all the others were nailed shut for security. The walls of the villa were thick; you couldn't hear anything, or see through the blacked-out windows.

There were always staff cars parked outside, and bikers who came and went with attaché cases and self-important gait. For now, Villa Orsini was Battalion HQ. A big, solid sprawl of a place, with outhouses, barns, all the remnants of a farm. From here, the battalion's activities and actions were recorded daily in the ops journal, the sad parade of dead and MIAs passed to regimental HQ.

Here was mapping, paperwork, supplies, discipline. Here was where they decided how many patrols went out and to where, whether they were reconnaissance or ambush (though you learned quick to adapt). Battalion intelligence also lurked inside, guys poring over the contents of said attaché cases, and the intel the scouts brought in. There was a message centre too, with runners from each company, and phone lines that connected to Company HQ.

In his journal, Frank had drawn the villa as a massive spider web, forged from heavy cable. Spools of phone wire went everywhere the Buffaloes went; the guys in the comms platoon never stopped, continually laying new lines, fixing the ones bust by boots and bombs. Communication was what they fussed about – and fucked up – most. Every night, the Buffs got a new password, and every night, Axis Sally got hold of it too. She was able to tell you all about your casualties, in between bouts of jazz.

Yesterday, Frank had done a stint in the villa. 'You got a firm voice, Chap,' the lieutenant told him, 'and battalion clerk's got the shits.' He spent the whole time bartering with regimental supply for more ammo. The 370th had been missed off that month's allocation. He'd managed to scrounge a few hundred rounds off the 1st Armoured. Good guys – for peckerwoods. You said it to their faces; it was a joke.

Bunch of peckerwoods in there now. Villa Orsini stank. The house was kept perpetually dark, so it wouldn't be a target. No electricity, just guttering candlelight, and the smell of sweat and melting tallow. Come on. *Don't let me down, Bear.* How long did it take to write a message out?

'You, soldier.'

'Yessir.'

A white officer stood there, complete with regulation clipboard – plus one unregulation civvy, with a camera round his neck.

'My friend here's doing a piece for – who was it again?'

'*Washington Post.*'

'That's right. *Washington Post.* We want a picture of some Negro soldiers with the VIPs when they come.'

'The who, sir?'

'We got a Congressman and some British politician coming in for a photo opportunity,' said the photographer. 'Lucca makes a good backdrop.'

'You needn't explain yourself, Harry.' The captain was scrutinising Frank's nose. 'What's your name, soldier?'

'Chapel, sir.'

'Well, Chapel. You look like a smart boy.' An airy motion of his clipboard towards the photographer. 'This type, yeah? OK, soldier. I want you to round up half a dozen of your cleanest, neatest colleagues and have them assembled by the front gate in twenty minutes. Here.' He handed Frank a card:

**Captain Dean Pringle. Office of War Information.
Press Liaison**

'Any problems, you get your sergeant to come find me, right? Now, chop-chop. And, Chapel.'

'Yessir?'

'Go for the lighter-skinned ones, yeah?'

The reporter tried to speak, but the officer hustled him on. Frank made to salute, then brought his hand down in a slo-mo punch against the wall. Fuckwit. Saw Comanche, coming over with his puma-walk. There was a new feather in his helmet, a black one that shimmered like oil.

'Hey, Chap.'

'Hey, Com. Nice plumage. Wanna be in a picture?'

'Say what?'

'Only joking.'

Comanche nodded towards the villa. 'Spooks still in there?'

'Spooks?'

'The Oh-So-Secret squad. Driver said he could get me a box of Toscanos for Bear.'

'Don't know. Bear's in there anyhow.'

OSS were a shady crew, with a direct line to the President. No one was sure what they did or how they did it, but they'd been drafted in to deal with the various Lucca factions.

'Signing up more natives, is he? I reckon Bear's on a retainer.'

''Scuse me, men.' Another officer in an unsoiled tunic and polished boots eased by them. He carried a bundle of Italian newspapers. 'You boys know where I might find a spare duffel-bag? Unmarked.' It was their very own Captain Dedeaux. Rare to see him out in the open.

'Hello, sir.' Frank followed him into the villa. No challenge from the sentry. 'I think I saw some yesterday, sir. Give me two minutes.'

'Sure. I'll be in here, soldier.' The guy didn't even know his name. When Dedeaux opened the door to what was once the parlour, Frank heard Vita's voice, high and animated.

'I don't care. If you take me now, I do it.'

'Vita? You alright?' Bear was there too. 'Sarge, you done here?' Frank spoke direct to him. 'Only I'd like to take this young lady back to her family now.'

The boldness of him. Three of them sniffing at her: Bear, Dedeaux and another peckerwood in civvies. Had to be OSS; they got a kick out of dressing like peasants. On the table lay a radio transmitter, in a small black valise with wires and a dial. Neat set of headphones too. There was a map and some white paper beside, on which was sketched a curve of hill, a thin track, a line of bricks.

Vita stood. 'I'm ready.' Sharp around the edges. Luminous with purpose while the rest of the room was dull. Wasted. Anywhere else was wasted space. That was the truth. Maybe she could write him, and he could send her dumb doggerel on V-mail. He knew where she lived. And, when war was over, he could come find her. A bug fluttered round the candle on the desk. Bear coughed. Dark rings on the underarms of his shirt.

Francis Chapel was not yet nineteen years of age. He had not yet graduated, did not have a girl. Frank's life should be on the cusp, should be busting with new things, new people, and it was. It's just – they were the wrong things. They did not reach into the future the way he'd supposed. Where he thought there'd be a path was holes, blockages, folks falling through the holes, Frank not catching them. The world was not going to be his for the taking, no matter how wide the smile that met it. *Home is where you are missed, Francis.* He guessed his mother was describing love, how it had to hurt for you to feel it, properly. He couldn't hardly love this girl, had known her half a day, but it was bolts of proper pain he felt, thinking how she was here, now, a handreach from him, and how, in time he'd forget her face.

'Can he take me, please?' Vita said, pointing at Frank, and he glowed with her. She shut the suitcase.

'PFC.' Dedeaux put the tip of his foot to the door, pressing just enough that Frank could feel the door against his breastbone. 'You was told to go fetch me a duffel bag.'

'Excuse me, sarge? What's going on?' Tight spurt of fury in Frank's throat; him swallowing it down. Those transmitters were what they parachuted behind enemy lines. He noticed, too, the masthead on the pile of newspapers. *L'Italia libera. Fuck you, Bear.* He had wanted to help Vita, not put her at risk.

The OSS guy took his toothpick from his mouth. 'Anyone ask you to speak, nigger? Go get the bag.'

'Why are you giving her the transmitter? Sir?'

'That word you call him?' said Vita. 'I am no stupid. Apologise, else I won't help you.'

The OSS man removed the suitcase from her hands. '*Arrivederci* then, *signorina*. Because this is the US Army. And we do not apologise to niggers.'

'Sir.' Bear spoke, his craven smile making Frank sick to the guts. 'Sir, I'm sure the young lady didn't mean it. We just josh like that, ma'am. Don't mean nothin', so it don't. Now, you want to get to Barga and we want to get this little bundle there too. Way I see it, that's a win-win. But Chapel here won't be going. Captain Dedeaux will take you as far north as he can get.'

What the fuck did that mean? Frank's teeth were hurting. Jaw muscles dancing. *Ten-shun, nigger.* Another private came in, carrying a duffel bag. It was Luiz. 'Sir. Believe you were looking for this?'

Dedeaux dumped the newspapers inside the bag, handed it to Vita. He thought she shook a little, but it could have been the candles. If the Krauts found her, did she know she would be shot? She looked straight at Frank.

'Please tell my nonna where I am gone?'

Frank nodded.

'And if you could take them a wee bite to eat?'

Dedeaux took Vita's arm, led her past where Frank stood. She brushed her hand against his, once and only briefly, before she slung the duffel across her shoulder and took the suitcase from the OSS operative. The three of them left the villa.

'Sarge. What the fuck you doing? She's just a kid.'

Bear gripped Frank by his lapels. 'You want put on a charge, boy? Don't never cuss at me. She wanted to go, OK? It was her idea.'

'Bullshit.'

This time, Bear did strike him. Frank felt his cheekbone explode, his head crack on the wall behind. 'This is a fucking war, Chapel – not some kinda tea party. Every step we take forward is 'cause a folks like her. Who you think tells us where the mines are? Where the Krauts is massing; their weak spots? Old guy walked in this morning with plans for the entire west half of the Gothic Line. In his goddam fucking shoes.' He pulled Frank off of the wall. 'So, you stop thinking with you fucking dick. Start being a fucking soldier.'

Shoving him out the door of the villa. Drench of sunlight, everything brilliant lemon-white. The heat was flooding under his shirt. Head thumping. A mix of rapid movement and time slowing down, so that when he looked in vain for the captain's jeep, the hard yellow light tricked him into thinking it was still parked up. But it wasn't. Frank watched the cloud of dust moving on the road out of camp. Taking her away. He kept on watching, staring at the sun until his eyes burned. Then went to find some light-skinned black boys.

Chapter Fifteen

The americano said he'd drop Vita near Mozzano. Beyond were German lines, German snipers. The jeep sped through a blasted landscape, lines of sunlight washing over ruins; no longer meadow or mountain, but carcass. The trucks and trails of mules moving on it were like ants. Forward and back, forward and back. She was a piece of driftwood, buffeted by the steady, far thuds of bombs.

The americano wore thick sunglasses, stared resolutely forwards. Vita had already agreed to take their little black box home. He had no need to charm her any more, and she had no desire to talk.

She had seen what Nazis did to her father. What did they do to women?

She should never have left Barga. Vita had lived through four years of war. It felt like a hundred. It was forever men who thought they held all the cards. Men who marched and shot and starved people, while women waited to be saved. That's what they thought, behind their sunglasses and their swastikas. Well, maybe she wanted to take their radio. Maybe she wanted to do more than wait for others to decide her fate. Or her mother's.

Had that boy been part of their charm offensive? Francesco, who was the saint who loved animals. He was beautiful, smooth like a film star. He was the only soldier she'd met who smelled of soap instead of sweat. Chestnut-hard when she brushed against him.

She let her eyes shut. When she stood on the highest branch of her tree at La Limonaia and dropped her body forward to catch the next branch, there was a single, glorious point in air where neither feet nor hands were on any solid thing. You were entirely held by sky; it caused your skin to fizz away from itself, your blood to crackle as your belly rose, voluptuous.

Francesco. She had wanted him to drive her to Barga, and he had wanted to, Vita was sure. He had looked at her in a way she did not think possible.

They reached a small river, a row of floats strung across the current. On top was a series of planks bobbing from one bank to the other. The stumps of a previous bridge stood alongside; ghost-limbs. The contraption swayed as they drove across.

'OK, ma'am.' The americano's voice was loud. 'I can take you no further, capeesh?'

The reek of smoke hung everywhere. The view was unfamiliar. High, wooded hills ahead, with stone houses clustered on the sides, but it wasn't anywhere she recognised.

'Where is this? I thought I was going to Borgo a Mozzano?'

'No can do. Full of Bosch. No way we can cross the Serchio.'

'How no? Ponte della Maddalena is still standing.'

The soldier looked blank. 'What's "stawnin"?'

'*Standing.* When I came past.'

'It's not safe. You'll get yourself killed if you go back that way. See over there?' He pointed further up the hillside to a church tower, surrounded by roofless ochre houses, serrated against the bright blue sky. 'That's Pescaglia. Our guys took it earlier today. This is as far north as I can go. Keep going east into the hills, and you'll be OK. You can find a way to cross the river further on.'

Vita's eyes smarted. She needed to be home. Mamma was half-demented; she could say or do any number of things, would stand up to a battalion of Nazis if she thought they'd wronged her. What if Vita got lost? She only knew the way from Mozzano.

The soldier tapped the black suitcase. 'Remember. Find a man called Tiziano and give this to him. Or, better still, Captain Bob. You got that?'

'*Sì*. Tiziano or Bob.'

'Better take this too.' He passed Vita a piece of paper, stamped with a red cross.

'I'm a driver?'

'Sure. Just write your name on the line. Means if you break curfew you got an excuse.'

'Do I no need a motor for it to work?'

'Jeez, I don't know, lady. I'm trying to help you. Find one of those – what you call 'em? Misery cords?'

'*Misericordia.*'

'Yeah. Ride in one of them, they'll let you go anyplace. Even Krauts don't blow up the Red Cross.'

The paper hung in Vita's hand.

'You don't wanna help?' He raised his sunglasses onto the top of his head. 'Man, you people. It's your goddam country.'

Her teeth caught the inside of her lip. Tugging the skin, but not breaking it.

'You gotta distribute these too.' He handed her the knapsack from the backseat.

'Where?'

'Anyplace you can. Trains, cafés. Just don't get caught, OK?'

'*Sì.*'

'Good girl.' He patted her bottom as she got out of the jeep. Vita froze, her knuckles stuck to the door. She fought the urge to slam it on his fingers.

'The other one. How come your pal called him that name?'

'What name?'

'Nigger. Is not a good word. Why do you call him that if he's one of you?'

''Cause that's what he is. Don't you go getting any ideas about our niggers. Just 'cause we dress 'em up in uniform, don't make them one of us.' The soldier unrolled a stick of *cingomma*, popped it in his mouth. 'Gum?'

'No.'

'OK. Well, I gotta go. Good luck.'

Vita watched the nape of the man's neck beneath his crew cut, how the bands of flesh jiggled as the jeep drove away. Her chest felt packed with jangly fragments. If she didn't walk carefully, they would pierce her.

The climb to Pescaglia was gradual. As she reached the foot, the track split. Long columns of smoke drifted from the blackened town. Clouds were forming over the forest-clad slopes. Harvest time was always changeable: a tang of rust in the air, then a squall could rush from nowhere. Vita moistened her lips, trying to get the taste of smoke from her mouth. She avoided entering Pescaglia, kept the sun behind her. If it was going west, then she was going east.

Insistent birds called across the valley. Walking on the open track, the sharpness in her chest increased. She felt as if she were travelling naked. She hoped Frank would tell Nonna where she was going. He would, though. He would. A quiet and foolish thrill ran through her. Imagine walking out with someone as beautiful as that. At passeggiata, hearing swishes as folk spun on their heels, their hard-clipped comments delivered sotto voce. Imagine not giving *un fico secco* for what they said. Perhaps if a man gazed on you like that, like you were made of gold, then you wouldn't care. Perhaps.

The rush of being drawn down a long alley – had she imagined the pull? Bracken tore her stockings. She had trusted that beautiful boy, trusted the sparkling feeling he'd given her, and he had led her to rude, pink-necked soldiers.

The hillside was a web of faint tracks. She kept to the widest path, swinging round one tree trunk, then another. Came to another junction, where a concrete bunker stood like a little mountain chapel. There was an unglazed slit at the front, just wide enough to look through. Deserted. It stank of urine. One upturned chair and a metal tripod within. She'd seen tedeschi rest their machine guns on tripods like that. A rubber hose was coiled on the ground. If you could make zoccoli out of old tyres, you could do something useful with that.

'Hoi!'

A man's voice, yelling in her ear. Flurry of movement; a hard arm coming up and across her neck. No feet, no ground, Vita's legs flailing, trying to kick out behind, but she couldn't get a breath, couldn't get a breath to scream or shout, he was crushing her throat, pulling her arms up higher than they could go, the slit of bunker disappearing, ground looming as she bent forwards, away from the pulling, slamming.

Slamming her head back, into his chin. It was the last thing she remembered doing.

Vita woke with a splitting headache. Eyes down, on weirdly clasped hands. Her wrists were bound in front of her, but it was a limp, half-hearted effort. A square of moonlight shone on the earthen floor. A man said, 'She's awake.'

She turned her head towards the noise. Bright shaft of pain. Feet shuffling.

'Who did this?' It was a woman's voice. She pulled the rope loose, started yelling. Lots of yelling, the man joining in. At least they weren't Germans. Vita felt more floaty than scared.

'Can I get a drink?'

'That depends. Zippo here thinks you're a spy. Are you a spy?'

Vita craned up at the woman. About Renata's age. Hair scrunched under a headscarf; thick, black brows. Fists also scrunched. Wiping her nose with the back of her hand.

'Why? Are you?' There were three of them: the woman, a man with crusted blood around his mouth and an older man. Both males sported beards. 'Why did you tie me up?'

'Just, you broke my brother's nose.'

'He grabbed me!'

'Well, what are you doing here?'

Vita looked around her. 'Where's my stuff?'

'You mean the radio transmitter? Ah, well, see, we had to requisition that.'

'Give it back!' Vita got to her feet. Nobody stopped her. 'It's not for you. I've to pass it on. Who even are you?'

'Pass to who?'

Fumbling for the name. 'Tiziano?'

The three of them sniggered. 'That useless prick? Nah. It'll definitely be safer here.'

'We need it in Barga.'

'Says who?'

'The americani.'

'You working for them?'

'I'm not working for anyone. My mamma's been arrested by tedeschi. I need to get to her.' There was her knapsack, bundled in a corner. No suitcase.

'What for?' The woman poured water into a wooden cup.

'Helping my papà escape.'

'And did he? Escape?'

'I don't know.'

'Where have they taken her?'

'Castelnuovo. I think. I don't know. Look, I was in Lucca, now I need to get back to Barga. An americano gave me a lift. In exchange, he asked me to take the radio to some man called Tiziano, and that's what I'm doing, right? He says they need it to "communicate across the lines".'

'We already do,' said the woman. 'Without americani help. We do it every day.'

'Good for you. You won't need my transmitter then, will you?'

'Sit down and shut up.' The woman shoved her. Vita shot her hand out, landed heavily. A judder went up her forearm, reigniting the pain in her skull.

'Maybe we'll keep you. Use you for a prisoner exchange.'

She tucked her hands into her armpits. 'A prisoner exchange? Me? Yeah, swap me for what?'

'I'm not joking. This is not a game. I have lost a brother, a husband.' The woman squatted. 'And these.' She splayed her left hand on the floor. Gaps where her index and middle fingers should be. 'So if you're stupid enough to wander in here with gear we need, you really think we're going to ask permission to take it?'

'What if we need it more?' Vita was shocked; she couldn't look away from the absence of those fingers. 'I thought Pescaglia had been liberated. Are we not on the same side?'

'How do I know which side you're on? What's your credentials?'

'Credentials? My name's Vittoria Guidi. I'm eighteen years old. I just want to get home. Find my mother and hand over the transmitter like I was asked.'

'But who asked you?'

'I don't know. Some American soldier. At the army camp in Lucca.'

'Why were you in Lucca?' said the younger man.

'To see my nonna.'

'Did you take anything with you?'

'Apart from my sister and a bike, no.'

'And you left your sister there?' said the woman.

'Well... yes. Surely it's safer there than in Barga?'

'You tell me. How involved are you with the resistence there?'

'I'm not. God, I'm just a girl. What can I do?'

The older man laughed, a nervy, clipped-off noise that jangled against the concrete walls. He and the other one shuffled out as the woman stood up. Vita braced herself to be struck again.

'You're right. You have tits. What could you do, except make babies and pasta?' She waved her arm. 'Except, how about sabotage? Recruitment? Hiding weapons, running a safe house? Sending messages, taking observations, creating false papers, moving prisoners of war?' As she spoke, the woman held up her disfigured hand. 'One tip. Don't salvage detonators from German hand grenades. They tend to go off while being dismantled.'

She topped up the water from the jug. Offered it to Vita. She smelled earthy, as if the fresh air was inside her skin.

'I'm Dina, by the way.'

'Thank you. Look, Dina, I have to go. I'm terrified what they might do to my mamma.'

'It's not my name, you know. It's short for La Dinamitarda.'

'Dynamiter. Nice.'

She sat beside Vita. 'If you're going to be a partisan, you need a nickname. For security. If you make notes, use the radio, whatever. Give your real name and you're dead. Your family too.'

'Why do it then? If it's so dangerous?' Again, Vita was drawn to that terrible, glamorous gap in the woman's hand.

Dina pulled her knees into her chest. 'You know how you're feeling about your mamma, your papà? You want to kill someone, don't you? And that anger will give you the strength to do what you need to do.'

'But that's my own family. You're risking your life to help people you don't even know.'

'What are you doing now? You don't need to take that radio to reach your mother. The americani will never know.'

'I suppose not.'

'It's a choice that's been made for you. By them.' Dina's eyes shone. 'Who have you lost already? Even if you do nothing, you'll still lose more people, more places. So what are we preserving, if we don't fight? The old Italy has gone.' She took a long draught from the jug. 'This Tiziano. You know where to find him?'

'I'm not sure. Maybe in the forest?'

'Well, don't go looking.' Wiping her mouth. 'Tedeschi search for partisans in the mountains all the time. You've seen the low-flying planes? They're spotters – though they'll machine-gun you too, if they think you're worth it. Make straight for where your partisans are, carrying your little case, and you'll be waving a flag at the enemy. Best to get a message out, have them come to you.'

'You saying I can have my little case then?'

Dina laid her hand on Vita's back. 'You can, amica mia. As long as you let me find another case to put it in. Better to look like a refugee than a spy.'

It took Vita most of the night to get to Barga. Dina and her brothers walked with her for a while, taking turns to carry the suitcase. The battered beige was less suspicious. Plenty of laden folk trudged Italy now; a river of refugees carrying entire worlds with them.

'We've work to do,' said Dina, when they left her. 'And so have you. Night-time is our friend. And remember: my call sign is La Dinamitarda. If you need help from the south, just give me a shout.' She hugged her. 'Viva l'Italia.'

Vita continued walking, using the North Star as a guide. Occasionally, she'd stop and rest, but only until she felt herself drifting. To be discovered sleeping would be fatal, give her no chance to collect herself. Already, too much time had passed since Mamma was arrested. Up and down the twisting paths, pebbles spitting into her zoccoli so often she gave up trying to fish them out. She learned to move her toes and heels till the pebbles slipped unnoticed, into or away from her flesh. Gradually, she stopped feeling anything; not her feet, legs, her blistered suitcase-lugging hands. Numbness overtook the chill of mountain air, and the vague, unspecific fear gnawing in her gut. She kept warm by thinking of the americano, imagining that he was watching her, approving each time she stumbled and righted herself. It made you warm to have a face like that in your mind.

Dawn seeped. Her bones less cold. Slow, slow, the landscape shifted black to grey, from opaque to veiled to radiant. The sun rose on a place she finally recognised! She could see Monte Forato. Her breath made clouds, joining the morning mists as the way ahead yawned on and on. Finally, she began to descend, the far eye of Forato watching.

She followed the Serchio until she found a spindly footbridge. Far across and up, she could see the Duomo's square tower clinging to the hill. A burst of energy quickened her feet until she were almost running. The suitcase barged and battered her shins; she would be covered in bruises, but it didn't matter. She was nearly home!

Once, a circus had set up in the gorge below the old town. Clowns and jugglers, all of it stunning, but it was the tightrope walkers that amazed Vita, their teetering-running-burst to safety just at the end, and the sigh of the crowd in relief. She ran like this now, into Barga, began to package her adventure, how she would spin the tale. First, she would go to the Monsignor, have him speak to Generale Utimperghe. Maybe even go to Castelnuovo himself. Yes, she'd plead with him to go straight there. What an idiot, to leave her fate in others' hands. Papà would never have abandoned her mother, and she would have to be Papà now. Mamma was fragile underneath. Vita would protect her, for all those years her mother had protected her. Even the city itself; she wanted to throw her arms round Barga's walls, because she'd seen what might be coming.

She climbed Via dei Frati, entered the old town by Porta Reale. There were others moving through the streets: a carter and his mule, a woman setting lemons on a tatty piece of cloth. Curfew must be over. She took the vicolo that led towards the Canonica. Safe within the stones of Barga. The alley, bending and narrowing to deeper shade, then a reassuring streak of sunshine, marking the opening of a wider street. She wanted to kiss the walls. Breathing hard, heaving her awkward suitcase with the knapsack stuffed inside. One last, confined set of steps. At the final turn of the stairs, Vita stopped. Directly in front of her was an armoured vehicle. A squad of fascisti had positioned a machine gun in the middle of the street.

Panic slithering, stomach to spine.

They were stopping folk. Asking to see their papers. Vita faltered, her feet iron weights. She was visible, too late to slip away; if she turned, retraced her steps... She couldn't make her feet move forwards. Fumbling for a grip on her suitcase. Trying to catch herself. They would find the transmitter. Even newspapers would get her arrested. One static second became two. Gritted teeth, her fist tight round the handle of the suitcase. Not scared. Tell yourself you're not scared. She continued to walk towards the fascisti. Casually. Unquickening her step. Right hand. Palm up. 'Eja! Eja! Alala, boys.' A cheeky wink.

The soldiers grinned. One doffed his cap, another whistled as she sauntered past. 'Ciao, bella.' They stopped the man who came after her, a poor protesting soul, but Vita did not look back or break stride, did not run though every sinew was screaming *get away*. Dry mouth. Wet eyes. Blinking, blurring, walking through her town like it was spiked with landmines, with spectres that would pounce from every door. Just one more street and she'd be safe. No harm could come to you in the Canonica.

'*Oof.* Watch where you're going.' The voice was gruff. Familiar.

'Nico?'

The old man took off his spectacles. 'What are you doing here? I thought you were in Lucca?'

'I was. Nico. My mamma's been arrested.' The tears broke, properly then. Nicodemo put his arm round her.

'I know, I know.'

'I need to speak to the Monsignor.'

'You can't. Not now.'

'But it's an emergency. I don't know what they'll do to her.'

'Vittoria. The Monsignor is with the generale right now.' Nico glanced behind him. 'There're spies everywhere. The Monsignor knows, child. Things are very urgent. Go home, sì? He's doing what he can. But if we ask, we don't get, you understand? It's all changing, Vita. Please. Go home.' His bony fingers held her wrist, drawing her closer. 'With care. Because I know you didn't take that suitcase with you.' He raised his voice. 'Father will be sorry to hear you are ill. He'll come to give you comfort when he can.' Nodding once, in dismissal.

The suitcase felt hot in her hand. She turned from the promise of kind words and weak soup that had been sustaining her, on through the old town, down to the crossroads and up the path that led to Catagnana. To La Limonaia, which would be empty.

It was. Shutters shut, no life inside. The Pieris' doors were closed too. Smokeless chimney. Down below, old Sergio's house was also shuttered. It would rain soon. Who would organise the harvest? Who would crush the olives and grapes? Across the valley, the Duomo bells chimed nine. She took the spare key from under the lemon pot on the terrace. The kitchen was cold; no heat to the stove, no bread smells in the air. The table, scrubbed and clean. Mamma might have marched off to fight the Nazis, but she'd washed her dishes first. Vita walked from room to room. Leaf-shadows flickering on the walls, that intermittent light her tree gifted to the rear of their house. All the beds were made. Mamma had put fresh sheets on them all. Upstairs, on top of Cesca's bed, she had arranged her dolls, which had been Vita's, in a neat row.

The lack of life inside the house was unbearable. Mamma was its ticking heart. The girls had outer realms of school and woods and light, Papà his workshop. Mamma was food and bustle; she was the fire in the hearth, the tongue that lashed you into shape, and, yes, she went to market, she went to the Massaie Rurali, she went to church, but all these things were distractions from the business of being here. Of literally being home.

Vita went into her parents' bedroom. Lay on the quilted counterpane. Patches of wedding dress and smocked baby rompers, the blue silk thread that bound each carefully shaped fragment in a pattern of hexagonal blooms. At the outer edges it remained calico, waiting for new threads to be stitched. She wanted so much to crawl into those crisp, bleached sheets, just pull the covers over her head and make the world go away. Sleep would not be helpful. Neither would pulling the ends of Mamma's shawl across her face. Just five minutes. Then she would be refreshed.

Vita woke some time after noon, wrapped in twisted sheets and sweat. The fronds of a dream tugged at her. There'd been a high barred window; Mamma's face tight against the bars. The point of her chin protruded through slices of metal, Vita could see it still, cutting the thinness of her mother's flesh. Could hear the voice telling her: *Leave some light with your mamma.*

In the kitchen, she went to start a fire. Wash first, then food, then she'd work out how to get a message to the partigiani. Joe would have known what to do. Maybe the partigiani could get a message to him. If Joe came home, then she wouldn't be alone.

That wasn't a reason to want him.

She reached for the matches. Felt guilt creep. She was thinking of the americano again. He was like a song lodged in her head. She blew the remains of the ash into a pile. Underneath, balled in the grate, was a letter. Vita recognised those bold loops and lines of blue. It was Nonna Lucca's writing. She pulled it out.

Dearest Elena,

I write this with the best of intentions, although you rarely appreciate the wisdom of my counsel. But in this I cannot be silent. Your notion of removing Vittoria from school is most wrong-headed. She is clearly a bright girl. And while it is true that bearing children is the foremost duty of any fascista woman, it is not always the most fulfilling. There is no shame in a mother having education, indeed there is much benefit from it. Perhaps if you had been more attentive to your studies and refined your thoughts, then you would have considered your own marriage prospects

Here, it stopped; the paper torn and browned. She wondered what her mother's reply had been. Carefully, Vita folded the remains of the page, to be used in evidence. For a brief, beautiful moment, she allowed herself to think of a day when her future might be discussed again, the family sitting at this table. Mamma flicking her apron at Papà, Cesca squabbling—

She sensed movement, the kitchen window darkening. Saw the profile of a person, watching her.

'Who's there?'

Flinging the door open, and, as it was slamming into the wall, thinking she should be locking it instead. An unknown man stood on the step, his hand outstretched.

'Vittoria? Don't be alarmed. You have something for me?'

She did not invite him but he came in anyway, slipping round the door and closing it. Vita's first impression was mostly hair: big, tangled beard, sheepskin gilet, long tresses under a knitted cap. Bare, furred legs beneath knee-length shorts. Red shorts. He bore a shepherd's crook, and a rifle tucked inside his gilet.

'Who are you? Who told you to come here?' She tried to fill the room with her voice.

'A mutual friend.' He raised his cap. The centre of his head was bald.

'What friend?'

The man smiled an apology. 'You have a delivery? A suitcase?'

He spoke very formally; even in her distraction, Vita realised he wasn't Italian. British? She switched to English. 'Tell me who you are first. You Tiziano?'

'Ah! A fellow Brit! No, dear. I'm not Tiziano. I'm his boss, so to speak. Captain Bob, at your service.'

'In they shorts? Aye, well, I'm the Queen of Sheba.'

'Indeed. Actually, your countrymen call me *Capitano Chiavapecore*. Strong sheep-man. Because of my fleece?'

Vita felt her face go hot. She didn't say anything, for fear she'd be obliged to explain that, while 'pecore' did indeed mean sheep, unfortunately, 'chiava' meant fucker.

230

'If I could possibly get that transmitter?'

'What is in it for me?'

'Beg pardon?'

She had slept for only a handful of hours. Her family was torn and scattered; she was hungry, scared, but more than that, she was furious at this oddity standing in her kitchen. To flash your bare knees like that; him, a grown man. It just seemed very rude.

'You need something. I need something. My mother's been jailed. My papà too. They've got them in Castelnuovo. If I give you the transmitter, you could help. Arrange a prisoner exchange?'

What Dina said partisans did.

'Or,' said the capitano, 'I could hit you across the face with my rifle, break all your teeth and take the transmitter anyway. Stopping only to torch your house as I leave.'

Her stomach shrank. If she spoke on her out-breath, her voice would remain steady.

'And why would you do that?'

The relish of his violence, how he flicked from benign to menacing; it was a smooth, practised thing. The way she'd seen Papà crack his rifle, lift-aim-fire, and then smile again, and be Papà. Men did that when they had weapons, as if their skin slipped off.

'Why indeed? Because that just would not be cricket, dear, would it? Nor would you playing funny buggers with me. So, where is it, please?'

'Case.'

'Beg pardon? Speak up, there's a good lassie.'

'In the suitcase. In the front room.'

'Jolly good. I'll just go and fetch it, shall I?'

She shrugged. Hotness under her skin, in her eyes. Clenching her fists; she was an impotent joke. The man returned in seconds.

'Cheerio then. Take it those newspapers are mine too?'
He secreted everything inside his gilet. You could probably secrete a sheep in there. She felt his gaze land, briefly,
on her.

'Plucky thing, aren't you?'

'I'm gonny ask you again. Please will you help? My
papà, he was taken in the *rastrellamento*.'

'The men from here? Oh, they've already been sent to
Germany, dear.'

The floor tilted. Vita dug her fingernails deeper into
her palms. She could see the hazy ghost of her nose, of her
top lip as she swallowed.

'What about my mother? Her name's Elena—'

Captain Bob was checking out the window. He wasn't
really listening to her.

'Elena Guidi. She was arrested for kicking a German
soldier. I think she might have bitten him too—'

'Guidi, you say? Is Guidi your name?' The capitano
swivelled. Smiled at her, and it was a horrible smile, it
was the most horrible face of the several faces he'd already
used, standing in her kitchen. Because it was real. Gentle.
He was being sad, she could see sadness in his mouth and
eyes; in the extension of his arm as he touched her, so that
when he finally spoke, it was as if she'd already known
what he would say.

'Oh, my dear. I'm so sorry. Has nobody told you? Elena
Guidi was shot this morning. Just after nine, I believe.
They always hold their executions at nine.'

Chapter Sixteen

By the time the light rose fully, it was done. Smoke could be seen from miles away; it might have been chimney smoke. Or a bonfire. Or dust as the Panzergrenadiers rolled out.

All summer, the refugees had followed the hard mountain light. Old women, scared Jews. Babes in arms and children who could barely toddle, yet knew, instinctively, to be quiet. Hundreds of them, gathering in remote hamlets, trudging there on jagged roads which veered to the plunging edge and back. Far in the distance, a flash of sea. Viareggio was somewhere on that winding coastline. Older folk could remember trips there: looming promenades and art nouveau hotels.

Air-dropped leaflets littered the tracks. Full of exclamation marks. *People of Italy! Help us help you! Work with us to block the Bosch retreat! The Allies have got your back!*

La Resistenza handed them out. Men who knew the land, knew the locals; they could melt and drift like clouds. But they needed the folk around them too, for food, shelter, bandages, eyes. They needed people's donkeys to tote their makeshift bombs; they needed women to walk through a German patrol, fuse wire hidden in their skirts. At the very least, they needed trust.

But Kesselring was clear. All resistance was to be punished.

Kesselring. A sharp sting of a word, which caught in people's throats like phlegm. The steady summerlight shone on other leaflets. *Traitors will be shot. Earth will be scorched. Ten Italians will die for every German killed.*

Each cluster of hilltop towns had their band of partisans, and the folk who lived alongside. All that summerlight and weeping rain, turning on the earth as three thousand souls were slaughtered. Why would Sant'Anna be any different? Joe had thought it would. Why? Because it was beautiful and remote, clefted in the rock? Because the light was so high here it might have shone from God Himself?

The light had tumbled over the 16th SS Panzergrenadiers all summer, as they mopped up partigiani. It shone with them along the Gothic Line, the Apuan Alps, the Versilia hills. And it stared unblinking as the partisans fought back. With every indignity that was inflicted, why would you not? But the Nazis were so efficient, they went beyond being men of their word, and the light rose wearily on a day that required no German deaths at all, to provoke a massacre.

On a soft summer morning, four columns of Panzergrenadiers marched up the mountain to Sant'Anna di Stazzema. They arrived at first light. Villagers fired a flare to signal the usual unwelcome guests: folk hid their grain, took the animals inside. Some men and boys fled to the woods. It would be another rastrellamento. Because you don't get reprisals for a thing you haven't done.

Ah, but Kesselring was canny. Why wait for a partisan strike at all? If you have no villagers to shield the partisans, you have no village from which an ambush might be launched. Why had they not thought of this earlier? It seemed that retreat and the high mountain air were clarifying German minds.

The Nazis arrived in Sant'Anna, and were brisk. In the climbing morning sun, they shot dead everyone they encountered. Rounding them up into barns: villagers, refugees, the old, the tiny. It didn't matter. They killed in batches: machine-gunning groups once they'd herded them in. Grenades were tossed in cellars, homes set alight. Entire families butchered. More than a hundred souls gathered outside the church. Parishioners on their knees, praying. The sore mountain light poured on the priest, pleading with the soldiers to kill him and spare his flock. He was first to die. Point-blank, before the soldiers turned their machine guns on the rest.

Babies died that morning. Eight pregnant women. The bodies were piled in a heap. More than five hundred bodies. Pews were ripped from the church to make a funeral pyre. And then the soldiers sat in the sun to have their lunch.

Light bled on executed dogs, pigs, an old donkey. It bled on scattered brooches, on trinkets and wedding rings and toys and photographs. Mostly photographs, which people had held to their breasts when they knew they were to die. If the light could have shone on their words, it would have filled the skies with *Remember me*. Instead, the light burnished a gold-branched candlestick, lying in the dust. It gilded the Panzergrenadiers as they finished their eating and their burning, and rolled efficiently onwards and down.

No birds sang at Sant'Anna. Puzzled light broke through palls of smoke that lay in every pleat of sky, in every crease of earth. Illuminating unhuman humps with half-hearted covers of rags, placed there when the men returned from their hiding places.

Light touched the men as they wept and knelt and lifted their loved ones up and dug out their grief and the light blazed on, baking them, tempering liquid to silt, tempering grief to blocks of square and solid rage. They dragged the animal carcasses from the human. Strong light shone in their eyes as they cut down partisan bodies hanged from trees, friends of theirs – and strangers too, some foreign boys who had come to help. When the sun was as high as it could go, an old man brought blood-warm wine. They drank it in the shade, backs turned on the mass of earth. Some grimaced, although the wine was good. Light cast the shadow of each man as he slugged it back. Wiped his mouth. Picked up his spade. Began again, until all the bodes were underneath the soil. There was no priest to bless them, but he was in there with them, and maybe that was blessing enough.

The blue Alps soared, endlessly catching the sun. The light had run to the highest mountain. Where else was there to go?

Chapter Seventeen

Overnight, the rains came. That dense, dark scud above the mountains which told you summer was done. Yes, it might be warm again, you could get lovely autumns in the Garfagnana, but the sun was no longer a given. From this point, every day would be changeable; the rains would lead to snow and sharp-toothed winds. The quality of light would lose its lustre, blue thickening to grey, with no flicker to it.

Only afterwards was it that Vita noticed. How a piece of her died with her mother.

When war began, it was the whisper of the untouched. Whenever you saw a family read the noticeboards, see their son's name and dissolve. *How can they bear it?* Now, almost every Tuscan had been visited by death. It was true, what Dina had said. To keep going was just a reflex. The bearing, the coping, wasn't brave. It was an alternative to dying.

The Nazis refused to let them have the body. Vita was denied the right to bathe her mother, to dress her in her finest clothes. The Monsignor travelled to Castelnuovo, to plead that Elena Guidi might be allowed to come home.

He was directed to a patch of new-dug earth in the back-yard of the police station. *Our apologies, Father. But you see, it really is not possible.*

Vita cried for Mamma until there were no tears left. Sick and thirsty, she'd fall asleep for a few hours, then wake, and the well would be full and she'd cry again. Hollow bones, hollow heart. Those first days were a blur; it was still a blur now, but in the blunt immediacy of the pain, Vita padded herself with doubt. If she hadn't seen Mamma, then perhaps she was not dead. It was a wicked tale; it was someone else's mamma. The Monsignor tried to send word to Lucca, but the route was now blocked; even to priests.

'We have to tell Cesca.'

'I know, child, I know.'

He took Vita to the Canonica, ensconced her in the little room that had been Devora's once, before Vita replaced her. Some days he brought Sister Cristina or Mother Virginia, who fussed and made her drink cloudy tisanes. Other days he stayed with her himself. Those were the days when she wept the hardest. He would sit, worry-ing the folds of his neck. 'I did everything in my power, Vita. I begged Utimperghe, I met with the German commander—'

They felt like stories he was telling to console himself.

'Will they kill my father too?' It was better to know these things than imagine them.

'No. They're to work as builders, I believe, or in agri-culture. I'm sure your papà will be on a farm, with his experience. And when the war is finished, he'll come home. Here.' He offered Vita some kind of torta. He kept tempting her with sweetmeats. 'This is good. They call it strudel.'

'They?'

'The Germans.'

'You mean murderers.' She handed the pastry back. 'An eye for an eye, Monsignor. Do you believe that?'

'I think of you the way I would a daughter, if that had been allowed to me.' Succumbing to the strudel, taking dainty bites between sentences. 'I hope you are not contemplating doing anything stupid.'

'Yes, Father. I mean, no, Father.'

He looked at her obliquely. 'It will end soon, child. The Allies are almost here.'

She believed him. The roar of artillery was constant, coming from the mountains of Pescaglia. The paths Vita had walked were impassable, which meant any chance of reaching Cesca was gone. People like Dina still lived and fought in those hills. Even if they dodged the bombs, they couldn't escape the terrible noise.

Three weeks after they murdered her mother, the Nazis opted for a show of grace. Without warning, a horse and cart arrived at the Canonica. Vita was scrubbing the doorstep; the repetitive movements soothed her. She straightened, watched the driver deposit one passenger – a bent old man, nothing but skin and bone – and a roll of carpet, which the driver shoved unceremoniously from the end of the cart. The old man screamed obscenities; the driver shrugged, then pushed him into the mud too.

Vita went to help him. The man was Sergio. Confused, dirty. Unable to do much except press a tiny object into Vita's hands. She looked down, saw the slight and endless circle of an iron wedding band. *For you. She said for you.* Then Vita noticed the sweet stench bloating the air. The carpet had unrolled slightly to reveal a hand. Oval-shaped fingernails hanging.

She didn't recall much more.

They buried Mamma the next day. They had no choice. As usual, it was raining. They walked through mud and distant guns, down to the camposanto. Set low, slightly apart from the town, it was its own village of statues and tombs and crosses which grew like trees. Vita saw only blanks and hardnesses. The nuns had filled Mamma's rough coffin with sweet rosemary and thyme. Vita walked behind in a borrowed black coat. Renata and Rosa, and women from the Massaie Rurali followed. Sergio was too weak; he'd gone to a cousin in Diecimo. But he'd told her how Mamma had followed the rastrellamento. How she'd kicked and bitten her way into the police station. Only old, weak men had seen her fight, though. Papa – indeed, all the strong ones – were already gone.

There was no horse to draw the bier, so Signor Nutini and his grandson from the bakery pulled the load. Shelling from the mountains was heavy, and the Monsignor suggested they go straight to the cemetery. He would still do all the proper Latin prayers. But no bells. Bells drew attention to you.

'Your mother wouldn't want you to be hurt.'

Vita's veil hung over her eyes, limiting her vision. She could only see fragments. Deep shadows cast by gravestones. A rope of muscle on a hand, bulging as the coffin was swung. A long black hole and a pile of mud. The bright tip of Nicodemo's patient spade. Rain that was kind and whispery on her cheeks. A crazed and wounded animal in her breast. You couldn't see that one, not till you closed your eyes. The bend and crick of her knee, the damp cloy of the earth she flung. The black line rimmed there afterwards. The ever-present thud of war.

You would drown if you kept weeping.

The dullness in Vita was quiet. Static. Every day, she walked in the garden of the Conservatorio, the paths and lawns where schoolgirls once played, given over to vegetable beds and barrels to catch rain. The rain ran down her hair, her neck. It was the saturating type, that Joe would call smirr. She liked its gentleness on her face. Damp felt kind. She missed her family, missed the comfort of home. Who was comforting her sister, stranded with Nonna Lucca? Part of her prayed the Monsignor's messages would not get through. She should be the one to tell Cesca. This, all of this, was her fault. If Joe had not defended her—

Stupid, stupid Joe. She had *told* him not to.

Oh, this fluid, guilty rage she felt. She beamed it like a lighthouse. Daily, the nuns invited her to pray. Daily, she declined. *I am too angry, Mother*, she would whisper. You could say that to Mother Virginia.

The nuns set her little tasks: sorting clothes for the refugees, mending altar cloths. Dusting, again. Taking clean linens to a labouring mother – there was a panic, Sister Agatha was already there. Sulphuric smells, her bloodied hands seizing the basket of cloths, not allowing Vita through the door. Life and death, how quickly it blurred. Dissolving like water into land.

Linen delivered, Vita continued walking, down to the crossroads in Barga. It felt good to be away from priests and nuns. As usual, L'Alpino was packed with tedeschi. Frequently, it was a raucous place to pass, especially if the commandant was playing the piano. No more genteel trumpet concerts, this was wild saloon music. *Plenty oom-pa-pa*, the barghigiani laughed. But it was a false, glazed laughter, and most women avoided going that way at night. Today, they were using the bar as some sort of command post. The tables had been dragged together, a series of maps laid on top, weighted with ashtrays. A string of lorries was parked on the verge, with cabling piled on the flatbeds. Every so often, teams of soldiers would march up and run a big skein of cable from one of the drums. Others carried off wooden crates. Three women stood under the big tree by the crossroads, surveying the action. One of them was Signora Nardini, her mother's erstwhile friend. Arms folded, they were talking animatedly.

'How can they do this? We've been so hospitable.' It was an old lady from Piazza Angelio speaking, Vita forgot her name. The third woman was her spinster daughter, Angela, named imaginatively for the square in which she lived. Angela ran the Piccole Italiane when Vita was a little girl, drilling them daily with gusto. Always a bitterness about the woman; even her enthusiasms were grim.

'Exactly. We've caused them no harm – and this is how they repay us.' Angela spat on the ground. Then she saw Vita, and the three of them whipped their heads round. Paused in their gossip, the word *traditrice* unspoken on their lips. Folk thought her mother was a traitor. Good fascist women did not get themselves shot by Nazis – no matter the provocation. The Guidi name had developed all the dark glamour of Dina's missing fingers. Vita remembered then, why she stayed with priests and nuns.

Defiantly, she joined them. 'What? What is it they're doing?'

'Mining the bridges. That one's a sapper.' Signora Nardini elongated this new word.

'Why?'

'To blow them up, of course. All of 'em.'

'It's a farewell gift. Bloody swine.' Angela spat again.

'That's not fair. They have to do it,' said Signora Nardini. 'To stop the Allies following them.'

'Are the tedeschi leaving?'

'Officer!' Signora Nardini ignored Vita, calling to a blackshirt, who was also observing the Germans. 'Officer. Are they really going to blow them all?'

'Afraid so. It's getting worse every day.' He gave a sad smile.

'How "worse"?' said Angela's mother.

Like children grasping sand, as their prizes slipped away, the Nazis were gripping harder. There were whispers in the Conservatorio even, when they thought Vita wasn't listening, of other executions in lonely places – whole villages worth of people, the gossips said. Folk tightening their mouths. Praying the rumours weren't true.

The soldier shook his head and strolled off. *How dare you?* Vita wanted to yell. His pretend sorrow at the coming destruction – the Brigate Nere were facilitating it. They'd worked with the Germans to bring Barga to this state. Chaining her like an animal, and now they were going to hurt her more. Barga without bridges was impossible. The way the town was contoured to the rising land, the gaps and gullies she straddled. Destroying her bridges would not just seal her off from the outside world, it would divide her from herself. From Catagnana to the crossroads, from the Giardino to the Castello walls, and the Arringo beyond, Barga's bridges were her veins.

Vita left the three women, still muttering behind their hands, to walk back to the Conservatorio. Enough of the real world. The outer doors of the church of San Rocco stood open. Music floated out. Across from the church was the red-roofed casa where Sister Agatha was fighting for two lives. The walls of the house ended where the foot-bridge to the old town began. They surely wouldn't mine Ponte Vecchio? No truck could get over it, you could scarce get a mule across, and the gully below was so deep. The destruction of this bridge would just be for spite.

She could see tedeschi engineers working on the next bridge up. Behind that one were the arches of the ancient aqueduct. What about the new one, which pulled the water Barga relied on from the hills? If they wrecked that, the town would go thirsty as well as starve.

She pressed her ear to the inner door. She could hear the Monsignor droning. Despite the heaviness on her, she smiled. He never stopped giving succour to his people. Patches of sky shone in a puddle. A waft of guttural song lifted from the church, out into the piazza. Male voices united in their cause. German voices. The Monsignor was within, giving the Nazis Holy Communion.

The air spun like fraying linen, flickering over her eyelashes. Frequently, her tears came like that, spilling without effort. Folk no longer stopped if you cried. Their grief was finite, and reserved for themselves. She crossed the road, hammered on the door of the red-roofed house. A perspiring Sister Agatha answered. There was a high keening coming from somewhere beyond the hallway.

'Tell the Monsignor... just tell him I'm away. I'm going back to Catagnana.'

Vita turned on her heel. Walked down through the Giardino, in the direction of home. God might not take sides, but she did.

As the houses of Ponte di Catagnana came into view, she saw tedeschi loitering on the bridge; more underneath, making a piercing noise with a drill. She tucked her shawl tighter and strode on, averting her eyes from the decay of Signor Tutto's shop. The men seemed more concerned with leaning over the side of the bridge and pointing. There was no reason not to cross, no roadblock.

It was her bridge. She was almost over before a soldier stopped her.

'Where you are going?'

'Home. Catagnana.'

'Papers.'

She handed him her identity card.

Comune di Barga certifies that the person presented in the photograph below is Vittoria Guidi.

Height, hair, eye colour, address, everything. The man was stripping her with his eyes. 'Fine. Move. And stay on the path.'

'Enjoy the trip,' called another. 'But you must decide if you will stay up or down.'

The drilling ceased. A loud burst of laughter floated after her, as she made her way to La Limonaia.

She sat a while, in the quiet of her empty kitchen. The house was cold and damp, a smell of onions coming from the sink. Her heartbeat felt irregular; too rapid to stay inside her ribcage. She busied herself with chores, stoking the fornelli, cleaning the floor, anything to make the house seem alive.

When dark fell, she went outside. Let her mind dissolve into the vast dome of sky. Thick, blanketing black. That was what she sought. Being up here, away from people, made you feel gone from the world. It was a good, empty feeling. One by one, above La Limonaia, the stars came out. Bursts of distant brilliance. Yesterday and tomorrow, glimmering alive, then dead, and in between, nobody really knowing you. Who you are. Folk seeing the colour of your eyes, your hair. Knowing how tall you were certainly, and if your nose was straight, but not seeing *you*. How could you ever know? It wasn't possible.

The starlight deepened, coming in swirls and milky cascades. She wondered, suddenly, if they shone on the americano; if he was even still alive, and felt a fresh, unexpected gout of fear. She tried to remember what he looked like. To recall that daft, soft pause where she'd thought she was falling, and being caught.

How many had died for this war? All those thousands of dead restless souls – where did they go? Where was her mother? Was she the air Vita breathed? The stars, that stared impervious as the world consumed itself below?

The night grew cold. Vita took herself inside.

Chapter Eighteen

In the morning, Renata came down with some cold polenta. 'I saw smoke. You have to eat.'

'I will.'

'Come to ours tonight, eh? Some of the girls are getting together. Nothing special.'

Vita shook her head.

'I'm glad you're home. That's a good sign, Vita. Life has to go on.'

'I know.'

'Please come to Sommo. It'll do you good.'

'I'll think about it.'

'Alright.' Renata pushed the plate of food towards her. 'But listen – don't veer off the paths. They've been laying mines in the woods.'

All day, Vita waited for the sound of bridges tearing. The Germans must have changed their minds. Perhaps Kesselring was more civilised than other Nazi generals. They'd not blown up Lucca, had they? Under his command. Under his command they'd—

Vita pushed her hands deep into the sink, water breaking across her forearms. She would not go there. A few more days, and the Germans would be gone – then the cowardly Brigate Nere would flee too. Brave *americani* were marching onwards. Men like Francesco. *Frank.* It sounded honest; like biting an apple. All those soldiers she'd seen in Lucca; in days, hours perhaps, they would free Barga, and the war would pass them by. Once more, she tried to remember the americano's face. The image was cloudy. His moustache was clear, the curve of his mouth. And she thought she might recognise his eyes. If they looked at her in that hungry way, then, yes. She would know him again.

She watched her shape move in the window. Was hers a face you would remember? Smudged and dark, she assessed herself. Too thin, too sharp, but her mouth was full. Outside, the trees shimmered. Soon the leaves would fall, and the underwater light of La Limonaia would be done for another year. Winter-bright would come instead, with her chestnut tree a skeleton, and Vita, alone in a house that should be full. She opened the window, and it was as though the evening had been pushing there, desperate to pour in. You could smell the cut of the harvest, the long drill of disturbed earth. The sky, thickening, shifting, and the thought pressed again, of the americano. The girl in the window was tracing her collarbone. Why did he lodge below her breast like this? Joe had never made her feel this way. Not close. But then, Joe was real.

The girl's mouth changed to something soft. Her nipples quickened, hardened. She wondered what happened when men and women lay together, and how it would be if she died untouched, if the liveness inside her simply withered and passed away. Who would she tell of the things inside her head, foolish, lovely things she wanted to share? Who would come for Vita and save her, tear her enemies with their teeth, if she withered here alone?

The damp from her hand settled on her smock. She shook herself into some sense, closed the window. Maybe she should go up to Renata's. She was suddenly hungry; all she'd eaten was that cold polenta. She'd go early though. The tedeschi patrolled at dusk, sniffing like truffle-hounds. Vita put on her zoccoli and donned her shawl.

You could hear the music before you reached Sommocolonia's steps. A badly played fiddle, and raucous singing, coming from the first of the piazzas. Little Giuliano, of course, scraping his bow. The clicking, heel-stamping sound of dancing came. When Vita got to the top of the rampa, she could see the flash and turn of wrists held in the air. This was more than a few girls; the piazza was in full festa mode. She could smell the candy-scent of roasting chestnuts. The dance the village girls were doing – hands low and push, and swoop, then twirl. Had she missed the chestnut harvest? But there they were: baskets of nuts. How was that possible, if you couldn't walk freely in the woods? Platters of mushrooms too, flecked with fresh herbs. And strange, dark bread and a kind of cabbagy salad. Where had all this food come from?

'Oh, you came, Vita! I'm so glad.' Renata was carrying a plate of – Vita wasn't sure. Pale, sliced slugs? 'Come and sit by us.' She pointed to where little Rosa sat with the lady who ran the fruit and vegetable shop.

'Is that sausage?' Vita poked at the dish.

'It's really nice. *Bratwurst*, I think.'

'*Bratwurst*? From them? Are there Germans here?'

'No. Not yet. But there might be a few coming. Don't worry, just the nice ones. You know, the boys who did the concerto, and a few of their mates. We promised we'd show them what a festa was like—'

'*Tedeschi*? How could you?'

'Vita, they've been really generous. Look at all this food. I mean – do you have a problem with me feeding my daughter?'

'But...' Her throat hurt. It didn't feel real; none of this felt real. 'Renata. They shot my mother.'

'*They* didn't. Guards in Castelnuovo did. Might have been Brigate Nere for all we know. Vi, I'm truly sorry about Zia Elena, you know I am.'

'Well, why didn't you stop her then?' she shouted.

'Why didn't you?' Renata shouted back. She shook her head. 'Look, I'm sorry, Vita. But this is war.'

'The Germans took your father-in-law.'

'Yes, and the Allies took my husband. Gianni's in some stinking POW camp, and I'm here. Trying to survive. You seem to forget, Vita, the tedeschi are on our side.'

'Our side?'

Their faces were tight-close, Renata's lips stretched thin and white. 'Yeah, well, with you lot, who knows.'

'What's that meant to mean?'

'You, your dad.' Folk were looking over. 'Bloody Giuseppe too. Just stop pretending, Vita. You can't *be* Scots–Italian. You're either one thing or the other. You not get that? Gesù – do you think they'd have taken half of Barga away if Joe hadn't—'

'Fuck you.' Vita slapped her hand wide; the dish upended. The air was filled with falling bratwurst and a spatter of *Guten Abend* and *Buonasera* as a stream of German soldiers trooped into the piazza. Vita's hand shook; the skin of her fist stretched so fine it shone.

Renata knelt to retrieve the sausage. 'You'd better watch yourself, Vittoria. A foul mouth is never a nice thing in a woman.'

Vita stared round the village square, at the gleeful, breathless dancers, at the German soldiers bearing bottles and cigarettes. She looked at the old women frowning at her; at the kids like Rosa, wide-eyed and sunken-bellied, clamouring for *kuchen*. The familiar felt foreign. The air full of whispers. Mice hiding. Owls arguing, trees crouching at glints of steel.

She took a glass of wine from a table, waited quietly in a corner of Sommocolonia until the rampa was clear of tedeschi. Fifteen or so of them, legs planted wide in chairs dragged from houses to accommodate them or legs akimbo as they stood to survey the dancing girls. A few of them were officers, greatcoats worn casually across shoulders or draped on the backs of chairs. Little Giuliano started up a new tune, and there was a rush to dance. Renata untied her headscarf, shook out her hair. Then, deliberately fixing her eyes on Vita, she extended her hand to one of the slick-haired officers. Formed her mouth into clear, slow words. 'You dance?'

Vita downed the wine. A few empty chairs, piled with coats and hats, blocked the rampa. She pushed them to get past. Blurry smudges of gaberdine and black leather. A gun belt slung underneath. Careless, the way it was left hanging, and who's to say where the actual gun might end up, the brown-handled pistol of an officer who can't even be bothered to secure his weapon, the pistol all sleek and evil, perhaps it wanted to do good and that's why it was shining there, and it was the matter of unthinking seconds to pull her shawl down over the gun belt, unclip the little leather flap and slip out the gun.

Sommocolonia shrank tiny-wee, the pistol burning inside her shawl. This must be what hunters call tunnel vision; this narrowing of the world to a single shaft. One step, two steps. Polished glimmer of a brass lamp swinging; the open door of a house. She saw a soldier touch his moustache and yawn; an awful bustle through the hallway. One poor woman, crying as another soldier dragged her by the hair. A buzzing sound filled Vita's head, and she realised the woman was laughing, not crying, at the soldier untwining his hand from her hair, pouring wine across her unbuttoned breast.

It was like watching Hell. Vita began to run down the steps. In through the trees, away from paths and people. Night was coming, and this was a nightmare. No idea what to do with the pistol scalding her skin. Her feet fell on the hollow woodland floor, twigs snapping and breaking like gunfire. Weaving between the shadows of the trees, balancing on roots and rocky edges. Rims and margins were less likely to be mined. She touched the tree trunks as she passed, because wood was meant to be lucky. All the low snuffles and coos, the squeaks and scrapes of nocturnal life, worked to slow her breathing.

She came out on the road, beside the wayside chapel. It was a shrine to San Rocco, open at the front so any wayfarer could leave offerings, or rest on their journey up the hill. A painted Madonna sat under San Rocco's icon, a votive candle flickering below. The light brought the statue's face alive. Time and the elements had chipped her; you knew she wasn't real, but there was a substance there, from all the tired hands that had touched her. A cloak so blue it made your throat ache, and her sad face, forever looking at her feet. How many prayers had been offered up to this Madonna? They hadn't thought to bring her to the sagra this year. Vita picked some of the wild thyme that grew everywhere, laid it on the ledge.

'For my family.'

Then another voice floated, in the shadowy, pale air. More soldiers.

Her hand hovered over the pistol. There was an alcove behind the statue, where folk would leave corn sheaves and wine for other, more ancient, gods. It was a forbidden practice. She gripped a handful of shawl, reached for the Madonna.

'*Still stehen!*'

In her panic, she knocked the votive from its place. Dropped the gun. She fell to her knees, sweeping out her hand to reach it; finding only air. Then her fingers hit hard metal.

'You! What are you doing?' This voice was Italian.

'Praying.' She drew the pistol closer.

'Stand up.'

The bent head of a praying woman, offering alms. Vita's head swam as she rose. Shawl wrapped tight. '*Bitte.* I have to get home.'

'*Nein.*' Two soldiers, right behind her. One of them was smoking.

'Scusi?'

'Is not safe. Papers.'

Careful hands, moving down to reach her documents. They were in the side pocket of her dress. A good, wide pocket. Slow, slow slide of her fingers. Letting go, the sly trigger trying to snag her finger.

'Here.' She withdrew her papers, the rustle of them deafening.

The smoker shook out the folded document. 'Veet-orra. Vittoria – is victory, *ja*? So you pray for our victory?

Ha.' He clapped his hands, cigarette ash and sparks flying wide.

'Hello again.' The other figure came closer. It was the Brigate Nere soldier from earlier. He took her papers from the German. 'Where are you off to?'

'Catagnana. Just down there. I've got to get home by curfew.'

He clicked his heels together. 'Signorina, you look… unwell. Let me accompany you.'

'No! Honestly, there's no need. I'm fine.' She willed her voice not to break. The pistol waited under one single wisp of fabric, rubbing on the curve of her hip. Surely they would see it?

'Ah, but there are *parmigiani* about in the hills tonight.' The blackshirt sniffed the air. 'You can smell their cheesy feet on the breeze. *Zehen von käse, ja?*'

His companion also sniffed. '*Ja, ja. Käse. Das is gut.*' He laughed, but his face was terribly weary. He carried his helmet, dangling it in his hand, and stood to the side of her, frowning. Sweat in Vita's eyes, she kept wiping them, kept repeating the action because it was the only thing she could do, a rabbit staring at a hunter's gun; there was a burning urge to urinate, to turn and flee. Her foot must have brushed the fallen votive, for it clinked and rolled, Vita confused. Petrified by his frowning. She began to stoop.

'*Nein, nein.*'

The German gripped her arm. The pistol a hand reach from where he held her.

'*Bitte.*' He retrieved the votive. '*Das is nicht gut.*'

Vita couldn't speak. The Nazi struck a match. Relit the candle. Gently, he positioned it so it was central before the Madonna. Replaced Vita's thyme at the front.

'*Das ist besser.*' He frowned again, eyes flitting as if he were counting. 'Um. *Wir…* we…' Fiddling inside his collar. 'We *alle… ein kleine…* hope?' He showed her the crucifix he wore round his neck. 'Little hope, *ja*?'

'*Ja.*'

The Italian soldier leaned back against a tree. 'I had a *kleine* hope there would be pretty girls to dance with in Sommocolonia. '

'Please,' said Vita. 'Enjoy your evening. I must go home.'

'You're not going to the festa?'

'No.'

'Shame. And you don't fear bandits?'

'Me?' She winked. 'Nah. I'm a mountain witch. I just draw a magic circle round the house and they keep away.'

'Oh, witches are the worst kind.' He tipped his cap to her. 'You take care, Vittoria Guidi.' Carefully, carefully, folding her papers. 'Watch out for wolves.'

'I will.'

Head low, she picked her way downhill. The path zigzagged round the contours of the slope, then doubled back, so the men were directly above her. She heard the German say, '*Momento.* I too… would…'

'Klaus. We've a party to get to. Might be our last chance.'

'*Ja*, but… I cannot… *nicht recht*. Was not right, Rossi.'

'Sant'Anna?'

'*Ja.* Is too… *Bitte.* To pray. *Fünf minuten.*'

Sant'Anna? Vita held her face against gnarled tree bark. Cold down her spine. What had happened at Sant'Anna that would make a Nazi pray? She waited for other words to come, or for the German's shout as he looked down and saw her there. Felt the night close round her. Faith used to be like breathing; it brought rhythm and purpose. But where had prayer brought her? Here, to a forest, alone, in the dark. Words and prayers and ritual and promises. The ground seemed to undulate. If she opened her eyes, the sensation grew worse.

There was no one. No one was coming to help her.

Hardly breathing, she crept back up the path.

The chapel was maybe ten paces away, on the other side of the track. Two candles danced, casting faerie light. The Nazi's head was bowed; she could see the tension in his neck; the little tick of life there, above his high collar. He was alone. Vita eased the pistol from her pocket. There was no way of telling if it was loaded; she only knew how a shotgun worked. Crouching low, she pointed the nose of the gun, testing her index finger; hardening her knuckle until it was a solid knot. One press would crack open the dusk, and his skull. What happened in Sant'Anna? Tell me. What did your people do?

What did Nazis always do?

Her finger twitched. One press. It would bring an avalanche of running feet.

Who was left to care?

The soldier moved, and the shadow changed, passing over the Madonna's face. Vita lowered the pistol. Still crouching, she watched him walk away.

She felt so alone. Cradling her face in her hands, trying to think, and to not think. Knowing what must have happened, in her bones.

The partigiani. Joe's friends. They had contacts. They would know.

There was a grangia in the mountains, a bothy the goatherds used in summer. There were hidden, inaccessible clearings too, where charcoal makers hid from their wives. Whole weeks they spent there, being carbonari instead of fathers. Papà had taken her once, when she was little. It was an excuse to camp out. The men brought dry pasta and eggs, cut branches into even lengths and stacked them into earth-clad pyramids taller than themselves, with a hole at the centre to set the fire. Then they would ignite, and wait. *You must burn it slowly to make it strong*, said Papà. *If you rush, it will turn to ash.*

There were many places where men could contrive to be absent from home. When you thought about it, the partigiani were not so hard to find. Simply climb into the forest. Of course it would be to their boschi the partisan men returned. Vita was careful; no eyes or aeroplanes followed her. She knew these woods as well as anyone. And, if you are a mountain witch you can see small differences, can *smell* them; how the grass is flattened, here. How these cut branches truncate just there. Threads of red wool adhering to a mossy trunk.

The forest spread itself across the hills and valleys of the Garfagnana, turning from oak and chestnut to spiky fir as the altitude increased. She climbed for nearly two hours, the rain changing to an icy sparkle. The grangia lay somewhere outside the treeline, on the plateau stretching ahead. She took a breath, left the shelter of the forest, into open ground. Waiting for a shout, a gun crack across the dark.

It was too early here for snow, but she could see velvet shelves of white, packed and sparkling in the moonlight, all along the spires of the higher alps. Endless chains and peaks, shimmering into fairytale. Finally, she saw the shape of the grangia up ahead: a mound of stones, almost a trullo. Clever partigiani. They had fringed the roof with pine branches, so it was camouflaged from above.

Vita was thirsty. Her cheekbones tingled. Up here, on the horizon at the edge of the world, the darkness receded into faint, washed greys. She waited. Her thighs, fists, tense. In the bone-coloured sky, an owl swept in circles.

She made herself move on. Walk boldly. They were on the same side.

There was a man by the side of the cabin, skinning a rabbit. He squealed as Vita approached, flinging the bloody carcass at her.

'Stop! Who goes there!'

'Fucksake, Puccini!' A man in a red beret came from the shelter, rifle first.

'What do we do, Lenin? Do we shoot her?'

The cold night settled on her shoulders.

'I don't know. Do we shoot you, bella?' The man tilted his gun.

There was a third figure inside the cabin. What if it was Captain Bob? He would kill her, calmly, and resume his cleaning or map-reading without pause. But she could see no hairy knees within. Her black suitcase sat unashamedly in the centre of the floor. 'I wouldn't recommend it. See that? It was me brought you that thing. Ask Captain Bob. And I've brought you more goodies too. If you're nice.'

The man inside was sitting on a heap of pine branches, absorbed in whittling wood. There was a little camping stove too, filling the room with smoke.

'Like what?' said Puccini.

The legendary transmitter got her through the door, but it was the unveiling of the pistol that got her trusted. They let her sit in their cabin, drink their horrible coffee. The one called Puccini shook her hand. 'And you just took the Luger? From his coat?'

'I did.' Vita coughed in the smoke. 'And I want to do more. Please. Let me help. Teach me how to use it, for a start.'

'Out of the question,' said Lenin. 'This is men's work.'

'The girl is brave,' said the wood-whittler. 'To come up here alone.' He nodded at the pistol. 'Resourceful too. I think she has a good heart.'

'What if she's a spy? Eh, girlie? How d'you even know we were here?'

'I used my initiative. Plus I've been here before. With my papà.'

'Who's your papà?'

'Mario Guidi. I'm Vita.'

'Christ,' said Lenin.

'Who?' said Puccini.

'You know Mario. He made the cavity cart.'

'Oh, Mario MacCavity! The Paisley boy?'

The whittler wiped his knife on his trousers. 'So… if Mario's your dad…' Vita saw him glance at the other two. The cabin smelt of unwashed men.

'Then Giuseppe Guidi must be your—'

'Tiziano will never agree to it,' said Lenin quickly. 'We can't decide without him.'

'For Godsake!' Vita kicked her foot out, spilling their coffee pot. It rolled across the cabin, spattering dark globs. 'Don't you understand? I've got nowhere else to go. No one left.'

'Do you know, then? About your cousin?'

'Fucksake, Puccini,' said Lenin.

Vita stared at her wrists, at the fluted bones there. 'I saw you once before, Lenin. Didn't I? You were in that ambulance with Joe.' Smoke stung her eyes, the dry skin on her lips. 'What happened? Will you tell me about Sant'Anna?'

Puccini took her hand again. 'It was a massacre, bella.'

Voices, rumbling. Vita, hot, then cold. *Merciless.* Airless. Smoke-filled faces. *Five hundred souls.* The wall of voices kept battering her: *very quick*, Puccini, then Lenin, and *revenge* and *next time*. The clammy cold kept coming, clouding together, so the cold became shivers and it felt like water was in her ears, her mouth. Vita bit down, focusing on the stove light. Her teeth hurt. Dario had baby teeth, scalloped and neat. Marino's teeth were crushed against the big ones forcing their way in. He would have tried to protect his brother. Vita knew he would. Carla too. And Joe would have tried to save them all.

'You owe us then.' Her breathing was sore. They seemed surprised she'd spoken.

'Owe who?'

'The bloody Guidis. We've sacrificed my father, my mother and now my cousins too. And people like Signor Tutti, and – even Andromeda.' And then she was weeping, weeping for a brave old donkey.

A rough hand patted her knee.

'You want me to die too? Because I have nothing, and nobody left. Please. I need to do something. To... fight all this death.'

'The Bloody Guidis.' Lenin scraped up the coffee grounds with the lid of the pot. Bits of dirt and leaf mould came too. 'What?' he said. 'It'll add to the flavour.' Then he smiled, briefly, at Vita.

Puccini nodded.

'So,' said the whittler. 'I'm Fredo by the way. You want to be a staffetta? Work with us?'

She scrubbed her eyes with the heel of her hand. 'I do.'

'Ah, girlie,' sighed Lenin. 'Be careful what you wish for.'

'You want some vinata, stafetta?'

'She'll need a code name.'

'How about Dolcezza? That's what Guiseppe called you, wasn't it?' said Lenin. 'Dolce Vita. How's that for a code name?'

Vita took a raw swig of the wine-gloop. Her tongue felt thick. 'Sure. Why not.'

Lenin began handing round small pills. 'Simpamina. For energy. We've a long night ahead of us. Not you, Dolcezza. We're meeting with the Allies.'

'Tonight?'

'Yup. They've made it to Bagni di Lucca. Hopefully with some decent radios. No offence, but your transmitter's rubbish.'

'Why don't you rest here, then go back down when it's daylight?' Puccini saluted her. 'And await orders, soldier.'

Too spent to argue, Vita nodded. They were mumbling and arguing as they left. She didn't know if it was about her. Didn't care. She extinguished the stove. Better to freeze than choke. Lay on the pine fronds, vinata-porridge filling her with dopey, alcoholic warmth. It softened her limbs and pushed out the clamour, the imagined scenes she could not bear. She just wanted to be numb. Concentrating on the smell of woodsmoke. She thought of favourite foods, but food led back to family and—

The door juddered, letting the wind through. Vita drank the vinata to its sloppy dregs. It was like blood clots. The wind song outside turned to cries, Joe's cries, the children's. All of them dead because of her. She wedged the door shut with her foot. Shoved her hands into her eye sockets, and clung to the image of the americano. It was a new, good memory. Keeping his face behind her eyelids, pressing him over the fiery reds and bursting white comets and whatever else came into view. Finally, she lay back on the pine boughs. Finally, she fell asleep.

Exhausted, Vita slept through the roar of the bombardment that grew deeper and nearer in the night. On a mountain top, the wind moaned louder than guns. Vita slept through the first of the morning bells, the Duomo ones that tolled in the valley below, warning the townspeople of impending doom. She slept through the movements of the German scouts who scurried from the Duomo's campanile and sped off; she slept through the self-important bustle of the Brigate Nere as they closed their headquarters and fled Barga.

At the second carillon, Vita woke. Barga's bells were telling time. They were giving her people thirty minutes' grace between the sound of the bells and the blasting of the bridges. Plenty of time for folk to grab everything they loved and run away. Plenty of time before the wail of the drill gave way to small explosions, then to gasps and tearing and creaks as the dynamite was shoved deep in and Barga's guardians prepared to die. As Vita was climbing back down the mountain, she heard the bells toll on, a funeral dirge to guide her home, while down in Barga, people were boarding up their houses, chucking furniture, linens, children, dogs, onto carts, their panic filtered with deep grief, with anger, murmuring old curses as they passed tedeschi sappers.

People gathered in the safe places they could find, with friends and neighbours, with family and refugees. The bells stopped. Silence fell. And the silence was worse than the drilling, because the silence became a well into which the people poured their dread, their impotent rage, until the air fizzed with the silence; it sparkled like a lit fuse, even as the Germans were lighting their own fuses, were standing back to admire their handiwork, and then the silence exploded in a terrible, grinding roar. Barga gasped, heaving as her bridges' keystones flew up, hurled down, smashing past the campanile, into the Duomo door, ripping up Piazza Angelio, tearing into Angela's mother's house with such a fury that half the house fell, the ugly floral wallpaper of their salotto revealed to all. Barga's streets were pounded and doused in broken brick, smashed tiles, wood, twisted shutters, the pirouette of crackling, live wires. Homes and shops beside the bridges were blasted open; even the church of San Rocco, where the tedeschi had worshipped, teetered on collapse.

From the Giardino to Barga Castello, the town lay wrecked and split. The pretty ravine they called Fontanamaggio, verdant as a park, became a massive slag-heap, filled with debris and straddled by the stumps of broken bridges – including Ponte Vecchio, which they needn't have hurt at all. The sole remaining bridge was at Porta Macchiaia; a single thread by which the town hung together, given grace to remain.

By the time Vita was nearing smoke-dusted Barga, the Germans had rumbled out of town. *Is it really true?* whispered the townsfolk, hardly daring to believe it. Perhaps this pain would turn to a blessing. If they were free, they could rebuild. But war is not clean, nor fair: the older folk knew this, and refused to see a silver lining. Their pessimism was rewarded moments later, when the bridge at Catagnana was blown, the aqueduct destroyed. *Thank you for having us*, waved the tedeschi as they left.

A pause. A vacuum opening, a few heartbeats when their city was their own. One week of dazed nothing, like gauze on a wound.

Then came the first of the bombs.

Autumn 1944

Chapter Nineteen

'Don't touch that,' said Comanche. 'It's his girlfriend.'

'Fuck off.' Frank raised his head. He was lying on his back in the mud. 'And put it away. I don't want it getting wet.'

They were bivouacked outside of a place called Piano. Cue bad jokes about music, and acting in concert. Bivouacking was just camping with no tents. Moving day on day, it didn't make sense to pitch up properly. A shakedown in a foxhole, under a tarp if you were lucky, a sojourn beneath a dripping tree if you were not. Four hours on, four hours off, in grey, incessant rain. Sometimes you slept standing, propped against a wall with your helmet down. To most of them, sleep, real sleep, was a half-forgotten promise, but that was no bad thing, because the hazy, mouth-furred blur that rocked you on meant functioning in a half-life, where you were never sure if what just happened was dreamed or real. And that offered occasional absolution.

Routine was: no routine. Morning, night, no longer mattered. It was the inching forwards and the flushing out which counted, daily, hourly. Aggressive patrolling against the backdrop of shells, rifles, machine-gun echoes ricocheting through the sodden hills. Sometimes you were bait, luring Nazi stragglers, the snipers who lurked trigger-happy. Sometimes you were bulldozer. Your day's labour could be trying to take a rocky outcrop above a river: two steps forward, three back. Run and duck. Two steps forward. Retreat. Four steps, charge, skip over your dying colleagues. And hold.

Seravezza had been the worst. Fanging its way into Frank's brain whenever he closed his eyes, taking on different, venomous shapes. They had reached it in a pitch-black thunderstorm, rain teeming, sky louder than any guns. Four hours to get two miles, and every inch of them terrifying. Krauts firing their cannon from on high, incessant, deadly; the river a swirling madness, impossible to ford. So blind in their fumbling movements that every crater was a crevasse; tipping two feet in the dark felt like thirty feet in your head, cloying mud and lightning all fuelling the disorientation. Men drowned that night. The town itself was shattered. But securing it was not their aim.

Seravezza sat below Mount Caula. Caula was the prize, so important that Colonel Sherman himself came to wish them well. The commander took pains to tell them the Germans would machine-gun them as they climbed. *Stay silent and unexposed.* Sure thing, boss. Try staying silent as you're scaling a mountain in the dark, actually climbing up ladders lashed to rock, armed to the teeth, while your buddies cry and fall beside you, slipping, being shot in the back, while your front is lacerated by the cliff face and the rain whips down and the wind howls up. Shrapnel stuck to your skin, hot metal searing as the shells explode. Cordite burning up your throat while a cloudburst of explosions on the ridge became a waterfall of fire, of pouring black and orange, so all you could do was huddle in and pray for it to pass.

Frank wasn't sure how many men they lost that night. But they never made it up the mountain. In the first-aid station afterwards, they'd been baying for blood; Frank's was the type that could mix with anyone's. Automatically, he'd offered up his arm to the doc, to the white officer screaming in the bed. Heard his spit-flecked words. *Don't give me no nigger blood.*

Two steps forward, three steps back. Yet, somehow, the Buffs kept nudging forward. As they limped across the Tuscan countryside, the Krauts melted back. Frank couldn't help but wonder if they were being led to a cliff edge.

While the Buffaloes were fighting their way up the Serchio, the Brazilians were battling to take Lama di Sotto, a fierce-toothed ridge of serrated mountains. The Krauts had all kinds of cannon hidden there. Dragons, maybe. *Lama* meant blade, Vincenzo said. He was their go-to guy, a teenager in bare feet who had tagged along with them since Lucca. The quartermaster found the kid a pair of boots, and now Vinnie followed the Buffs like a love-struck pup. He translated for them, briefed them on the terrain, the towns they passed through. *All fascisti bastards*, he'd say of one innocuous village, urging the men to rest up closer to the next one. *Nice girls there*, he'd grin. *And grappa.* Vinnie's advice was good. Frank had watched, powerless, from a foxhole way above a village they'd been told to avoid, as a truckload of GIs drove in. And were instantly ambushed by Krauts, firing from the surrounding houses. Encircling and mowing till nobody moved. He'd made it down in time to help collect their dog tags.

Out near Bologna, the Buffaloes had managed, briefly, to break through the Gothic Line. When the news came, guys here went nuts. But nowhere had been breached since. All along the lines, the German defences held. They had the soar of the mountains behind them, and reserve after reserve pouring in, while the Buffs slogged on with no rest and few supplies.

A raindrop splashed on Frank's forehead.

'Man,' said Ivan, above him. 'That girl got wet plenty times, I reckon. Look how she crinkles.' He shook the paper. 'With your jizz.'

'Fuck *off.*' He made to take the picture, but Ivan was too quick. He'd been rifling Frank's tunic for smokes. Found the little sketch instead. Frank had done several drawings of the girl, one after the other, trying to capture what it was he'd seen. But she was elusive. *Vee-toh-ree-ah.*

He slept with that name, rolling it around his mouth. He would dream the rolled-up sweater he used as a pillow was her hair. This small, square pencil sketch was his best attempt; it was her face half-tilted as she'd turned to say goodbye. Whip of hair across her mouth, the spike of chin and sharp, straight nose which balanced out the cheek-bones; it was more a sense of her than a likeness. Flash flash flash. She was a blade, slicing mineral-lit air. The girl was all glimmer at the extremities. She was not real.

'What she called?'

'She's called mine.' Frank cuffed Ivan on the side of the head, the way he might cuff Willis. Keeping it cool. 'Now give.'

'Whoah, man. What you doin'? Don' hit a brother like that.'

'You ain't my brother.'

'No?' Ivan crumpled the sketch, deliberately mangling it in his fat-fuck hand. 'You make me real sad. Boo-hoo.' He made to blow his nose into the paper. Frank knew Ivan wanted him to charge head down into his belly. Gather a mob of cheering grunts. Oh, the exhilaration of losing yourself in mindless assault, with an audience to see your finest work. Plenty of guys loved it. Unless you got mentioned in dispatches, who'd record your warrior status otherwise? Staying alive didn't make you a good soldier, any more than hiding did. When every waking minute in this fucking war was unfinished business, it was no wonder guys went insane. From day one, Ivan had been a jerk. He was always switched to self-destruct, unless he could get others to do it for him. Since Seravezza, Ivan was rage personified. He would rant at the wind when the guns went quiet, punch walls when he couldn't punch people. He was pretending to wank into the picture.

Comanche put his hand on Ivan's shoulder. 'Just give it mothafuckin' back.'

'Hark at the corporalle.'

'Corporeal.'

'Corpodick.'

'Suck my dick. Give.'

'You boys!'

'Sir, yessir.'

They stood to attention as Captain Dedeaux appeared. The man was always louche, hands in pockets, shoulders slumped. He poked at Ivan's mummy bag with his polished toecap.

'What you all hollering at?'

'Hollering, sir? Us, sir?'

'Yessir, you, sir.' Dedeaux stuck his chin in Comanche's face.

'Not us, sir.'

'You in charge here, boy?'

'Yessir. Corporal Barfoot.'

'Well, Blackfoot. How's about I break up your little party? You go find your good ole sergeant and tell him I need two men dispatched to the 366th. As of yesterday.'

'Yessir.'

If the Buffs weren't being whittled by injury, they got fucked up by transfers instead. Frank had lost count of the number of platoons turned to squads, of battalions plucked to scrawny companies; men, good men, who disappeared in the night to fill a need in some other unit.

'Two more of you dumb fucks disappearing. And I'm still s'posed to...' Dedeaux kicked Comanche's rifle over, 'Ain't all the reasons you disappear, is it?' He circled behind Frank, sniffing like a hog. 'No, sir. I can smell it. Oozing. Wha's your battle-cry, soldier?'

'Um... Deeds not Words, sir?' Frank could smell liquor on the man's breath.

'Bullshit. Will I tell you what your motto is, huh, soldier? Huh?'

'Sir. Yessir.'

'*Unass the hill!* Because the black man is afraid. All you boys do is run and hide. Why the Good Lord painted y'all shit-brown. So's you can hide you miserable goldbrickin' nigga faces in the nigga-fuckin' mud.'

As motivational speeches go, Frank had heard better. Like Axis Sally, you just tuned Dedeaux out.

'Don't I know you, boy?'

'Sir?'

'Ain't you the nigger gave me grief back at Lucca? 'Bout some *puttana*?'

Frank kept his fists tight.

'Sir,' Comanche interjected. 'PFC Chapel is an excellent soldier, and a key member of our squad, sir. I can personally vouch for his integrity and—'

'Hey, Blackfoot. Good for you. Guess we found ourselves our first volunteer to go supplement the 366th. As you were, men.' Their captain mooched off. An insignificant fuck whose uniform wore him. If you were on neutral ground; if Frank was one on one... You could snap Dedeaux's neck like a twig.

'Give me the fucking picture, man.'

Ivan relinquished the drawing to Comanche, who gave it to Frank.

'Coulda bust your mothafuckin' balls anyway, Chap.'

'That right?' Ivan was big, but he had no finesse. Frank did chin-ups on the shower rails; he did daily push-ups and crunches, no matter how tired he was. Ran when he could, even if it was just sprinting loops in a field. Comanche offered to shoot at his feet, to speed things up. He couldn't keep clean, but he could keep fit. Self-respect, order, that extra push that got you over the hill – it was his own version of Ivan's need to provoke. Unspilled energy had to go someplace.

'Chap,' said Comanche. 'Go get some fresh air, my friend.'

'We're in the fresh air.'

'Well, go breathe someone else's air for a minute, yeah?'

Comanche had been doubly promoted: PFC first, then leaping over Frank to corporal. Frank was glad, he honestly was. There'd been a bunch of promotions after Seravezza, commendations too, but Frank hadn't covered himself in glory. He'd barely survived. *No, son. You Bearly survived.* Bear had found him clinging to an overhang of rock. The fear had got to him. It wasn't the Krauts, it was the height; an angry blast of vertigo spinning his brain, so the fall had seemed more alluring than the climb. It was Bear who unprised his fingers, who shoulder-shoved his ass, bawling, bawling, until Frank was thawed enough to shift.

'What can I do, sarge?' he'd asked afterwards. 'Next time. We're in mountain country.'

'Don't look down. And have someone you trust behind you. Another sergeant would've shot you, baby bear.'

Least he and Bear were cool again. Frank still hadn't forgiven him for Lucca. But he knew Vita hadn't been duped. She would have walked over broken glass to get to her momma; Bear simply offered a smoother path.

He lit a Lucky Strike. He never did go to her nonna's house. Sure, he took a crate of food with him, tins mostly so's they'd keep, plus as much fresh stuff as he could purloin (the quartermaster did deals with the locals: fresh greens for army sweaters). Frank went there all right, ready to knock on the grandmother's door. Was one doorstep away from the blackened bell-pull when he'd glanced at his wrist as it flexed towards the button. The colour of him. The line that sliced dark to light. To Vita's nonna, he was a Moor, an enemy on several fronts. Along with wonder, Frank saw the filthy looks the Buffaloes ignited. The cusses and forked *cornuto* fingers. The grandmother couldn't speak any English. How could he explain where her granddaughter had gone; it would be too upsetting, she most likely wouldn't eat the food; he was talking himself into this being the only practical solution. Kidnap someone's little girl, and leave a basket of cookies. His momma would be proud. But that's exactly what he did. Left a crate of food and a scrawled note. Slunk away. He figured Vita's sister could translate.

Dear Vita's nonna, please accept this food from the US Army. Vita is very very safe (he underlined the verys) *and she tells you PLEASE not to worry. She has gone to Barga and will be home soon.*

He had signed it: '*A friend*'. For 'friend', read 'dick'. The woman would be frantic with worry. But Vita was resourceful; she would get a message to her grandmother. If she'd made it home.

She would. She had to. The girl was smart.

No fucking way was he going to the 366th. Being with your buddies was the only endurable thing about this piece-of-shit war. With every advance the Buffs made, the front was shrinking to a smaller, denser field. Both sides playing volleyball by hurling bombs, but one side was pushing, pushing against the net while the other side got crammed against an unforgiving wall, all that concentrated fury trashing everything on the court. Yeah, it was a crap analogy. Frank was an athlete, not a poet. But it was what he drew in his journal; a bouncy image in which to hold the chaos. Vita, and thousands like her, were caught someplace in between. He'd asked Bear if the transmitter had been used yet, did OSS know these things, could he ask Dedeaux, could he find out maybe? Gently, Bear had tugged on Frank's ears, touched Frank's forehead with his own.

'OSS don't exist. And neither does that dame of yours, nor that little black case. You mention it again and I will skin your ball-sack to make me a pair of winter mitts.'

The skies were no longer warm. The air had a sharp, iron tang to it now. Frank blew a smoke ring. *Perfetto.* The ring floated in a halo, over a mountain flanked by towering, pewter clouds. Guns thumped on in the next valley. Constant, heavy bore through the ground beneath your feet. They called it the death rattle.

'*Buonasera.*'

Comanche perched on the rock beside him. 'Spoke to Bear. He says to ignore Dedeaux. Just keep your head down and your mouth shut. We're getting trucked out in one hour anyways.' He lifted the cigarette from Frank's mouth, took a drag.

'Yeah. Where to? Venice?'

275

Frank helped prepare the nightly maps meant to clarify enemy positions and Allied gains. Communications flew between local command posts and divisional command; you would expect there to be a cohesion to all this activity. Yet frequently, the Buffs would find themselves on the brink of reaching some town they'd been aiming for, then get pulled back miles and miles, ordered to make for some other random point instead. Reason for these abrupt changes never came. Ensconced in the hotels of Viareggio, Fifth Army Command's ambitions knew no bounds. Nor sense.

'Relieving the Brazilians,' said Comanche. 'Out near that Lama Ridge?'

'So where they headed?'

'Fuck knows.'

Frank was fascinated by the Brazilians; that easy blend of black and white slick-smart troops who spoke Portuguese and fit with everyone. The Italians loved them, the Yanks loved them. And they seemed to love themselves too.

'Gonna be right on the Gothic Line. Some place called Barga? You heard of it?'

Frank's mouth went dry.

'Between us and the Bosch they been blasting fuck out the place. Christ knows what state it's in. But it's of stra—'

'—tegic importance.' They finished the sentence together.

'But, more important than that,' said Comanche, 'it's sock day! Ain't nothing can't be cured with a fresh pair of socks, my friend. Hey!' He nudged Frank's elbow. 'You OK?'

'Sure.'

'Well, come on, sock-buddy. Let's boogie.'

Frank ground the Lucky Strike beneath his heel. Veins fizzing. The Buffs were going to Barga.

Chapter Twenty

October 16, 17, 18, 20, 25, 26

Vita ran her finger along La Limonaia's kitchen wall.

When the Axis soldiers left Barga, there had been one week of peace. The occasional German patrol would return to forage the ruins like feral beasts, then slink back to their hillside lairs above Sommocolonia, and on the mountains all around. People blinked. Emerged. They thought about rebuilding.

The partigiani moved in, Tiziano taking the reins, a new Commissario, he wore it well. Then, as quick as it came, the eerie peace was broken. Partisans put down their rifles and raised hammers instead, smashing or prising off every mention of Fascism, tearing those angular posters from walls. Men were beaten, women sheared. Vita overheard Renata's name mentioned as Lenin and Puccini searched La Limonaia for scissors. 'No,' she told them. 'You do not touch her.'

'She was at a party—'

Vita had removed her scissors from Lenin's grip. Deliberately drew the point of the blade across his fist.

'You. Do not. Touch. My cousin's wife.'

'Calm down, girlie. I presume when Joe called you Dolce Vita it was ironic?'

'Ironic as your beret, amico.'

She took no part in retributions. A fortnight after the Germans fled, and Barga was occupied again. Vita couldn't have left even if she'd wanted to. Occupied or liberated, it didn't matter, the song remained the same. The overture: a cheering crowd welcoming the troops; this time, the multi-hued Brazilians, who tooted horns and rode on trucks adorned with pictures of the saints. They threw coloured sweets as if it were a circus, told everyone to stay indoors. Why, when they were free? Except they weren't.

The Brazilians ousted Tiziano – though he insisted they were working in partnership. The timpani resumed. The Brazilians were a magnet. And the pounding bombs began.

October 27, 29, 30, 31

Thudding from every side, directly onto Barga. They were in the crossfire of a music which had no conductors. Worse than it had ever been, because now it was on top of you. You'd fall asleep to the double-bass of shelling. Wake to the cymballing of bullets. And endless, endless rain. Some local men got to work on patching up the aqueduct, and were shot by German snipers. Three barghigiani died when their homes were hit by shells. Days later, six more perished. A few more days, and you almost stopped counting. Except Vita did not. She wrote them on her kitchen wall. All the days the bombs hit.

November 3, 4, 5 – cannonball on Duomo

It was her way of staying sane.

Shelling camposanto (can't even rest in peace).

She'd scribbled this, then thought it crass. But it would look less bold if she scratched it out, and Vita was earning a reputation for boldness. She was running a partigiani safe house, for Godsake, right under the noses of the enemy. There were too many tedeschi on Lama di Sotto ridge for the mountain bothies to be safe any more. But La Limonaia was tucked in the overhang of a halfway hamlet, at the end of an empty road. A couple of conta-dini with hoes, a shuffling man with a cart of hay? You'd expect to find these folk on a farm track.

The partigiani said Vita should return to work at the Canonica. 'It's ideal,' Lenin said. 'But keep living up here. Means you can move freely between Barga and. Catagnana, no matter who's in charge. We can use that. Plenty food stashed at the priest's house too, I bet. You can swipe some of that for us.'

'There's not actually.'

Lenin waved a dismissive hand. 'And you'll get the gist of Comune meetings – especially now they're shutting Tiziano out. Eavesdrop on the Monsignor too. Find out which side he's on this week.'

'That's not fair.'

'Isn't it?'

Today, then. She would go back to the Canonica today. She picked up the sack by the door. The rain had stopped, briefly, but the damp remained. It dripped from rocky outcrops, fell inside her clothes. Patched zoccoli were no barrier against the sodden forest. But the old pair of Papa's trousers she had belted tight? Who knew a seam cut through cloth could be so liberating? Vita loved the clean flap of fabric as she strode, no petticoats to encumber progress. Walking with purpose lifted her spirits. Moss glistened, trees were strung in jewels. The earth smelled new. She heard a voice inside her say: *Another dreich day, Dolce Vita.*

No, she thought. I can't face another dreich day.

Guilt came, mingled with the sadness that happened when she woke or washed her face or stepped in a ray of watery sun. Always the waiting pit. She had tried to write to Cesca, many times.

Darling Ces,
    Mamma is dead. Joe is dead, and Carla and the boys, and the Tuttos and probably Andromeda too. Papa is in Germany and I am here. I love you and I miss you. God willing, I will see you soon. Look after Nonna.
    V x

Vita hefted the sack onto her shoulders. She never sent any of the letters. Touching the paper hurt. Everything was raw. Things you didn't even know were there would lurch and trip you unawares. So she shrank into herself. Whenever an unguarded memory stabbed her, she taught herself to shrink more. She found it useful to wear her mother's ring. When the world got too bright or boisterous, it was a point on which to focus, condensing everything to one small circle, which she could weigh and hold. It allowed her to shut out every other distraction. Because grief, loneliness – these things were distractions.

They didn't keep you alive. If you laid out what was lost in some infinite line, to try to make sense of it, it reared up to strike you like a whip.

Sometimes, she made herself go even smaller, until she was inside the iron band itself, and the band was round the whole of her; sometimes it became the spinning cylinder in which Joe had made gelato. Cold, dark metal wrapped in ice, with Vita safe inside.

Leaves skirled at her ankles. Above, a clear hollow of sky was framed by dark branches. She felt the familiar, soft give of earth; then the forest floor began to rumble, before the artillery boomed behind Lama di Sotto ridge. A staccato of gunfire in retort. Couple of kilometres off, at least. She was getting good at judging distance. If you waited too long, the fear of walking anywhere could paralyse you.

It was good to be busy. To focus on the hour before you, and nothing more.

Vita slowed as she approached the swollen Corsonna. The rubble from the blown-up bridge lay where it had fallen, an island of broken stone creating two rivers from one. At first, you could ford it, using the debris as stepping stones, but the autumn rains had made the river much deeper and faster. The Brazilians had erected one of those temporary pontoons to get their trucks across. Helpful for the locals, but it also meant Ponte di Catagnana was a target, an ideal narrowing where, from the German vantage points above, enemies could be picked off one by one. It was crucial, when approaching, that you looked as civilian and unthreatening as possible. Even then, you crossed with your heart raging harder than the torrent below you.

She picked her way over the swaying bridge, waiting for the mosquito-whizz of a bullet. It was fine. All quiet; so quiet you could hear your own breath ease through gritted teeth.

Barga was caked in brick dust. Some of the modern villas were still intact; others had been blasted flat. Cinema Roma nestled within a film set, where facades and walls stood with empty air behind. Trucks packed with Brazilian soldiers passed her, along the rubble-strewn roads. There were so many. It wasn't the normal movement of supplies; it felt like another evacuation.

Ponte Vecchio hadn't been repaired, so she had to go the long way, up by Porta Reale. More Brazilian troops marched through the old town, moving down the streets in squads. They carried full knapsacks as well as rifles, tin cups clinking in time with their boots.

When she saw the Monsignor again, Vita wanted to cry. He looked thinner. Of course, she didn't need to appease him; he received her as he always did, with one raised brow and a tiny sigh. His spine no longer seemed ramrod straight when he stood, but he embraced her, whispered, *Welcome home.* And she held on to him until the threat of tears had passed, and they could be normal again.

'Pantaloni, child? Really?'

'They are practical and serviceable, Monsignor. Like me.'

The Conservatorio had become a barracks and a hospital of sorts, too full of humanity in which to breathe or think properly. There were Brazilian officers and refugees sleeping in the basement of the Canonica as well, beside the wounded. But the upstairs and the kitchen remained the Monsignor's domain. And it did feel a bit like returning home. The nuns hugged and petted her. Vita was given Brazilian coffee, then put to work. They were using the Monsignor's study to sort out clothes for those who'd been left with nothing. There was something nostalgic about the nuns' fastidious approach to compassion. It was almost fascista: checking lists, counting garments, assembling appropriate bundles.

'It's the only way to make it fair,' said Sister Agatha. 'Two jumpers per child under ten, one jumper and a coat for the rest. Or just a jumper if we run out. And they only get them if they have a chit.'

The nun's belly rumbled as she bent to fold a large blanket.

'What time is it? Have you eaten today, Sister?'

'Me? No. I am sustained by prayer and hard work.'

'Why are the bells not ringing?' It dawned on Vita: she'd been there for ages, in the lee of the Duomo, yet not a single doleful clang had sounded.

'*Mah*. The Brazilians told the Monsignor to suspend them. All the bells. And the organ. Clocks too. They think it encourages spying.'

'How?'

'They believe some barghigiani are sending signals to the Germans. Coded in our bells. I ask you.'

What a genius idea. Too late for the partigiani to adopt it, unfortunately.

Vita had brought a load of stuff from La Limonaia: dresses, shirts, any old children's clothes she could find. At least five pairs of yellowing bootees. It seemed her mother was a terrible one for preserving baby wear. She could feel the nuns' hesitation as she smoothed and folded the contents of her family's wardrobe.

'Might as well let some poor soul get the use out of these.'

Trousers spilled over jackets and dresses, legs and sleeves curled in empty apostrophes. The flatness and the perfumes of the jumbled garments were terrible. Deft, decisive, her fingers barely touched the various fabrics as she divided them into big and small. She wanted them squashed into bags and gone. Her hand turned over a calico shirt; it was a small thing, made with a deep hem for letting out. She shook it open, and an embroidered blue rabbit danced on the yoke. It was the nightshirt Dario had slept in.

The Monsignor's desk began to shake. Then a deep, low sound filled the room, not especially loud, yet it seemed deafening, far closer than the thuds behind the mountains. The force blew the study window open, shattering a pane of glass. Sister Agatha seized Vita's hand. Began to recite the rosary. Vita could pinpoint the bang exactly, to a fizz of firework light, and the magnificent circles of blue, green and yellow that flared as the mast of a power-line cracked down outside.

Falling missiles punctuated their hours and days, every one of them like a hard, banging punch. It was difficult to describe the complexity of sound when the bombs came. Exploding thunder and whistling kettles, screaming air and chiming glass. Afterwards came human sounds, and the low crackle of flame licking the debris clean. The war did not discriminate. Ambulances, schools, farmers in their fields.

The nuns stood immobile, waiting for the noises to summon them. But the power-line must have been the only target, for it remained quiet outside.

Bombs and dynamite. Scarlet blood and spurted cries. Actual, lethal firepower held a strange energy. In its aftermath you got this wild, invincible rush – you were vulnerable, yet you survived. Such a clever energy; they must pass it down in their marching and their songs, so that, when the old made war for the young to fight, they passed them this energy too. Vita tingled with it now. Alive on the frenzied energy of not being dead. She regarded her hand, her brown fingers, Sister Agatha's pale ones and the white calico beneath. If there was nothing but a brief, brutal life ahead, surely you should live it?

She broke the silence. 'May I have the scissors, Sister Bertilla?'

Quickly, she snipped a square from the hem of Dario's nightshirt. Tonight, she would stitch it into her mamma's quilt. The nuns returned to their sorting. She would find something of Joe's too, some grubby scrap left in the cave, maybe a ribbon of Carla's, or she'd embroider all their initials on a patch. Or something. A daft, pointless action, but it was something. There was a phrase, nagging at her. *You must name the dead.* Was it the Romans or the Greeks? Greeks, probably – Papà was always extolling ancient Greeks. To give them peace, you must name the dead.

'Vita, dear.' Sister Agatha closed the shattered window. 'Watch you don't stab yourself with those shears.

By late afternoon, all the clothes had been bundled and collected. Sister Bertilla had swept up the glass, and pinned a scrap of material over the broken pane. The noises from Sister Agatha's stomach had become embarrassing. Vita went to the kitchen to see what food there was. She wasn't sure she was still the housekeeper. However, she was a daughter of the Canonica, was she not? In this free-for-all, it was her kitchen as much as anyone's.

She took one of the copper pans from the stone ledge, opened the larder. A couple of sad purple turnips rolled on the shelf. Rainwater in the barrel, some chard she'd found in the garden; it was a feast, and… she edged her hands along the topmost shelf. Nico was too bent to reach up here, and she wasn't sure the Monsignor ever went into his kitchen. Her fingers closed on a bag of barley she'd stuffed there ages ago. Mamma's ring dug into the pad of skin below her finger. It would toughen up soon.

Vita chopped turnips, rinsed the barley in a sieve. The Brazilians had extended their rations, allowing each person three hundred grammes of flour a day, plus beans and chickpeas and milk powder. No doubt the Monsignor had foregone his share, or given it to the nuns. That man. Where was he anyway? No one had seen him for ages. Vita was just setting the water to boil on the fornelli when Sister Agatha came banging into the kitchen.

'Vittoria! Come, quickly. The Monsignor is here, with new guests.'

'Well, I don't know how much I can stretch this soup by. How many?'

The nun twisted butterfly hands beneath her chin. 'I'm not sure they eat soup. I don't know if they eat cooked food at all actually. They're *Mori*.' She dropped her voice as the Monsignor's own voice spilled down the corridor.

'In you come, gentlemen.'

The kitchen door swung wide. The Monsignor appeared at the head of a group of soldiers, American soldiers, Vita recognised the colour of their uniform from Lucca; it was the heavy green of pressed olives. Six of them. Black-skinned and smiling, one who doffed his cap while the others merely stood there, the glowing light from the fornelli illuminating the round, yellow-green patches on their shoulders. *Bufali*. The Buffaloes were in Barga.

Chapter Twenty-one

Barga. Twisted, dark November streets. Sheer grey and broken stone. Tall walls made of mountain, mountains made of wall, of moisture-packed clouds at high altitude, and great vistas of valley that were beautiful still. It was a battered place; a town of smashed-up bridges and jagged gaps.

Two days of rapping on doors and taking roll calls. It didn't feel much like liberation to Frank. Bear said the Brazilians had been too polite; that if the Allies were going to flood this place with enough men to truly take Jerry out, they'd need every spare bit of accommodation going. In pidgin Italian, the Buffaloes tried to work out who lived where. If their basement kitchens or their weird, hay-stuffed lofts weren't occupied by a family of five, then they were prizes for the US Army to commandeer. 'Don't put folks out on the street though. We need 'em on our side.'

OSS warned there would be a deal of resistance. These northern mountain towns had been Fascist strongholds, and in the powderkeg shadow of the Gothic Line, you must assume your friends wore two faces. They trudged through the old city, stepping over scorch-marked chair legs and blackened metal, which might have been prams once, or bikes. An old woman washed her one remaining window, while a man brushed the front step. Children kicked stones, built castles in wreckage. A duo with dirt-smeared faces fought over a cheese rind, until their mother came out and slapped them both. Rubbish was heaped in piles, possibly sewage by the stench. The Buffaloes marched down through the skinny streets of the old town, canteens clinking in time with their boots. Occasional snatches came, of that jagged Scottish English that made Frank's ribcage split to wings, and his head would turn and he'd search for her, even when it was a man's voice and he knew he was being ridiculous.

Always that electric, storm-scented air.

'Most Scottish town in Italy, this,' said Bear as they patrolled the shuttered alley of a little hamlet downtown. 'Did you know that?'

'How come you did?' One eye on the thick-forested hills above. Russet hills. Somewhere high up, a dog barked. Pockets of life coming in on a sharpened breeze. The leaves on the ground shimmied. Soon it would snow, Vinnie said. Maybe so – Frank had seen a consignment of white snowsuits arrive earlier, and that in itself was unnerving. Supplies never arrived on time. The officers kept saying: *We need to break Jerry before the snows come.* The sky wasn't dense enough, surely? But what did a Berkeley boy know about snow?

'Make it my business to know these things.' Bear cleared his throat. '*Significant migration, due to the poverty-stricken Italian diaspora journeying to Scotland in the late nineteen hundreds.* History, boy. Is the key to tomorrow.'

'Very impressive.' Frank kicked the door of an empty shop. Its walls had been daubed with crude yellow stars. 'Clear.'

Ivan went upstairs. 'Clear,' he called. 'Could maybe billet a dozen guys here.'

'Yup. Gonna open me a little travel business when I get home,' said Bear. 'Battlefield tours.'

Frank rolled his eyes. 'Who the fuck will want to remember this?'

'You'll see, Chapelley. You'll see. Ma'am.' Bear tipped his helmet to an old woman who crouched, blank-eyed, in the next doorway along. She flapped thumb and fingers together, like a kid making shadow-pictures of a duck. Then the sour tang of urine hit them. People here were surviving, not living; depleted to the point they were more reflex than human. Same sunken features Frank had seen in Naples. Wasn't just hunger making their faces thin. You could see their postures reflected in their town: bowed, battered. Dying from the inside out.

With the utmost care, Bear's squad navigated the pontoon the Brazilians had erected across the river, conscious they were the sole moving dots on the landscape, visible for miles above. But there were a couple of villages on the other side of the river they needed to check. One in particular was getting a lot of radio traffic. Sommocolonia. Whoever held Sommocolonia held riches. Beyond it lay Lama di Sotto, the ridge to which Jerry had fled. From the river, if you cricked your neck, you could see Sommocolonia's towers, teetering on the summit of the jagged slope. Mountain? Hill? How did you gauge size, when this entire panorama was peaked with unending rows of dragon teeth?

These forays were to gather intel about enemy movements, assess the local populace, the terrain – you were literally charting the lie of the land. And they were also tentative pokes. Toe-pokes, how you would poke a sleeping beast, prodding and prodding until it stirs and roars.

'Your pretty black ass is bait, boy.' Bear blew Frank a kiss. 'Git along, li'l hossy.'

Indian-file, they moved along the mule track that scissored round the mountain. Overhangs of rock, undergrowth that could be fathoms deep: plenty of ambush-happy spots. The Brazza boys had been all the way up to Sommocolonia, but the dumb fucks were so keen to get relieved, they'd given themselves a headstart. Who knew what leakage had occurred in the interim, while Sommocolonia lay unguarded? Could be full of Nazis by now. After about a mile, the track split. Frank checked the map.

'OK. Down here we got a village called Catagnana. Do it now or on the way back? Or do we separate and do half each?'

'No. Let's stay together. How many houses?'

Frank turned the map around. 'Dozen, say. Plus a little church.'

Bear led them down the road. 'OK, Corporal Comanche.'

'Yes, Sergeant Bear?'

'You take Chap and Ivan and do this side. You other boys, come with me.'

They worked their way down the higgledy street. Houses clung at different levels, anchored and carved just wherever the rock would fit them in. Most had a full complement of occupants, several with more than one family squeezed in. Judging by the parlous state of Barga, folks thought it was safer to hide out in the mountains. Not when the offensive started proper though; all these poor suckers would need to flee again. Godknew where.

In the tiny village square, a cat slept in the thin light which drove through hammered-iron clouds. In what showed on the map as a church, a little schoolroom had been set, a bunch of kids teaching themselves spelling from a chalkboard. One of them offered the Buffs some water. They declined politely, moved on, past a decent-sized villa that was shuttered and empty. Frank marked it on the list. 'Casa Pieri'. A rickety farm further down the slope also looked vacant. They'd check that later, get a local to guide them, in case of mines.

Last one. Right at the end of the track was a red-roofed house with blue shutters. A ceramic tile on the wall declared its name: *La Limonaia*. A pretty house, framed by the forest and with a terraced slope out front. The view across the valley took Frank's breath away. Reams of rolling land and purple-blue mountains, Barga ruddy and intact from here, not grey at all. One mountain in particular dominated the horizon; it was cut clean through with a perfect circle. Like a watching eye.

Comanche opened the door of the house, banging at the same time, for courtesy.

'US Army,' he shouted. '*Americani. Va bene, va bene. Amici.*'

There was a small hallway, then straight into the typical Italian kitchen. Wooden larder, big stone sink. One door in, one window – no, two doors, there was another door leading out back. Frank was sweeping the room, not admiring the decor. Those boys being shot while he watched from on high? They'd been on reconnaissance too. Through a fug of cigarette smoke, he saw a gang of men, sitting round the kitchen table. Instant alert. Six of them, three Buffs. The men had unkempt beards, and the haggard, tan faces of guys who lived wild. *Partigiani*. A teenage boy in baggy trousers was stirring a pot on the stove. Like several of the men, he wore a hat, but not the traditional beret. More what you'd call a baker-boy cap, too big for his head.

'Stand up, *signori*,' said Comanche. 'Hands where I can see them.'

The oldest of the men tipped his chair back. 'On whose orders, *americano*? You are guests in our country.'

The dry click of a trigger. 'How about I say "*per favorino*"?' Ivan, leering. Licking his lips like a madman.

Frank lifted his hand but did not touch him. 'Cool it.' You would not physically touch Ivan when he was holding a gun.

The boy at the stove glided his head, his neck, to face them. Her face. Wild hair piled under the cap, Frank's belly bursting in stars. A restless whispering, climbing inside of him. He knew it was her, it was Vittoria, because he was freezing cold and sticky. Palms of his hands, his spine. The thin line of moustache on his upper lip, beaded with sweat. Ivan, the room, the partisans, all fell away. It was only him and her. Did she not know him? *Look at me, baby. Not them. At me. Ignore everything around you, these soldiers in your home and fix on me. See me.*

The space between where he stood and where she stood was contracting; she was looking into him. Hard throb of blood. Through him. Looking at the tableful of men. The older man slid a revolver onto the table. Folded his arms. Vita spoke to him in rapid Italian. He replied in English.

'My name is Tiziano. Commander of this brigade. And you are?'

'Corporal Barfoot, sir. US 92nd,' said Comanche. 'We're sorry to interrupt your meeting, but we need to make sure this area is safe.'

'As do we, *caporale*. I have laid down my weapon. Tell your men to do likewise.'

'No can do, I'm afraid,' said Comanche. 'We need to see your papers.'

Vita slammed her spoon on the rim of the pot. 'This is Tiziano, you understand? You must know him. Yous lot liaise with him all the bloody time. Bloody eejits.'

'Jesus, man.' Ivan was jangling to hit someone. His knuckles twitching. 'What the fuck she speaking? Crazy bitch. You sit on you ass—'

Frank nodded at the commander. '*Sì, signore. Mi dispiace.*' He too laid his rifle on the table. 'Please advise your men we are friends. But our commander insists we check the papers of every male we encounter. We mean no disrespect. I'm sure as a commander yourself you'll understand the need for security – for your people as well as our own.'

Tiziano inclined his head. Another burst of unintelligible Italian, or it might have been perfectly understandable, but Frank was aware of nothing except his own concentration on Vita. He would not exist – he, this, would make no sense – if she didn't look at him. Eyes downcast, she continued to stir her pot, flushed with the heat of cooking.

One by one, the partisans produced their documents. Some had a variety of cards: ambulance driver, a permission slip from the Military Hospital, denoting a Repubblica soldier home on medical leave. Clever. The best was held by Tiziano himself. *Ente Italiano Audizioni Radiofoniche* – the state utility company. A pass like this gave the bearer access to a van, equipment, permission to roam outwith curfew.

Comanche handled it beautifully, shaking each man by the hand and addressing them individually as 'Signor Molti Nomi'. One partisan was some kind of Slav, but even he got the joke. Ivan stood, dumb, as gales of laughter swooped around him. More high-speed Italian flying in the kitchen, which Frank couldn't understand. A cold dullness was forming inside of him, like he was being frozen even as the *partigiani* thawed.

'*Parlate inglese ora, compagni*,' said Tiziano. 'We were just about to eat. Do you care to join us?'

'Um, no, thank you, sir,' said Comanche. 'We need to be heading on.'

'And you may not have enough to go round.' Frank said it pointedly, as a way of trying to make Vita engage. She was on her tiptoes, reaching for some bowls on top of the dresser. Her shirt was pulled out of the waistband of her trousers; glimpse of honeyed skin stretched drum-tight over her hip bone. He wanted, so bad, to press his face into its sharpened curve. Just to die there.

'Nonsense,' said Tiziano. 'This is a house of miracles, eh, Dolcezza?'

'Well, I need to feed the children first.'

'You can get anything here, gentlemen. Food, detonators, fuse wire, forty winks – you name it.'

'Everything except a hot bath.' Vita delivered a theatrical sigh to the assembled men, her back very definitely to Frank. 'One thing I want most in the world.'

'Sorry, ma'am,' said Comanche. 'We only brought some cans of corned beef.'

'Corned beef we take,' said Tiziano. 'Not that your food is not delicious, Dolce Vita.'

'Our Dolcezza is a magician.'

'*Eccellente* cook.' A man in a red beret raised his beaker to her.

'Actually, there is one favour you might do us.' Comanche proffered his most charming smile. 'We're looking to billet some of our soldiers.'

'Out of the question,' said Tiziano. 'We need hundred per cent access to this house. Many goings and comings, *sì?* Plus there is the issue of morality. Only this young lady lives here. We cannot have a group of soldiers—'

'*Specialmente quei sudici Mori!*' interjected the man with the beret. A few of the others laughed.

'I can protect my own honour, thank you. And this is my house.' Only then did Vita meet Frank's gaze. 'I can billet three or four of your men in the *soffitta*.'

'You watch, Dolcezza. Remember what happen to Romola Pierracini.'

'Oh-ho. *Bordello di Vita, arriviamo!*'

'*Basta!*' Tiziano clapped his hands.

Frank had understood enough. 'That won't be necessary, miss, thank you. We can use the two empty houses beside yours.'

'Sure.' Comanche took charge again. 'Would one of you gents mind accompanying us down to the old farmhouse, help us figure out where the mines are? Then we'll be on our way. And, sir, I apologise again for the interruption. Command should have told us you were here.'

'Your command does not know all my safe houses. And I would appreciate if you do not reveal this one. With the best will in the world, our safe houses are vulnerable soon as they are identified.'

'You have our guarantee, Commander,' said Frank.

Comanche stared at Frank. But it was Tiziano he was talking to. 'Sir. I'm afraid I can't promise that. It's vital we get a full understanding of the terrain we're defending – and its occupants.' Smiles all locked down now. Just weary, tight lines of mouths. Excepting Vita, who seemed more fluid somehow, as if she'd softened one degree, was bending inward like the branches of the tree outside, which made the light move in slats and ripples. *Bend towards me. Please.*

'I won't go flagging it up,' said Comanche. 'But my report will have to state this as a "friendly" area, sir.'

'Indee—' Tiziano did not finish his sentence, nor the gracious bow of his head. In slow motion, a smooth wooden stick with a bulbous spill of grey came spinning through the window, Frank never could recall if the window had been opened, but it must have been a bit, because of the cooking maybe, and the fuckers had been up that close they'd been able to push it further, lob in this firestorm. He observed its neat trajectory, heard the shout 'Grenade, grenade', the curve of it gliding over the sink, him with his big catcher's mitts, the college athlete who never missed; he felt the thick, fiery impact of it on the heel of his hand, felt a groove along the girth of it, and with far greater force than it was ever hurled, he flung it straight back through the kitchen window at the instant machine-gun fire began to spit and stud the walls; so down, down onto the flagstone floor he threw himself, bringing her with him in the hardest of tackles, and she was so fine and thin, he was bracing his elbows on the flagstone floor so his full weight was not upon her, heard the blast outside, glass like diamond dust, thick smoke – *Thank fuck it was a smoke bomb* – and there was a second of suspended gold; her breast a breath from his, swelling and falling, the imperceptible second where they clicked, they fit, and then she had wriggled out through the gap and was running for the door. Yelling, and he was after her, but she was smart, this girl; the men had taken up position at every window and on their knees outside, one partisan lay dead in the dust already, two others were in pursuit, clambering over a smouldering, screaming Kraut, which was where the grenade must have landed, way over by the empty Casa Pieri, man, that was a good throw, and Vita was taking aim, with a blunt-nosed shotgun, she would drop, fire, then run; Frank let her go as he and Comanche swept their fire across the road. The German patrol was as small as theirs, and the Krauts were sandwiched, now that Bear and the guys had come out from the other side. Ivan, insane Ivan, running screaming with his machine gun, zipping line after line of silver bullets, Bear yelling to *take some prisoners*, then Ivan fell, was lying in the road, count one, count two, how many gaps between the thunder and the lightning?

'Cover me.'

Two, three hundred yards at most, Frank ran in a crab-crawl. Under continuous fire, dragging the dumbass Ivan back towards La Limonaia, Comanche still firing, an eternity of shooting until Bear hollered: 'Cease!'

The Buffs stood still. The echoes of their gunfire ricocheted in the basin of the mountains. Waiting for a response. None came.

Four dead Germans. Two prisoners, a dead partisan (the Slav one). A bleeding-thighed Ivan, cussing to the heavens, a whooping, smoke-wreathed Bear, being introduced to Tiziano while simultaneously on the radio, and yelling, *Ist mehr? Is there more?* at a hog-tied German boy. Frank sought out Vita. She was in the schoolroom with the kids, had them all cowered behind the altar, her up front by the door with her gun.

In his head, he could see her standing there even after they'd trooped the kids out and safe home, after they'd locked up the church and radioed for transport and marched their prisoners down to the pickup. Standing in her own glow. She had said 'Thank you', and he'd said something like, 'Did you get your mom?' But she'd only smiled, a sad smile, and still her glow had not left him, nor let him in. Frank held her by her elbows, because he'd thought she was going to faint. Escorted her home. All

the occupants of Catagnana were to be interviewed: stand-
ard practice after an ambush. He volunteered to take the
statement from Vittoria Guidi.

They sat outside on the terrace as the autumn sun
began to set. Ten minutes before the Buffs moved out of
Catagnana. Another patrol had gone to recce Sommo.

'We'll need to go in when it gets dark,' said Vita.
'Curfew. Else your men will come and shoot us.'

'No, they won't.'

'Ach, well, someone will. La Limonaia is burned now.'

'Burned?'

'Canny be a safe house? Not now *tedeschi* have been here.'

'Yeah, but none of them got back to base, did they?
No comms on them that I could see. So your secret's safe.
Nobody knows this is a hotbed of—'

He was making a joke of their bravery. And she was
moving away from him again. He had minutes left. 'Why
did you pretend you didn't know me?'

'I don't.'

'But you do. You did. In Lucca?'

She shrugged. 'My mother's dead.'

'Oh, Vita. I'm so sorry.'

'Germans shot her.' Her jaw worked down on itself.
Hand flicking her hair behind one ear; one slight movement of her hand, and then she was brittle. Like glass.
A glass silence fell too. They concentrated on the curious holed mountain on the far side of the valley. Barga
spread below, the square tower of its cathedral defiant
in its straightness. Long land that concealed men and
arms, given a final burnish by the sun, until the earth was
blood-coloured, the mountains gilt-edged. This was her
view, every day. Frank thought of his momma, how she
would love it here. The speckled cough of gunfire came,
high and far away.

'And your dad?'

'My da? Jail. Germany.'

'Shit.'

'Aye.' She rubbed a strand of hair from her eye. 'How could you no have come here sooner? Just a few weeks sooner.'

'We've been—'

'And how can yous not stop bombing now? You know how many days Barga's been hit? Thirty. Thirty bloody days non-stop, by yous *and* them. Why? What have we done? You say you are our friends?'

'Vita, it's just war. Collateral damage. Because you're in the middle.'

'I know that.' She nodded towards the mountain. 'You like our Monte Forato?'

'Sure.'

'Two sunsets. You get two sunsets there. Two shots.'

'Yeah, right.'

'Is true. If you are still here in January, you'll see it.'

'Deal. January. Once we've won the war.'

'Aye.' Vita kicked at some pebbles on the terrace. Beside her was a small tree in a terracotta pot, its fruit shrivelled and black. 'But I only believe in things I see now. No promises.'

'No?'

'Nah. Just believe what you see. Things are true. That's all.'

'You can see the sky.'

'So?'

'Well. The sky's not a thing. How does that work?'

'Vittoria!' It was the partisan with the red hat, leaning out the window. '*Basta! Vieni dentro!*'

'*Scusi?*' Frank wasn't sure what the guy was saying, but Vita ruffled herself, like an angry bird.

'*Tiziano ha bisogno di te.*'

She made a face. 'I'm away in. You done interrogating me?'

'For now.'

Frank lay in his billet that night, in some broken-down farm outside of Barga. Listening to the calls of night creatures, thinking how he could have died today. And that he had found her again. Vittoria. On a stained mattress to the left of him, Ivan rolled and groaned. By candlelight, Comanche wrote a letter. Luiz was in the corner, cleaning his rifle and humming a jazzy tune. Bear was someplace in Barga, with the prisoners. One of them was just a kid, as young as their Vincenzo. Did the US Army torture kids? He felt his lips retract. Fuck, yeah. Blowing a smoke ring at the ceiling. He was getting good at it. *What did you learn in the war, Daddy?* He tried to recollect Berkeley and the guys there. Were there flags on the wall of his college room? Triangular pennants of a football team?

Maybe Frank could stay here until January. She would believe in him till then.

Chapter Twenty-two

November 14, 15

Three barghigiani dead, many injured.

Vita's tree waved skeletal fingers. The shutters were open so she could keep an eye on the track outside. It was cold, the light in La Limonaia's kitchen tinted blue. She chewed a fingernail. Skin grimy. She probably smelled. She rubbed Mamma's ring across her lip, and tasted metal.

Barga no longer felt real. Vita walked through its streets on padded air. Senses taut, heightened like an animal's. Frank was moving in her town. Where was he now? Where was he when that last bomb howled? The splintered sounds of war had become more wicked, because they might hurt him too. In the day, she searched for him. Hot and fretful at night, thinking how, if she met him again, she would explain, then glimpsing him, just once, in the Conservatorio and clamming up as she balanced bedpans, and he, in a group of Buffaloes, laughing and chatting and stopping and turning. *Knowing* that she watched him.

Vita had run to the pump outside, inarticulate curdled nonsense playing in her head. Impossible to explain; she didn't know why she was ignoring him. *I was shocked to see you.* See, that sounded like she didn't want him here. *It's like I was punched. I am scared you – they – might laugh at me. I'm an idiot.*

By the time she'd gathered herself, returned to the hallway, Frank was gone, and then a bleeding family limped through the doors, and it was *stazioni di azione*! Water, bandages, chair. Some of the older folk weren't up to moving, so the more able took turns to bring food, ease bodies to prevent bedsores and – where possible – hobble them through to the buckets the nuns had lined up in a flagstoned store. Sheets were a rarity – anything decent had been shredded into bandages – so it was imperative to keep bedding clean. Whenever a poor soul had an accident, you were mortified for them. Dignity was another thing the barghigiani lacked.

November 22

The numbers spewed beyond the madia, onto the wall with the sink. When that wall was used up, she would write them down the other side of the window too.

November 24

The tail of the *4* dribbled slightly. She rubbed it clean, screwed the cap back on Papà's fountain pen. There was no ink left, so she'd been using watered-down paint.

'I don't know why you do that, Vita. It's morbid.' Renata sat at the kitchen table, shelling fagioli. 'Rosa, stop eating them!'

'But I'm hungry.'

'We are all hungry.'

Renata and Vita had reached a truce. Though neither apologised, a small pot of heather appeared one morning on Vita's doorstep; a great-great-grandchild of the plant Zia Antonia brought back years ago from Scotland. Vita was grateful, for she missed her friend, and loved little Rosa. They didn't replace her sister, but it was nice to have some life about the house.

'Am bored, Mamma. Can I go out and play?'

'Only if you stay on the terrace. And put on your coat.' Renata brushed the pods into another pot. 'Boil these, Vita, and you can wring some soup out of them. Oh, did I tell you I got another letter from Gianni?'

'Good. All well?'

'Yes. But he's been asking about his dad. What do I say? Have you not heard anything at all from Mario?'

'No. Nothing.'

'You should ask the Red Cross lady to chase it up. The one at the Comune. I'm going to.'

'I will.'

Vita thought of her papà, alone in a Nazi cell or maybe bunked with Orlando in the outhouse of a German farm, while Orlando's son languished in an Allied prison. All of them Italians. *Viva l'Italia!* That big swirly banner folk were clinging to. Where six weeks ago the Monsignor was giving Communion to the Germans, yesterday he was with the americano chaplain, singing hymns at the piano.

'What about Francesca? Any word from her? I heard they might open the road at Borgo a Mozzano soon.'

'Really?' Vita didn't tell Renata that she slept in her sister's bed some nights, high in the soffitta. When she woke, in the slow drift up from sleep, there was a moment she could convince herself that Ces was curled beside her, and they'd been dreaming.

'Vita.' Rosa spoke quietly, shyly, lingering at the open door.

'Shut the door, piccola. It's freezing.' Today had brought the first of the proper snows, which would make movement difficult for the partigiani. Snow meant tracks, and tracks could be followed.

'Vita.' Rosa's voice had turned urgent. Vita looked up, the movement rapid, stars behind her eyes becoming pin-dots in the blue-white glare.

Aware of each single hair rising on her forearms. The heartbeat in her ears.

Frank stood in her doorway. Waiting, unsure, the freezing, ice-feathered afternoon beyond.

'I thought you might need some medicines,' he was saying. 'Bandages, a little morphine?'

'Thank you.' *Thank you, thank you, thank you.* The air was full of friction, sparking bright, clean shadows on the empty walls, replacing the leaf-light now the leaves had gone. They both knew he could have brought the medicine to the Conservatorio.

'Fancy a walk, did you?' Immediately, she was sorry, because he looked away, shy-like and stupid. 'Is a long walk up. Would you like to come in?'

'No, it's fine. Hey, hi there.' He crouched down to Rosa. 'Would you like some candy?' He offered her a small packet. '*Caramelle?*'

'*Sì!*'

'Rosa,' called her mother. '*Vieni qui.*' She pulled on her shawl, lifted her basket. '*Stiamo andando a casa.*'

'Renata, wait!'

'No. *Ogni volta che vengono qui, si soffre di rappresaglie.*'

'What she say?' asked Frank.

'Nothing.'

Rosa spoke through crunching. 'Aye she did. She say: *Every time yous come near, we get…*' The child made a gun shape with her forefinger and thumb. 'Bang!'

'Rosa!' Renata took her hand. '*Vieni.*'

'Cheerio then. Thank you for my candy-melle.' Rosa crammed in the remains of her sweets as her mother marched her out.

'Cute kid,' said Frank. 'Also fluent in *scozzese*, I see.'

'Her papà is my cousin.'

'Is that true? What her mom said?'

'No, just ignore her. Renata is a wee bit… conflicted. She doesny trust you.'

'No?'

'Nah. Thinks you're gonny steal our chickens – no that we have any left – and attack us in our beds.'

'She *fascista*?'

'*Sì.* Well… no really. Same as most folk, I suppose.' Vita couldn't tell him everything Renata had said. Her friend, who thought the Moors were *filthy black beasts*. Hadn't both their families gone to wipe them out in Abyssinia? But here they were, *walking on their hind legs amongst decent Italians. Thieves and rapists, the lot of them.*

'Hey, I'm sorry. I shouldn't have come.'

She felt a thread pulling out from her chest, tugging and unravelling at the thought of him gone so quick.

'No. Let me get you a drink.' She fumbled at the ladle; she'd scooped buckets of snow this morning and boiled them. Strained through a muslin, it was drinkable. The well in the piazza was out of bounds after the dead dog got chucked inside. The fascists were blaming the partisans, the Allies blamed the Germans. A petition had been made to the Comune to have it removed, but that was a week ago now. If someone didn't sort it soon, Vita was going to climb down and drag it up herself.

'Here.' Her thumb bumped his as she passed him the scoop.

'Outta this?'

'Sì. Unless you got a terrible disease?' She folded her arms. 'Or you think we do?'

She saw his teeth, poised on the edge of a smile, and a sweet surge came over her. Standing there, with the terrace all laid out, Papà's carved bench empty.

'Well, if you won't come in, I will come out.' She grabbed the first thing hanging on the peg – Mamma's fur coat. She'd taken to wearing it when she went to chop wood. Mamma claimed she'd worn it to the opera as a young woman. Vita hadn't believed her, unable to connect her mother with the glamour of furs. But, occasionally, the faintest waft of Mamma's perfume would rise when Vita swung the axe. Being inside the furs, having the coat hanging in the kitchen, you could pretend Mamma had just this moment taken it off. That she was animated. Not in a dark box at all.

'Hold on.'

Vita placed a yellow jug on the kitchen windowsill. A sign for the partigiani. If there was no danger, the jug stayed on the sill. If tedeschi had passed recently, she took the jug away. Sommocolonia had returned to being a no-man's-land. The Germans still moved freely on Lama, and the highest mountains behind. But sometimes they crept below the line too, using the trees for shelter. Like a church, the forest offered its protection to everyone.

She spread some fur over the bench so it was dry.

'Very grand.'

Frank sat beside her, a pleat of animal skin and a hand-breadth between them. There was a flickering in the hollow where his cheekbone met his temple. She wanted to reach out and smooth it away. He was skinnier than she recalled. Eyes narrowed against the brilliant sun. The Valle del Serchio was hushed today, crisp snow making everything pure. The earth was shadowed blue, but striped in rows of fiery sunlight, as if it were burning with cold. Bright, bright air, making smoke when they spoke.

'There's a saying my papà taught me: *All fur coat and nae—*'

'What?'

'Nothing. Is rude.' She glanced sidelong at him, just as he was glancing down at her. A glimmer there. Snowblinding. It felt like the world was falling, dizzy with the brown tumble, the cool blue rip of the sky. Then the sore, familiar beat began, of gunfire beyond Lama.

'Here comes the background music.' Frank closed his eyes. There was a slight tremor in his knee; she could feel it run through the wood they sat on.

If you were up by the Arringo, the oldest part of Barga, you'd hear the *thsh-doom* of German bombs, falling all the way to the coast. Coreglia, then Trassilico, then Coreglia again. Then the Allies, thundering their reply. Fornaci, Castelvecchio, Fornaci. Mornings might begin with a tearing explosion, then a rain of salty white powder; fall-out from the destruction of Bologna. *It spreads that far?* the people would say, although they were simply words. The barghigiani had ceased to be amazed. Ceased to feel much beyond indifference. Even when the sirens wailed, there was no longer panic. When the snow fell, there had been no rush from children to tumble in its glister. Barga was crystallised.

'I'm sorry,' she said.

'For what?'

'When you came here before. Kidding on I didny know you.'

'Oh, yeah. That. Why did you?'

'You did the same.'

'No, I didn't. I just... I was waiting to see. If you remembered me. Oh, man. Honestly? I was shit-scared you wouldn't.'

She'd not been able to explain to him, yet here he was, untangling her thoughts, laying them out so it didn't matter. He thought the same things she did.

'Me too. Anyroad. I'm sorry.'

The shoogling in his leg had stopped. 'OK. Well. I'm glad I came, then.'

'Glad it was worth the trip. So, how come you escaped? You allowed out on your own?'

'I got a very kind corporal. Said it was an errand of mercy. The rest of the guys were heading to Albiano, so I hitched a ride. I wanted to tell you...'

Her stomach clenched. Monte Forato stared back at her; a glittering mirror-peak of ice.

'We've been told to evacuate everyone from higher up the mountain. Not here, not yet. But I thought you should know.'

His pinkie finger curled into the fur, so close to her own hand. Were they touching? If they were, she couldn't feel it; her hand didn't feel like her own, all of her felt set apart from itself. Maybe Vita was in the mountain with the sleeping shepherd, watching, and it was her mirror-self here, with Frank.

'Is that so you can bomb here?'

'Yeah.' He stared at his fingers.

'I canny bear this,' she said. 'I have lost my mamma, my cousins – I've no seen my sister for months.' She smoothed her hand through the fur. 'How many people have you lost?'

'Don't know. I've stopped counting.'

Looking away from him, she could feel the snow-bleached light run down her face. And then, from nowhere, he spoke. He spoke, suddenly, to her of home. Of tall palm trees springing from arid desert sand, of coyotes that howled on the breeze. He talked about raccoons and cougars, the Sierra Nevada rising in an orange glow. He spoke of his little brother, of grey stone buildings and high white towers, of the pillared porticos of Berkeley, where she tried to picture him in a buttoned-down shirt and knitted tank top (he described it as a vest; she wanted to envisage every last drop of him, but 'vest' made her think of Papà's semmit). With perfect stillness, Frank stared beyond Vita's mountains and talked to her of sequoia and giant redwoods that would dwarf her chestnut forest; of the multitude of pines which spiked the Californian sky. How he loved that sharp resin smell you got up here, how it reminded him of family vacations in tents. *You stay in tents?* said Vita. *In America?* And he mumbled how plenty of the boarding houses would not take Negroes, and had she ever eaten a potato baked in its skin? How he missed eating cream cheese off of Ritz crackers, which his momma thought was the height of sophistication. How his momma and Willis would love this view.

'My mamma loved it too.'

He took her hand, and her heart slipped sideways. Then it was Vita's turn. She told him how the Etruscans had come here seven hundred years before Christ, scaling the Apennines, building roads, growing crops of olives, mining the land for ores. How they filled the wide spaces between the Arno and the Tiber, creating art of gold swastikas and easy beauty before Greece and Carthage and

Gaul and Rome came pouring in, and, after them, the Goths, Byzantines, the Lombards, the land all chopped up and fought for and cut and pieced together again until Tuscany was part of Italy. She told him about Paisley and the Scotland she'd never seen. She paused then. Thinking of Joe, and a life in a rainbow-glassed café. Frank's hand was still in hers. But no guilt came.

She felt an unexpected release.

'One day, I'm gonny be a teacher.'

'Yeah?'

'All those things there are to know. As many as the stars – what is the word? Inspiring? Is that, you know, when you are filling someone's brains with thoughts – but so they think them for themselves?'

'Yeah.' He smiled, but he wasn't laughing at her. 'That's the right word. Inspiring.'

'Is thrilling. I think you can do anything maybe, if you can think for yourself. My papà taught me that. He said that is what is wrong with the world. When people don't.'

'Your pop's a smart guy. So, was that you set up the little schoolroom?'

'Aye. Just weans from here and Sommo. They canny get over the bridge to school, so me and Renata take it in turns.' She sighed. 'I love knowing stuff.'

'Me too.'

'Did you know, we have singing wind caves beneath the mountains? La Befana lives there.'

'Who's that?'

'Och, she's like your Santa Claus. An old lady, who missed the birth of Christ. So she brings gifts to good children.'

'Not real then?'

She shrugged. 'What is real, Frank?'

'I like it when you call me Francesco.'

His voice was low. It felt like needles shuttling through her, flying in and out, tightening all the fibres.

'How?'

'I dunno. Makes me more exotic, I guess.'

'You don't think you are exotic enough?'

His thumb was stroking the base of her thumb. His pulse in time with hers.

'And see up there?' she said. 'Monte Forato? That's really a sleeping shepherd. He is waiting for his true love.'

'Your hands are very soft. For a *partigiano*.'

'*Partigiana*. Is soft fae the olive oil. I've to mix it with balsam to make holy chrism for the nuns.'

'Vita.' He pressed her hand, let it go. 'Tiziano says you're friends with them. The nuns.'

'You been talking about me, Buffalo?'

'Maybe you could go stay there? In the Conservatoire.'

'Conserva-*torio*.'

'*Mi scusi*.'

'I have a room in the Canonica anyway. If I need. But I don't need.'

A flock of aeroplanes droned towards the coast. For every action there is a reaction.

'You do, though. You need to leave here.'

'This is my home.'

'But you don't have to stay right here. In the line of fire.'

Monte Lama glowered behind them, the final bulwark of the Gothic Line. Pummelled daily by americano fire, as men destroyed what they could not have. And now he was telling her they would bomb its foothills too. So desperate to take Lama, they would eradicate whole mountains.

'Where? Where do I go? To not be in the line of fire? You want to tell me to go way up to Sant'Anna? Well, my cousins tried that – and they got slaughtered. You want to tell me to go back to Lucca and starve to death?'

'Don't, Vita. Please.'

'Did you take food to my sister, Buffalo?'

'I did.'

'And? What did she say? I havny heard a word from her. Or Nonna.' Vita pulled her knees towards her chest. 'I miss her.'

'I worry about you.'

'Me too.'

He worried about her. Jewel words falling from his glittery breath. She could see them in the snow. *Worry* would be ruby red, and it would be smouldering, definitely. Frank took out a little notebook and a stub of pencil. Write it on the page, she thought. Write: I worry about you. There. She could trace over it with pen later on.

'I thought you were gonny stay up here anyroad? How come is alright for you?'

'Nope. They decided against it. So you're even out-toughing the Buffs.'

Whatever Frank was writing was taking an age. He kept glancing over the valley, as if it was out there in the snow, the thing he wanted to say. The notebook rested on his lap. She realised he was sketching, not writing. Chin, nose. Eye. Her hair blowing. The twin peaks of Monte Forato, gliding easily over the paper.

'You know, when I'm back in California, that sky up there you see? That'll be the same one I see. Same sun in the day, same stars at night.'

'My nonna says stars are dead folk. The brightest ones are folk you've loved.'

'Yeah? That's beautiful. So, maybe when I'm looking up, I'll kinda be here. Or wish I was back here, at least.'

'Why would you wish that?'

He glanced at her face, sketched another line on the page.

She and Frank continued to watch the horizon, and the skein of army trucks that moved on the road below. Her legs chilled, then her backside. Soft dusts of snow began to fall. The silence between them grew; the space they'd opened making them awkward. Vita smiled at him; she couldn't help it. He dropped his pencil. Daft, that. To smile and have him flutter like a foolish boy. But it made her feel fine and calm until she realised he was collecting up his notebook and she noticed how long his hands were; sleek and dark with the little notebook slid inside, and she was undone. Her lips parted. Tongue catching a snowflake.

'You got one there too.' His finger brushed her eyelash. She held her mouth open for more snowflakes. Unmoving, staring at white sky, leaden clouds, him, tracing fire down her cheekbone, across her collarbone, almost at the top of her heart, her heart which rose to meet his hand, and the heat of her breast. Surely he would sense it? This singing inside her?

'Think it's time to go meet my ride.'

She could barely hear him. Frank's head was down, he was doing those fumbling-checking actions that signified departure.

'Would you. . .?' Her throat felt harsh, as if fine-glinting sand had been poured there. 'Come back here? Afterwards?'

'Sure I would. It's stunning.' He got to his feet. 'Even when I'm getting my ass shot off, I feel free here. We get thanked. People share their food with us. At home, there's places I can't go into, folks who won't let me speak, that think I'm a dumb—'

'You think is any different for me? I canny walk in my own hills, my own forest. I'm no allowed out at night—'

'But that's not the same thing. This is temporary. Mine is forever.'

'So's mine. Even if I make it all the way to Scotland, I'm still a lassie. And everyone hates the Italians.'

'That's not true. You guys make great ice cream. Everyone loves your ice cream. Anyhow,' he said, 'everyone hates the coloureds way more.'

Vita was emboldened. He made her brave, and he was leaving anyway. She stood, held her arm to his. 'No that much difference, you know.' She licked her finger, rubbed it on her skin. 'See? Even under the stour.'

'Stour?'

'Dirt. Am still brown underneath.'

'Yeah, but you're the right side of brown.' He pressed the tender underside of her wrist. 'You're tan.'

'So are you.'

'No. This kind of brown is black.'

'Who gets to decide?'

'Ah, Vita.'

She thought then, that he was going to kiss her. But he simply breathed against the top of her head. 'Think about what I said, yeah? It's gonna get much worse here up in the next few weeks.'

A shadow moved behind them. They split apart, fast as grass cleaves when you run your nail up its shaft.

'Lenin!'

'*Buonasera.*'

Lenin looked hellish. He wore a grey raincoat, with the collar torn. Filthy red beret, long beard, his eyes pink with tiredness. She hadn't seen him in a week; there had been too much tedeschi activity for the partisans to come down. Poor soul. How he must wish to be clean and warm in his house, or walking freely in the park. To not have frostbite on his cheeks.

'*Mi scusi.*' He was staring at Frank. '*Possiamo...?*' He indicated they should move inside.

'Is fine. We speak English? Remember Francesco?'

'*Sì.*' Lenin nodded, passed her an oilskin-wrapped package. Inside was a small black box, marked *Siemens*. '*Ecco. Apparecchio Acustico.*'

'Hearing aid?'

Lenin rolled his eyes.

'Ah! *Grazie.*' She unfastened the back. The workings had been scooped out, the cavity filled with an AC/DC power-pack.

'Vita! *Non qui!*' Lenin laid his hand across hers. The transmitter she'd brought from Lucca was dumped in her soffitta, awaiting repairs. Perhaps this would do the trick.

'This should make everything clear.' She smiled, but Lenin did not. 'Is it not a bit risky? Coming down in the afternoon?'

'Hear you got medicines?' Pointedly, in English.

Frank adjusted his helmet. 'Man. I didn't realise we were being spied on.'

'We need morphine. *Disperatamente.* Tiziano ask many times already for your soldiers to help.'

'It's fine, Francesco, don't worry. The *partigiani* often keep an eye on La Limonaia.'

'*Certo.*' Lenin faced the Buffalo. The Italian was a fraction taller, but Francesco could have blown on him, and he would waft away. 'Good asset here, *americano*. And we like to keep it. No attention drawn to La Limonaia, *sì*?'

Vita's skin bristled.

'No Mori on your *terrazza* perhaps, Vittoria?'

'I'm sorry. I should go.'

'No, you should not. This is my house.'

'Please. I have no wish to fight,' said Lenin. 'Dolcezza, another flock of sheep to be delivered. Tonight possibly. And more Alpini move in. There is news of it on the wires.'

'See?' Vita turned to tell Frank that 'sheep' was code for a parachute drop – yes, it was a stupid code, because they had no sheep here, goats would have been better, but it was Captain Bob who wrote the code, which was uselessly non-specific, because it could mean men or supplies or both. And that Vita would be needed to co-ordinate the response: finding hideouts or food for those who needed it, arranging transport onto higher ground. If Alpini troops were being brought in, that meant the Germans were mustering reinforcements – did he hear that? How she knew those words? 'Mustering'. 'Reinforcements'. See, she was a soldier too. She turned to say, *This is why I need to stay here. Under these bare trees, taking strength from hard blue mountains. It's like I drink it, Francesco, and it makes me strong. In my own house, where I'm the last of the Guidis.* Up here, she could breathe freely. Keep the faith. Not Church-faith; it was a covenant, between Vita and her family and the pulse of roots and rocks and time and all the folk who'd ever lived, or would live, here. *It's why you fight too, isn't it? For something more than yourself?*

She turned to say all of these things to Frank, that he would understand. But the americano had gone. Tucked under the fur of her mother's coat was the torn-out sketch from his notebook.

Chapter Twenty-three

'No! No, I tell you. I tell them all. You must take them away!'

'But, sir, they're here for your protection.' Frank tried to remonstrate with the priest. Such were the duties of an assistant squad leader which, as of yesterday, was what he'd unofficially become. A domino spill that had seen Lieutenant Garfield make captain. Again. Man, how it stuck in the throat of Dedeaux. 'Don't think this is on your ability,' was his farewell, to a guy who'd saved his ass daily. 'It's only a field promotion.'

Frank was pleased for Garfield, but sore they were losing him. Garfield got the final word, climbing into his jeep. 'Yeah, *Dwight*? So how come no one's promoting you?'

'*Caporale!*' said the priest. 'Are you listening to me?'

'*Sì, sì.* But I cannot move these guns.' Frank looked in vain for assistance from the gunners, whose corporal had just sliced his shin open and was being helped off to the medics. Several large-calibre guns had been positioned in Piazza Verzani, near the cathedral. It was an excellent position; gave them a clear high view over the valley and up towards Lama.

'They will draw fire to my Duomo. Always I tell you people and always I am ignored. Don't you understand?' The priest waved his wide-brimmed hat. Spectacles frosted with condensation.

'I'm sorry, sir. There's nothing I can do. *Mi dispiace*.'

'But we are coming into Advent. Where is your compassion? All of you! How many hundreds of hits already on this town? Look! Look around you.'

Where once were streets was tumbled rubble; great chunks of wall and roof paved the roads and alleys. A channel had been cleared down the centre, so folks could pass. It had the effect of making the street into a dry, stony riverbed. Battered buildings clung to one another, or gazed down on their collapsed, ashen neighbours whose shredded brick pitched into gapes where upper floors should be. The drape of snow softened it, but only in the way sculptors softened funeral monuments with marble cloth. The gable end of a restaurant stood boldly on its own; further down, the portico of an old *palazzo* led to a crater. A family shuffled past, wrapped in overcoats and scarves. The eldest boy was trying to drag a pram full of possessions over a fallen rafter.

'Sir. This is war.' Frank stamped his feet, vainly, to get warm. 'And most of the fire is coming from the German side.' Republican troops too, he wanted to say. Italians. *Your guys*. But did not. The priest was not shouting at him, Francis Chapel. He was yelling at a black boy; an upstart soldier who was engineering the final destruction of Barga, and who, in the natural order of things, should never have been telling this venerable old preacher what to do. Frank got that.

'Here. *Mi permetta*.' He took hold of the pram handle, to give the kid a hand. The priest followed him.

'Yet your men are also mining Porta Macchiaia. Even our German friends did not stoop so low. It is insupportable. Is there no honour amongst you Moors? I demand to speak to an officer.'

'I'm the most senior personnel here, sir.'

The boy with the pram blinked. His family swept around him, gathering child and pram into their midst, then trundling on. Was Frank shouting?

'You are a coloured *caporale*.'

And I ain't strictly no caporale. But to go into the vagaries of field appointments in times of war would not endear Frank to this enraged man.

'I am the Monsignor of the Duomo.'

'Monsignor! Ah.' Frank smiled his smile, trying to shift momentum. 'You a friend of Vita's, then? Vittoria Guidi?'

The priest's expression darkened further. Frank was glad he wasn't Catholic – to give your confession to those furious brows. Man, His eyes bored into the meat of you. Sucked out your marrow and decreed it wanting. It would be safer just to sin.

'Me too, sir. I too am a friend.'

'If you were a friend of my housekeeper, you would not be doing this.' The Monsignor returned his flapping hat to his head. 'Your guns are pointing directly towards her home.'

Frank knew that fine. He bent to tighten one of the ropes round the gun carriage. Which was why he was going back up to Catagnana, just as soon as he got this emplacement battened down. Fuck being a PFC assistant squad leader. He was going to be Santa Claus.

La Limonaia was quiet when Frank got there. Almost dusk. He checked round the perimeter, found the back

319

door unlocked. Nobody home. Well, he'd plenty of time. Three hours till he was on patrol again. Three hours to make the place nice; to douse Vita in sweetness, then, when she was mellow, he would argue his case. Jesus, he would get down on his knees if it persuaded her to jump in the jeep and come with him off this damn hill. Right now, a squad was mining the pontoon over the Corsonna. The guys at the front were due to fall back, pulled away to cover another flank considered even more threatened than this one. By tomorrow, or the next day, this whole area would be unmanned. Might be vulnerable for a few hours only, but Frank knew they'd blow even the temporary pontoons to protect Barga if need be. And leave Sommo and Catagnana to their fate.

He could order Vita to return to the Conservatorio, kidnap her, or he could convince her. What he wanted, above all else, was to make her smile. To give her a gift, a real thing, not just a handful of supplies. Foraging in an abandoned house, he'd found an old tin bath. Frank knew the power of a good soak. What she'd said she wanted most, what she dreamed about. So tonight, when Vita came home, the bath would be waiting for her. Hell, they could all take a bath, her and that other dame and her kid too, if it persuaded them to move off this hill.

He'd brought new soap and a clean towel. Borrowed three burners and a little gasoline to heat the water. The candlelight danced on the stove, shining up the enamel to alabaster. It wasn't pretty, but he figured in front of the stove was the best place, so the air would be warm around her. Was only a hip bath, and she'd long legs to squeeze in there. He'd like to have used the parlour instead of these hard surfaces and tiles, but no way could he carry the bath through to empty it after. From here, they could drag the tub to the back door, drain it outside.

Took him twenty, thirty pitchers to fill the thing. He didn't use their precious water. The burners he'd stolen from the quartermaster served two purposes: to heat the water yes, but also to melt the snow. In and out he trooped with his shovel, tipping snow into the cauldron and topping up the gasoline and trying not to think how much fuel he was using. Frank worked through yawns and heavy eyes, through frostbitten fingers when his mitts got too wet. Four hours on; this was his four hours off – he should be sleeping or eating. But it would be worth it. Shit. What if she didn't come home? He carried on, fashioning a screen from kitchen chairs, with a tablecloth over to keep the draughts away. He couldn't keep the water warm forever. What a waste. Maybe all the *partigiani* would pop down soon for a dip, seeing as how they kept watch over La Limonaia.

Frank was looking out for her, was all.

He sat on the remaining kitchen chair. Laid his head on the table. Finally, when he was just about to turn the burners off and leave, the back door opened. Rather, it exploded in a flurry of snow, a female yelling: '*Per terra! Ho una pistola!*'

Frank hit the deck. A blunt and gleaming shotgun pointed in his direction. 'Vita! It's me. Francesco!'

'*Gesù*. What you doing, lunatic? I could of shot—'

'I'm sorry, I'm sorry.' Pulling himself to his feet. 'I thought you'd be here earlier, OK? When it was still light. Man, will you put that down? I just wanted to...' He tailed off, stepping backwards so she could see the surprise.

Vita didn't speak. Her bottom lip moved, like she was chewing a bad taste. Frown lines deepening. Gently, he took the shotgun from her hands, laid it on the table. She swallowed, it was a precursor to freaking out... Shit, he had got this wrong, wrong; she was insulted, raising her face to seek out the top of the big wooden cupboard. Was she searching for some implement to hurl?

'Hey, I'm sorry. It was just you'd said how much you'd like a bath. I didn't mean anything by it.'

'No. You did.' Her voice was liquid. 'You meant kindness.' Small inclination of her head. '*Grazie*, Francesco. And thank you too, for my picture.'

'Sure. Well. Was just a sketch. I'll do you a better one. Look, best get in while it's still warm, yeah? There's fresh soap there – only lye, I'm afraid, I couldn't get nothing scented – and the towel's new too.' Embarrassed, rambling. Grateful she wasn't mad. 'You can keep it,' he added lamely. 'Hey, I'm gonna wait outside till you're done. Make sure no one disturbs you. Plus you'll never lift the tub on your own.'

Her chin jutted. Cute.

'Vita, *I* can barely lift it.'

'How long did this take you to do? Heating the water. Where you even get the water?'

Frank raised his hands in submission. 'It's not yours, I promise. I brought a couple gallon cans. And snow. Mostly snow. I made sure it was clean.' He had picked out every piece of grit and twig as it melted. 'Don't worry. I only used a little bit of your wood. I'll chop more. I borrowed some burners and fuel from the cookhouse. But I'll need to take them back.'

'You carry them all the way up here?'

'Yeah. Well, no. I stole a jeep. But I brought in all the snow. Tons of it.'

She shook her head. Then something wonderful happened: a luminous, tearing waterfall of laughter ringing from her throat. 'This is amazing.'

'Right. God. Good. Get in. I'll go outside.'

'I canny believe you did this. For me.'

'No problem. Be a lot easier if I didn't have to drag it halfway up—' He bit his tongue. Chiding would not work. 'OK. Well. Enjoy. Bath's all yours. I'll wait outside.'

'Is freezing! No, don't be daft. Just wait in the *salotto*. Or my room maybe, it's warmer. Is the one on the left.' She pulled off a mud-caked boot. 'I won't take too long. You'll need to get back – Frank. Have you had no sleep?'

He shrugged.

'Go lie in my room. Please. Just rest your head for a wee while.'

'You get clean, then I mess your bedsheets? Nah. I'll just sit in your lounge room.'

'*Salotto*.' In the candlelight, she was glinting: a wild, sweet, elvish thing, stirring water with her foot. Casting spells.

'Salo-*toe*. I've put a clean dress out for you too – I'll leave it by the door.'

'I wear *pantaloni* now,' she shouted.

Frank left as she was undoing the little buttons at her neck. He wished he hadn't seen that. He carried a candle through to the *salotto*. It smelled musty. When he sat on a cushioned settle, the damp came through his woollen pants. He retraced the actions of her fingers, her thumb pressing out the button from its loop, her hand stretching down towards the next one. Held his skull in his hands. Two walls and a door away, Vita was naked. It was no use. He walked into her bedroom. The window here wasn't shuttered. Blue snow-light, washing the ceiling. He put the candle down. Opened her wardrobe, and the smell of her slapped him. He had not thought this through, that they would be here alone, would never have... never have... Oh. Pushing his face into a long cascade of fabric; the sound of the sea in his ears. He walked round the room. Stroked her counterpane. Her pillow in his arms. There was a frond of green lace, a hair ribbon maybe, tossed over her mirrored bureau. He held it under his nose. Put it in his pocket.

Returning to the dark hallway. Kitchen door was fast-shut. Slivers of light on the floor and on the hinges. The only glow was inside that room; it was spilling from the cracks, the long crack in the place where the door and its hinges did not quite meet the jamb. Dirty-hating, the way you dirty-hate your hand as it slides into your pants when you are a kid and God is watching, but it slides in nonetheless; it is driven by the piston of your hammer-fist heart, the same thing that was driving him now, driving his filthy cheek into the crack of the door and the line of his sight lining up with her limbs, unsure at first of what he could see: a tan curve. Elbow or knee; no, it was shoulder. Oh, Jesus Christ, it was turning. It was breast.

The flat of his hand, slamming against the door. He heard Vita shout, but he opened it anyway. This wasn't them. Kept his eyes screwed shut, aiming to formulate a reason, a way to try and say it and not be dirty. Couldn't hear her any more, fuck, man, he must be terrifying her, and this was not him, he was not a monster. He would never, ever hurt her.

'I want to see you,' said his voice.

Crystal clink of water. Air brittle. Breath held.

'I swear I won't touch you. I swear.'

'Alright,' she said at last. 'Alright.'

So he came inside. Couldn't swallow, couldn't think right. Slid against the wall, slid downwards till he was on the cold floor. Then he opened his eyes. Thought she would be looking away from him, that he'd shamed her, and it was already too late. But her gaze was direct in his. Level. Holding his eyes, she ran the yellow soap down the length of her leg, ankle to shin to thigh. Folded it into water. Began to wash her breasts. Cupping her suds-filled hand over right, then left, pouring the pitcher high to rinse them. Drops of water hung from her nipples, her pale nipples, her untied hair wet across her face. She tossed it back and in that generous, practical movement, he glimpsed the sun as it splits blurred cloud. Heard the slow drip of moisture. He knew that there would be no one else.

Vittoria stood, faced him. Soaped the dark triangle between her legs, but it was a demure action, made him think of Venus in that picture, when she's rising from the waves, then just as quick, she was down again, pouring a pitcher full of water over her back; that neck lowered, he had seen every bit of her unwrapped for his delight, and it was still her neck that sent him demented.

He got to his feet. Didn't speak, just held the towel for her to step into. Vita, so still and so quiet. Frank wrapped the towel around her, wrapped his arms around the bundle of towel and drew her in, the fine, brilliant angles of her. He felt his knees give, but she caught him as he caught her hair. Handfuls of soaking hair, half-hummed whispers, and then he kissed her. Not a long kiss. But perfect.

'You go get dressed.' His throat was hoarse. 'I'll drain the tub.'

'OK,' she said.

'OK? Make an *americano* of you yet.'

'Can-*a*.' She brushed her lips against his nose. '*Americana*.'

He turned away to let her get dried properly, shy again after the boldness. But her bare arms came up from behind, under his own. The damp heat of her, pressing through the back of his shirt.

'Francesco.' Breathing it in his ear. 'Love me.'

'Oh, Christ, Vita. I do. I love you.'

'We might no be here again. '

Only then he understood. He turned round. Holding her. Kissing her eyelids, her cheeks, butterfly kisses until she started to shiver. Laying her on the kitchen table, gentle as he could though there was a heap of junk and tools there, pushing them off with his elbow, half-gone with the wanting of her. Her mouth on his, his open shirt grazing her skin, then his flesh was touching her flesh, and she took him close into her. Far and far in the close dark kitchen, with the hard snow arrowing the window. Slower and closer. Slower and closer, cast blue and gold by tiny flames. Belonging to no one but themselves.

Dazed. Sleepy murmurs; a coming-to that glowed. Frank stretched, running his hand along her hip. He kissed her shoulder.

'I need to go, baby.'

'Not yet.'

They watched moonlight shift in a slow waltz over the tiled floor. The snow had stopped. He put his fingertips on his heart. It hadn't. Everything had a different light to it though.

'I got to get back, or they'll put me on a charge.'

'Of what?'

'Being AWOL. On account of how we're all yellow-bellied cowards.'

She moved onto her back, put her cool hand on his face. 'No way. *Americani* are brave. Everyone knows that.'

'Not the black ones.' He kissed her breast. Unbelieving that it was his. Was it? 'I swear they're desperate to court-martial someone.'

'That is just daft.'

'It is.' Hand under her neck. One final kiss, his brain speeding, spinning that this was true. He'd woken, and it was true. 'Will you please come down with me, baby? To Barga, like I asked?'

Wrong thing to say. She sat up, dragged the towel off of the floor and put it round her. 'I got things to do here. Important things.' A hank of hair fell loose into her eyes. She was so beautiful. Sullen and belligerent.

'Vita. Winter is closing in. There's rumours Austrian reinforcements—'

'No rumours. It's true.'

'Yeah? Well, clearly you're better informed than me. So, in the next few weeks, this place is gonna get blasted to fuck. You understand that?'

'*Sì.*' She was still perched on the table, but hunched. He rubbed at her shoulders, her eyelids half-shutting.

'Then why won't you leave Catagnana?'

'Because if nobody lives here, then…' Her beautiful face was flushed and rosy. 'By Christmas we're gonny win.'

'Says who?' He needed to get dressed. She was coming off of this mountain if he'd to carry her over his shoulder. Act out a scene from those Nazi posters.

'Everyone.' She jumped from the table. Bare feet padding on the tiles. 'We just need one final push.'

'Vita. I'm begging you.'

'Can you get a message to Lucca? Are there ways?'

'I guess. Yeah, sure. We got a mail run goes there twice a week. Hey – you want to go back to your nonna's? It would be way safer than here.'

'And never see you? You want that, Buffalo?' She was fiddling with something on the counter of the big dresser. A cutlery canteen? In the dim light, he could only see outlines.

'No. 'Course I don't.'

'By Christmas, I promise.' Her words were flat, almost detached. 'I'll only stay up here till then.'

'What if that's too late? What would your sister do without you?'

'She would understand.'

'I thought you said you miss her?'

'Of course I do. But I have to do something. Same as you.'

'It's not the same.'

'How no? You can help my country but I canny? If I am at La Limonaia, at least I feel useful.'

'What about the Conservatory? You've been helping the nuns.'

'I'm no a bloody nun!'

They both started laughing. Frank paused, mid-button. 'True.'

'La Limonaia is a safe house. Is a safe house because of me. The *partigiani* won't let me fight. All I get to do is make polenta and deliver documents and ferry folk up and down. Canny even get this stupid thing to work.'

He came over, but it was just an excuse to slip his arms through hers. It wasn't a cutlery canteen; it was the suit-case OSS had made her carry. She was poking at the radio transmitter inside.

'Shit, Vita. You oughtn't to have that on view.'

'Doesny work anyroad.'

'Battery gone?'

'I don't know.' Her backside arched slightly into him. He was growing hard again. Was she worth going to jail for? Undoubtedly.

'Let me see. Sometimes the components can get corroded. You got a screwdriver?'

'Aye. Think you shoved it on the floor.'

'Oh. Yeah.' He felt full and light, as if his blood was effervescent. The radio set filled the entire suitcase. Frank opened the front plate. Orange dust fell from a nest of wires and bulbs and fuses.

'See? Rust.' Beyond that, he'd no idea, save only that Vita's admiration was trained on him. 'OK. Deal time. You come back with me tonight, and I'll take this to one of our wireless guys. They can make music come outta thin air. If they can't fix it, no one can. And if no one can, we'll get you a new one.'

Peach-skin nape of her neck. His hand, braceleting her wrist. He ran his thumb over the fine nub of bone. 'Vita. Please—'

She jerked away. 'Don't. Please.' Patted the back of his hand. 'Don't you see? If the *tedeschi* make me leave La Limonaia, then... there's nothing. For any of us. What will we come home to? This is for all of them. No just me. What if they are restless? Maybe you try to find comfort in the places you once loved.'

'Who?'

'Sorry. Ignore me. I... my da says I haver.'

'Haver?'

'Talk mince. Look, please. Can you not fix it now?'

'I'm not an expert.'

'But you are.' She kissed him. 'You're brilliant. Please just try? I don't want to take the radio away to Barga. We need it here. They've to send a *staffetta* to Castelnuovo and back every time we want to pass on information. It's dangerous.' She pulled out a rusted coil. 'Is it just that spring? Can we no find a new one?'

'Careful. Don't pull it. You got any clocks, watches?'

'Maybe in that?' She pointed to the radio, sitting on a shelf by the stove. 'Canny use it now there's no electric.'

The candle was guttering. The ticking of Frank's watch grew louder. 'Vita. Baby, I honestly don't know what I'm doing.'

She flashed keen, sharp teeth. 'Me neither.'

'Did you change the battery? I thought the power supply on these things was self-contained?'

'Don't ask me. It was Tiziano.'

'What about fuses?' He twisted a dial marked *megacycle*. 'You been playing with this? You shift it to a higher frequency and it can cover hundreds of miles.'

'No. Tiziano said not to touch it. *Tedeschi* can triangulate your position.'

'Ooh. Get you.'

She stuck out her tongue.

'OK, I give up.' He blew on the coil, shoved it back in. 'I gotta go or Dedeaux will—' Immediately, the set began to crackle. 'Hey. Alright! We did it.'

An awful static hissing. Frank moved the dial slowly, trying to pick up any traffic. Yips and woofing, a howl like a whole kennel full of dogs trapped inside the transmitter.

Fsshhnon lo farà mai il popolooshBuona sera. Gelato ragazzo sta trasmettendo Gelato raboO Boom. Eich spreche . . .

'Joe!' The radio fizzed, then banged. 'Get it back, get it back!' She was shouting at Frank. Smoke was rising from the suitcase; he could smell burning.

'Shit.' He pulled the wire out.

'Get it back!'

'I can't, baby. Hey.' She was crying. 'Ssh. We'll get it fixed. I swear to you, we'll sort it.'

'No. No, I'm sorry. Stupid.' Her hand was up, rubbing at her face. 'Ghosts. I thought I heard my cousin.'

'Yeah? Maybe you did—'

'No. Joe was killed. At Sant'Anna. Oh, I'm sorry. Don't know what I'm thinking – I feel… my head is all fizzy, know? Inside. Like I have—'

'Like you are in love?' Kissing and kissing her.

'*Sì.*' He could feel the buzz along his jawline. 'Like I am in love.'

Ten minutes to muster. If he drove like a dervish, he could do it. Frank Chapel could do anything with Vita at his side. Fate was a car crash, and the jury was out on God, but all the long lines of convergence, of dawns rising and stars coming out while the world ripped itself apart, had brought them together in this room. He would take her from this place, from every bad place. He was going to love her and look after her. Fuck it, he was going to marry her. Take Vittoria Guidi to his momma and make her proud. But first, he would get her to Barga.

'Vita, I'm begging you one last time. Come with me. Let me keep you safe.'

She hesitated a moment, her fingers lingering, lifting up his hand. Holding it to her breastbone.

'No, Buffalo. My papà also says I am thrawn. I will go to the Canonica tomorrow, because it is my job. But I am not leaving. You already have made me safe.'

The air hummed between them, musk-sweet.

'Guess "thrawn" means pig-headed crazy?'

'Aye.' She went to open the back door. A strange, orange-coloured moon hung in the sky, making the snow blush. 'Look. La Luna Rossa.'

He kissed her. 'I have to go. On duty in ten. But, just so you know, this ain't over.'

'Good. Because I don't want this to be over. Ever.'

Chapter Twenty-four

The blood moon followed the pull of the tide, trailing peachy fingers over the Versilia mountains, over the salt air of Viareggio. It glanced through an open door, where a man turned a dial and a lightbulb dimmed. Two sleeping children were swept orange as the light passed the skylight and on, over a promenade filled with Allied soldiers and burned-out buildings, over beaches lined with gun emplacements instead of deckchairs. It tinted an art deco palace, coaxing blackened walls back to ice-cream bright; it orbited the anti-aircraft guns and sandbags guarding a domed hotel; and it shafted colour on all the ruined factories and shipyards, on the wide streets and cluttered sea. Spilled fuel gleamed on wide flat water, as the coloured moonlight bounced off warships and mines, as it coated twisted railtracks and the wrecked railway station by the canal.

La Luna Rossa followed the man, followed him leaving the sleeping boys. He was almost running, running and running, because he was always running; a child under each arm, he couldn't save them all but he could save these two, his two, *I won't let you fall*, but he was running and running and leaving them all to die.

Only he wasn't. Joe was carrying a cabbage, round and fat as the moon.

The blood moon passed him passing a group of Buffalo soldiers outside a bar. Muffled in their greatcoats, laughing and drinking, yellow light spilling as more came out, folk shushing: *La porta! La lanterna!* Two of them began a duet; voices strong, tuneful, *Have Yourself a Merry Little Christmas*, and Joe listened to their words, and the melody hurt. So did the giggling women, who nodded at the Americans, and laughed at him. At the state of him in his shiny trousers with the arse near out, and his dirty old coat. But he didn't care. Aye, maybe he wasn't fighting. But what did they know? What did any of them know?

He hated using the radio. Always brief, to avoid homing in on their position. No need to invite the Luftwaffe over. But his heart still raced. People, noise; anything could trigger the fear now. At least he was doing his bit. *Hope and warnings, Gelato Boy. That's what we broadcast from here.* The Viareggio partisans had been kind to him. The news tonight was not. Thick lines of enemy artillery were on the move towards the Serchio Valley. Towards Barga.

From the promenade, La Luna Rossa shone into a side street. It glowed on the Hotel d'Ancona, and its sweeping, generous gardens in which La Proprietaria kept the refugees no one wished to rehouse. Abandoned animals. Terrified cats and dogs, beloved horses, the occasional cow. Joe unlocked the gate. A donkey brayed a low welcome, trotted over; she was a strong, stocky girl, who nudged his coat, while two ponies came for a nosy. The moonlight turned peach to red as a chain of dogs barked inside the hotel, and he shared out the greens. The two ponies bunched into the huddle. He was flanked by flanks. Lovely, good-smelling flanks.

He rubbed the space between the donkey's ears. Those stocky legs had carried two children across the mountains. The blood-tinted light covered him as he laid his head along her backbone, his cheek into her fur. On their journey here, he had slept this way sometimes, dozing in an awkward angle even as they stumbled forward and up and down.

It was Andromeda who'd found them. Paying him back for untethering her, as the bright tracer fire flew in unending vomits, Sant'Anna's barns ablaze before the gunfire strafed. Joe kept seeing the bounce of curls lit by flame, and the woman diving after. Seeing her fall and fall and a child's hand in the dirt. He kept seeing himself grasp the hand, pulling Dario by the wrist, Marino under his arm, bucking, struggling; so hard to hold them as they arched to reach their mother, but he kept running forwards, trying to outrun the whistling bullets, leaping over others who had fallen in the mud. He couldn't save them all.

The moonlight poured on his spine. Joe had no recollection of how far they'd run. At some point his legs must have given out. Then it was daybreak. It seemed obscene that light still rose on Tuscany, but it had. The swollen sun shone in his face; he was in a cave, could see a crescent of daylight in the cave mouth, and the donkey licking moisture from the rock.

Joe couldn't get those days to form any shape. Blank swathes where he'd thought of his mamma's winter coat, of nothing but following its thick grey folds. The children sobbing. Wet mist. Andromeda had carried them all at some point.

The donkey's back bumped his chest. His finger was throbbing. His trigger finger. He'd caught it in a buttonhole of his coat, been winding and winding a loose thread round. It had turned an ugly purple. He had to go. Men from here, *partigiani* with no connection to Barga, were rushing to her defence. La Proprietaria would look after the boys too, if he asked. He was making them an excuse, when they were the reason he should go.

Joe flexed his fingers, feeling pinpricks as the blood coursed in. Then he took out his pen, began to write. He told La Proprietaria who the boys' next-of-kin were, and about the café in Paisley. If it was still standing, he wrote, it should be left to the boys.

The blood moon blinked. Slipped below the sea.

Chapter Twenty-five

Vita woke to the smell of snow, and a deep, unfurling content. Unaware at first of why.

Squeezing the tenderness between her thighs. Edging her backside off the mattress, trying to get used to this new feeling. It was like her bones had shifted slightly, then realigned. Bolts of cold shot up her leg, foot striking frozen linoleum, sending jitters all the way to her teeth. She didn't care. Inside was on fire.

Chittering, she got dressed. Chipped ice from the basin on the washstand and splashed her face. Stared in the mirror at strange, wild eyes.

Fingertip-slow, he'd traced the front of her. Candlelight on his hands and the brown of him and the fawn of her, making a pattern of satin folds and overlap. Each pore opened in the chill as she recalled the whorls and tightness of his hair. He was fragile, this Francesco, he was tender hair and skin, he was brittle bone and smooth and rough; she had felt every bristle as it pocked her flesh, his tongue pushing past hers, undoing, tasting salt and sweat, the press of hard on soft, then feeling nothing but the shivers and her body correcting itself, until she was not able to think at all.

Why then? Why would Joe come back to haunt her then? Hearing ghosts had unsettled her. Guilt for a dead boy who would never get to love. Guilt was like being caught in a snowstorm. All the flurries and hints of light that would disorientate you if you let them; would have you lose sight of where you were headed. Guilt was what kept the nuns pure and lonely, and made boys like Pietro climb on a war-bound train, and made her think she should be grateful, grateful and ashamed that Joe had killed two men, when she'd begged him not to.

The americano was not like that. He was the first person who did not decide what was best for Vita. Francesco listened to what she wanted, and that made her love him more.

She had had her fill of ghosts. Vita breathed on the silvered glass. Put her lips to the haze and kissed it. The trick was to keep breathing.

Leaving Catagnana felt like flying. Monte Forato blazed in the winter sun. Saucers of ice crackled as she walked down the pitted track. Every vibration pushed at the heat in her belly, at the melt of her limbs. She picked her way over leaves which reeked of decay when you kicked them, while the wind rubbed the black-stemmed trees. Ice gave way to slush. Swathes of forest on either side of the valley had been denuded – blasted, or chopped and dragged off for whatever hellfire the war required. Trees split white as bone.

Vita let herself into the Canonica's kitchen. The ashes in the fornelli glowed. She gave them a poke; felt sparks where her legs rubbed. Put water on to boil. The sisters were at chapel, she could hear them singing through the dawn, could hear the faint, gorgeous ting of the glockenspiel that held their single note. The Monsignor shuffled overhead, floorboards creaking as he got up and moved about his room. A flashing thought came of his scrawny white ankles; that underneath his nightshirt he would be naked, everyone was naked. What a waste, not to share your body. Every person who'd ever lain with their lover – why did they not scream it from the rooftops never stop grinning and hugging themselves? Why was the whole world not singing?

'It's you.' Nico shuffled in, rubbing his eyes. 'Not hear the door then?'

'Nicodemo. Buongiorno.' She went to kiss him, but he evaded her grasp.

'You deaf, girl? There's somebody at the front door. I'm not going,' he grumbled. 'It's too cold.'

'Certo. Keep an eye on that water for me, will you?'

'Better be for coffee. I hope you're not wasting it on washing your hair or something.'

Click-clack along the hall to the front door. It was a Buffalo, a handsome, thin-faced man with a feather in his helmet. Frank behind him, wide-smiled, coy, and her flustered. Afire. How did you make your face say things you couldn't find the words for?

'Morning, ma'am. Is the Monsignor in?'

'*Sì*. Please. Come in.'

The Monsignor was coming downstairs anyway, fiddling with his collar. 'Vita, I have three funerals today. I need you to – ah, a delegation. Such an honour. And before la prima colazione too.'

Frank had brought real cheese and white bread for the Monsignor, who received the gifts graciously. 'Put this in the kitchen, Vita. And can you muster up some coffee for our guests? Perhaps find some of the chicory essence?'

'Sir,' said the one with the feather. '*Per favore*. We brought you this too.' Offering Vita a gaudy tin. She

338

tucked it on top of the parcels of food, holding everything steady with her chin.

'May I help you, ma'am?' Frank stepped forward.

'No, thank you.' The Monsignor changed to speaking in English. 'My housekeeper is perfectly capable.' She saw him pointedly look, then look again, at Frank. 'Now, gentlemen. Shall we go to my study, or do you prefer to conduct business in this raging draught?'

There was a sprig of winter jasmine protruding from Frank's breast pocket.

'Hurry along then, Vittoria.'

Back to the kitchen, balancing her load. Of course Nico had not stoked the fornelli. Vita stabbed urgently at it, added another block of precious charcoal. Stupid water. *Boil*, damn you. By the time she'd made the coffee, put the bread and cheese on a plate, they had gone. Her heart slowed. Only the Monsignor sat in his study, prodding gloomily at one of Sister Agatha's pottery owls, which stood on his desk.

'Well, our liberators have spoken. It seems we are to billet a quantity of Mori here now.'

'Oh.'

'Doubtless they won't even be house-trained.'

'It was nice of them to bring us some food, though.'

'Easy enough to give away things that are not precious.' His untwinkly gaze bored through her. 'It's probably stolen.'

'Monsignor, I don't think that's true.'

'They are simple men, Vittoria.' He bit into a piece of cheese. 'But not always good. Tell me. Did you know them at all? The taller one perhaps?'

She picked at a corner of the bread. 'No, father. I don't think so. Shall I take this away then?'

'Well, I certainly don't want food that bears your fingerprints, Vittoria. Stop that! Tell Nico he'd better start clearing a space in the basement for them. You might help? If you have no prior engagements?'

'Sì, Monsignor.'

She closed the door, anxious to escape. The man was unearthly. Did God whisper gossip in his ears? Well, maybe God should pay more attention to all the bodies littering Barga instead. The tray was shaking; she laid it on the hall table. The whole tense length of her, shame-filled. Who had seen them?

Her knuckles drove into hot, hot cheeks. Why would God make a thing so beautiful, then make it bad? Nobody could have seen a thing. The Monsignor was simply testing her. The Sacro Cuore above the coat stand looked down reproachfully. A miniature San Cristoforo joined in. Vita shook out her hair, long and knotted with the smell of Frank. The entire hallway smelled sweet. On the table, part-crushed under the tray, lay the jasmine, wrapped in another page from his notebook.

Got 24 hour pass, starting 5. What's for dinner? x

She snatched it up, lest some greedy watcher see.

All morning, Vita skimmed above the Canonica's dusty floors as she worked. She floated across the piazza to glide the corridors of the Conservatorio with more grace than all the sisters, and the diamond-hard knowledge that she knew something they never would. Never had a housekeeper moved so beautifully, dancing an unseen dance. Until it was four o'clock, and she calmed herself. Walked slowly to the Monsignor's study with a cup of coffee.

'Monsignor, I'm not feeling so well. Can I go home?'

He looked up from his papers. 'What ails you, child?'

'I just feel... not myself.' The telltale heat in her cheeks again. The Monsignor removed his glasses. Stared at her. Staring and staring, willing her to break.

'Vittoria. May I speak freely?'

'Of course.'

'Sometimes, our grief can feel very much like fear. And in our fear, there is an intensity – a panic, if you will – that makes us not be ourselves. Nor act like ourselves.'

Even when he lectured, the Monsignor was kind. He used his goodness like oil; carrying and easing, his underlying gleam making things better. He was a good man. Yet he could say those things about the Buffaloes.

'Father, it's women's pains that I feel.'

'Ah.' His coffee cup clattered in its saucer. 'Well then. Hurry along.'

There was no pleasure in upsetting him. But the pleasure she felt inside obliterated everything else.

From five in the evening until five the next, La Limonaia was their own. No vase in the window; instead it sat on their dinner table, filled with winter jasmine. Vita had gathered porcini at the rim of the forest. Stolen a handful of farina – taken it from the mouths of starving refugees – to make a batch of fine-stringed pasta. Frank brought wine and unpleasant, dry biscuits. One hour lapped into two, one kiss became a river, a sea of tenderness and crests and riptides pulling. They woke, walked barefoot, Vita wound in a blanket, the fabric trailing over her breast. Frank, tugging the fabric slowly from her, Vita hooking it over his neck to pull him in, thumbs pressing his collarbone. They lay, tangled, kissing murmurs, her resting against his beating heart, the ball of his foot nestled on her shin. And when they rose again and ate, naked, at the table, they barely broke contact, his hand between her thighs, his heavy-lidded eyes on the flex of her muscles as she moved.

'Keep the shutters closed,' he whispered.

But Vita did not wish to live in the dark. Conscious that there may not be many days when a husband and wife could love and cook and laugh. Even when they weren't touching, she was sharp to his presence; no matter where in the room he was, their thoughts caught hold of one another. It felt like spinning in a tunnel of light. When Vita looked back on that perfect day, it was unbroken light she recalled.

And when it was time for him to leave, she wept.

'Come with me, then.'

'But you won't be in Barga.'

'I will till noon tomorrow.'

'Then where?'

'They're sending us to Gallicano.'

'How long for?'

'Few days? A week maybe.' He rested his head against her cheek.

'Then I will be here till you come back.'

They agreed to meet in the morning. One last kiss before he left. She arrived in Via Mura before Frank. The bulk of Barga's walls made the street somehow clandestine. Vita leaned against the wall, enjoying the cold of the stone on her buttocks. Her whole body felt alive. She heard the low putter of an engine; could see the top of a khaki windscreen bump into view. Frank was driving. Her mouth ran dry; a beat when his eyes found hers. Vita raised her hand, enjoying the lushness of movement, because soon, at last, in perhaps thirty seconds, he would touch her again and—

There was another person with him. A mirror-hand waving. Not her own. Smaller, with her mother's oval fingernails.

Francesca. Defiant Cesca, sitting in the passenger seat. Scarlet-rimmed eyes.

'Francesca!' Vita ran towards the vehicle.

'Surprise, *bella*!' Frank jumped from the jeep, and his easy smile was too wide, too satisfied. 'I volunteered to do the mail—'

Her hand flew up, striking his face. 'Why would you bring her here? I told you, *no*. Is bloody raining bombs. Even to risk the road – you don't get to decide for me. You're just as bad as Joe. *Gesù*, she was safe in Lucca. What were you thinking, you stupid Moor?'

The words made little spears in the air. Her palm, smarting. Pain like a tuning fork down her veins. Frank's poor face. His eyes. The hurt bursting there was incredible.

She put the back of her hand to his cheek. 'Why did you no speak to me first?'

'Whoah.' Cesca caught Vita's wrist. 'Well, Frankie One. For *mia sorella*, can I just apologise?'

'Take her back,' said Vita. 'Right now. Get in the car.'

Cesca lifted out a bag.

'You hear me?'

'Aye. And am ignoring you. Cheers for the lift, Frankie One. Oh, and the Buffalo patch. I'll sew it on my jacket!'

'Sure thing, Frankie Two.' Frank kissed her sister's cheek. Got back in the jeep, his gaze fixed ahead, on the wall. 'Stay cool.'

'Did none of yous bloody hear me? You did this to keep me down here, didn't you?'

'Leave him alone, Vita. I wanted to come; he didn't drag me.' Cesca slung her bag over her shoulder. 'At least he gave me a choice. You have a very kind man there. Only one that's bothered to tell me what's happening with my own bloody family.' But Frank was driving off, away from them. 'Bye, Frankie One,' Cesca shouted in English. 'Mind and bring more sweeties.' He didn't look back. She switched to Italian. 'You are one rude cow.'

'What did he say? What did he tell you?'

Clouds passed the struggling sun, turning the stone bleak.

'Cesca, did you know? Did Nonna get the Monsignor's letter?'

'About my mamma being dead? Yes.' Harsh set to her sister's face. 'Oh, and thanks for all yours, by the way. Words from my big sister were such a comfort.'

'I couldn't...'

'Couldn't be arsed? Fair enough. Why would I need to know Papà's in a Nazi prison either, or that my cousins got butchered? What would be the point in bothering to tell me that?'

'He had no right...'

'I *asked* him, Vita. You any idea how awful it's been for me, stuck in Lucca? Hearing all these rumours and knowing bloody nothing?'

'I was trying to protect you. And don't swear.'

'I'm not a baby! And you're not my mamma.' Cesca's cheeks blazed like apples. 'You're not in charge of me.' Shoulders rigid, only her throat moving, up and down. 'You left me behind. You know I hate Nonna.'

'You don't hate her.'

'See? That's you again. You don't *know*. You're her favourite, not me. Anyway, you just left me, you didn't even come back and tell me you were going. Nothing.'

'I couldn't.'

'We thought you'd been kidnapped.'

'But did Frank not come? To Nonna's house? He said he'd speak to her.'

'Nope. We got a few tins of corned beef left outside and a note. That was it, Vi. A three-line note. Nobody to answer questions or calm Nonna down. Zio Cesare ended up coming to Lucca, she was in such a state – that's the only reason I could leave. Because I wouldn't have left Nonna on her own, Vita. Not like you.'

'Nonna wasn't on her own. She had Serafina – and you.'

'But I'm just a stupid kid. That's what you keep telling me.' Cesca's eyes glistened. 'You said you'd gone to save my mamma, and you didn't, so how can I believe anything you say again? It's you that's the stupid kid, not me.' Rocking, holding herself, caging in her tears. 'I want Mamma.'

'So do I.' Vita pulled her close. 'I miss her so much.' Cesca's face filled her vision, and the black, deep tears came on again.

'Oh, Vita. We've lost them all. The babies were so little. I can't believe I'll never see Joe again. And Mamma... I've been praying so hard.'

'I am so, so sorry. I promise I won't try to replace her.' Vita kissed her. 'And I will never leave you again. No matter what.'

She felt Cesca's shoulders relax a little. They stood awhile in the shadow of the wall.

'Did you tell Nonna you were coming here?'

'Yes.' Indignant. *I'm not a coward* was left unsaid.

'What did she say?'

'"My brave girl. You are all my brave girls." Then she went to write a letter for Mamma. I think she'd have come here too, if she could.'

'You mean a letter for me?'

'Nuh.' Cesca wiped her nose on the cuff of her shirt. 'For Mamma. She wants it buried with her.'

'But we already... We had a funeral.'

'Without me?' Her sister withdrew.

'We couldn't wait.'

How to explain: the papery fingernails on their mother's hand? Livid. Vita knew it described anger, but it meant a colour too: the hue of absent life, which Vita could never unsee. She put her arm round Cesca. 'We'll go to the grave. We'll sort something. God, I thought about you all the time, Ces. But we didn't even know if you'd got the Monsignor's letters.'

'Well, we did. And we sent letters back.' Her sister's lips were pale. Tinges of blue beneath. 'Lots of letters. At least some of them worked. They let Mamma come home.'

'Thanks to the Monsignor.'

'And Zio Cesare. He said he'd speak to people – and he did.'

'Who?'

'I don't know. He's working in something called "Transitional Liaison" now. Very well connected. He brought lots of stuff with him to Nonna's, food and that. I know he's an arse—'

'Ces!'

'Well, he is. But he's broken-hearted about Mamma. So's Nonna. But she couldn't travel and he couldn't leave her.'

'I thought Cesare would be in jail by now. They've been rounding up all the Fascists in Barga.'

'Serafina says he's a "fixer".'

'Well, as long as he stays to look after Nonna, he can fix anything he wants. Ces, you're shivering. Come on. Inside. Mother Virginia will want to see you.'

Cesca held her in a filthy, dark stare. 'I told you. You are not in charge of me.'

'No. But I am a bossy cow, so move it.'

One week passed. Became two. The weather grew colder. No Francesco. Vita, drooping, dropping a precious jar, seeing the last of the farina spill. Quarrelling with Cesca over who was more tired. Hearing boots outside. Stiffening. More drooping.

'You should have said sorry, you know.'

'To who?'

'Your Buffalo. You should have apologised before he left.'

'Shut up, Ces.'

'Grow up, Vita.'

Fighting with her sister was good; a straightforward, familiar pleasure. Patterns brought comfort. Vita wondered, when they were old women, would they still bicker like this; sistercode for knowing a history no one else did? Only they would remember Joe's daft jokes, or how it felt, when Mamma sung you to sleep.

They went to the camposanto, to watch Nico carve their mother's name on the Guidi stone.

'They won't have a proper grave, will they? At Sant'Anna.'

'Nope,' said Vita. They were sitting on a wall, in low winter sunshine which gave Nico a halo as he chiselled. A dog barked, delighted at the uncanny, cold quietness of the day.

'I keep feeling worse. Like I'm falling down a well.'

'I know.' The sky began to darken. Aeroplanes were carouselling in the distance. Long smoke trails wove together at different heights, their trails like twining plaids. 'It was my fault,' Vita said quietly.

'What was?'

'Joe, Carla – everyone. If it wasn't for me, they wouldn't have been in Sant'Anna. Not then. And if it hadn't been for me, Papà would still be here.' She hunched up her legs. 'And Mamma.'

'Well, that's just a load of. . . Vita, why would you even say that?'

'I just think it. I think it all the time. Joe shot the blackshirt—'

'Because of him. Joe shot that blackshirt because *he* wanted to. God, Vita – it's always got to be about you, hasn't it?' Her sister's scorn was forceful. Hurtful. She turned her head to tell her so and Cesca crossed her eyes, then burst out laughing. Her laughter was infectious. Nico looked up at the noise.

'We should've brought some food,' said Cesca. 'Had a pity picnic.'

'I really hate you sometimes.'

'No, you don't. I am the light of your life.'

'That's what Papà called Mamma.' They both stared at the grave.

'Yup.' Cesca swung her heel against the wall. 'D'you think it ever goes away? This ache? Or do you just get another layer of sadness dolloped on for every person you love?'

'I don't know.'

'Do you love him? That Buffalo?'

Vita focused on the great wheel of sun, ignoring the winged shadows. Made her face inscrutable.

'You look like a smug cat, just when I mention him.'

'No, I don't.'

'You're doing it right now. And you light up like a fire-fly when he's around.'

'How would you know? You've only seen me hit him.'

'Exactly.' Cesca nodded towards the grave. 'Whose example d'you think I'm going by?'

Way above them, in the steel blue sky, one of the planes peeled off.

'Don't lie to me. Life's too short, Vi. Do you?'

'I do,' Vita said softly.

'Ha! I knew it. More than Joe?'

'Oh, Ces. It's nothing like that.'

The plane moved like a lazy snake, down past the towers of Sommocolonia, easing left, circling round.

'Folk were always going on about me and Joe. But it wasn't – I'm not even sure it was Joe's choice. I'll always love him, same as you. He's... He was my family. But, see, with Francesco...' Toes curling, the heat of her skin in the cold, cold air. 'God, I can't explain. It's like there's a candle inside me. Don't say anything to anyone. Please.'

'It's alright, you know. He's really handsome. And nice.'

'He's a Buffalo.'

'So?

'So, it's different. Plenty folk don't like the Moors. Here.' Vita got up. 'Give me Nonna's letter.'

'Thought you said it would be sacrilegious?'

'Nico.' Vita went to where the old man was working, chewing his tongue as he concentrated. 'This is a letter from my nonna. She wanted it buried with Mamma. Please?'

The errant plane drifted wide, snaking back in the direction of Barga. A lazy, yawning snake, its great underbelly gaping as it dipped across the Serchio. Drifting, drifting.

Nobody moved.

'We should get inside,' said Nico.

Tearing echoes rang across the valley, before a brilliant, slow explosion lit up the sky and turned the air from grey-blue to orange. All three of them stood mute, staring at the terrible colours. The rest of the planes disappeared.

'Where was that?'

'Gallicano, I think. Oh, give it here, child.' The old man snatched the letter from her. 'But do not tell the Monsignor. Now get indoors, the pair of you.'

'He likes you,' whispered Cesca. She was pretending to smile, but her lips trembled. 'I thought Nico hated everyone.'

The roaring in the sky diminished. Gallicano. Where Francesco was.

The days, and the bombs, continued.

December 4, 5, 6

Francesco had been wrong. It was not safer here.

The Conservatorio was a desperate place. Almost no water, little food. Despite stuffing rags in the gaps, the wind blew through holes and glassless windows, freezing the sick and homeless gathered inside. The sisters did their best. An old man had rescued the rabbits from the Asylum, and they were stinking out the cellar. More mouths to feed, but the Monsignor said the rabbits in turn would feed more mouths, and Vita was not to grumble. She couldn't bear to look at them. Her mamma would have slapped her for her sentimentality. Cesca said she'd feed them when the old man grew too sick to move. Cesca was braver than Vita. She was also an excellent nurse. She would aid the nuns with lint and salve, fold bandages, thread needles with a dextrous touch that Vita lacked. All Vita did was drop stuff. Whenever boots crunched on a fragment of Conservatorio window, that jangling feeling started again, her breast filling with glass. Shaking floors, gullies, mines: the very earth you walked on was not safe.

An unexploded missile brooded in a house below the Duomo, and there was nobody to move it.

Almost impossible now to reach Catagnana. Whenever she tried, Buffaloes she didn't recognise would stop her at the bridge, turn her away, and she'd give up protesting. Ask instead: *Do you know Francesco? Francis Chapel?*

Sometimes they'd laugh, say, *Hey, baby doll. Why you wasting time over him. He bailed, sugar. I'm here. How 'bout me?* Other times, they'd frown and ask her name. From where had she got her information? Was she *fascista*? *Partigiana?* But Vita was nothing. Her absence meant the House of Miracles had ceased to perform.

She prayed for a real miracle. On her knees in the Conservatorio chapel, clasping her hands over her trousers. Several girls had taken to wearing men's clothes since the Mori appeared. The nuns had been encouraging it, doling out breeches and dungarees.

'They are not all bad,' Sister Agatha whispered. She was sitting in the row behind where Vita was trying to pray. 'These Buffaloes. But they do have questionable gallantry. I had one of them propose marriage the other day.'

'To whom?' said Sister Bertilla.

'To *me!*'

'Well, two of them offered me some army boots.'

The nuns continued to chatter as they waited for the Monsignor to begin. If it had been Vita whispering, they'd have chucked her out.

'You should have taken the boots, Sister. We have great need of—'

'No, dear. *Sell* me them. Not gift. They care too much for brandy and chickens, I think. Now, physically, they are unattractive. But with their hands full of cans and cigarettes...'

'Sisters!' The Monsignor cleared his throat. 'A little charity, per favore. We must appreciate the more primitive nature of the Moors. It can't be adequately controlled by moral education, you see. Even their spirituality is a little... wild.'

Vita left them to it. What did they know about anything that was real?

December 11, 12, 13, 14

Closing doors, windows, closing your eyes, offered no protection from the winter storm. *Der Wintergewitter.* Beyond any mediaeval siege Barga'd suffered, she was being systematically battered to the ground. Her people were trapped. The americani, terrified of spies, had posted roadblocks at Borgo a Mozzano, prohibiting movement in or out. The near-dead were an exception – if escorted by military personnel. Even refugees could no longer leave in search of shelter or food. Jeeps and soldiers zooming everywhere, huge wheeled cannons, and boots, boots, forever rumbling past. None of them Frank's.

Vita slept with Cesca in the small room at the Canonica. At night when the bombs fell, they were meant to shelter in the cellar, but going outside panicked Cesca. So they would just hold each other, and wait for it to pass. Afterwards, Cesca insisted on opening the shutters. Together, they would count the stars until she was calm.

December 17, 18, 19

The thudding, demented war music screeched on, intensifying as more soldiers assembled. The promised Buffaloes arrived to take up residence at the Canonica – but they were white, not black. *Officers*, said the Monsignor approvingly. These men brought their own food, and didn't share. Partisan battalions too were joining the Americans, lending support from all sides – they were coming from as far off as Viareggio, Tiziano said. Vita met him one day in town, leaving a meeting of the Comune. He wore an air of desperation. She asked how the partigiani were faring.

'Ach, everyone has perpetual coughs. We are all aches and rheumatism and strength to be preserved.'

'Why are there so many soldiers coming here?'

'Does it make you feel reassured?'

'No.'

He lowered his voice. 'We're to make a massive assault on Lama di Sotto. This is the big one. The *final push*. But you must not say; not to a soul.'

'What can I do to help?'

'You are serving here, Dolcezza. Soon, there will be no more subterfuge. Our men are mustering. We're coming into the light.'

Truth or rousing battle-cry? A new commander had arrived, Tiziano's position in the hierarchy slipping even further. '*Pippo.*' Tiziano sniffed. 'That's him over there. With his bodyguard.'

Vita could only see heads and bright berets, swinging into a US truck.

'They've made his battalion part of the Fifth Army. Autonomous Patriots. Ridiculous name. You keep safe, Dolcezza.' He kissed her on both cheeks. 'Stay here and do your best.'

She surveyed her pitiful basket. Four large mushrooms and a meatless bone. This was her best. How was she to feed twenty mouths with that? Their basement was filled with refugees and strange Buffaloes, the Conservatorio packed with wounded souls. There was no longer any currency in using the Monsignor's name, because there was nothing left to buy. Soon, very soon, they would starve.

She made her way back to the Canonica. As she climbed over the fallen lintel of a house, a boy stepped out. Gallus lad, chewing gum, and affecting an American accent.

'Hey. You Vita?'

'Who's asking?'

'Vinnie. Work with Comanche and the guys?'

'I don't know what you mean.' He looked dodgy. Could be after her mushrooms for all she knew. 'Let me past.'

'Got a message from Frankie.'

Vita halted. Gripped the boy's collar. 'Is he alright? Is he alive?'

'Sure he's alive. Says to tell you he'll be here at first light.'

'Thank you. Oh, thank you.' All the brittle glass burst out of her, a thousand cleansing splinters of relief. Not realising how sore they'd been until they were gone.

'Yeah. Ran into a bit of trouble over at Gallicano. But we whipped their motherfucking asses. Scusi.'

'Don't be sorry.' Light flashed on distant Monte Forato; the crimson bleed of sunset, and a little burst shot through her heart. If you stood, and concentrated hard, the world was still beautiful. 'You keep whooping their... whatever-you-said asses. Did Frank say anything else?'

'Nope. Just that.'

Vita went to bed that night to dream of love. But she dreamed instead that she was inside the sunset. Its amber glow was part of her, and she was reaching, stretching into rays, letting sky rise past her as the earth kissed, granular and warm. The air was pounding, like the coming of a stampede.

A dull heave woke her. White-whining hurricane of paper, frosting eyelids. Salty, crashing waves. Vita, slow.

Stupid.

One second of muffled calm; of faintly ringing air that billowed with the soft give you get when snow falls, then she leaped from her bed.

Flying roof tiles and sheets of glass were crashing past the windows.

Far away, Cesca was screaming.

'Where are you?' Couldn't understand her own words, tongue twisted, ears packed with... feathers? Soap?

The walls of the house were bowing out. The skewered ceiling, the high void of it senseless – she could see the Monsignor's dressing gown flapping at the sky. Grit pattered her face, the powdery, falling ash dusting everything white.

'Cesca! Cesca!' Words falling, echoing.

'I'm here,' shouted her sister. 'I'm stuck. Help me.'

She pulled Cesca from under the upturned washstand. Broken mirror glistened on her skin, bright blood dripping.

'Can you move? Wiggle your fingers.'

'It's just cuts.' Cesca was flicking off the glass. The ceiling, all cloudy, muffled gapes. Blood trickled into Vita's eye. She hauled herself over the debris, yelling up at the gap in the roof. 'Monsignor! Are you alright?'

'Vittoria?' Quavery, old, like he hadn't yet put on his persona.

'Hold on. I'm coming.'

She tried to open the bedroom door, but it was stuck. Icy air whipped her face. Hammering on the stubborn wood, seeing her fists rattle, hearing only dull thumps.

'Nico! Nico!' She could smell burning; her ears suddenly rushed and piercing, Vita wincing at the whimpers above, the cries coming from the families crammed below.

'Get out of the basement,' she shouted, stamping on the floor. No windows there, only wooden stairs leading up, to what? Kitchen, to the storeroom, to the kitchen where she could smell burning. Gesù. If the kitchen went on fire, they'd all be trapped.

Then women's voices came, ringing. The sisters, calm and patient. Mother Virginia calling: *We will get you out.*

Ragged air, curtains blowing like spectres. The wind eddied leaves of white paper, chinkling glass and crisping flames. Bangs and confusion below. A nun recited the rosary through the open ceiling.

'Is the Monsignor safe?' Vita shouted.

'Sì.'

The Canonica yawned and the ceiling groaned, bits tumbling further through the hole. Other, deeper voices arrived, pounding boots and smashing doors. Americani orders: *On the count of three.*

Feet and fists.

Stand back, stand back.

Two of the white Buffalo officers were reaching inside. Hands, arms, finding theirs. Lifting her, carefully, out to the starless sky.

They were lucky. A few bashes and gashes. Nico was cut by jagged wood, but there were folk injured far worse. Vita saw Lenin and Tiziano, running past with a makeshift stretcher. Soldiers doused the flames in the kitchen, using a rain barrel and blankets, the Monsignor walking himself out, albeit with a sister at either elbow. The soldiers moved them all away from the unstable wall, round to the Conservatorio. The poor sisters, their building had been struck too, but it was a glancing blow. Sister Agatha knelt on wet cobbles, nursing a casualty: the wooden Nativity she carted to the Duomo each Christmas. Beside her, Buffaloes laden with rifles and packs were tending to a little boy, blood pumping from his head wound. Cesca ran to help.

'He'll need to go to hospital. Sarge, can we get this kid to Pisa? Like now?'

Vita knew that voice. Hard to see faces, in the smoke and bitter dark.

'Francesco!'

His tin cup clattered as he spun round. 'Vita! Baby. Are you OK?'

'I'm so sorry.'

He had grown a beard. It sculpted his beautiful mouth, his cheekbones. Made him strange, alluring. She ran her hand over his features. Smoothed his brow. His straight, fine nose. She could feel a wound on the side of his cheek, a patch of torn and part-healed flesh. 'What happened to you?'

'Think that's bad?' he whispered. 'You should see my butt. Hey! Your head. You're bleeding.'

'Is nothing.'

'We should get you to hospital too.'

He held a square of handkerchief against her temple. Around them, small fires raged and timbers fell. The sky seemed to droop and bevel. This must be how an earthquake felt. The sucking in and spitting out. The crack appearing. The little boy was carried past, arms limp. She imagined Barga receding as she sped in a truck towards clean linen and a quiet bed, watching her valley collapse.

Vita laid her head against Frank's chest. Smoke coiled into house-shaped spaces, a hard and amplified tingling in her skull, her tongue tasting dust. Only this clear, bright bubble. Through the push of his heartbeat and the hissing containment of her ears, she thought she heard a man's voice. Low, resonant with fury.

È disgustoso.

Then the bubble ruptured and the crackling, whooshing, rustling dark, and the shouts and the moans, broke through. Her head pecked side-to-side, trying to see who'd spoken.

'Baby. Hold still.'

Blood pumped again, hot into her eyes. Frank went to wipe it, and a fist came crashing down, striking his hand away.

'You! Are you goddam deaf or goddam disobedient?'

Immediately, Frank released her, sending Vita stumbling against the man who'd hit him.

'Get your whore off of me, nigger.' The man shoved her against a wall; a white soldier, the Buffalo patch prominent on his arm. 'Know why they call 'em booby traps? 'Cause they all got the pox. Gonna send you one of two ways – a bayonet course or the goddam grave.'

His words ebbed and flowed around her. Vita, dazed, waiting for Frank to react. But he just stood there, clenching his fists.

'Listen up. Y'all hear me, men? I repeat. You Buffaloes are no longer to fraternise with – nor fuck – the locals. Do I make myself clear? Spies, fascists and thieves, the lot of them.' The officer yanked at Vita's arm again. She thought it was the fat-necked one who'd driven her to Pescaglia. 'Go make out with one of your own, *puttana.*' She didn't understand. A thin, chill moment where she thought Frank must speak. Then, through the smoke and debris, Mother Virginia appeared, like a tiny, furious crow.

'Filthy.' She pushed the officer. 'You, away. *Avanti.*'

'Hey, sister! You stay outta—'

'Leave her alone, ya big bawbag.'

Cesca stood in front of Vita. Barghigiani were assembling in the shadows and the smoke. You could *feel* folk watching. Mother Virginia draped a blanket over Vita's back. She drew it tight, wanting to hide herself entirely. Only then did Frank step towards the officer, but another soldier, the feather-capped one she'd seen before, blocked his path.

'Yes, sir, Captain Dedeaux. Roger that loud and clear. C'mon, Chap. Move it!'

Without protest, without looking at her once, Frank let himself be led away.

Chapter Twenty-six

Frank, Claude, Ivan and Comanche, walking four abreast through the tail end of Barga. Luiz and Bear up ahead. Frank, tight and hard as iron, his lover's blood on his hands. The fury filling him. Fuelling him. Next chance he got, he would kill Dedeaux. Easy enough: just slip your trench knife behind the windpipe and jerk. Comanche's nails dug into his elbow.

'Fuck, man. You can let me go.'

'Your lady friend all right?'

'Yeah, Claude. Thanks.'

'She the dame you been beating yo' meat for, Chap?'

Always best to ignore Ivan.

'Wild one with the hair you was butt-pumpin' back there? You and Dedeaux share her?'

'Fuck-up, asshole.'

'Can't say I recognise her from your crappy drawings.'

'She's fine,' said Claude. 'What she called?'

'She's called Vita, Claude.'

'Ooh, Vee-ta,' Ivan sang. 'I'm gonna eat her.'

Frank had blown it. 'Course he fucking had. What would Vita understand about orders? About white men, standing on your neck? Jesus. Those beautiful long angles of her, lit by flames. Seeing the planes of her cheekbones melt like they were wax. Watching the whole of her face cave. He'd never get to trace the pulse of blood that ran through her neck again. The vulnerable uplift where he'd pushed at her hair, wanting to bite down, to own her, there, in the burning street. His battle-hardened body screaming *just fuck her, man.* While she was hurting. Bleeding. Real hard, Francis. You let a peckerwood humiliate her, without saying one single word.

The violence tightened. It was under his breast, his tongue; it smarted his eyes.

Surrounding him were boys full of bluster, thumping, gouging, mutilating their way into being men. Doing it with bristle-sharp pride. In a hamlet above Gallicano, an old Italian had led them to a farm. Nodding and pointing that, *sì, this was it.* No *tedeschi* there now, of course. But the family inside had been feeding German officers. *Traditori.* Making dinner for them night, after night. Worth questioning, *sì*? On the approach, Frank shaking their guide's hand, *grazie, grazie*, the Italian being reluctant to shake his in return, pulling away, that familiar crawl of disgust at *americani* uniforms coating Negro skin, *man, fuck 'im*, the upstairs window already open though it was cold, his brain ticking from curious to—

Drang and drang and drang and drang: the machine gun had ripped from inside, a fucking set-up, the guys in front mown down, metal shaving his face, Frank just quick enough to fly out a tackle, bring the Italian to his knees. He had used the man as cover, letting his skinny body take the flak. Afterwards, when the position was secure, the dead and wounded Buffs dealt with, the Italian was still breathing. Frank had taken his knife and gutted him.

He bit down on his lip. He had wanted Vita to make him clean.

'Sarge,' said Luiz. They'd stopped outside Barga's whore-house, an unobtrusive *casa* that was part of an old mill. 'We got five minutes, yeah?'

'Not for in there you ain't, boy. You not hear *il capitano*?'

'I gotta go say my goodbyes. There's a little *chiquita*—'

'I'm sure those ladies will survive without you.'

'Serious, sarge. I left my wallet in there. Kinda had a tab going...'

'Jeez-Luiz. Five minutes.'

They leaned on the wall of the bordello, each man pretending there were not soft skin and willing mouths beyond the scarlet curtain. All Frank wanted was Vita. In the warm crease of neck he wished to bite, he would find himself. *Frank Chapel. Berkeley Campus, University of California. A regular guy.*

Bullshit. Frank was a liar. Every soldier with a pulse lies. They lie when they pretend to be two people, to split the Jekyll from the Hyde. They lie when they spit at fear, or fake nonchalance at the screams, or feign disinterest at the point they no longer hear them. Man, that is when you should be screaming loudest of all, when you are going, going.

Gone.

A troop of *partigiani* came down the street. When they saw the Buffs, they nudged one another, began to march. As if they were signalling: *We are the soldiers. Not you.* Frank closed his eyes. Asleep, awake, this metamorphosis of skin to scales would eat you up. Was this his life now? Was this it? Muddy snow, snowy rain, shitting and shoot-ing, being caught on barbed wire. Giving hills numbers and running up, getting shot at, slithering down. Snow-dampened booms, hot earth hitting skin and your trigger finger bleeding, blood gone ice with cold. Huddled round fireless campfires, your back against your buddy's back, so that when you spoke to one another in low voices, you spoke into air. Speaking to the mountains. Different answers came different days – mostly crashing shells, or polar indifference.

'Chapelley, a word.'

'Please, sarge.' Frank looked at Bear. 'Not now.' A leadenness had come over him, glossy black like crow feathers, and he'd the sensation that if he tumbled into it he would never stop falling.

'You got to leave her be, you hear?'

'OK, bros. I is done.' Luiz emerged. Hand raised. 'Gimme skin, Ivo.'

'Ooh, Vita. I gonna eat-huh. Ooh, Vita—'

Bear cuffed the back of Ivan's head. 'OK, children. Let's move.'

For the rest of tonight, they were detailed to hole up in Ponte, keep an eye on the bridge. Krauts had been making forays down the mountain in their absence; man, the Buffs were stretched so thin right now, one sneeze and the line would bust. They were almost out of ammo. Difficult getting anything through the lines. Mule skinners were working day and night to transport weapons and rations to the troops; they were literally scaling mountains for them. Fattening them up for the kill.

Bear kicked the door open while Claude circled his rifle wide, taking obs on the hills. Luiz rolled inside, flamboyant and dumb. *Clear. Clear.* They were using an abandoned shop, the one with the yellow stars. Two upstairs windows, facing front.

'Oh, Vita.' Ivan was dry-humping the door frame. 'You taste soo sweet.'

'Can I get a minute, sarge?'

'Ain't gonna bail on me, Chapelley?'

Frank fished out a pack of Lucky Strikes. 'I just need a smoke. And a break from that piece of shit.'

'One minute. Else I gotta come kill you, baby bear.'

Frank hunkered at the side of the building, where it jutted and joined onto the next one up. *Boom. Schwwsh.* White flashes on the mountains. His whole body hurt, the sound was inside him too, trying to explode itself out from under his thick black hide. He wished he could hear silence again. *Schoom-whish.* Trying to make the dark hush. Trying to recall his momma's scent. He drew the smoke deep inside his lungs, holding it till his mind went blank and dizzy.

From nowhere, a crunch slammed the side of his head, booted feet knocking him sideways, flash of red cloth as a forehead butted him, hand clamping over his mouth. Punching on his throat; he was choking, could feel the sharp tip of his cigarette burning through his neck. '*Non toccarla*, Moor,' a voice hissed. '*Capisci?*'

The pain bloomed through his cheekbone, cluster-blasting behind his eye.

'Vittoria Guidi.' From the corner of his swelling lid, Frank saw a dirty red beret. 'Leave her alone. *Capisci?*'

Another punch, hard into his balls. Pain cleaving from his groin to his belly, and a deeper toothache pain beneath. He welcomed it.

Kick me more. Fucking do it. Finish me, man.

The guy released him. Frank curled, speechless, on his side. Focus on the stars. Breathe. He waited, cheek freezing on the hard earth, until his assailant had disappeared back into the dark. Then he hauled himself up, limped inside.

'What the fuck happen to you?' Ivan grabbed his rifle. 'Who did that?'

'I fell.' Frank eyeballed Bear. 'Guess I gotta be more careful, sarge.'

Bear eyeballed him back. 'Guess you do, baby bear.'

Next day. Late afternoon. Frost gilding the ground. No Krauts had snuck down to Catagnana, but no Buffs had come to relieve the nightshift neither.

'Can't feel my feet, man.' Luiz jigged up and down, the wooden floorboards creaking.

'I can't feel my balls,' said Ivan.

'We got to stay here another night, sarge?' Claude was pissing, elegantly, out a window. 'You think the captain forgot about us? We ain't got no food or water left.'

'No radio neither.'

'No, but we got this.'

Comanche had discovered a locked door under the attic eaves. Containing one accordion, a trumpet-thing, assorted other instruments and a stash of clear, sharp-smelling alcohol. Bear wouldn't let them drink it.

'Know what, children?' The sergeant struck a match. He had kept this one stub of cigar unlit in his mouth all night. 'I'm gonna make me an executive decision. If we are still on our lonesome by the time I'm finished this smoke, we hit the road.'

They returned to Barga through the beginnings of a snowfall, Ivan sharing surreptitious glugs from one of the bottles he'd liberated, to discover the 366th Infantry Regiment had arrived. A bunch of unloved bastards whose own colonel just quit. First time in action, they'd been mostly guarding airfields since June. Not their fault they were green. But it seemed the newbies were getting acquainted with L'Alpino rather than relieving them.

'You boys go get a drink. Get warm,' said Bear. 'I'll find *il capitano*. S'all gone to shit since the lieutenant left.'

L'Alpino was rammed. Full of 366ers. These new men made Frank awkward with their excitable voices, their undimmed eyes. Their casual ownership of this town. Vita's town.

'Frankie, man! Baby! You're looking swell.'

'Charlie?' One of the new guys was his college mate from Berkeley. Oozing backslaps and high-hands of familiarity. Frank didn't know why it made him angry, but it did. He slammed down a shot of brandy.

'Love your cute l'il beard, Frankie. Hey – you know we called this one the Urgent Virgin in college?'

Frank necked Charlie's beer.

'Hey, man! Get your own.'

'Thought you were pleased to see me, Chaz?' His words slipped into one another. He was so tired. Should really get some food.

'Urgent Virgin,' whooped Ivan. 'Man, I love it.'

Comanche shook his head, slung Frank another shot.

'Yeah, but the Urgent Virgin done popped his cherry, I do believe. Ain't that so, Chap?'

Fucking Ivan. Comanche laid his hand on Frank's arm. 'Ignore him. You wanna go get some chow?'

Frank shook his head. Poured another brandy. Fuck it. The room was getting cloudy; fugged with smoke and... His hand jerked, spilling another man's beer.

'Ho! Watch your—' The guy stopped. Moved away. Fuck him. Fuck them all. The *partigiano* who beat Frank up was one of Vita's lot. Maybe she sent him. Maybe she really hated him now. Man. His hand was bleeding. How'd that glass get broke?

'Right, men!'

Frank tried to focus. Why was Bear standing on the bar-top?

'She doesn't want me, Com.'

'Keep it down, man.'

'Listen up! Colonel Sherman wants to brief us on transition. Officers are already present. Get yourselves sober and your asses shifted. Right *now*.'

Fast-marching through the old town. Seemed Comanche had him by the arm whenever they swung a bend. They assembled inside a cramped *palazzo*, in an odd, tall salon stuffed with horsehair chairs and opulent couches, with two long dining tables and assorted stools. As if every missing stick of furniture in Barga had wound up here. Dedeaux had been to the barber's; blond crew cut, hair sharp as sharp. Shame *il capitano* wasn't. Check him out, swaggering up front, trying to crawl up the colonel's ass. Frank was so thirsty. The alcohol had dried out his throat. Colonel Sherman said a few words, the usual rousing platitudes, then, for reasons that were misty, but involved *being straight from the horse's mouth*, handed over to Captain Dedeaux, and departed quick as he came.

Dedeaux sipped a glass of rum while he spoke. Mean bastard kept his liquor close. 'I'll make this quick. Most of us will be waving bye-bye to Barga very shortly. I'm delighted to say, we got ourselves some fresh black blood.' He smacked a startled 366er on the back. 'You boys are all most welcome. Plus, I believe the injuns are heading in soon to join the fun. Proper ones. Not your woo-woo kind.' He actually ululated, sucking his hand over his fat, stupid mouth. 'But firstly, I need me some volunteers. A few brave boys from the 370th to hang around and augment the 366th.'

Bear's hand went up, middle finger slightly higher than the rest. To the untrained eye, it looked respectful.

'Suh?'

'Yes, sergeant.'

'May I ask how long these volunteers would require to stay behind for? And what would their detail entail? Sir?'

'I was coming to that, McClung.'

'Like fuck you was,' mumbled Frank.

'Captain, may I?' Lieutenant Fox stepped up. Fox was the 366th's forward observer. Guy looked like a film star, slim moustache and steady eyes. Frank would've liked to know him sooner. You could tell his men rated him. At L'Alpino, he'd been surrounded by a bunch of them, hanging on his every word.

'As you men know, winter is closing in. We got OSS reporting Mittenwald troops advancing at Monte Uccelliera, and more of Kesselring's men moving into Castelnuovo. Clearly, momentum is building. So. We need to strike at them before they strike us. If Jerry's thinking like we are, he won't want—'

'Bullshit,' said Dedeaux.

'Excuse me?'

'Bullshit. Fifth Army Command have stated clearly they can see no indication of an enemy attack. Jus' spies planting false intel – to scare the crap outta these chickenshitters.'

There was the bullshit, right there. Everyone knew enemy activity was increasing. Partisans had spotted Monterosa too; that fearsome hybrid created by the Fascists, of ex-Royal soldiers and raw recruits. They sure weren't coming to visit their moms.

'OK, sir,' continued Fox. Barely blinking, running over the top of Dedeaux, so smooth the prick was taken unawares. 'Well, what we do know is, we need to take Jerry out. Take Lama di Sotto, take control right along the Serchio, before their reinforcements have time to amass. Therefore, our aim is to march two platoons up to Sommocolonia, where we'll meet with a local partisan platoon. From there, ideally we'll march onto Lama di Sotto itself. At the same time, two other Buffalo companies will head to Bebbio and Scarpello, so we're in position to facilitate a multiple, co-ordinated attack. Of course, there are no guarantees. The terrain's extremely difficult, the enemy, within their Gothic Line, are incredibly well-ensconced—'

'I'll do it,' said Frank. 'Suicide mission sounds good to me.'

'On your feet, soldier,' said Dedeaux. 'You some kind of clown-show? Aiming to fuck up my men's morale?'

Frank sat where he was. 'Sir, I am one of your men. And, if you ask me, it's—'

'Suh!' Bear got to his feet. 'I guess I can volunteer my squad. We all familiar with the terrain, and with the type of enemy action to expect. We'd be happy to accompany you 366th gents up to Lama Ridge. And,' projecting his voice, 'straight on over the other side. Let's kick us some Kraut ass!' he hollered. 'Let's kick 'em way over the mountains and back to fucking Krautdom come!' Fist pumping as his other hand administered a warning jab to Frank's temple.

Bear slapped him harder when they left the briefing, Buffs spilling into freezing Barga, plenty 366ers still whooping. The rain had turned to sleet, roads and steps were shiny-slick. A corporal skidded down the sloping street, gaining speed. Fell on his butt, to claps and cheers. A young woman stepped disapprovingly over the corporal's legs.

'Hey, college boy,' said Bear. 'You *fixing* to get court-martialled?'

Frank shrugged.

'Here.' Bear offered him his hip flask. He took a swig. Took another. A-fucking–other. Felt the burn tear through him, splashing and searing his empty belly. Empty world, empty stares: him staring out, that passing woman staring in. Frank almost wished the fierceness would return – would welcome a blast of it, but it was all held inward. Or maybe it had died too.

'Easy!' Bear wrestled the brandy off of him. 'What the fuck is wrong with you, Chap?'

Frank knew that dame. It was Vita's sister. 'Hey, Frankie!' he shouted. 'Hey, wait up!'

'Leave the kid alone, Chap.'

The girl skipped around. 'I don't want to talk to you.'

'*Scusi*, signorina. Chapel, get you sorry ass back to base. Go get cleaned up.'

'Sarge.' A 366th corporal broke in, clutching a map. 'You gotta sec? I can't find where we s'posed to be.'

Frank slipped round the huddled Buffs. Following Cesca through slender, winding streets towards the edge of town. Sparkling walls towered either side. Shuttered nothings. He was in a ghost-maze.

'Frankie! Frankie One, please. Wait up.' His voice reverberated.

'You are pished. Away home.'

Frank's eyes filled with sudden tears. A dripping, persistent uncertainty at first, then they were coming so thick they felt like a storm. A lightning storm. Home. Electricity pulsing through his brain, black holes where his family, his life, should be. In the centre of the storm, alone, was him. One day, when he was an old man, all this would be surreal. His memory would fade and he would forget the intensity of this moment, the rub of the boots that tore his heels, the perpetual damp resonance round him like shadow. If he could forget the softness of his momma's skin, he could forget anything. Forget why he was here, when here was a circle of forever, a wheel on which, daily, you ran. But Vita had come and made it right. She was everything.

'Is Vita—'

'Go away!'

'Cesca. I'm begging you. Jus' tell me. Does she hate me? I gotta know.'

'Hate you?'

'I gotta see her.'

'No way, pal. You *stink*. You stay well away.'

'But I love her, Frankie.'

'Well, you've a gey funny way of showing it.'

So busy jabbering over her shoulder at him that she too succumbed to the hazardous ice. Of course, being a sure-footed Barga girl, Cesca only slithered. Enough to make her glide into him.

'Frankie, please. I'm sorry. I should've kicked the shit outta Dedeaux. But he's my captain, and—'

'It's no *that*. Here, your eye's all swolled up.'

'What? Yeah, I know.' He waved dismissive fingers. 'One of Vita's pals.'

'*Vita's* pals? Who? Mother Virginia?'

'Nuh. The Commie one.'

'Lenin? Aye, well, no wonder.'

'No wonder what?'

'He *seen* you, Frankie. How could you?'

Frank shook his head, vigorously, and the whole street began to slide from under him. 'I don't get you.'

Cesca hoisted him by the arm. 'That's the problem. You don't get any of it, do you? She loves you, you eejit. And you've went and broke her heart.'

Chapter Twenty-seven

Christmas Eve. Hour of the final Novena. Vita reached beneath the table, for the basket of candles. The Duomo was filling, folk shifting, silent, over pink marble tiles, to the places they'd always stood. Midnight Mass was at four o'clock this year, because of the curfew. She unrolled a waxpaper cone, to count the remaining tapers. Surely then, the duelling guns would cease? For one night, they would get a respite from constant fear and noise. Christmas Eve had fallen on Sunday. You couldn't get a day more holy.

December was nearly done, and the barghigiani had endured. Relentless shelling; day upon day where folk died and the skyline changed irrevocably as another palazzo vanished, or the campanile at Albiano fell.

She shook out the waxpaper. Only three tapers left. No candles in the Conservatorio either. This was no good. There had to be light on Christmas Eve. She put her shawl over her hair.

'Ces! I'm away to find some candles. Five minutes.'

Her sister nodded. She was binding pieces of Joseph together with straw from the manger. He'd come off worst in the shelling. Vita went down the rampa, to the warren-like streets of the old town. Treading carefully, a deep crust of snow lay on roofs and cobblestones. That little droghiere near the Comune might still have candles, if she said it was for the Monsignor. She'd say he'd light one specially for them. Worth a try. What Vita needed was a magical emporium, a shop like Signor Tutto's. Frost rang beneath her boots. The soles offered little grip; they had worn so thin, she could feel the ice coming through.

She stared through the grids and shutters of the empty shops she passed, trying to picture last year, when those same stores had been filled with Christmas bustle, folk haggling over the last of the panettone. Rations had been saved, small, secret parcels stashed and the bells were pealing from the Duomo in obstinate joy. Mamma was alive, war was still beyond their mountains and the night was for Baby Jesus, for the children. This afternoon, a handful of people poked in the few shops that remained, darting like furtive rats. The droghiere was shut. She pushed her forehead into the window grille. Piles of screwed-up paper on the floor, the type fruit came cushioned in. No baskets of oranges and lemons. No dark green leaves of carciofi, nor papery chillies woven into a plait. If she concentrated, she might fall like Alice through the mirror, spin headlong into a topsy-turvy world that made more sense than this. In the windowpane, she saw a man behind her. Tall and fine, he was a long, dark dancing line more brightly dangerous than any fuse. The freezing metal of the screen tingled, rusty on her skin.

The man at her shoulder was not really there; he was a warm imagining which ran up her spine. He had loved her and she had let him. Why not? She'd no mother, no father. Who was there to care? Why should she not lose herself in pleasure, when it was so scant in the world? And so what if it was lies? If he had betrayed her? Deliberately, Vita tried to make it a small, angry matter, a thing of animals and defiance. Placed spikes round her heart like mines, because whenever she let her guard down, a mouth of such misery and want consumed her. She hadn't room for it. Loving folk brought pain.

She watched the reflected activity across the street. Comune officials packing boxes into a car. More rats. Vita turned from the window. Her gaze shifted across the road. A US truck was parking beside the Comune car. Two military policemen jumped out. They approached a young woman who was doing the same thing as Vita: staring into an empty shop. Grabbed an arm each, and started tugging her towards the truck.

'Help me!' she pleaded. But nobody intervened.

Their friendly liberators had begun arresting Italian women, to check them for disease. All it needed was a finger pointing, a whispered *con un moro*.

'Dirty bitch,' said a passing man. Vita bowed her head. Perhaps she would be next. Mother Virginia's fury at the Buffalo capitano had taken the edge off any accusations. But people talked. Renata suspected, for one. And Lenin. Her cheeks felt hot. The US truck drove off, peeping its horn, forcing the Comune officials to scatter. There were a handful of other women already in the back, clad in robes and nightdresses. Le donne perdute. The women you never spoke about, never acknowledged if you passed them in the street.

Puttane.

He hadn't wanted to say it, at first, Lenin. When he told her. About the Buffaloes he'd seen at the bordello. Vita placed her cold palms together. Blew on them. *Sì.* The lightest, twisting hiss. *Sì*, he'd said eventually. *The Moor from your terrace. He was there too.*

It had nothing to do with her.

Nothing had. She felt entirely detached. Anger cooled to steel. This was war. Transactions were how you operated. Firm-binding circles become spidery lines, cut adrift and shapeless.

The Buffaloes had claimed him.

Vita climbed the hill, towards the Duomo. She would learn not to care. Her feet skidded on black ice. She braced herself, pressing the side of a high, louring wall, using the gaps between stones as handholds. She should have stayed in Catagnana. In Barga, she was impotent. A refugee, tended to by nuns. As the days grew darker and smaller, so did Barga's streets. They were claustrophobic, dusted with their own remains. Each streak of sky above each vicolo was thick with ash. Her breath puffed in front of her, hot then cold. Hanging now onto the low hedge, slithering up the Duomo rampa. A pamphlet stuck to the sole of her boot. She peeled it off. One of those horrible ones the Luftwaffe were dropping: a half-nude woman encouraging the *Boys of the 92nd* to *Slip over to Jerry!*

Vita stamped her boots, entered the cathedral by the side door, which gave onto a thin, vaulted corridor. Cesca met her, smiling fit to burst. 'I found some tapers.'

'Did you? Great. Well done.'

The lassie was bouncing on her toes.

'It's not that exciting.'

'Someone's here to see you.'

Her heart slipped like a fish. 'Who?'

'Oh, someone. Someone tall, dark and handsome.' Her sister dragged her under the graceful arches.

'No. I don't want to see him.'

'Vi, please. Hear him out.'

It had been four days. She felt sick. 'Where is he?'

'I'm here.' Frank was waiting for her in the shadow of an arch. Vita fell forward, lost herself in olive drab and oilskins. Then pulled back.

'I'll leave yous to it. I'm away.'

Vaguely, Vita heard the door into the sacristy opening, her sister going through. Frank took her face between his hands. 'You're too pale. You been eating?'

'No really. Oh, Francesco.' Stroking the roughness. 'Was I not enough for you?'

'Did Cesca not tell you?'

'Tell me what?'

'I didn't do it. Baby, please.' He caught her wrist. 'We don't have much time. You got to believe me.'

'What? That it doesny matter? You and your friends, in the whorehouse?'

'Vittoria, I've never, ever—' He stopped. 'OK.'

Her stomach, falling.

'Twice, I have been to a whorehouse. But I never did a thing either time. I swear. The other night, we were just waiting on Luiz. Outside, I promise. And the first time was months ago.'

'Months? Not here?'

'God, no. Way back in summer.'

'Before Lucca?'

'Yes, before Lucca. Of course before goddam Lucca.'

'And you never—'

'On my momma's life. I just... let the lady have a nap. Before she had to – do the next guy, you know?'

Lightness swelling. Becoming tears, at the waste, the *waste*. At how you can choose what you believe.

'Francesco.'

She loved how the tip of his tongue touched his teeth, how he thought before he spoke. How his eyes became so bright and vast that it was like staring at the sun. She buried her nose in his neck. He smelled of smoke and snow.

'I *missed* you.'

'I love you so much.' Her hair shivered under his mouth. 'I love all the colours of you.' Kissing the top of her head. 'Here, where you're *cioccolata*.' Tilting her neck so he could reach her collarbone. 'Here where you're *caramelle*.' Lifting the underside of her wrist to his mouth. '*E latte*. Here's good too.'

Through the door, in the body of the Duomo, the Conservatorio piano played. She and Nico had dragged it up the rampa this morning. The Monsignor's baritone resonated, practising his singing; determined this service would be perfetto for his flock.

Tu scendi. A faltered note.

Francesco began to unbutton the top of her blouse. 'I love this bit, where you are creamy *caffè*.'

Tu scendi dalle stelle

His lips nudged the swell of her breast. Kissing her out of her senses, as though the sky had swung, dreadful and wonderful, and she was lost.

'I love you, Vita.'

'I love you.'

The outer door creaked. Clutching her shawl to make herself decent. The quick light of a match, then an American drawl. 'Gotta split, Chap.'

'I'm coming. Vita, I have to go.' But he hesitated, closing the door again so the two of them were the only two creatures in the universe. Laced his fingers between hers.

'What does that song mean?'

'"You descend from the stars."'

Holding one another. Strong arms. Frail bone. The seconds ticked by. Holding hard curves till they were softer than your own shape, until you didn't know where the ending of yourself began. That was a fine thing. To feel another's body contain your own, and the bright, slow shine of it wind round and through the pair of you. Being that close. If the boys who were Germans were allowed to do this tonight, if the boys who were Jocks and Tommies and Austrians; the Indians, the Fascists, the black boys and the white, the americani, the partisans. Just allowed to kiss their sweethearts and be quiet and kind with them for one last time, then they'd want to hold them for always, she thought. There would be no more fighting.

'We're going up the mountain tonight. To Lama. One last big push. So they say.'

'I heard.'

'I don't know if—'

'I love you, Francesco.'

The outer door was pushed open, with more urgency this time. 'Chapel. Shift your ass, that's an order.'

'I'm coming, Com. Vittoria—'

She put her finger to his lips. 'I love you.'

He nodded. Then he was gone, and Vita returned to the music of the Duomo. The Monsignor raised one hand to her from the piano as he played. His cheeks were pink, he looked happy. Fortress on the outside, soaring within. She loved him as well. Loved everyone, everything. The high, glorious echoes, the veined marble floor, here, this carved stone of the pulpit, this great square basin with majestic lions for feet. Cesca had left the tapers beside it. Vita moved them onto the altar, dipped her head before San Cristoforo. Three metres tall and nearly a thousand years old, his wooden form dominated his cathedral. After this Mass, the Monsignor said he was to be stored for safe-keeping. How could that be? It was their saint who kept them safe. She stared up at his crude jaw, his golden crown. At the boy king seated on his shoulder.

San Cristoforo, who carried Christ. In sieges past, the barghigiani would parade this statue round the city walls, to scare the enemy and fortify the defenders. Arrow fragments were embedded in his wood. San Cristoforo should not be hidden away.

She walked backwards from the altar. Don Leoni tutted as he took his chair: he didn't hold with women anywhere near San Cristoforo. Well, tough, old man. Needs must in times of war. The organist was sorting his music at the piano. Around a hundred folk in church. They were just about to start, Nico fussing with the Monsignor's stole, four chierichetti waiting to process down the aisle, when a volley of shots rang out. Some distance away, but loud enough to remind you, lest the uplift of music and incense, the audacity of warm bodies come together in love, had encouraged you to forget. A few nervous blinks, but the congregation continued singing, the organist playing the piano with bravado. Vita searched the cathedral for her sister, saw her with some schoolfriends. She went to join the girls, and the side door from the corridor opened. For a wonderful second, she thought it was Frank returned, but it was a group of partisans. They did come sometimes, to receive Holy Communion. Usually, they left their guns outside.

'I'm sorry,' she whispered to a man strung with cartridge belts, edging in next to her. 'But you'll need to—'

The partisan took her hand. 'Buon Natale, Vittoria Guidi.' Beneath the cloth cap, Dina's face shone. Dina from Pescaglia. She kissed Vita twice, leaned over to shake hands with Cesca.

'This is your sister, I can tell.'

Vita felt the church swell, grow larger than anything outside. With her friend on one side and Francesca on the other, they stood to greet the (premature) birth of God.

Later, when the music had died and the people filed out, they shared a bottle of grappa behind the Duomo: the Guidis and this bunch of undesirables. The Monsignor would be furious – at the brutta figura, and because Vita and Ces were meant to be serving an early supper for the priests. But the sisters and Nico could manage what meagre offerings there were. Of greater importance was feeding the refugees and the sick, and Vita had seen to them before she left.

'You sure it's safe here?' They were clustered directly under the wall of the Duomo. A contingent of Buffaloes shifted more sandbags round the gun emplacements, fiddled with tripods, adjusted heights. Snow fell, scurrying the dark mess of the soldiers' footprints. Vita kept looking, but he wasn't there.

'We're fine. That shooting earlier, it came from over there.' Dina pointed in the direction of Campo Sportivo. 'Miles away. So, sister partigiana. You up for this?'

'For what?'

'Battle.' Dina frowned, as if the answer was obvious. 'How else will we kick the tedeschi out? Brofferio Partisan Formation.' She saluted the dozen ragged men they stood with. 'At your service.'

'Me? No.'

'You can hold a gun, no?'

'Well, yes. Grazie.' Vita took the bottle of grappa from Dina's brother, bypassing Cesca. If their mother were here, she would tan their backsides. 'Dream on, Ces. You've had one sip already. You don't understand,' she said to Dina. The grappa tasted foul, but she swallowed it. 'I can't fight. I've got Cesca. I'm all she's got.'

'I do understand. I have a daughter. In Pescaglia.'

Vita tipped the bottle to her mouth again, shocked. Sunset scudded across the mountains to the west, sending flares of pink and gold light into the air behind the snow, the clouds lit yellow underneath. The twin peaks of Monte Forato melding into the form of the sleeping shepherd.

'I'd like to bring her here one day. To see your double sunset.'

In response to Nature's show, a volley of guns fired on the other side of the valley, behind Lama, where it was already evening. Strings of red and azure bursts illuminating the sky.

'It's like angels dancing!' shouted Cesca.

'Or they're shooting at the stars.' Dina's brother flourished his gun.

The shine of light grew watery until Vita couldn't see. She realised she was crying. Overwhelmed and frightened.

'What's wrong, amica?'

'Just ignore her,' said Ces. 'She's in lurve.'

'Shut up.'

'With an *americano*. He's going up there too.'

'Sì? Well, come with us then. We leave tomorrow. Nothing's going to happen then. It's Christmas Day.' Dina took back the grappa. 'We'll have a party in Sommocolonia, get some rest, devise strategy – for God-sake – you're a local, you know those hills better than anyone. Salute!'

'Vita, *please*,' said Cesca. 'Renata and Rosa are still up there. It must be fine. You said it's worse down in Barga. And I *hate* being with the penguins. They'll just make us pray all day.'

'See?' Dina wiped her mouth, thrust the bottle at Vita. 'We'll join up with your brigade, liaise with your americano, then next day – we strike! Plenty of time for you to come back down. Or come with us to Lama, if you decide. Come on, Vita. To be there when we liberate Tuscany. What a story to tell your grandchildren.'

'I can't. I'm sorry.' She returned the grappa to her friend. The snow was getting heavy, soaking through the weave of her shawl. 'C'mon Ces. Let's go home.'

'That's what I want to do, Vita. I want to go home.'

'Fuck it. You live, you die. That's it.' A kind of gleaming madness had come over Dina. She waved her hand, spilling grappa, splashing her comrades with it. Some of Dina's men were chatting to the Buffaloes, who'd stopped work, were nodding and joking with the partisans. 'Hey, Vita,' shouted Dina's brother. 'What's this big guy saying?' His arm was slung round a tall americano. Cigarettes were being shared.

'*Ancora, ancora.*'

'Repeat what you said?'

The americano struck a match for his new pal. 'Tell him I say: *We all bleed the same.*'

Dina smacked Vita's arm. 'Ho! So, where's it going to be? Where do you want to do your living, Vittoria Guidi?'

'Vi, *please*, please. Just for tomorrow? Then we come straight back down. You can fetch Mamma's fur, and we can get her big quilt. The patchwork one. Please. It can be my Christmas present.'

'Alright,' Vita yelled into the fading day, louder than she meant. 'Alright, then. We'll go.' So loud, it might have floated all the way up to wake the stars. Might even have burst into flame. Found a long dark fuse, and followed him all the way up to Sommocolonia. Or it might just wake the giant.

Chapter Twenty-eight

The Buffaloes left when the moon was high. Bright air, snapping underfoot. Pin-quiet; Frank's brain slooshing inside his skull. Echoes of the next footstep and next and next, the creak of your pack, your boots, and the infinite replications of the man moving next to you and the man next to him, all those neat, soft ripples, widening out and rising up and splashing wide, filling this whole vast valley with

You.

The you that was praying to be invisible, in this high bright moon, on this scrape of path and trees. Luiz up front, scything for mines; then Ivan, his hood flipped with his helmet pitched on top like some overdressed doozy, hefting his Bangalore pipes, which would blast through barbed wire like a bullet through flesh, one pop, then bam – bits flying every which way. One blast, one scream right now and that was you, hollering. 'Hey! Over here, guys! Hey, Krauts! We're right here.'

They'd know soon enough.

Two platoons of them, Foxtrot and Golf, snaking their way through the foothills below Sommocolonia. *Fear not*. The Buffaloes are coming. Maybe one day some of the suckers marching alongside Frank would return here, come on vacation with their grandkids to a land lush with olives and sun, and discover they'd named this long drag after them. Wouldn't that be something?

Soldiers up ahead were whispering. Not Bear's men. They were deathly quiet. It was the new guys. Frank cursed as he stumbled on a tree root. Twice his ankle had gone and buckled on him. Their low jabbering unsettled the air.

Vita unsettled his bones.

He was aware of each movement, how his tendons flexed and his muscles pulsed; he was aware of the night call of troubled animals. His blood leaped at the slightest thing, on the cusp of boiling over. Fat smacks of snow batted his eyelashes; he could see the crystals in them, dripping in raw lines down his face. He bowed his head. Against the snow, his bootprints made shadows, great savage holes which retained their shape for less than a minute. If he looked back, he could see the muffled whirl of snow fall in, eradicating the marks he'd just made, only for the next man to muss up the cleanness with his own stamp.

'Hey, Frankie. Cheer up. This is it, huh? The big one. Get your mojo on.'

'Charlie – keep it down.'

Clear, ferrous tangs as the snowflakes struck his mouth. Falling in globes, not heavy, but busting on impact into almost-rain. Soon, it would be through them like a wicked spell, chilling from ground up and neck down. He had walked this path several times; he'd driven up this steep-sloped terrain, sat on Vita's terrace. Viewed this land from on high. It was part of her, so it was good and fruitful and kind. He'd always been careful and he'd always come back down. Tonight felt different. It had been quiet today, but quiet wasn't always good. Quiet gave you spaces; spaces and vacuums that filled with swirls and ghost-men, forming images you thought you'd locked up tight. Quiet gave you a thin sheet of paper and a pen. Gave you jitter-bugs in your gut, assholes whispering in your ear.

What exactly were they marching to? Dedeaux had been on fire at the final briefing. *Trust no one, boys. Your arrival has to be a Kraut Christmas surprise. You got me?*

Suh. Yessuh.

The enemy are everywhere. They're that shopkeeper you josh with, that kid you give candy to. The belladonnas you insist on fucking. These people are Fascist to the core — it's their religion.

Had he meant to send them forth with resolve and pride-filled breasts? All he'd done was made them jumpy. From the minute the company left Barga, Frank felt like a kid inside a nightmare. Every building, every clutch of hayricks could be monsters. The circling hills with their ripped-up trees? Tombstones. He saw gaping faces in the snow. He wasn't sure, if there was to be an after, how you would trust things just to be things again.

He pressed his lips, trying to taste Vita on him. He knew fine why he felt this dread. Love, and the simple terror he might lose her again.

The snow had stopped. They were deep in the forest, the darkness between the oak trees thicker, branches obscuring the moon. Small points of light from occasional stars stabbed through, spinning on their way to someplace else.

'Hold!' A mittened hand was flung across Frank's belly, and he, automatic, hit the next down the line, and the next and the next. Why they broke you down in training, so you'd be no body but *the* body. The spit on his lips freezing. Leg cramps. A tiny turn of his head, either side. No one was looking. Frank inched his foot on a fallen tree trunk, grotesque with pleated vines. Nice just to rest the muscles in a different way from down. This ceaseless stomping, heel to toe on miles of foreign soil, up foreign hills. Past foreign faces that would've shot you back in spring. Yet he would stay here in a heartbeat. A leaf grazed his forehead. He wondered if 'corps' came from 'corpse'. He would like to know words again.

Lieutenant Fox moved forward. The fact he was here, marching in the midst of them, that his driver and radio-man were walking with him too – it was a kind of loyalty unknown to Dedeaux. Having dispatched his men, that redneck fuck was most likely headed to Viareggio for some R and R.

'Hey, Frankie,' said Charlie. 'How about you conjure—'

From nowhere, Bear flicked Charlie's ear. 'Bit of shut-the-fuck-up you don't get, *bwoy*?' Not stopping though, the sergeant never lost pace, just kept bouncing up and down the line like this was what he lived for, the bulk of him everywhere – in your face, at your back. Frank's eyes doing pantomimes at Comanche. Comanche turning away. You could tell he did not care for Charlie.

'On' came the command. The path lifted here, a high arch with the ground falling steeply to one side. On with their careful shuffle – very careful now Frank could see the sheer rock drop and how this flank was so exposed. Across the valley, at the corner of the sky, Sommocolonia revealed herself again. The moon was behind the big tower; it was a horror film, or the cover of one of Willis's comics. Behind Sommocolonia lay the long ridge of Lama di Sotto. Beyond that, the Krauts. Or maybe not, maybe they were swarming on their bellies right now, crawling over the ridge, between the trees. Coiled inside Sommocolonia, playing dead. Thank Christ, Vita was safe in Barga.

With every glimpse of Lama, Frank's lungs grew tighter. Behind him, a line of men. Sixty of them, strung like paper dolls. What was better? he wondered. To be the first to fall, or to be behind and see it coming? Leaves squelched under churned-up snow. The path narrowed through the trees, Frank ducking under half-torn branches. The weight of his pack pushed him forward as they moved downhill. The plan was to make it down to the river, then cross near Ponte di Catagnana.

'Hold.'

Flat of Comanche's hand on his belly, Frank's on Charlie's, Charlie's on Claude's. In the moonlight, he could see where the trees became more sparse. Like a curtain opening on scene two: *The Road*. Whichever way they went, they'd need to cross the road at Ponte, the one they'd been avoiding. Against open tarmac, you were flat-out exposed. Bridges meant mines and tripwires, even bridges you'd checked yourself not twelve hours past. They would cross upstream, way behind the pontoon, where it was shallow enough for their line to get across. He flexed his toes inside his boot. Three men went forward – Fox again: that guy was straight up. You'd want him at your back, if he weren't so damn good up front.

They were brave, all these guys were brave. Yeah, like you had a choice not to put one boot in front of the other while every cell of you was screaming *no*. Man, what is brave about just existing, just holding all the damp insides of you, the liquid bowels and leaping heart in a thin bag of skin, skin you know is fucking fragile and will bust and split and let your life force out? No, what is brave is turning round and walking back to Barga. To Vita, who loved him. A noise came up from his mouth. If he saw her again, he would ask her to marry him.

He felt Comanche's hand. A sliver of foil. Passing him some gum.

'You OK?'

'Sure.'

When you stopped, you remembered you were tired and cold. Not his job to think. Frank had learned when his mind could cruise. To accept those gracious seconds where your body carried your brain. You were a limb – hell, a digit – of this body, you were a drone in the hive. Soon enough the dance would start again and your switch would be flicked. He stared across the darkness. The moonlight caught like white fire: tips of trees, a fingernail of light on a curve of rock. Painting on the mountain tops, spilling into the valley, where it pooled like ice and snow. Stare hard enough and it became an illusion, a lake of light that was not really there. You could just step out into its coolness. In some far-off shack, a dog howled.

'On.'

Slithering down the slope. Get across the river, then double back to the mule path that would take them up to Sommo. First: make it past the strip of houses that ran along the road.

'Is that Ponte then?' Charlie, sotto voce.

'Yup.'

'What a dive. More like No Point-ay if you ask me.'

'Nobody did,' said Comanche.

Slowly, they moved in threes and fours, backs tight to the trees, face-on to the open road. Beyond the bridge, the river was a little wider. All the rain and snow had made the Corsonna run deep. Sliding, clattering their backsides down the pebbled bank. Bear first, testing the depth; but he was six-six, *and that ain't no benchmark,* said Luiz.

Bear's one finger, pointing. A mouthed 'In'.

Rifles up. Shit, don't forget the handgun acquired from Vinnie, no questions asked; waist-deep water, only everywhere was swirling higher than it should, a month of rain and snow and mud filling up, faster and faster, making soil thick and water hard. A constant firecracker of sucked-in breaths, *Jesusgodalmighty*, the ice ripping up your veins. Frank stood, trying to be solid in the flow. Legs sinking, could no longer feel his feet. *Don't look up.* He was a little boy again, lying in bed with the dreadful certainty that eyes lived inside the darkness. Watching him. One fragile chain, cast across the waters. He waited for Jerry's artillery, but it didn't come.

'C'mon, man.' Comanche touched Frank's elbow. 'Gotta move. '

Twenty seconds to make the other side. Hands stretching to pull you up the bank, and your frozen, sodden pants scalding your thighs back to life. 'This way.' Bear's hand on your shoulder, counting each man as he shoved them on. Skirting the other side of the road, facing the chestnut woods they'd just come down through, round one neat bend, and there it lay. The track to Sommocolonia.

'Wait.'

Frank sheltered into the rock overhang. About ten of them had grouped, hidden from view by the sheer hill rising over them. A muffled thunk; Ivan resting up beside him. The Bangalore torpedo he nursed was fifty feet long when full-grown, packed with pounds of TNT. Five-foot lengths of threaded pipe, which you screwed together and assembled along the way.

'See how high I had to lift her? She is *heavy* tonight. Love to meet the asshole who invented this bitch.'

'You say that every time.'

'I mean it every time too. Hell. I am shit-sick of climbing.'

'Yeah.' A deep bass – it sounded like Claude. 'Wonder how many of us be coming back down?'

'You shut the fuck up, farm boy.'

Frank reached for Ivan's arm. 'Enough.' Felt Ivan pull away, go close in Claude's face; Frank could see the sleepy eyes, the slow-jowled surprise that anyone was even listening to him.

'Don't be saying that, OK? You get that? You get that, stupid nigger?'

'Hey—'

A fist swung, then a rifle butt, then Bear sliding in from Godknows where to crack skulls (it was a literal skill of his) and silence them with threats of lynching.

'Now get your miserable asses in some semblance of order, stand tall and get climbing, you hear? Claude, what the fuck you doing, boy?'

'Takin my socks off, sergeant.' Claude hopped and swayed, one boot heel in one meaty hand. ''Cos they're wet.'

'Fuck, Comanche, just you keep beating on him 'stead of Ivan.' Bear straightened his doughboy. 'OK, my children. Santie's coming.' Teeth, gleam-sharp in the moonlight. 'And a Merry Christmas, one and all.'

No one spoke on the way up. Only rasping breaths and crunching snow. The terrible silence of no guns firing intensified. *Fucking bring it on, why don't you?* But the Krauts would not come out to play. On and on, gliding upwards: maybe they were ghosts already. And then, like herald angels, US guns started firing on Lama di Sotto. Great spits of colour soared above the Buffaloes' heads. In turn, the Germans hurled their fiercest response down onto the banks of the Serchio. Back and forth, like kids aiming to holler loudest. Soon it seemed as if the entire Lama ridge was set ablaze. An appalling brightness illuminating their climb, shining their faces gold. Black shadows roared from incandescent trees further up the mountain, but still the Buffs ploughed on. None of it was aimed at them, this stream of men cowed and moving against the rock. *Tell yourself that.* Tell yourself you are inured to everything. You have to. Lesson one trillion and one: pretend to enjoy the light show.

Then, as ominously as it began, the pounding stopped: a few final stutters of ya-boo firing before both sides bowed out, returned to sullen gloom. Even the moon had given up and gone to bed.

'Was that cover for us, sarge?' whispered Claude. He sounded younger than Willis. For a painful second, Frank thought of his brother, tucked up and waiting for Christmas. He should've sent him something. When he got back down, he'd sort it. A picture maybe? Yeah. Willis liked when Frank drew stuff. He could make up a little frame with twigs and wrap up that sketch he'd done of Pisa. And he still hadn't finished that picture of Vita. He couldn't quite recapture the lithe sketch he'd made on her terrace.

'Guess so,' said Bear. 'Either that or it was Santie's sledge backfiring. Now shake you little tush, Claudette, because, in case you ain't noticed, that's our cover ceased. Hup, now! Hup! Fly, my children.'

Hup two three four. Hup two three four. Dark lightening to grey. One final hairpin and the track they were tramping became flanked by a tall stone wall, rising to the left of them. The Buffaloes had arrived. As dawn broke on Christmas Day, they entered Sommocolonia.

The silence continued. Up the cobbled slope to a little piazza with a fountain, their rubber-soled boots sliding on the icy ramp. A platoon of partisans was already waiting. They'd taken up a command post in Casa Vincenti – nice family, who hovered, anxious, in the background as the partisan lieutenant greeted the Buffs. Sommati. Just a young guy. He assured them all was *bene*. Suggested they make their command post at Casa Moscardini.

'Is at the foot of the fortress, so you have good vantage. You can use La Rocca for observations.'

'Sure.' The scene of normality, the casualness of the villagers as they woke to the day and headed across the square to visit family or the little church there, made everyone relax. *Stand down, boys. Nuthin' doin in Sommocolonia.* Lieutenant Jenkins, the 366er in charge, lit a cigarette. Turned to Fox. 'John, you want to go with some of Sommati's guys and check that out?'

'Call me Pier,' said Sommati. 'Please, I will take you myself.'

Jenkins split them into squads, told them to disperse throughout the village. Bear took his own squad. Frank felt his jaw ease as Charlie headed off with a group of 366ers.

'So. We digging foxholes or what, sarge?'

'My, oh, my. What a view. Foxholes you say? No way. Is Christmas Day, Francesco. The bad Bosch is having themselves a rest. And you is friends with the locals. So you, my golden chile, is gonna get us quartered in a nice, comfortable *casa*.'

'Hey. I don't know no one from Sommo, sarge.'

'Nah.' Luiz nudged him. 'Catagnana's where this boy lays his hat.'

'Fuck up.'

'Now, children. You won't get no presents if you don't play nice. How about that lovely lady over there? Good mornin, ma'am. *Buonio Natalio.*' Bear bowed in the direction of a woman who watched them from the foot of the cobbled ramp. It was Renata. She chucked her own chin with her fist, then walked away.

'Reckon that means "I'll go get some coffee on"?'

'Nope.'

'We goin stop her? What if she a spy?'

'Claude, baby. There's 'bout a hundred assorted Buffs and partisans milling round up here. Try as we might, we ain't gonna keep that secret for long.'

'Ain't you worried, sarge?' Comanche passed round a pack of smokes. 'Most of the 92nd been sent to the beaches now, not the hills. What if we don't surprise Jerry? What if they surprise us?'

'Nah,' said Luiz. 'OSS said the Krauts were gonna launch a massive hit two weeks back – and they didn't. Those guys don't know what the fuck's going on.'

'But HQ have moved our reinforcements back—'

Frank took a light from Comanche. 'Yeah. To fucking Lucca. A bunch of tanks. What use is that to us?'

'Suck it up, baby,' said Luiz. 'We is the thin black line.' He started doing a stupid jig, ass waving in time to some unseen beat, and from there it all went a bit crazy. Bear passed around his hip flask, to *wet Baby Jesus' head*, then Sommati returned with the village priest, and an invitation for them all to go have Christmas dinner at Casa di Mazzolini di Catagnana.

'Very ancient family, you know,' Sommati said earnestly. 'Lords of the Castle of Sommocolonia.'

As if the Buffs might refuse a free meal. Not only was there to be food laid on, but the villagers would like to welcome them to Christmas carols and a sung Mass too. Even the boys who'd no religion crammed themselves into the tiny church. Not Frank. He and a few others remained on guard outside the service. Wasn't that he never prayed. He just didn't know what to say. He cleared off the snow, sat on a wall, a quiet niche that gave a decent view of the approach road, and the ridge above. Let himself be still, enjoying the throb of the singing seep through stone, the sunlight on his skin. Wasn't in the slightest warm, but Frank wanted to accept every coming hour as a gift.

He thought about Vita, how she got up each morning and looked for ways to make her world better, even as it crumbled in. He wished so bad that she could know his world. The real one. Man, he wanted to show her California, take her to Santa Cruz. Imagine if they were on the boardwalk. The grainy snow crystals under his fingers could be sand. Those faint, persistent thuds might be sounds from the amusement park. Or they could be lying on a towel, him massaging the skin across her belly and those thuds might be the blood in his ears. Oh, God. Did she know that he ached when he was near her? Had he told her that?

He opened his eyes. Looked properly at the cobbles that formed the walls of these hilltop homes. Chosen and laid in patient patterns. Each one, considered, balanced, same as the terraced streets on which they sat. He watched the 366ers move a gun carriage into place, blurred his eyes so's they disappeared. Some mediaeval man – no, way before that, Vita said this place was Roman – OK, some guy from antiquity, had stood right here, scratching his head, angling his foundations to get the best of shade and sun. Knowing that when he planted a settlement and raised his family here, they'd be sheltered.

Soldiers were the lucky ones. They had some kind of freedom. Yeah, they got shot, but so did these folks. Least the Buffaloes got trained for war, got to run in like heroes, move on. They'd a fighting chance to be primed and prepared, while the folks here scrabbled to survive. War came to them, they didn't bring it. Men like Frank did. He tried to imagine how he'd feel if men arrived at his momma's house and beat her up. Shot his little brother. It wasn't difficult, he didn't believe even the dumbest Buff here would find it difficult, because you thought it any time some brother got lynched down South, or a coloured student was beat up on campus. You thought about fury and revenge. You thought all the pumped-up bullshit they tried to make you feel about war.

'*Buon Natale, figlio mio.*' Church door was open, folks milling out. An old lady took his hand. Warm. Real warm. She was smiling with her whole two teeth. '*Per la pace.*'

'*Per la pace*, ma'am. For peace.'

She patted his cheek. The warmth in his hand came from a hot chestnut she'd placed there. A man was roasting chestnuts in a skillet over an open fire and he'd never noticed. Some sentinel Frank was.

When the Buffaloes left church into the wintery sun, more locals queued to shake their hands, offer the sign of peace. The chestnuts kept coming – *caldarroste*, Sommati told them, and the meal at Casa Mazzolini had now become a dance party. *Vieni, vieni.* As the troops were ushered towards the big Mazzolini house, Frank could hear the low boom of shells falling closer over Barga. He didn't want a party. What was the point, unless you could sit with your sweetheart on your lap, kissing her in full view of the whole of Sommocolonia?

Salute! Grappa was passed, the local throat-shredding firewater made with all the bits of grape they didn't want in their wine. Numbing his throat. They took it in turns. Some Buffs danced, some Buffs ate. Some patrolled the perimeter of Sommocolonia's walls. A mix of villagers danced in the large hallway with them, old ladies and little kids, young women in pretty dresses. Frank was surprised to see so many villagers had stayed. Had he called it wrong? He'd thought dragging Vita down to Barga would protect her. But mountain rock was way stronger than brick or stone. He snatched at the grappa as it did its second rounds. Wanting to drown out all that tender heartburn. Apart from Willis, he'd never needed to keep anyone this safe before.

The partisans began to sing, old mountain songs the locals joined in with. Even stone-faced Renata was thawing, you could see the flesh of her arms jiggle as she swung them high, linked to the old boy next to her. A beautiful atmosphere permeated the room, of caring, pride. Joy, almost. You didn't have to understand any of the words to know they were healing one another. One drink more and you could feel power drawing up through the earth and rock. When they stopped for breath or a change of tune, the occasional burst of gunfire might fill the pause, but these mountains echoed, and it was distant enough not to matter. Perhaps they had chosen not to care, not to count the seconds between to see if it was coming closer. The grappa, the flurry of limbs, was making his head buzz. No, it was the room; there were knots of consternation: he could see Sommati nod at Jenkins, could see Bear go over, cigar in hand as he gesticulated. Shake his head at a piece of paper they passed between them.

Frank couldn't make out what they were saying. He was surrounded by 366ers, all sore about their colonel, and bellyaching about General Almond.

'Almond. Soft white nut.'

'Man, the shit he gave us when we got here. *I did not ask for you, and I do not welcome you.*'

'Yeah, we heard,' said Comanche.

One of them flipped his knife to open another bottle of wine. 'Is all fucked up, man.'

'I hear Almond call us monkeys.'

'Well, I *know* he called us goats.' Charlie, wedging himself into the group, and instantly bringing the centre of it to him. 'Stood right there, in my white jacket, filling up their glasses. Amazing how folks can talk right through you when you're serving canapés. Ole General Almond, dining out on the novelty of his nimble Negroes. "Sure-footed as goats, those culahd boys".

Like he was Hannibal leading his elephants across the mountains.'

'Ah say, suh.' Luiz held his mug with his little finger pointing out. 'Use 'em niggahs at night, and they be damn-neah invisible.'

Jenkins and Bear joined the group. The laughter dissipated. 'OK, men. Message from 370th Infantry HQ. We've to retire from assembly area. Order to attack Lama has been countermanded.'

'Say what, lieutenant?'

'Postponed, leastways. So we're gonna rest awhile with these good folks. Hold our positions and await further orders. I want intensive patrolling. Reinforcement of all existing defensive positions.'

'Reinforcement? Jesus, sir. You think they expecting a hit on us right enough?'

'Possibly,' said Bear. 'The request to intensify defences is a direct Field Order from General Almond hisself.' He read from the paper. 'We got to *reinforce, organise, occupy and hold present position, at all costs*.'"

'Only we ain't supposed to know?'

'Well, I guess they figure most of us can't read,' said Bear, handing the sheet back to Jenkins. 'Hey, Lieutenant Sommati. You been recalled?'

'*Sì*, I have. But I stay here with my men. We wait for comrades from Versilia and Pescaglia.'

'Appreciate that, sir.'

Most of the 370th were at Molazzana and Calomini. Most of the Division were focused on the coast. Apart from Bear's squad, the two platoons of the 366th, and the all-singing company of partisans, this was it.

'OK.' Jenkins spoke to one of the partisan soldiers. 'Corneli is it, yeah?' He was scribbling something on the bottom of the order.

'*Sì.*'

Jenkins tore off the bit he'd been writing on, folded it over. 'I want you to take this message to our command post at Barga, *sì*? Tell them it's urgent. *Urgente.* Tell them we need more troops. I've been trying to radio the fuckers back, but there's no reply.'

Sommati nodded at his man. '*Attendere la risposta.*'

'Sarge?' said Frank. 'What should we do with these folks, then? Evacuate 'em?'

'Where do you suggest?' said Sommati. 'America?'

'We keep them company, I guess.' Bear took out a slim box. 'Cigar, anyone?'

There was a flurry of noise and fresh snow, the door of Casa Mazzolini crashing wide. Frank thought it was Corneli leaving, but it was a new crowd of people pushing in. Reinforcements already? How was that possible? A deep voice shouted, '*È qui la festa?*'

In trooped a dozen *partigiani*, headed by a woman flourishing a machine gun. They entered, bellowing, '*Oh bella ciao, bella ciao, bella ciao, ciao, ciao.*'

What was it with the *partigiani* and song? The entire brigade was topped and tailed by women: machine-gun lady at the front, another two at the rear, one in furs, another part-hidden by her hood. Which was really a patchwork quilt. One of the women closed the door, subduing the heaving snow. The other shrugged off her rainbow cloak. It was Cesca. It was Francesca and his Vita. Wearing a wet fur coat. Smiling straight into him like a bullet through his heart.

Across the hubbub she grinned and waved, Frank, spilling his drink as she blew him a kiss.

'Marry me,' he mouthed.

She shook out her hair, scattering diamonds, and came over.

Chapter Twenty-nine

Sometimes it is the smallest thing. 4.15 a.m. on the 26th of December. Vita swirled the coppery liquid in her glass.

'Here, you want more? Right up your street, scozzese.' Dina poured another tumblerful. The scene in Casa Mazzolini was surreal. Twenty or so people lounged on couches, on the floor. Rifles were propped against the wall, beside a pile of Buffalo backpacks. A man and a woman danced in front of a table, which held a half-devoured wheel of cheese and the remains of some roasted meat. Although shuttered from the outside, the high-ceilinged room had been lit by several coal-fired acetylene lamps, which cast slender, rearing shadows into the wooden rafters.

The whisky tasted delicious. Papa had never let her try his precious stash. 'What is it?'

Dina's brother looked at the bottle. 'Bourbon? *Ameri—*'

'—*cani?*' said another of her squad. 'Beware of men bearing gifts. Guard your wine, your women and your chickens. Oh, and the going rate's four americani cigarettes if you want un pompino.' He pushed his tongue deep into his cheek to illustrate the point.

Vita put her glass down. Feeling the golden slide of it go all the way. For a lovely second, there was only her and this soft heat in her gullet. All night, she had been good. But the bourbon was making her loose, unguarded. Comments like that were why she must stay alert. She had talked to Frank, she had danced with him and his friend Comanche, then with Lenin and Tiziano and the dashing Pier Donato Sommati, because that's what you did at a party. Nobody could hear her heart hammer when Frank moved close. Or know it was for him that she laughed, or touched her hair.

Half-shut eyes; tasting the rasp of burned toast, then syrup. But she was growing anxious. Desperate to unwrap him, this Christmas present she couldn't have. *Listen to yourself.* Such appetites must be unwomanly. These *pantaloni* were unsexing her, and the thought suddenly became very funny, and then she was giggling to herself, Dina frowning, then giggling too.

A knot of Buffaloes passed, Frank among them. She sensed him there, conscious of the heat on the back of her neck, his hand trailing on her shoulder – then he disappeared out the door. She looked round. Apart from the Balestri lot, there was hardly anyone she recognised. Cesca had gone with Renata and Rosa to get some sleep, Renata waiting pointedly for Vita to come too, but there was urgent *partigiani* business... Vita had to talk tactics with Dina... *Aye, right,* said Cesca as they left.

The eerie dance of light on the walls, the snores of the strangers surrounding her, were unnerving. It felt subterranean. As if the room was waiting for death. Did he mean for her to follow?

One touch. Sometimes it is the greatest thing. She pulled her fur around her, climbed over a sleeping Buffalo and went, shivering, into the cold. Frank stood directly outside the door.

'*Ciao, bella.* Want to go for a walk?' His fingers grazed hers.

Clusters of Buffaloes were dotted on the streets, building barriers, priming guns. Just as many stood smoking cigarettes.

'Yes. But not here.'

'Where then? We can't go far.'

Up beyond Piazza San Rocco rose the Via del Saltello, the ancient drove road that led across the mountains. She could see the outline of the redbrick customs house which sat on the brow of the hill. For centuries, the lords of Sommocolonia had gathered levies there, growing rich from the passage of trade. It had given this place power and status. A group of shadowy men were carrying something bulky towards the building.

'Follow me. Secret place I know.'

She led him away, across the hazy grey shapes of the piazza and down the steps beside Renata's house. A single Buffalo stood guard at the bottom, rags and foliage fluttering from his helmet. His white snow-cape flapped as he aimed his rifle.

'Halt!'

'Ginger. Be cool. It's me.'

'Hey, Chap. *Signorina.*' He winked.

Vita stood to one side as Frank tried to persuade the soldier to let him through.

'No can do.'

'But the lady needs to get home. I said I'd escort her.'

'Orders, Chap. We got a perimeter guard all round the village.'

'I can vouch for her, man. She ain't no spy.'

'Can't let no one in nor out. Not even cute ones.'

'C'mon. We just need to get some air.'

'Jus' need to get laid, you dawg.'

The forest edge loomed, trees stark against the cloud-washed moon. Vita pulled the fur collar closer to her face. Tugged Frank away, back up the steps.

'Hey, baby, I'm sorry. He didn't know you could understand him.'

She shrugged, glad of the dark to hide her humiliation. 'Would rather your people saw us than mine.'

'That 'cause you're ashamed of me?'

'No,' she said. 'I am ashamed of me.'

She led him back to Piazza San Rocco. There was a hunger there. Not just in them; in everything. Night-time yet, but a paler version of itself: banks of deep grey were beginning to creep from the east, you could see day coming, tentative fingers pushing into the star-studded black of elsewhere. Soon, it would be too bright to stand here so brazen.

'Where were you taking me anyhow?'

'I wanted to show you our truffle grove.'

'Classy. You know, after the war we could export them. Make our fortune.'

'You want me for my money? Some families have olive plantations or vineyards. Us Guidis have fungus.'

'I was serious, Vita. What I said before. I want you to marry me.'

She put her finger on his lips.

'Is only special people can go there.'

'Is that so?'

'*Sì*. Best place in all of the Garfagnana.'

'What's Garfagnana?'

'This.' She spiralled her hand at the wooded landscape surrounding Sommocolonia. 'All the trees. In Etruscan it means *enchanted woods*.'

Veils and ribbons of cloud passed the moon. An owl cried on its night-sweep for prey. She wondered if it was the same owl she had seen up on the plateau. How far did they roam? Stubborn, still-hanging leaves shook on the nearest trees as a rumble of artillery came from the far side of the valley. They crossed the square, past a cigar-smoking Buffalo shouting at two partigiani. 'No, *grazie*. I already made my peace. *Buonasera*, Chappelley. Hey, sweetheart.' It was Frank's sergeant.

'Sarge.'

Frank half-shielded her with his body, but it was too late.

'Vita, ain't it? Is me, Bear. *Bono notto*. Come translate for me, will you, kid? These two just arrived from Viareggio, but I can't figure out a word they say. I think they're asking if I want prayers.'

One of the strange partigiani was patiently repeating himself. 'Will you tell this idiot we have new intel. From a priest.'

'Who?'

'Don't know. We met him on our way here.'

'What was his name?'

'You deaf, girlie? I don't know.'

'Don't call me girlie. I'm partigiana, same as you.'

His companion spat in the snow. 'Cristo. No wonder they needed reinforcements. All they've got is Mori and ragazze.'

'And now we have old men from Viareggio too. So.' Her breath glittered. 'You want to tell me what your *intel* is?'

'The priest asked if we were going to Sommocolonia. He said to tell the Buffaloes that a German attack is imminent.'

'When?'

'Tomorrow.'

'Tomorrow as in today, or tomorrow as in tomorrow? It's the middle of the night.'

Time was confusing. Who kept track of actual hours now? Folk inhabited a netherworld, stalking their own hills like wraiths, digging animal holes in which to circle and snatch an hour of sleep.

'Tomorrow as in tomorrow. Twenty-seventh,' he said. 'Guaranteed.'

Who to trust if you cannot trust a man of God? Vita translated. The sergeant sucked on his cigar. 'OK. Let's go pass that on. Guess we can stand easy for a bit. They got time to deploy more troops up here at least.' Bear nodded at Frank. 'And maybe we will get some of these folks evacuated when it's light? You gentlemen come with me. *Veni, vidi.*'

'What?' The partigiano shook Bear off. 'Where is the fat Moor taking us?'

'Lieutenant Sommati's in charge of partigiani,' said Vita. 'But I don't know where he is. If you go with the sergeant, he'll find him.'

'There's more of us from Viareggio, up by the Customs House. Place is a shambles – we're all just hanging about, waiting for instructions.'

'Well, I know they were needing reinforcements up at Montecino.'

She saw Bear lean into Frank, say something in his ear. Vita pointed up the hill. 'You know the low ridge of pines directly above the village? First in the firing line, if the enemy comes from Lama.'

'Nope. Don't know where Lama is either. I told you – we're not from here.'

Frank came to stand slightly behind her. He hooked his little finger onto hers, insistent. The wind funnelled through the piazza. Vita could feel the iron weight of the sky, and them, so tiny beneath. The snow flurried. The vastness was overwhelming. A rush of fear passed through her, and she told herself it was just the wind.

'Honestly,' the other partigiano said. 'You spend days trudging through blizzards, and this is the thanks you get. You should've told that stupid comm-op to get stuffed, Bruno. The foreign one. He said you lot were crying out for reinforcements.'

'We are.' She could feel the sharpness of Frank's hip against her backside.

'Jus' any time you like, Vita-bella,' Bear drawled in English. 'Tell 'em there ain't no rush. Not like there's a war on.' He relit his cigar.

'What did he say?' said the one called Bruno.

'Look, just go with Bear, find Sommati, and they'll give you your orders. If you're lucky they'll give you whisky too. A wee dram?' Vita said to Bear, in English.

'Sure, sure.' The sergeant gave Bruno a hefty back-slap. 'Come meet the family, *amigos*.' They headed for the ramp that led to Casa Mazzolini.

'You want to go back with them?' she said to Frank.

He shook his head.

'What did Bear say?'

'Nothing.'

'Tell me.'

'"You got one hour, boy. Use it well."' He smiled, and didn't look at her.

'Ah. Well, see, time here is different, Buffalo. *Molti secoli o un anno o un'ora.*'

They walked to the next level up, casting shadows on the houses and the thin, cobbled streets. Snow-quiet and empty. A shutter flapped.

'I love when you talk Italian. Don't have a clue what that meant. But it sounds pretty.'

'It is a poem. About here.'

'Sommo?'

'No, Barga. It says ... *let me look a bit more at... things that are many centuries, or a year, or an hour old, and at those clouds that disappear.*'

'OK. Swell. Still don't get what that means.'

'You a college boy and all.' She put her arm through his. 'I think it is saying that here, now, contains many times, you know? Things that last for a second and all of history, and what is moving and coming. Is all here.'

'Well, all I know is you're here. And you're all I need.'

He swung her round, pressing her into the length of a wall, kissing her eyes, her mouth.

'Wait. Not here.'

'Vita, you're killing me.'

'Please.'

She couldn't explain. It felt tonight as if she was walking to her fate. If her legs were blown from beneath her or a bullet met its mark, it would be because it was time. The street here was so narrow you could press your hands against the walls on either side. When she was little, it was a badge of honour if your limbs could span the gap. Vita used to go one better, wedging herself off the ground with her arms and feet. *See if you can hold for a count of ten.*

Round the corner, the passage split into two separate cobbled lanes. Which way? She held Frank's hand. Followed the last of the moonlight.

Pale light yawning. A figure walked through Sommocolonia, trying to get a sense of how many Americans were stationed here. He hoped it was hundreds. This street was so narrow you could press your hands against the walls on either side. Round the corner, the passage split into two separate cobbled lanes. Which way?

Sometimes it is the smallest thing. The call of an owl. Joe followed it. At the end of this lane was a paved terrace, which overlooked the eastern flank of the mountains. If the Buffaloes hadn't found it already, he'd suggest the Viareggio partisans should bag it. A fine vantage point for the coming day.

But someone had found it. They'd even found the wrought-iron chair on which the Widow Giotto used to sit with a cat in her lap. Two entwined bodies were straddling the chair; he could see a naked black arm, pushing up the pale flesh of a woman's spine, her undone blouse cascading from her hips, into a nest of fur. The black arm rubbed up and down, long fingers massaging the bony ridge of her arse. The woman groaned, grinding her backside to his thrusts, the side of her breast gleaming. Joe should turn away, but he couldn't. Transfixed. Sinewed black biceps. Her white elbows raised to hold her hair to the waning moon, then she was bowing, bowing onto the man's chest, him loving her. Joe moved from the doorway he sheltered in. The woman was murmuring *Ti amo* as the sky exploded in a shower of red and blue light. A flare, sent high above the enemy positions on Lama di Sotto ridge. Their swaying became rigid.

'What was that?'

Sometimes it is the greatest thing. A voice. Joe felt it as a slow, bright impact, even before the colours fell from the sky and lit her stricken face. Did he make a sound then, or before?

'Joe?' Vita was holding on to the black man's shoulder, looking backwards. 'Giuseppe? Giuseppe!'

'Vita.'

'Oh my God.' She clambered off the man she sat astride, tugging at her clothes; the soldier was pulling his shirt close, and her, but she was off, up. Tripping on her trousers, throwing her arms round Joe, her bare nipples pushing and spreading into his chest, but he shoved her away.

'Christ, woman. Cover yourself.'

'Joe!' She was still unclad. The black soldier stood over her, trying to hide her bareness with the furs. 'It *is* you. Oh my God.' Fists at her mouth she was weeping. 'It *is* you. Francesco. Is my cousin Joe.'

'You get the fuck away from her. Now.'

The soldier held his palms wide. 'Hey, man. I love her. This is not—'

His words were drowned by a shower of noise and light, comets streaking, streaming in long, earthbound arcs that began to speed and crash around them.

'Incoming!' yelled the soldier. 'Get down.' He threw Vita to the ground. 'You got a gun?' he shouted. 'Hey! You! Joe. You got a gun?'

Tracer bullets burst onto the hillside, over a group of figures, less than a mile uphill. The whish-whish-whish of mortars started. Black towers of earth rising as missiles hit the ground, sky screaming with pink and yellow flashing veils of light.

'Not here,' he shouted. 'At Casa Mazzolini.'

'Take this.' The soldier set a pistol on top of the metal chair. 'Keep her safe.' He bent and held Vita's face between his hands. 'I'll come back for you, baby.'

'Where you going, Francesco?' She latched onto his wrists.

'There's enemy movement over there,' said Joe. 'North of us.'

'Got it.' The soldier wasn't looking, though, he was whispering: *I love you, I love you*; then a grinding screech as a wheeled cannon was dragged past the end of the lane, and Joe's knees were dunted by the soldier scrabbling by him, to reach it. Thick white smoke. A mountain range ablaze. Howitzer shells whistled in, shredding trees, igniting houses. Joe could hear men screaming. Vita snatched up the gun, went to run after the soldier.

'Vittoria! Stay here!'

'And die in a doorway?' she yelled. 'I need to evacuate Renata's. All the weans are there. Come on!'

'Renata will—'

'I love you, Joe.' Racing to the top of the alley, past an army medic, the red cross on his helmet slipping as he tended to a figure on the ground. Vita could see the rear of the cannon, Frank's crouching scuttle as the cannon moved, then a shrill whirr made her recoil, and the medic was prone too, felled by a sniper's bullet as a huge blast hit the alley and a wall tumbled to block the entrance.

'Joe!' Cordite coated the roof of Vita's mouth. Bullets snapping like ripping teeth. Hails of brick and twisted metal flying, windows exploding, her breath in ragged heaves.

'I'm alright! Just get out of here.'

Choking smoke filled the air; she could no longer see him, or Frank. There was a volley of huge explosions on the Saltello above Sommocolonia; Vita colliding with running bodies.

'Gesù, what was that?'

'Minefield. Think the Krauts just found it. Hey, Vita!' It was Lenin and Tiziano. Lenin kissed her forehead. 'Gelato's alive! Did you see him?'

'Yes! I can't believe it!'

'I told him to go to Montecino. We've got a big machine gun parked there. Come with us.'

'I need to find my sister.'

'No,' said Tiziano. 'What you need is a fucking gun.'

'I've got one.' She held Frank's revolver aloft.

'Cesca will be fine,' shouted Lenin. 'She's a Guidi same as you. We've walls to defend, so move it, comrade.' A bowl of flame ricocheted down the twisting street. They dived for cover in a drainage trench as a mortar exploded in front of them.

'Hold fast. Hold fast.' Tiziano was signalling up at one of the houses. Urgent drilling of a machine gun. Vita, burrowing her body into the earth. Grit-filled air in gulps, hearing cries and screaming all around.

'Hold fast!'

Running boots. Troops moving and dropping, moving and dropping. Americani in formation, come to get them out. The guns drilled on; it was a factory of noise, ha! If this was your work, your daily work; soil spitting as the bullets struck, she was becoming hysterical. An uninjured woman, screaming wild. Beside her, Lenin reared, firing at the sky.

'Save your fucking bullets!' Tiziano shouted. 'They're too far away.'

Lenin slumped. Thank God. That man never usually listened to sense. Vita twisted her neck to say as much. Saw a piece of meat. Saw a blue-boned knob at the end of a joint lurch towards her, and it was Vita, it was Vita's own body that broke Lenin's fall. The torso's fall. Yelps and cries, a Buffalo's contorted face, telling her to *fucking move. Leave him, leave him!* What the soldier was telling Vita, what Vita was telling Tiziano, who was trying to lift the Lenin he could reach. *He's dead, Tiziano. Come on.* Yellow-pointed arrow-flash. Rifles, bullets. Running low.

Dawn came as they were sprinting for their lives.

First light, making every day anew. How it glows and climbs, up here, where the far sky billows. The subtlety of its incursion, forward, onward, until it erupts into piercing life and rolls across the hours. Opening them, offering them, gobbling them, sweeping them away, and each and every living thing in its path will gain or lose that day. From the 3rd Company Hoch, tedeschi who were only following orders, who were trying to make their frontal attack on Sommocolonia from the Lama di Sotto road – until they hit the ring of mines there, to their mates from 2nd Company, creeping round from the Mariola Forest, who had been so quiet, so stealthy. Yet the detonations of their dying friends were what shocked Sommocolonia to its senses, made it bristle and turn outwards and be alert to the creeping threat below.

Light defies gravity; it floods resplendent, brilliant, dazzling, clear over blue bone and black blood. And it shone over the furious efforts of the partisan outpost at Montecino. Surrounded by the clean snap of pines, they had been on guard all night. Just after five, the remains of the landmined tedeschi appeared in the draw north of Sommocolonia. The partigiani had a Browning, some rifles and an ancient machine gun. They had their wits and their love of their land, which fed their blood and kept them light. They battered the sky towards Lama with fearsome fire, the smell of sweat and snow and gun oil thickening, the sting of hot metal cartridges hitting wide-eyed faces as young boys wrestled with old guns. Lieutenant Sommati from Livorno hunkered with his men as the dark mass of the enemy flowed in rivers down the mountain, as the missiles heralding them scudded in a *son et lumière* show, blanking then blackening light, and it made Sommati think of the jerky movements of actors in the movies, and how he wished that his twenty-three years had been filled with more joy, because there was nothing wrong with fun, and if he had the chance he was going to

He never had the chance. His men laid a blanket over his body and carried on. Tossing sandbags. Lining up grenades and fattening their beasts with ropes and ropes of bullets, toiling with bleeding fingers to keep the tedeschi from penetrating from the north. For a long time, they did. American mortars joined the efforts, along with small-arms fire from Casa Moscardini, at the foot of La Rocca where the Buffaloes had their command post. First light shone on them, steadfast in the ancient fortress. On Lieutenant Fox and his radioman, who were positioned in La Torre, the highest tower for miles. From there, the Buffalo observer and his men could direct the US artillery down in Loppia, urging them ever closer, as the German threat spread and spread.

First light gleamed on Vita, who was invincible, invisible, as she leapt from ledge to ledge to reach her little sister. The horror of poor Lenin; that could have been her, right next to him, but it was not, it was not, and her cousin was alive and her lover loved her. She sclaffed down to the Biondis' by rock instead of road, in time to see clever, sullen Renata, who had Francesca by one hand and Rosa by the other, fleeing down the mule trail. A thread of refugees was taking to the lower slopes; they would make for Catagnana. Vita leaned over the parapet of the Biondis' terrace, but did not call out. In this amphitheatre of guns, who would notice? If Cesca looked up, Vita would follow. Her sister kept going, and Vita was glad, indeed, she was alarmed by the adrenalin, sparking like rising smoke. She had no encumbrance; could return to the fray with her wet furs and the pistol that was Frank's. Knowing he was here, somewhere, watching over her and watching the streams of flickering fire from

412

on high and the guns pounding so hard that the earth vibrated through her belly, that they were fighting this together, terrified and quick and alive, being inside the splashes of watery green light and criss-cross red, white snow, grey sky, black burning trees, thrilled her.

It, this, was a test of faith.

'Do your fucking worst!' she yelled into the abyss. Throat raw, Vita hurled the words as far as Monte Forato. To the shepherd who was still asleep; he had been asleep for generations. Generations who'd held their beloveds while they watched the double sunset. Thousands of girls had got to do that.

'Fuck you! Fuck you!'

Other partisans were coming up the mule track, towards the village. The one at the front looked so clean, so upright in his running. His beret was too stiff. How was that possible? That animal-look. It was the soldier from the chapel. The fascista who had checked her papers.

Air suddenly wheezing, sucking itself away. Instinctively, Vita ducked as the light went out, americani shells crumping into the Biondi house, sending great lumps of masonry piling down, choking grey dust, clagging, filling up her eyes and mouth. Day leaving.

Daylight has no side. It welcomed the proud and sneaky Mittenwald as they coughed through grey dust to penetrate Sommocolonia's perimeter. Unleashed after spending Christmas hidden down in Pruno, a simple hamlet, where folk had heard their hobnailed boots in the night, but didn't want to look. The Mittenwald eschewed Teutonic helmets. All a hard-headed *jäger* needed was an embroidered edelweiss and a jaunty beret – plus some fake partisans to ease their path. Once they got in at the foot of Sommocolonia, it was a simple matter of kicking in doors. If a black face appeared, you shot it, howling like the Krampus, who brings bad gifts to bad souls. A slug of warming schnapps might loosen the tongue and your trigger finger too, so it was entirely understandable if accidents occurred. Civilians should have locked themselves in their cellars. That was the rule, and this was war. So, when the Alpine soldiers broke into the house at Via della Bulitoia and blasted a husband while his wife and children cowered, when an exuberant *Obergrenadier* machine-gunned through a closed front door and killed little Giuliano in his mother's arms, it was entirely understandable. The rolling daylight knew this; it was another passing hour.

One hour rolled into another, and for some the seconds were hours. By eight, nine in the morning, the waves of Axis troops, one hundred, two hundred, *incoming*, had driven most of the Buffaloes, and the partigiani, deep into the village. They were surrounded. Again and again, Lieutenant Jenkins radioed for help. Again and again, they said: *It's coming.* The Buffaloes set up two 81mm mortars in Via della Piazzola. Comanche and Bear urged their men on, Frank leaping to one side as a partisan was hurled from a window in San Rocco. *Jesus, man,* the Germans were that close, they were inside the goddam houses.

Three hundred enemy troops, fighting house to house, you would just dive and shoot and roll, dive and shoot and roll; if you kept up a forward movement, you could pretend it was momentum, could force your trembling exhausted limbs to lock, reload, your legs to run, although you never knew what you were running from or to, except once, stopping, kneeling to hold the hand of a dying girl. Feeling so sad she'd lost part of her fingers, 'cos she was beautiful, this woman who'd dressed like a man. And the searching, the constant frantic head-swivel searching for your own woman, whom you'd left because you were a soldier. A bullet struck a metal helmet – not his, thank God. Frank pulled a machine gun from its unattended wagon, firing into the house behind. Snipers remained unseen, magnifying the fear, compromising anyplace that might be safe. Freezing fingers. Smoke bombs and incendiaries. He turned to Comanche. 'You got any grenades?'

Comanche was lying across a wooden rafter. Helmet spinning. Blood pumped from one ear. Frank held two fingers across his friend's neck, but there was no pulse. Gently, he raised his shoulders, slipped one dog tag from the chain. Placed it between his friend's teeth before rigor set in. Bullets spraying from top-floor windows. Soft flesh ripping red, Comanche's torso bucking. Very calm as the guns spat and men screamed, '*Feuer.*' A friendly howitzer blew a hole through the house: Frank could hear the snipers inside dying. He tried to breathe in steady measures, the air more dust than oxygen. One deep heave, and he dragged Comanche's body behind a hill of rubble. Stroked his thumb across the eyelids. Closing them on Sommocolonia.

Another shell came in slow motion. Like being submerged, when an explosion falls near you. Sounds are muffled, you move in yawns. Daylight insisted on intruding, then, when all you wanted was to burrow down and cry, it got you to your feet, past Claude who was saying prayers, past the shock on his face at the waste, the waste. *God bless you, Luiz.* Frank put Comanche's feather in his own cap. Carried on.

Cold daylight struck the nineteen houses at the foot of the church, razed to the ground. It lit the way for US howitzers to hit the German mule trains coming down from Lama with more supplies, and for German machine guns to cut through the relief platoon the Buffs finally sent from Barga. Scything and scything till they gave up the ghost, and retreated. Lieutenant Jenkins watched them go.

By half-past ten, the sun was not quite in the centre of the sky, and washed in grey, which meant the glare from the snow was never blinding. It was in a calm, yellow light that the partisans at Montecino were shot in the back, still facing Lama and the oncoming tide. But La Rocca down below had fallen to the Mittenwald, who, efficient and neat, turned Allied canons into Axis canons. Italo and Riccardo, Giacomo and Albano: they never stood a chance. Pine-fresh daylight passed over where they lay, shone onto the Germans sweeping in to seize Montecino, where they joined with their *Brüder*, aiming Allied weapons onto *Amerikanische* targets.

The minutes ticked on. Light flowed and stuttered. Under palls of heavy smoke, Frank made it to La Rocca – where he thought his command post was – just as the Germans were swarming in. He threw himself into a redbrick building opposite. Found two other Buffs crouched inside.

'Hey, Chap.'

It was Ivan, holding a bleeding 366er.

'The Krauts have occupied the fortress, man. It's over.'

Scores and scores of the fuckers, roaming like bugs on a corpse. Frank laid his forehead against his rifle tip. A couple more rounds, then it would be fix-bayonets.

The wounded 366er was balancing his gun on the broken window-ledge. 'Lieutenant Fox is still inside. His driver and RO too. We gotta try and give him cover.'

'Shit. Where?'

'They've barricaded themselves in the tower. He told us to get out.'

Smoky daylight, as the bombs dropped close. Too close, too accurate.

'Fuck, man,' said Ivan. 'Why they firing so crazy? They gotta be ours. Jerry don't be firing on his own.'

Frank realised then that they had to move. 'Ivan. Put your arm round this soldier. Now. We got to get out.'

Thirty seconds. Twenty seconds. Running and scraping the 366er's toecaps in the dust. Churning like tiny mice on a wheel, clockwise, is that the way the world spins? Ten seconds, and brave daylight was shining in the window of the mediaeval tower, where Lieutenant John Fox was holding the phone attached by wire to the black box his RO carried everywhere. He repeated his coordinates. Thought of his wife and nodded at his men.

Fire it! Put everything you got on my OP. There's more of them than there are of us.

When dawn came round the next day, they found his body in the ruins of the collapsed tower, a hundred dead Germans surrounding him.

But this day was only half done. For now, it glared on the American artillery blasting friend and foe. It glared on Frank stumbling from under the bodies of his colleagues, on the walls come tumbling down. So many walls. In all the hours of combat, both sides fought to destroy Sommocolonia. None of them meant it. It was war. By the ruins of the Biondi house, Sergeant Bear McClung packed his wounds tight and manned a machine gun. For two hours, he covered the withdrawal of his men. Despite the blood in his eyes, he stood his ground, firing until his position was overrun. The sun had moved a little further on by then; it was after eleven when the two hundred German soldiers swept down the sheltered gullies between Scarpello and Bebbio, led by their Italian guides.

Only then did Bear retreat. Removing the gun from its tripod, he went firing from the hip, lugging the belt across his shoulder until his ammunition was done. The partisans who saw him fall did not understand his final shout.

Ain't none of you bastards got a light?

The troops flooded into Sommocolonia, *Viva l'Italia* roaring on both sides. Monterosa mixed with Mittenwald, Italian soldiers of the Republic, come to free their homeland from black devils and bloody Communists. In Piazza San Rocco, Joe slipped on a body as he fled. Cracking his skull on the cobbles. Dazed. Hearing bootsteps scrape. Smelling dark stone and burning meat. On his back, high noon, and the grubby sun looked him straight in the eye. A smudged face. Joe blinking at lapels that bore the green flame of the Monterosa. Head swelling in pain. He let his eyelids fall shut again.

'Hey, Gelato? Santa Maria – get up.'

Forcing them open. Daylight and the shadow of a thin, sharp nose.

'It's me. Pietro! Get up. Quick. Fucking run.'

Pietro from Albiano, who wanted to grow sunflowers. Before Joe could speak, there was movement on the sloping ramp, a Buffalo dropping to raise his gun. 'No!' he shouted as Pietro fell away, and the Buffalo snatched Joe up. More Monterosa piling down the street, the Buffalo hauling at Joe's collar, dragging him on, down the steps to the outer walls, to a heap of stone where the Biondis used to live. Ugly daylight lingered on the fleshy trails of the soldier sprawled there. It lingered on the tears in the dust down the Buffalo's face, down Joe's face. On the splashes on Joe's shotgun, which was stolen from a dead man. The gun was spent and heavy. Heavy enough to swing and smash into the face of the crying Buffalo, it would be easy; the soldier was bent, whispering over the dead americano, holding him in his lap. Joe's knuckles rippled, independent of his brain. You didn't need to think to kill.

418

Sometimes it is the smallest thing. The way the Buffalo cradled his friend, with the same care he'd cradled Vita. Joe knew fine which Buffalo this was.

'He wasn't going to kill me.'

'What?' The Buffalo looked vaguely at him. Eyes swollen.

'The soldier you just murdered. Pietro. He was from here.'

Noon found its pinnacle, tumbled forward down the other side, to the south-west ridge where the Germans were sealing off the last escape routes. As casualties mounted and ammunition ran out, the remnants of the Buffaloes were finally ordered to withdraw. Relieved light bleached a path for the scattered remains. Seventeen Buffaloes made it out. Daylight covered First Lieutenant Jenkins, who refused to leave his wounded men. Half the platoon could no longer walk. When the enemy closed over his position in the winter glow of afternoon, he was comforting another soldier.

Joe and Frank. They sensed the call for retreat, hunched as they were alongside Bear's body. Sensed the helplessness descending. Joe retched from taking too many breaths. He could hear the cries of soldiers waiting to die. The Buffalo, Frank, offered him a canteen of foul-tasting water.

'What do we do now?'

'Guess we keep fighting.'

'I havny anything left.'

Frank rubbed his eye with the back of his hand. 'OK. Help me shift Bear.'

'What for?'

'Might be a clip of ammo on him somewhere. Failing that, a cigar.'

Light is clear and cruel. Light is casual. Light is light. It birled; it let them birl the sergeant over and find a revolver, concealed in the rubble of Casa Biondi. It let them see the slim, unopened hand beside the revolver, the sleeve of fur. Steady light to help scrabble and heave out rock, to brace an olive-drab spine against a ton of distended wall while a Paisley buddy dug for his cousin, and guns tore up the street above. They found Vita breathing, protected by a wooden beam that had landed diagonally, wedged between her and the worst of the toppled masonry. Her lover and her cousin pulled her free, not knowing that moving her would make the bleeding start again. Joe let the black man take her; she wasn't his. She never had been.

'Vita, baby. Hey, girl. I got you. I'm here. I'm always here.'

The Buffalo held her and nursed her alive. He kissed Vita, breathing on her lips, her nose, her eyelids, enough for her to wake. *Francesco mio.* Joe couldn't bear to watch: her, smiling up, trying to reach out, and the soldier begging her to stay with him. Then he saw the stickiness of the fur, the spreading patch of blood.

'Frank. Frank. Look. We've got to move her.'

The Buffalo tore his shirt in strips, binding the wound in her side. Light was flickering, fading. Shouts of *Raus* and grown men crying. The enemy were winding their way through the village. Systematically. Efficiently.

'You go,' said Frank. 'Get her over your shoulder and fucking run.'

'What?'

'Take off your armband. And this.' Frank snatched Joe's beret from his head. 'You can climb down there, yeah?' He waved over the terrace wall. 'Man, come on. They're fucking coming.'

'Aye.' Joe stared at the drop. It was steep, but passable. If he could make it down a hundred yards of rock, he could reach the first of the smouldering trees. From there, the forest and Catagnana.

'Jump and I'll pass her down.'

'What about you?'

'Fuck me. They see you and her, just gab lots of Italian. No English – or Scottish. You're *sfollati*, right? Now go.'

Raus!

Vita's breath was shallow; it was a rattling bone of breath.

'Jesus, move it, man! They'll be watching me, not you. I promise.'

A machine gun drilled methodically. Joe vaulted the wall, dreeping down the other side till his feet hung above earth. He let go, landing on his knees.

'Right.' Joe stood. Held up his arms, wedging his feet against a fallen stone.

'I love you, baby.' Frank hung his own dog tags around Vita's neck. 'Always.' One last kiss, and then he returned her to Joe. Slow lowering. Joe on tiptoe. Vita moaning. When Joe hoisted her over his shoulder, she whimpered, the dead weight of her forcing him backwards, rocking on the cliff edge and clawing for balance. *Steady, steady.* Face against the wall. The brisk clink of tedeschi boots. The casual chatter of the victors, clipping down the broken steps to call on Casa Biondi.

'Joe.' Frank's hand dropped down from the parapet, but he could no longer reach them. 'I wanna stay here. You got that?'

'Aye.'

'OK.'

Whispered seconds, thick with love. Bright and terrible, the shadows coming on the Buffalo's brow. His stare locked on to where they were, as if it could not loosen its grip. Then he lifted the empty shotgun, took the pistol in the other hand and turned away. Unwavering day lit the flock of birds that were really mortars pounding in. It lit the bare-chested Buffalo on fire. Joe thought he heard a sigh of wind as Frank charged, yelling, towards the splintered staircase and the oncoming boots.

Autumn 1945

Chapter Thirty

'Vita! Vita!'

Picture the scene. Evening in rural Tuscany, and much excitement down below. Flurried dust and movement on the mule path told her two special visitors were almost here. From her chair, Vita had an excellent view of the Valle del Serchio. The jagged points of Barga's citadel broke the rhythm of the land. On the horizon, folds of plum-coloured cloud were making a curtain for Monte Forato. As if the shepherd's coming silhouette was the main show.

Joe must have some of her papà's talents, because he'd made her an excellent place in which to sit. The wooden seat was planed and sturdy, the ropes pleated so thick they were as strong as the chestnut bough from which they swung. Except Vita wasn't allowed to swing. Gentle nudging of her toes on the earth. That wasn't swinging. And if a late-summer breeze happened to catch you, draw you a little higher every time? So what, if you were careful?

She laid her hands across the crinkling in her pocket. She was so tired.

'Vita! They're here!'

Finally. Her little cousins, Dario and Marino, had arrived. She should go down and greet them; she would, shortly. In a minute. But even getting up here had fatigued her; it was a torpor she couldn't shake. She moved slowly now, often in a dwam. Often, a dwam was the nicest place to be; cosied inside her own head, where she was loved, not pitied. Ach, Vita wasn't even a good martyr. Not like the saints, who suffered so beautifully and never complained.

We've all lost someone we love, Vita.

Sisters. God love them. From her eyrie, she saw Cesca sweep up the boys, smother them in kisses. Joe too, the four of them in a single embrace. It was beautiful. That should be her down there. Vita was the matriarch now. But she preferred to gaze over Barga, remembering what was lost, from a distance. Not observing the actual desert there, the buildings buried in tall piles of themselves, sealed in the stone and tile and wood they once were. The Canonica. The Conservatorio, L'Alpino, Signor Nardini's warehouse and on and on and on. Shelled beyond recognition. The worst of it happened in the days after Sommocolonia, when Vita was still in Pisa.

They were very nice, in the military hospital. Stitched her up as best they could, and filled her with her second cousin's blood. Who'd have thought Joe was the perfect match, closer even than her own sister? After some time – she wasn't sure how long – she was able to be propped on her pillows, although they wouldn't allow her visitors. Nor would they let her search the Negro wards, laughing at the very idea, as if she might catch something. First night she was able, she climbed over the edges of her cot, but the tube thing they'd stuck in her got caught and there'd been a terrible mess of blood. When they'd seen

426

her so hysterical, a kind Florentine nurse relented, and promised to check their lists.

'Where is she?'

Marino was scowling up the hill, hand shielding his eyes in a man's pose. He'd got so tall. If you scliffed your toes and shimmied your backside as far as possible, then the swing-chair was entirely hidden from below, by the tree trunk. You could see folk, but they couldn't see you. Joe knew exactly why Vita cooried in her tree; he'd played enough games with her when they were children. She liked to think he'd strung the swing on this side, in this precise position, on purpose. Cousins. God love them too. Vita loved Joe very much. He said he loved her. Even got down on one knee to offer her his hand. *Then I can take you home. If we're married, I can take you home. Away from this.*

This. The expression on his face when he proposed, was part of the *this*. It was a queer, bleak look Vita engendered: a porridge of pity and scorn and brave smiles, of disgust, lust, sorrow, anger and relief. Oh, the quantities varied depending on who was doing the looking, but the ingredients remained the same.

Relief was the worst. The twist at Joe's mouth when she'd said no. Daft that, to think the boy she'd grown up with could be her husband. Vita had felt love as a column of fire and light, felt it and felt it still. She wished that for her cousin too. How could you settle for a life that was douce? Doused. She would rather have this lonely burn. Marriage to Joe would be a life sentence, for them both. Besides. She stole another glimpse through her nest of leaves. Joe had his hand on Cesca's waist, at the sweet spot where her hips were beginning to flare properly, and she was laughing as he spoke into her ear.

With most folk, the relief they showed was for the fact it wasn't them. In Vita's position. She arched her back further, until the ropes were taut. The wound beneath her scar pinged. Bare knuckles whitening. After the war, you had to start afresh; if not, if not to make your world anew, then what had been the point? It hadn't been to preserve the old, for that had gone. Nor to give hope to the young, because they had been sliced away. She let her head drop, staring up at the canopy of her riven tree. Shrapnel had shaved a couple of branches and partially split the trunk. Already, shoots were growing round the cut. A pair of leaves quivered as a bird shook itself.

She and Cesca had visited Mamma this morning, in the camposanto. Elena Guidi was going to get her husband home at least – and you took comfort in that, because you needed to. Papà had never replied to any of Vita's letters. The nice Red Cross lady said not to give up hope, that she would keep searching all the records of all the camps. And she had. Papà and Orlando Biondi were to be repatriated soon. Papà had been ill with pneumonia, but he was alive.

Never give up hope.

All that grace, for all the broken families. All those good and earnest souls who were trying to piece back shattered things. Who to blame, what to say, to which neighbours, who remembers, what to forget? Men who'd served their whole time fighting for Il Duce. Men like her cousin Gianni. *That's who I joined for.* Defiant shrug, and you talked no more about it. You didn't ask if he had known about Sant'Anna, about the Jews in Poland, those terrible camps? Signor Tutto's son Ronaldo came home, briefly. Vita and Ces tidied his papà's shop in preparation, as best they could. When Vita opened the attic, Signor Tutto's instruments were still there. Ronaldo took the violin. The sides of the accordion had been eaten by mice. He didn't stay. Far better to bury the fragments deep away. Smooth over, start again. The whole of Italy had been wounded; all folk could manage was this tentative, sore shuffling forwards. It was how Vita had been, when she first got out of hospital.

Mostly, folk let her be.

The children were only a terrace and a row of olive trees away. She heard Cesca say, 'I think she must be sleeping.' Then Marino's, 'Vita's bo-ring. Ces, can we do it now? Joe promised we could do it now. Please. She can't wait a-*no-ther* minute.' There was a strange braying snuffle, some crunching.

'Should we warn him first? Boys! Stop pulling her.' Cesca sounded so grown-up. Well, she was, really. Sixteen in a few months, and lovely with it. Cesca was definitely the best of the Guidis.

'No.' In the slight pause that followed, it sounded as if Joe had moved nearer to her sister. 'I've been waiting for this for so long. Let's just see it happen.'

'You don't think it'll be too much for him?'

'No. And we'll be there.'

Ces lowered her voice. 'Joe, that's another reason not to go. We can't leave him on his own.'

This circuitous conversation, which they dipped in and out of most days. Sometimes it included Vita, sometimes not. In Scotland, Joe had a boarded-up café waiting, and the flat above. Zio Roberto was canny, the deeds for it were his: a slice of Paisley sandstone, bought and paid for by Tuscan graft. For what was left for them here? Vita's belly rippled. She dabbed at her side, at the pinkish fluid there. Ces had told her not to come to Barga this morning.

It's Mamma's anniversary, Ces. Of course I'm coming.

I know. But maybe you shouldn't? In case it starts weeping again.

It never stops.

'Don-kee. Don-kee.' Dario and Marino had begun a chant. 'Wonky don-kee wants to go *HOME!*'

'All right! We'll talk about this later. How's she been?' Joe was almost whispering, but Vita's senses were finely charged. They were talking about her. The inflected 'she'; acknowledging that Vita was a shared problem. Speaking close-up and together, lighter somehow, for all their troubles, in a way they never were when Vita sat between them. Folk were not permitted to be happy in her presence; that was the rule.

'Same.'

She heard Joe sigh.

'She got a letter today, when we were down in the town. But I don't think she's read it.'

'From…?'

'Well, it was in with the Red Cross stuff. But it had a US Army stamp.'

'Shouldn't someone sit with her, then? She'll be—'

'Joe. I think she wants to be alone.'

Sisters. God love them.

'Can we have our dinner there?' said Marino. 'Can we take that chicken?'

'You brought chicken?'

'We did,' said Joe. 'Proper coffee too. The riches of Viareggio know no bounds. Och, why not? We can bring Vita up some dinner later. Right then, gents. Come with me and we'll get this old lady home where she belongs.'

'I love you, Dromera.'

'An-*dromeda*. Why are you so stupid?'

430

'Marino hit me.'

'Enough! Marino, you start behaving like a grown-up or I won't take you to the frantoio with me.'

Of course. Home in time for the grape harvest. The boys would love that, squidging their feet in all the pulp and mess. And Vita could teach them how to sweep the forest floor. She craned her neck, moving her jaw from side to side. Her teeth hurt again. No, she couldn't. Landmines.

A network of leaves and branches splayed above her. Cool green shadows, making dinted chunks of light fall on her outstretched arms and legs. This position probably wasn't good for her, but it felt so comfortable, held in stasis. Neither forward nor back, not earth or sky. The gashes of light overhead reminded her of being inside the Duomo, that first day she'd come home to Barga.

Pain-wracked, needing the Duomo's quietness. She was supposed to be sleeping in the Conservatorio, so the nuns could keep an eye on her. Sleep? With no intact windows and an ice rink of broken glass? Outside, the war had still been raging: bombs, shrapnel, the hiss and burst of bullets, shrieks of the planes diving in and out. Two days, Cesca told her. That was all it had taken after Sommocolonia, for the Germans to be ousted and the Allies to regain control. So much blood, for nothing. But it wasn't the Buffaloes who came marching back to save Barga; it was tall brown men in turbans with vicious, glinting blades.

Vita returned to Barga at the end of January. Their home had been struck by a shell; one neat hit and La Limonaia was almost lost. The Monsignor offered the Guidis his study, which still had a door at least. But Mother Virginia claimed Vita for the nuns. Did she know, even then?

The wind had raged down spacious hallways, tinkling glass teeth from putty gums. You lay, being cut by shards which blew in the gales spinning stairwells, ripping off tiles. Nuns stumbling and slipping on glass as they tended their injured charges.

'You must rest,' said Mother Virginia.

How? Metal crashing outside, the fragile Conservatorio pitching like a ship on the sea. Joe, brave Joe, who'd borne her through a war zone, sitting by her bedside. Cesca, somewhere nearby on duty. Vita's little nurse, whom she had to share.

'Where is he, Joe? Where's Francesco?'

'Ssh now. Just sleep.'

Vita was dizzy from the medicines they'd fed her. Not dizzy enough.

'Where is he? I thought he'd be here.'

'He's missing. Remember?'

'But where?'

'He's gone.'

'Gone where?'

'Vita, I think you know.'

She refused to know, refused to understand him. Lay rigid with the covers at her chin. Eventually, Joe had fallen asleep. By then, the bombing had stopped. In that quiet aftermath, Vita could not breathe. She'd found boots and a shawl, and ventured outside. Wild wind catching her hair, Barga sprawled in filthy slush, her walls and windows torn, rain coming in torrents to wash away the snow. Clutching her side, which was leaking a wee bit, Vita had climbed the rampa to the Duomo.

Make it stop, she whispered.

Appalled by the wretchedness inside. The Duomo's roof was smashed, marble columns broken. The beautiful windows in the Chapel of the Madonna were riddled with bullet holes, everywhere soaked and strewn with debris.

Make it stop.

No chairs, so she'd lain on the rainswept floor and sobbed until her kidneys chilled. The torn roof was an empty mouth, breathing onto her as the wind worked its way through blackened rafters, pulling light into the darkest corners of the cathedral. Grief pulled everything into a different shape.

She had lain, that dawn, on the floor of the Duomo, watching eldritch light that should not be there and stroking her ruined belly. Being in ruined things comforted her. Was she sorry? Not for one single second. Francesco had loved her and she him. Only she and whatever created this miracle knew it existed then, as she searched through the rafters of the Duomo. Wanting to melt into the ice water she was lying in, to evaporate when the sun came, or be swept into the wind.

The Monsignor had lied. He said the Moors had run away. Joe said they'd fought like heroes, that they fought on their knees for Sommocolonia. *Nonsense. No moral fibre. Not like these Indian chaps. You know where you are with them.* The Monsignor didn't want to listen to Joe. As time went on, he didn't listen to Vita either.

Puttana.

First time that was spat at her in the street, she jumped. Second time, she wiped the slevvers away. Third time, she set her face on the horizon and never broke her stride. Probably then, that the teeth-clenching had started.

Vita was pregnant. That's what saved her, so many times, from not stepping off the mountain, not dropping beneath the ledge where La Befana lived, being sucked into the Caves of Wind, going down further until she just kept falling. Vita carried a gift, so she only thought these things. She believed her baby would heal. Once it was born, he or she would be so beautiful that Nonna Lucca would write again, would recant her insistence that she could neither receive nor aid Vittoria, until she gave the child away. And Vita would write to Frank's mamma, tell her how he lived yet, she would find somebody to take a photograph and put it in the letter, she would seal it with a kiss.

When she was soundest in her dwams, Vita believed this baby would pull Frank home to her too. There were stories of men returning from the dead, from prison camps, distant places. Few boasted of such good fortune, not when so many suffered. They held their luck and their loved ones close, lit joyful candles. But it happened. And who had seen Frank actually fall? She would write to his battalion, to his president in America if need be. *Vita*, said Joe, *trust me. I was there. He could not have survived.*

The Florentine nurse was so kind. She checked the names of all the Mori who'd passed through the military hospital. She had a friend, she said, an administrator with Fifth Army Command. Based in Viareggio. The colour rose in her cheeks when she spoke. Vita patted her hand. 'Don't feel guilty that he's safe.'

As her baby grew, more of Barga collapsed. A message from the nurse found her, tracked her all the way to the Conservatorio, to the space where the Guidis were living, next to where San Cristoforo was seeing out the war. Cesca and Joe went for meals in the refectory, brought Vita's food back with them. Her choice. Being tired suited her.

The telegram was brief.

PFC Francis Morgan Chapel. Missing in Action. Sommocolonia 26 December 1944.

That could still mean he was a prisoner, or back in America, lying confused in some hospital. It was only March then. Vita refused to hear the lies about americani prisoners shot by tedeschi. She would write to the Red Cross, to the American Consulate in Rome. She would and she would... yet every time she sat to write, it was as if the ink froze in the nib.

I am a friend.
I was his wife.
I would have been his wife. We were lovers.

Nuns padding overhead. Invalids calling from their packing-crate beds. People cooking on stoves under the stairs, where a single line of graffito had been scrawled. *Noi vivi.* We still live. Sorrowful saints. The tick of a new-repaired clock, smashed cabinets full of owls. Finally, she had sought refuge in La Limonaia.

Oh, the pleasure of that climb, feeling her long limbs swing and the mess of Barga fall away behind. Violets were starting to peek through the soil, but she couldn't reach them. A new fence and a crude painted sign announced: *Pericolo! Mine Antiuomo!* Scars and debris, new weals on old land, but there were also rabbits again, and birdsong. Vita felt almost healthy. Her stitches seemed to be healed, though the ache in her side remained.

What had she thought she'd find in Catagnana?

The back wall of their house was gone, the top kitchen fallen into the summer one. Wild ducks roosted in the burned-out salotto, bird muck covering fragments of Mamma's curtains. Her boots crunched vitrified chunks. It was the glass from Papà's picture frames.

Joe had found her at the foot of her tree, wrapped in shawls and bent over a notepad. 'Enough,' he said. 'I was waiting till you were stronger. But... this.' He waved his hand at the visible swell of her belly. 'And now there are officials asking about him. Because of you.'

'Me?' She had rubbed a sheet of paper against her eyes, trying to mop her face, but only succeeding in streaking herself with ink. 'Then good. I just want to know where he is.'

'Where *he* is, where *he* is? What about me and Ces, Vittoria? Christ, *we're* here. We're living and we're trying to make you live too.' Joe grabbed her hand, pulled her from the ground. 'Right. Bloody come with me.'

Upside down in her chestnut tree, Vittoria Guidi dangled from her swing. The chain she were around her neck clattered into her ear. Her smock was becoming damp. The shooting stopped in April. Peace came in May. Mussolini and his mistress were strung by their feet from a Milanese lamp post, and the King transferred his powers to Prince Umberto. Mutterings came of republics, referendums. Italy, upside down, but free. Vita's arms tingled with the stretching, her shoulders popping. Her belly gurgled and bulged, the perfect angle of an elbow pushing up.

'You'll like this, baby.'

She flung herself forwards, swinging high into the air, wind and breath and head a-rush, up and down, up and down, in flowing, rhythmic contractions. On every up, she could see her family. They'd reached old Sergio's farm now, were unlatching the gate as Vita swung down. Another up, and they were on Sergio's track. The old man was opening his door; he'd a goat bell fitted to the gate, it was one of the safeguards his cousin had insisted on.

—*You're staying with us.*

—*I'm going home.*

They were all as stubborn as mules, the Bertinis. Down and down, with the breeze in her hair, the plum-coloured clouds speeding. *Hurry, hurry*, her belly was pulsing. *Don't miss the show – Ah!*

Sergio let out a cry, a joyous one. Beyond where the tips of her toes were, Vita saw the old man's face split until it was only laughing mouth, then it was hidden in Andromeda's pelt, and Vita was hurtling down, and, on the down, she gave a jump.

Enough.

Vita, and the baby, jolted. Deliberately, she didn't fall.

'Alright, wee one?' Stroking her belly. Stroking, stroking. 'D'you think it's time?' She brushed stour from her skirts. Her baby would know two languages; two cultures at least.

Vita turned from La Limonaia, where tiles were ranged in neat rows, wood stacked by the far wall ready for work on the new floor. Joe and Cesca had got the back wall up already, the roof patched so it was almost watertight. Good stone, good stock. But they were staying in the Pieris' house for now, who were still with family in the city. She wasn't sure they'd come back. Joe thought the Guidis could sell La Limonaia when he was finished. He'd have other mouths to feed as well as his own; she understood his worries. But La Limonaia wasn't his to sell. She went into Papà's workshop, retrieved the piece she'd been working on. Aware of great, dragging pulses drumming inside her body. She was tired of being a cow. Once this new life was born, she could have a new life too. Where folk did not stare and mutter.

This wee soul would always bear the mark of difference. Italy, Scotland, America. Would it matter where? Was there a place in the world that loved folk equally, that saw no distinction between the colour of a person's skin and the colour of their hair?

Vita made the climb to Sommocolonia slowly, pausing as the pains increased. Joe had taught her to breathe well, those nights when she woke yelling. The wound in her side ached, perhaps it would tear all over again. It was why the nuns wished her confined in the Conservatorio. One of the reasons. The Monsignor wouldn't look the road she was on. The sisters said he was working to find the child a good home. *He knows missionaries in Africa,* they said encouragingly. It was Cesca who stood up for her. 'The baby will have a home with us, thank you. Now, if you don't mind, we'll be returning to Catagnana.'

God love family. She put her hand inside her pocket. The letter she'd received this morning was still there. Unopened. Her other hand held the carved piece of wood. Vita was going to the place Joe had marched her to, when he told her what he'd done.

From beginning to end, Joe had told her it all.

'He saved us both, Vi.'

Her Buffalo soldier, standing tall. Going forward so that they might fall back. The sunshine filled her head, and Vita could see the scene. Francesco. She saw him every day, polishing the image to keep it bright.

'He wanted to stay here with you,' Joe said. 'He made me promise.'

In the dying days of the old year, the men were allowed to return to Sommocolonia. Joe went with them. Found more than half the village razed. They dug through rubble that had been churches and homes, gathering scattered weapons, and shoes and crockery; dragging lumps of stone from where La Rocca and the tower had been. La Torre, which had withstood earthquake and siege. All that remained was half of one wall.

The men tried to recover as many dead as they could. From the fields and hamlets as well as Sommocolonia itself, bodies were placed in black bags, laid in front of the tiny cemetery, and in the garden of the cottage at the foot of Piazza San Rocco. Then, Joe said, a cortège of jeeps carried them down to Catagnana, escorted by the 8th British Indian Division. Women lined the snowy route in silence. There were no flowers to hold, so they up held their children instead as the jeeps drove past, and old men removed their hats.

Francesco was not among them.

'He left you these.' Joe had pressed coldness into her hand, the coldness she wore round her neck now, which swung and clinked as Vita climbed.

'His dog tags. I thought it was in the panic, you know? We'd only a minute. But I kept on hearing what he said. *I want to stay here.* It was me that found him, Vita. Afterwards.'

She'd shaken her head, not wanting the detail.

'I think it was quick. Anyroad, when we were… you know. Sorting them. An Indian soldier told me they were taking the Buffaloes to Florence. To bury. Vi, I didn't bring him out. From the Biondis'. I laid him in my old room – mind the cave? Take more than a hail of mortars to destroy that place. I wrapped him in my coat, and I came back up when everyone had gone. Nico gave me a loan of his spade. Well, he caught me in the shed, but he let me take it. I just went: "It's for Vita's man," and he nodded, and let me take it.'

Joe had buried Frank here, where the heather grew. Vita grasped onto a tree as her body shuddered. She'd made it. Here, on the slope underneath the overhang where the Biondis' terrace used to be. Facing Monte Forato. Facing every double sunset that would ever come, watching the sleeping shepherd across the way. That had ripped her; the rightness of the place. Joe's kindness to them.

The pinkish seep on her side was spotting red. She'd need another poultice. Then a trickle started between her legs. It wouldn't stop. God, she was leaking everywhere. Patting herself, embarrassed that someone would see. But Sommocolonia was deserted. The sun was lengthening into fiery streaks; folk were done for the day, were resting. Few had homes to live in here; they went elsewhere at night. In the daytime, you'd hear metallic clatters and the zizz of saws drift down the mountain. Already, people were sending money home from all the distant places they had settled, to rebuild their village as it was.

It would be ages yet. Vita rocked on her haunches. First babies took days. Renata had assured her of that. She'd have liked her mamma's hand to hold all the same. Or his.

She knelt down to give herself extra purchase, then drove the wooden plaque she'd made deep into the soil. Papà would have done a better job, or she could have asked Joe. But she had wanted to carve it herself. It was only a slender thing; you wouldn't see it from a distance. But it bore his name.

She rested her fingers lightly on the grave, on the warm earth. 'We're here. You can sleep now.'

They hadn't let her climb to Sommocolonia for weeks. *In your condition.* Frank had had no one to watch the sunset with.

Is it time?
'I think so.'
Are you scared?
'*Sì.*'
But I'll be with you.
'I know.'
Wherever you go. You don't need to keep coming here.
'I know. *Oh.*'

The pain intensified, beating like a fist. From her pocket, she removed the letter. Tore it open, releasing his words, and the trace of him that was held there. And with the words came the thick purple smell of thyme, the musk of truffles and sweet chestnut, and every good thing this land had given her. The pain was sweeping her clear above herself, rocking her close, her and the earth and this vast, lovely curve that cradled them. The sky was magenta and vivid gold. Soon the stars would come out, in time for passeggiata. She felt a breath begin to sing. High and distant ringing, falling like metal rain. The bells were clanging from the Duomo.

She began to read.

24 December 1944

Dearest Vittoria,

Have I told you that I love you? Properly, bone-deep love you. You can never can tell someone that enough anyhow, but it's hard to remember if I did, when every day with you seems like a dream. But it's a dream where you woke me up, you know? You have made me a different person. A better one. I've seen war send men crazy, and I think I know why. It's because they don't know what they're fighting it for, because nothing makes sense but the blood and the pain, and who wants to live in a world of pain?

But I'm fighting it for your mamma. I'm fighting to keep your sister safe and bring your papà home. I'm fighting it for you.

I guess if you're reading this, then it isn't a dream any more. Not my dream anyhow. Not ours. I want you to know, if I have to die any place, then I'm glad I'm dying where you were born. Don't let them take me home. Tell them I want to stay near you. Because home is where you are loved. Tell my momma. Oh, Vita, I wish you could have met her. I wanted so bad to take you to California. I wanted to grow old with you, to see your smile on our babies' faces.

I wish we could have had more time, my beautiful girl. But you've given me a lifetime already. For all the misery and killing I've seen, I'm glad of this war, because it brought me you. It brought me love. So know that I died happy, Vita. And you go on and live happy. For me.

All of my love forever,

Your Francesco

The words bursting, jewel-bright, into hours. She stopped fighting. Let the tears come, quiet and steady. Let herself ride the pain, hide in the cool dips of quiet. Riding it quiet and forever, feeling its beat, following the tails of light behind her eyelids, all the pink-and-gold-crested waves that beat on and on and on.

When she opened her eyes again, the sun was almost gone.

You will always be loved, said someone in her dwam.

'I know.'

Time to go home.

'I know.' She stroked her mobile, cresting belly. 'I will. But can we watch the sunset first?'

And it came and it filled up the hole of Monte Forato, flashing blood-red beacons and ribbons of the most perfect light, bathing the hammered earth gold and the broken glass into diamond.

And everyone who saw said it was the most glorious sunset ever.

Paisley, Beginnings

'*Ciao, bella.*' Torri's great-uncle Dario is sashaying into the room.

Torri holds a finger to her lips. Nonna is asleep.

He waves his car keys; pretends, like a mime, to tiptoe. She adores Dario. He lives with his daughter in the flat above Caffè del Rio, has her gran's bouncy curls and the face of a very old cherub. With him is a man Torri has never seen before; he wears a beautiful overcoat, carries a small case. She feels an acute ping of embarrassment at the fluffy slippers she's wearing. *They're my mum's*, she wants to say. The man, well, he's lovely. He is tall, dark, handsome, and it isn't even Hogmanay.

'Who's this?'

'Hi.' The man offers her his hand. 'I'm Will. I'm real sorry to disturb you.'

American, so he is.

'Away and don't talk daft. Come in, son. Sit down.'

'Zio Dario, Nonna's trying to rest.' Torri looks to her parents, who wait behind the American in the doorway of Nonna's room. Mum smiles. Dario is the family's patriarch, and also their favourite, indulged *bambino*. Dad shrugs. He's not that much younger than Dario, but he's not an old father. Her mum keeps him young.

'She'll want to meet this laddie. Won't you, *cara*?' Dario pokes Nonna's pillow, causing her to start awake. Uncle Dario is cheerfully defiant around death. Not for him the stilted murmurs of folk who can only imagine the worst. He has the *me ne frego* of a survivor. He plumps his hands on widespread knees. 'Now listen you to me. This laddie – wha's your name again, son?'

'Will. Will Chapel.'

'Aye. This boy's got a plane to catch, so we've no time for nonsense. He come to see me the day – daftie's been sitting outside the hoose all evening, 'cause I was at the bowls, know, and Rina, she was... Och. Here. You tell them what you tell me, son. I'm getting all mixty-maxty.'

'Sure. I'll be quick. Look, can I just say, I'm truly sorry. I don't want to intrude. But Mr Giusti insisted.'

'Oh, come on.' Dario gesticulates like he's directing traffic. 'Here's you coat and wha's you hurry? She's no doing nothin except sleepin, sleepin. Are you, *cara*?'

'Dario, please,' says Mum. 'Let the man speak.'

'So. It's like this. My grampa...' Will hesitates, looking at Nonna, who has become alert, is pinned by his gaze.

'Chapelley?' she says.

'Shh now.' Torri holds the beaker of water to her mouth.

'Yes, ma'am. That's right. Chapel. My grampa passed recently. We've been clearing out his house, and we found a bunch of stuff that was his momma's.' Will opens his case. 'Some of it relating to Grampa's brother. Now I never met him; he died when Gramps was just a kid. But I've been interested in tracing my family tree for ages – I don't have any kids of my own, so I guess...' There's an exchange of smiles between him and Torri's mum, who is visibly falling in love with this exotic stranger in her

444

mother-in-law's bedroom. 'Well, I was coming over to Europe on business—'

'What's it you do again, son?' Dario folds his arms.

'I'm a banker, sir.'

'And you no married?'

'No, sir.'

'See. He's no married, Torri. Our Torri – she's a teacher.'

'Zio!'

But they both laugh. Will continues. 'So. In my great-grandmother's papers, I come across this little sketchbook, full of pictures my great-uncle drew. And I found this one drawing in it, for an address in Italy.'

Torri can't see the picture he's showing her mum.

'Now, my grampa reckoned the family never knew where Frank was buried, but he thought it might be near there. Anyhow, when I looked this place up, it wasn't so far from Florence. So, I thought I'd check it out, when I was over in Milan. In case anyone there had heard of him. But I drew a blank – the house is a vacation rental. So then...'

Nonna's elbows are pushing into the mattress.

'You want to sit up more, Nonna?'

Nonna's eyes are liquid black. It scares Torri. She hooks her arm under her grandmother's oxter. The man, Will, does likewise with the other side.

'Thank you,' Torri says, surprised. Nonna is transfixed by this stranger. Her mouth gapes wide and her eyes are crazy-flitting. They lay her against her pillows. Her weight is thistledown. Torri hopes she's not going to say something inappropriate. Will's skin is the colour of coffee. Has her nonna ever seen a black man? Well, of course she has – she sees one every day.

Torri looks at her father. The war baby. Abandoned, adopted; the story is left deliberately vague, buried in

445

the craters. But his skin is a shade darker than his brother's and sister's, with whom he shares the Guidi nose. They have talked about it, Torri and her dad. Is he not curious about where he came from, really? *I came from love* is all he ever says. This lack of curiosity intrigues Torri, the casual blend of her family; how it is accepted and never said and forever quietly present, adding to the flavour, swirling like Tally's blood on gelato. Actually, she loves it. Loves that she is Scottish and black and Italian and Celtic and Godknows what else, and that it doesn't matter.

'Och, c'mon. You worse than me, son,' Uncle Dario is saying. 'Mind the Pieris? Well, their Giuliana works in the bank in Barga, so your man here uses his connections, she checks wi her nonna, and Bob's you uncle – they gied him my address.'

'Can I see the drawing?' Torri asks.

She doesn't know why, but she is asking Uncle Dario, not this Will who owns the sketchbook.

'*Sì*.'

'Sure.'

Torri smooths the yellowed paper. It is a drawing of a house on a hill. The house faces a horizon of mountains, and the one in the centre has a great hole in it, like an eye. The scene is breathtaking. But it is merely a stage, a frame for the portrait of the young woman. The girl regards them from the foreground; a trace of Nonna, but the face is too long, too sharp. And the eyes are wrong too. Almond like a cat's. How they blaze from the page.

Dario slips his hand under Nonna's. Torri sees the transparent skin on Nonna's knuckles tighten, squeezing Dario. Gently, her great-uncle raises Nonna's hand, and presses his lips against it.

Torri reads the inscription below the drawing.

Ti amo. Il tuo Francesco
                    Per la bella Signorina Vittoria Guidi
                         La Limonaia, Catagnana
                         Frazione di Barga, Toscana

Vittoria Guidi. Torri stumbles over her own name, written there. Composes herself. There's a tightness under her eyes.

'Who's Vittoria?' she asks, at the same moment Will says: 'Now, I was asking Mr Giusti here was if you might know – Sorry. You go on.'

Vittoria. Nonna's always said it was chosen for no particular reason, they just liked it and Torri's never quite believed her.

'No. Please. Go ahead.'

'OK. Well, I understand the Guidi family used to own this place. Lee-monia.'

'La Limon-*aia*.' Nonna's voice is barely a phut of air.

'Francesca.' Dario hovers. 'Is it time, *cara*?' Then he looks at her father. The room is stifling, Torri wants to open a window. The sweet smell of chestnut mingles with fragments of thyme.

Will continues, oblivious to the delicate tendrils creeping through the room. 'Like I said to Mr Giusti, I found a grave for a lady that fit the name. Up by Sommocolonia? So I wondered if, seeing as you guys are Guidis—'

'Is no my place. Was never my place.' Zio Dario addresses everyone.

'Francesco.' Nonna's fingers flutter for her eldest. '*Vieni*.' Her eldest, her clever *professore*, who is named Francesco for his mother, Francesco who is a mathematician and draws like an angel and whom the twins always joke is her favourite. 'Vittoria.'

'I'm here, Nonna.' Torri perches on the edge of the patchwork blanket. But Nonna isn't looking at her. She's looking at the stars outside. '*Vittoria.*' Her tongue rasps on dry lips. '*Mio bel ragazzo. Bello, bello.*' Nonna strokes her father's cheek. '*Sei sempre stato amato.*'

'I was always loved. I know that, Mamma.' Torri's dad is crying, her brave, tired dad, and she is struck by how that curious line on his hand, the one that Torri has, that nobody else has, but this stranger Will has too, is the same, the same. How it cuts a line of pigment like the equator between dark and light, pale palm and deeper skin.

Zio Dario rubs his eyes; he looks so wee, she wants to cuddle him. 'You did find it, son.'

'Excuse me?'

'You grandpa's brother. Francis Chapel. Is on a wee wooden plaque, in the grass. You found his grave, Will. 'Cause our Vita's buried wi' him.'

'I'm sorry. I don't understand.'

Nonna is struggling to speak. There is an urgency about her, she is reaching up and it's as if that young, vibrant girl is reaching out of the frame. Dario quietens her.

'I'll dae it, Cesca hen. I'll dae it.'

He grips Torri's father's shoulder, pulls him in for one fierce kiss. 'Remember, *nipote mio.* You have always, always been loved. See, Vita wisny strong. Well, she was, she was. But no then. Oh, son. All we wanted was to keep you safe.' Briefly, he shuts his eyes. The room stills, until there is only a family breathing and the tissue-thin scent of chestnuts.

'She died just after you were born, Francesco.'

Then Uncle Dario begins to tell them a story.

Picture the scene.

Acknowledgements

Many people have helped in the making of this book. I'd like to thank my friends Helen Fitzgerald and Sergio Casci for leading me to Barga – and on up the steep hill to Sommocolonia; my friend Riccardo Pieri for his ever-generous hospitality and kindness; local historian Antonio Nardini for taking the time to speak to me; Carlo Puddu and Piergiorgio Pieroni for many historical insights, for showing me the museum at Borgo a Mozzano, and for revealing to me the Gothic Wall – inside and out; Andrea Vincenti and Anna Biondi for letting me access the museum at Sommocolonia; Julia Campbell Hamilton for some Italian translation; Sonia Ercolini, Comune di Barga and all the team who run Barga Scottish Week; Creative Scotland for their generous bursary which allowed me to travel and research in Tuscany; Angela Botti and Anna Maria Botti for local lore and language; the Museum of Resistance at Sant'Anna di Stazzema; Sara Moscardini and the Pascoli Foundation for kind permission to reproduce parts of *L'Ora di Barga*; my Rejects Book Group for chewing the fat over titles; my brilliant agent Jo Unwin, Milly, Donna and all at JULA; Gillian Stern for editorial excellence; Alexa Von Hirschberg, Marigold Atkey, Lynn Curtis, Terry Lee, Jasmine Horsey, Holly Ovenden and Lin

Vasey and all at Bloomsbury for making this novel come to life.

A number of books have also been extremely helpful. These are: *Buffalo Soldiers in Italy* by Hondon B. Hargrove, *Black Warriors* by Ivan J. Houston with Gordon Cohn and *Lasting Valor* by Vernon J. Baker, all of which give insight into the lives, indignities and courage of the Buffalo Soldiers who fought in Italy; *La Battaglia di Sommocolonia* by Dario Gianni and Vittorio Lino Biondi (translated by Anne Leslie Saunders), which provides a detailed and powerful description of the battle and its impact on the people living there; *Trapped in Tuscany* by Tullio Bruno Bertini, a rich mine of detail on rural living at the time; *Fascist Voices* by Christopher Duggan – a glimpse into the rise of fascism, from the people who lived it; *Partisan Diary* by Ada Gobetti (translated by Jomarie Alano) which gives a rare female perspective on the risks and rewards of resistance; and last – but also first – *Barga Sulla Linea Gotica* by Monsignor Lino Lombardi. My Monsignor is a fictitious character, but I like to think he would have been approved of by the real Monsignor, whose meticulous recording of day-to-day life and death in Barga was invaluable in the writing of this novel. Any mistakes, or elision of facts for the sake of fiction are my own.

As always, my biggest and brightest love and thanks to Dougie, Eidann and Ciorstan. You know what for. Everything.

Note on the Author

Karen Campbell is a graduate of Glasgow University's renowned Creative Writing Masters, and author of *The Twilight Time, After the Fire, Shadowplay, Proof of Life, This Is Where I Am*, which was a BBC Radio 4 Book at Bedtime, and, most recently, *Rise*. A former police officer, and council PR, Karen lives with her family in Galloway, Scotland.

karencampbell.co.uk

Note on the Type

The text of this book is set Adobe Garamond. It is one of several versions of Garamond based on the designs of Claude Garamond. It is thought that Garamond based his font on Bembo, cut in 1495 by Francesco Griffo in collaboration with the Italian printer Aldus Manutius. Garamond types were first used in books printed in Paris around 1532. Many of the present-day versions of this type are based on the *Typi Academiae* of Jean Jannon cut in Sedan in 1615.

Claude Garamond was born in Paris in 1480. He learned how to cut type from his father and by the age of fifteen he was able to fashion steel punches the size of a pica with great precision. At the age of sixty he was commissioned by King Francis I to design a Greek alphabet, and for this he was given the honourable title of royal type founder. He died in 1561.